Wilson indeed!

Steve Walsh

First published in England in 2019 by Sin Embargo Publishing.
Second edition published May 2021.

ISBN 978-1-9164861-0-2 (Hardback)
ISBN 978-1-9164861-1-9 (Paperback)

Printed and bound in Great Britain.
Sin Embargo Publishing

For more information visit www.wilsonindeed.com

"A dream you dream alone is only a dream. A dream you dream together is reality."

John Lennon

"Dreaming permits each and every one of us to be quietly and safely insane every night of our lives."

William Dement

"Dreaming is an act of pure imagination, attesting in all men a creative power, which if it were available in waking, would make every man a Dante or Shakespeare."

H.F. Hedge

Chapter 1

The Brimstone

Two miles south of Stockport lies the well-to-do village of Davenport, a comfortable notch on the commuter belt of Greater Manchester. The focal point is a railway station and according to the community website, 'the range of facilities within walking distance make Davenport a good place to live for those who don't drive a car'. Which is somewhat ironic, given the events I'm about to describe.

Sally Bennett was a small-boned twelve-year-old girl with a bright, full moon face, a clutch of freckles on the bridge of her nose and fine, silky hair that crackled with static. She also had a major problem with eczema. Raw patches of inflamed skin flared across the back of her legs, painfully visible above the cuffs of her school socks. The trolling on social media and bullying in class were inevitably making the skin disorder worse. Sally's guardian, her Auntie Kay, had made an appointment with the allergy clinic directly opposite Davenport station and they'd arranged to meet there.

"Perhaps you're lactose intolerant or it's something to do with gluten. Half an hour talking to an expert can't make the problem any worse, can it?"

Wendy Bellamy was married to a famous footballer and ticked all the boxes for the demographic of a yummy mummy. In the minutes leading to Sally's appointment, Wendy was driving her Range Rover along Bramhall Lane, a busy road that strikes a tangent with the frontage of Davenport station.

It was early afternoon and she was heading to Sainsbury's to collect the dry cleaning and something for tea. Emily, her two year-old daughter, was an arm's length away, strapped into her car seat, sucking noisily on a bottle of milk.

"Goodness me Emily! It's like you've never been fed. You'll make yourself sick gorging away like that."

Wendy tried to think if something was missing from her shopping list but a favourite song came on the radio so she started singing instead.

The exit from Davenport station spills onto a pedestrian crossing where Sally was waiting for the 'walk' symbol to turn to green. In other words, listening for the sequence of tones that tell someone engrossed in their phone it's safe to cross without looking up. Sally was deleting insults as the beeps started and the car to her right came to a halt. Stepping off the kerb, her heart sank on reading a tweet from the tormentor-in-chief comparing eczema with leprosy.

As the Range Rover proceeded diligently towards the station, from out of thin air, a yellow butterfly danced through a gap in the passenger window and settled on Emily's hand. The child spluttered in surprise, then half-threw, half-dropped the plastic bottle into the narrow space between the centre console and the side of the passenger seat. The Brimstone, an unusual sight for October, waltzed back out of the window.

"Emily, you're so greedy, you'll choke one of these days. Anyway, serves you right for dropping your milk. You'll have to wait now, till the traffic's stopped."

Wendy heard an infantile grunt and turned to her daughter.

Only the rubber teat was protruding from Emily's mouth. Wendy looked for the bottle. She could see white splatter on the mat in the footwell which meant most of the milk was now flooding the carpet under the passenger seat. It's virtually impossible to expunge milk from a nylon carpet, particularly in such a confined space, and milk dries very quickly. Come the next sunny day, the pungent odour of curdled milk was going to make it insufferable just to sit in the car, let alone drive it. The new Range Rover was as good as written off!

Wendy panicked at the thought, took her eyes off the road and frantically reached over to fish for the bottle. It was wedged in a tight gap and kept slipping through her fingers. The hulking vehicle continued onwards at twenty-nine miles per hour even though the lights were now on red.

Sally was over the halfway line when she felt the need to look up and check the cars to her left had also stopped. The part of the eye responsible for fast reactions and peripheral vision was wide awake and she recoiled instinctively.

Wendy finally hooked the bottle from its lodgement by inserting a finger into the open neck and returned her focus to the road as the inevitable came to be. She slammed on the brakes and screamed.

The car wasn't going fast enough to knock Sally into the air. Instead, the bumper knocked both knees from their joints which caused her to bounce off the bonnet like a rag doll off a tin drum. As Sally fell backwards, the sixteen-inch gap between the vehicle and the road, like a gaping mouth, swallowed her up. The right wheel drove over a forearm. The cheese grater surface of the tarmac shredded skin like pith from an orange. Sally's shoulder dislocated the muffler on the exhaust system which caused a pipe to fall and wrap itself around her leg like a helix. The Range Rover came to a halt without expelling her from the other end.

Sally lay unconscious, wrapped in the coils of a metal snake.

Though gruesome, the sum total of the aforementioned injuries was not life-threatening. Sally's petite build and the ground clearance of the four-by-four were fortuitous. Her left shoulder however, was more of an issue. As she was being consumed, a razor sharp burr on the engine's oil sump sliced through her school uniform and nicked the axillary artery near her armpit. The axillary is a major artery of the upper torso and carries a lot of oxygenated blood. Seconds after the car screeched to a halt, a rivulet of thick, crimson fluid began to flow over the black tarmac. As the tide advanced, life ebbed from Sally's body. Without urgent medical attention she had only twelve minutes to live.

All traffic in the vicinity of Davenport station quickly came to a standstill. Wendy was in hysterics and refused to leave the car.

"She's stuck under there, she's stuck, please take her away."

Pedestrians were speaking on mobile phones, urging the emergency services to get there as soon as possible.

"No, the victim isn't conscious. Yes, she's bleeding, Of course we've not tried to move her!"

A wonder woman in a hairdresser's cape with perming rods in her hair proposed lifting the car. The owner of the convenience store said that would be impossible. The taxi driver insisted it would be better to wait!

People stood on the kerb on both sides of the road,

impotent and useless, with hands cupped over their mouths and faces drained of colour. An elderly lady buried her head in the lapel of her husband's raincoat.

Four minutes later, a police car with reassuring, blue flashing lights nosed through the congested traffic and pulled up alongside the Range Rover. Someone gave the nervy young copper the grim details of the accident and it took a while for the gravity of the situation to sink in. Eventually, the policeman put a walkie-talkie to his bloodless lips. His mouth was dust dry, his eyes ablaze, like those of a cornered fox.

"Constable Edwards here. I'm outside Davenport station. There's been a road traffic accident. Urgent assistance needed. I think there's a girl under a car!"

"Yes, Roger that," came the reply. "One casualty, is that correct?"

PC Edwards really didn't want to reply, and for a brief moment considered doing a runner; but he was a bobby, a figure of authority; someone to depend on in an emergency. He dropped to the ground, peered under the vehicle and gagged. As he clambered to his feet his knees buckled.

Meanwhile, a valorous young couple had managed to extract Wendy and Emily and were leading them away from the scene. People were frantically looking up and down Bramhall Lane, listening and hoping for a sign of heavier duty help arriving.

Constable Edwards had only been on the force for three months; three months spent booking people for minor driving offences; he was blatantly unprepared for this. Blood crept ever closer to the soles of his shiny new boots and he took a step back.

"But there's a hospital just down the road," he pleaded with the sergeant back at the station,"I think she's dying."

"Yes, but the ambulance crew are not based at Stockport Infirmary. They're about five minutes away, fighting through traffic. Is there anyone there with first aid skills?"

"I don't know. How can you tell?"

"Look son, pull yourself together and find out, yell for a nurse or a doctor."

The policeman hooked his walkie-talkie back on his belt, praying for the chance to pass his baton of authority to someone else.

"Is there anyone here with medical knowledge? Please, anybody, I need some help."

The crowd of people surrounding the car shrank back in response as though making room for a hero to step forward.

PC Edwards yelled at a bus driver. "Ask your passengers. We need a doctor or a nurse. Someone with first aid skills."

Moments later, as if by divine intervention, the prayer was answered.

A seventeen-year-old student in jeans and trainers and a khaki-green parka with a fur-lined hood walked out of the station and stopped in his tracks. The clogged traffic, the clusters of grim faced pedestrians and the frantic policeman bore the hallmarks of a fresh accident and with no sign of an ambulance, what was the student supposed to do; stay under the radar forever?

Wilson Armitage stepped off the pavement and forced his way through the halo of bystanders surrounding the white four-by-four. He saw the trail of blood, dropped to one knee and peered into the snake's lair. The victim was a schoolgirl, four or five years younger than himself and seriously injured.

The policeman came rushing over.

"Hey you! What're you doing? Stop taking selfies you little sod!"

Wilson sprang to his feet and raised both hands, palms outwards.

"It's okay. I'm not taking photos. You were shouting for help and I've had medical training. At school. Manchester Medical School. I'm an undergraduate. She's losing a lot of blood. I need to get under there and take a look."

PC Edwards didn't know what to say. Was this lad for real? He didn't appear old enough to have experience of carnage.

Wilson sensed the uncertainty.

"Listen, I'm advanced for my age and older than I look and right now we don't have time for this. Maybe I can apply a tourniquet and stem the bleeding until the ambulance gets here."

Like a wind-up toy with a spent spring, the policeman blinked and stood motionless. Wilson turned to the onlookers. They stared back like waxwork figures.

"Jesus" he said under his breath.

Wilson shed his rucksack and parka and crawled under the car until only his feet were visible. After twenty-seconds, he slithered out, ran to the other side and wriggled back under again. He finally emerged, fingers dipped in red, and addressed the policeman.

"She's unconscious and I think a leg's broken, but her shoulder is the biggest problem, an artery has been cut and she's losing blood. I can see where the artery is, but I can't grip it with my fingers. I need something to clamp it with. If I can stop the bleeding, she might be okay."

The request seemed to turn the policeman's winding key

7

and he looked over to his car.

"Errr, I think I've got a thingy . . . "

And he just was about to go and fetch the thingy, when Wilson pointed to a utility belt. "What's that in there, in that black pouch? Is it a multi-tool?"

"It's a Swiss Army knife, the big one, with all the . . . "

"Yeah, I know. Give it to me!"

Wilson took the knife, pulled out the snub-nosed pliers, checked the spring mechanism and scrambled back under the car. The call for assistance came thirty-seconds later

"Officer! Can you get under here. I need your help."

After a moment for deliberation, and unable to escape public scrutiny, the policeman reluctantly did as requested. Wilson had secured the damaged blood vessel and was holding it tight in the jaws of the pliers.

There wasn't much room for three bodies and six elbows in the claustrophobic underbelly of the car, but the policeman manoeuvred himself into position nevertheless. The crumpled state of the poor girl made him wince and Wilson sensed his self-doubt.

"Come on. She's only a kid and she's depending on us. You signed up for the police, the responsibility, so this is where you do your job. Just hold this, exactly like this, with constant pressure, and don't let go. If you do what I say, I think you'll save her life."

There was a stare down in the aura of half-light as they carefully completed the handover.

"Keep a firm grip and don't lose concentration, even when they prop up the car."

"I won't man, I won't."

As the urge for fight or flight receded, PC Edwards, sensed

something other worldly about Wilson. This pimply youth who'd been able to stride through chaos with all the surety of a paramedic. There was a transmission in the steely intensity of the lad's eyes that hinted at a secret under restraint. As though the black orb within each iris was a gateway to something incomprehensibly deep. An obtuse thought accompanied the policeman's perceptions.

"You're not really at Manchester Medical School are you?"

"No, not that particular one," said Wilson, "but I have been to a sort of medical school. Managed to pick up enough, to know quite a lot."

"So who are you?"

Wilson thought about the question for a moment. He returned the policeman's gaze with a kind-of half smile.

"To be honest, I've no idea. But I'm working on it!"

Wilson then rolled out from under the car, leaving PC Edwards to do the award-winning work of saving a young girl's life.

"Hey! What's your name fella?" The question was directed at a pair of white trainers branded with a bloody swoosh. Wilson scooped up his parka and rucksack and ticked the box for no publicity. The policeman followed the trainers from his worm's eye view until they turned right at a corner shop. Then he heard the song of the sirens approaching and nothing had ever sounded so sweet.

Metaphorically speaking, every good story starts with a car crash. Something like the 'edge of a seat' opening to a blockbuster movie that has you hooked from the opening scene. However, I have a confession to make, the incident described above was no accident. It was stage-managed under the auspices of my watchful neglect, instigated by a Brimstone butterfly and *not* concocted for popcorn entertainment

On that fateful afternoon outside Davenport station, my shepherding of the flock engendered a curious circle of life in which the convex of Wilson's yang locked perfectly on the concave of Sally's yin.

And more to the point, Sally ended up in Stockport Infirmary, which was *my* objective all along.

So let me take you back in time, solely for the purposes of clarity on future proceedings. Don't be fooled by the soft underbelly of the next few chapters; the animal in the petting zoo will sometimes bite the hand that feeds it and a car accident can lead to a fatal pile up.

Chapter 2

Twelve years earlier

Wilson Armitage was five-years-old when he first spoke French. Unusual, because Wilson was English, his parents were English, and as far as they knew, their son had never had a French lesson. It was teatime, 29th of October 2005.

Wilson's seven-year-old twin sisters, Kate and Megan were sitting at the kitchen table playing with Bratz dolls. The process of changing tiny outfits on stringy, plastic bodies was tongue bitingly difficult. 'Two peas in a pod' was how Gloria, Wilson's mum, described the twins. Wilson's dad, Alex, was on the phone in the hallway correcting the script for some hapless cold caller.

"No, I've not been involved in an accident that wasn't my fault. This is the third time this week . . . "

We'll come back to Alex shortly.

Clearly, there's nothing remarkable in a five-year-old learning a second language; children at international schools take it as read. However, since Wilson was only just approaching the foothills of the ABCs, an attempt at Mont Blanc should have been unthinkable. More significantly, Wilson's French was not simply a string of words assembled from a 'Speak and Spell' game. Gloria Armitage was loading the dishwasher as Wilson placed his spoon beside an empty pudding bowl and declared:

"Mère, je voudrais que nous puissions avoir ce repas tous les soirs."

Which means, "Mum, I wish we could have that meal every night."

Gloria froze, like a heron appraising an odd fish.

Megan's doll slipped through her fingers and fell to the floor.

Kate's eyes almost popped out on stalks.

Alex Armitage, oblivious to the *éléphant dans la chambre*, returned to the kitchen table and took a seat facing Wilson.

Megan had been trying to click the press stud on a miniature jacket and was captured by the notion that the fitting would be the size of a satellite dish if scaled up to adult size. (Funnily enough, the concept would never leave her.) Reaching down to retrieve the doll, she decided to 'out' the elephant.

"Mum, I think Wilson just spoke French!"

Observation verified, Gloria returned to unloading the dishwasher and dirty knives were placed back in the cutlery drawer. Alex began leafing through a fishing magazine, his thoughts on the banks of a river somewhere.

"Speaking French are we Wilson? Excellent. That's your favourite subject, is it?"

"No, it's not my best Dad."

Wilson began pulling faces on the convex side of his spoon. His chin cleared the table top by five inches and his legs swung to and fro beneath the chair.

Alex looked up.

"So what is your favourite lesson then?"

Wilson didn't have to contemplate the question.

"Fire practice."

Alex rocked back on his chair, howling with laughter. The twins sniggered and snorted respectively. Even Gloria smiled, neglecting all thoughts of the outburst moments earlier. But they demanded her full attention when Wilson declared:

"Mais je ne veux pas être pompier."

And he clarified everything for his dumbfounded audience by announcing "I don't want to be a fireman, because I don't like climbing ladders."

Then Wilson ran his tongue around his mouth to remove any remnants of rice pudding, crossed his arms and sat back.

Alex Armitage placed his magazine on the table and leant forward. He was totally and utterly astonished.

Alex was six foot tall and lean, rather than thin. His dress code was tartan shirt over a white t-shirt with cargo pants and desert boots. A spiky mop of unkempt hair gave him the 'just got out of bed' look. Colleagues at work referred to him as Shaggy, as in, Shaggy from *Scooby Doo*.

Wilson's dad worked for British Telecom and when asked his occupation would often reply, "I'm the cable guy," which suggested he might climb telegraph poles for a living.

But what Alex actually did, was oversee the national rollout of fibre-optic cable that one day would offer super-fast internet to every household in the UK. So if a line went down, Alex would be sitting at his laptop rebooting the digital superhighway rather than driving round the M60. A PhD in Electrical Engineering was redundant in helping him comprehend the minor miracle that had just been performed by his son.

"I didn't know they taught you French at school Wilson? You know, to speak like a boy who lives in France?"

Wilson laughed as though Alex was tickling his feet.

"No Dad, all we do is sums and colouring in. We don't talk like we're France people."

"But how do you know those words Wilson? Where do they come from? Did you hear them on TV?" Alex's voice quivered and rose in pitch as he asked the questions.

Megan and Kate switched from parents to brother.

Alex turned to his wife.

Gloria wiped her hands on a tea towel and walked over to the table. She lovingly ran her fingers through Wilson's hair. He was small for his age, but that was the only evidence to suggest he was anything other than a typical five-year-old boy.

Alex turned to his daughters.

"Megan, do any of Wilson's toys speak French? Like that, learn to read computer thing. Can you play it in a different language?"

His mouth was asking the questions he thought would bring reassuring answers, but Alex was talking without thinking; what he'd just heard was not from a toy.

"No Dad, the Picture Computer's broke. The screen's all cracked."

"Wilson's being very weird," said Kate. She bit her lip and escaped to the comforting world of her doll.

Alex continued tacking into the squall.

"Okay, so how do you know how to talk like a French boy Wilson, if they don't teach you that at school? Do you have a friend who's French?"

"No Dad, I just know it."

Wilson's answer took the wind from his sails so Alex sat back, frustrated with his navigational skills. Gloria shot a concerned glance at her husband, who returned it with gravitas, courtesy of raised eyebrows.

Gloria's thoughts had been racing through a candidate

list of explanations, starting with the most rational before considering more disturbing territory. However, since nothing could be ascribed to the rational column, it was a one sided race and Gloria quickly moved to the dark side. An intruder had entered her kitchen.

Wilson's miraculous ability to formulate sentences in what sounded like perfect French, meant he was not normal. In any mother, the realisation that your child is *abnormal*, brings a surge of fear that runs through the body like an injection of ice. It took Gloria to an unknown place, far from the cosy world she'd inhabited a few, worry-free moments earlier and she blamed herself.

Yes, maybe I have been over-protective, living in my little bubble, never wanting to think about all the bad things that can visit a family – but isn't that what all good mums do?

She cupped her face in her hands. Fledgling possibilities were becoming fully grown certainties and her fingertips carried a sheen of tears. The fact that Wilson could speak French meant things would never be the same. He was autistic or seriously ill. Gloria imagined the inter-parent conversation outside the school gates.

"Emily already knows her six times table."

"Philip can tie his laces all by himself."

"Wilson can speak fluent French!"

She half laughed, half sobbed at the seeming futility of her protective, maternal intentions.

Wilson rested his chin on the table top and peered up at his mum. The message he deciphered from her features told him that speaking a different language had not been a good thing to do. Her mouth looked tight, her eyes were shiny and she was upset. So Wilson decided to stop speaking French and return to being the ordinary little boy he'd been minutes earlier.

Later that evening, Gloria interrogated the internet for examples of 'spontaneous speaking in French' and given the dogged tentacles of Google, it didn't take long to find examples of Wilson-like behaviour all over the world. The article she read from Time Magazine acted like a soothing balm on her troubled thoughts.

A True Story. Published 24th October, 2001.

Teen Wakes Up From Coma Speaking Fluent Spanish.

A Georgia, USA, teenager who suffered a head injury while playing soccer last month awoke from a light coma and spoke fluent Spanish for the first time in his life. Rueben Nsemoh, 16, shocked family members and doctors when he opened his eyes and began uttering sentences in Spanish, despite having known only a few words before his accident.

"It started flowing out," the teen told TIME on Monday. "I felt like it was second nature for me."

It's not unprecedented for patients to start speaking a different language or using different accents after a major trauma. In June, a Texas woman made headlines after she had surgery on her lower jaw and then suddenly started speaking with a British accent.

That case was diagnosed as foreign accent syndrome, a very rare condition in which people speak with a different accent, usually after a head injury.

As the day drew to a close, Alex Armitage activated alarms, switched the house to sleep mode and entered the bedroom of his son. Despite the internet evidence, he knew he'd witnessed more than a strange anomaly. To a logical, educated man, the night's remarkable event was beyond plausible explanation. Which meant only one thing: Wilson was truly different. In a dark corner of his mind, Alex opened the top drawer of an imaginary filing cabinet and inserted a folder, labelled: 'Incident One – Speaking French'. He suspected more folders would be joining it in the coming years.

He tucked the duvet under his son's chin and kissed his forehead. A gentle sigh confirmed that Wilson was sleeping contentedly, dreaming of who knew what – firemen, faces in spoons? Alex closed the bedroom door, switched off the landing lights and joined his wife for an autopsy on the evening's strange event.

A conversation between Gloria and Mrs Lord, Wilson's primary school teacher followed the next morning, but in the cold light of day, claims of Wilson speaking French were met with looks of concern for the mental health of the mother rather than the precocious abilities of the son. Mrs Lord suggested that Wilson's recently acquired habit of falling asleep during lessons and the dark shadows under his eyes should be of greater concern.

Alex Armitage didn't know that Wilson had indeed been dreaming as he adjusted his duvet at the end of that memorable night. Dreaming not of firemen or faces in spoons, but about school and a French lesson.

Wilson was sitting at a desk in Classe 6a of L'École.

A boy by the name of Cecil Didier sat to his left and Daisy Meadowcroft, a pretty girl with a ponytail, sat to his right. They were focusing on a large blackboard, on which a strict looking teacher by the name of Miss Angeline was writing a

17

list of French verbs.

A large glass vase, brimming with flame-red poppies stood blazing on her desk. Daisy was mesmerised by the flowers.

Chapter 3

The Market Square

Four weeks prior to the speaking French incident, Wilson had followed his usual bedtime routine of a bath, three chapters of Doctor Seuss and a goodnight kiss from Mum and Dad. At 7.45 p.m., as the hands on his Mickey Mouse alarm clock waved goodnight, Wilson drifted away. To the outside world, a small boy cuddling a toy giraffe was fast asleep, cloaked in safety beneath a Batman duvet.

Light sleep soon descended into deep sleep and sometime around nine thirty, a faint smile stretched Wilson's lips as his eyelids began to flutter. He was making his first journey to The Market Square where 'Rocket Man'; a surreal visual experience in three parts, was about to begin.

To help you visualise the opening scene, imagine the centre of a traditional English market town such as Ludlow in Shropshire or Abingdon near Oxford. In the good old days, market towns were the hub of the local community where farmers came to trade. So they had a spacious, open area at the centre, a market square, where townsfolk could buy fresh produce from a variety of stalls and handcarts.

The Market Square in Wilson's dream was flanked on all four sides by an assortment of period properties including a terrace of chocolate box cottages, rows of shops with bay windows inset with bullseye glass, an inn with a Tudoresque facade and an imposing looking bank building. The surface of the square consisted of smooth, rounded cobbles laid in a herringbone pattern. A wide, uneven pavement of foot-worn flagstones bordered the perimeter while four narrow alleyways marked the entry and exit points in each corner. Towards one end of the square, to the right, stood a magnificent Clock Tower constructed from blocks of local stone. The neighbouring structure to the left, was a pompous-looking chap cast as a bronze statue; possibly a Mr Ludlow or a Mr Abingdon. A granite slab war memorial, engraved with the names of the fallen completed the triangle. Flowerbeds bordered the trio and a pair of wooden slat, bench seats offered the perfect vantage point for watching the dream world go by. On this particular night The Market Square was also personalised with fantastical details, all rendered from an infant's imagination and reminiscent of a scene from *Oliver Twist*.

Wilson was standing in the shadow of the Clock Tower, turning full circle, his eyes agog, his mouth agape, taking everything in. He'd seen something like it in a film on TV, about a boy lost in London with no mum. Wilson stood in wonderment, he was in that movie.

Actors dressed in period costume were dancing across The Market Square in choreographed splendour. A dairy maid, selling milk from a churn sang "who will buy this wonderful morning?" Cheeky boys in tattered rags stole handkerchiefs from each other's pockets. The square was drenched in sunlight and everyone seemed delighted to be there. Wilson's eyes searched for the Artful Dodger, but another familiar figure grabbed his attention instead; a stern faced lady with streaks of ice-blonde in her glossy black hair. She was wearing red stiletto-heeled shoes, a slinky black dress and her sumptuous, white fur coat was speckled with big black spots. Ten Dalmatian puppies were yapping and running behind her. One of the puppies nipped at Wilson's shoelace and then scampered away. Wilson giggled as it stopped to bark at a troupe of penguins and the man with the sooty face tap dancing with them.

From the far side of the war memorial, five of Wilson's school friends, dressed as Roman centurions, marched into view. They were heavily armed, with plastic swords and bows and arrows with rubber suckers on the ends.

"Come on Wilson, we're making a gang."

Wilson didn't need to be asked twice, but as he lifted his foot and turned to follow, The Market Square shape-shifted.

Wilson's vision became blurred, images fuzzy and detail indistinct. It was as though someone had shaken a snow globe and the snow was settling on an entirely different Market Square. Wilson knew he wasn't standing in a real snowstorm though, because the flakes were huge and not at all like snow. More like fluffy balls of cotton candy. They filled the air like drifting clouds. He held out his hand to touch one, but it passed through his fingers without sensation.

At the same moment he heard a sharp hiss, like steam being expelled under pressure and his field of view became further obscured by a pall of smoke. Wilson turned his head to locate the source and the air cleared. He was in touching distance of the enormous engines of a space rocket. Vapour billowed around coils of pipes and valves, suggesting the gleaming white rocket was primed for take-off, bang in the middle of The Market Square.

Wilson peered upwards. The Clock Tower was still there.

But it had launched itself in an upward trajectory to match the colossal height of the rocket and a latticework walkway connected the two somewhere near the top. Stacked letters spelled out 'Apollo 11' but the middle 'o' was out of line and the American flag, positioned above the 'A', was upside down. Just as they were on the Airfix model in his bedroom. Through blasts of steam, Wilson could see two figures high up on the walkway. A Bratz doll was climbing into the landing module with Buzz Lightyear. Then something screamed past in a flash of blurred colour and a slipstream of warm air lifted him clean off his feet.

Wilson shook his head to correct his vision as the buildings framing The Market Square came back into focus. But now, hundreds of people were cheering from doorways and leaning out of windows waving an assortment of multi-coloured flags. To Wilson's right, beyond the rocket, a huge grandstand overshadowed the square. It stood five storeys high and was bursting with banks of spectators.

The ground no longer consisted of stone cobbles. Instead, it was covered with a smooth layer of compacted, black plastic. Several narrow tracks, about four inches wide and lined with shiny silver metal were set into the surface. The tracks ran the length of the square from the Clock Tower back up to a bridge at the far end. The bridge was a rickety structure built from plastic drinking straws and branded with logos including Castrol Oil, Firestone Tyres, Richmond Sausages and Peppa Pig. Wilson got the distinct impression he was standing in the middle of a life-size Scalextric track.

A large sign with the words 'Starting Grid' hung below the bridge and alongside that, a traffic light holding on red. Directly beneath, Wilson could make out a row of cars. Each vehicle was fitted with the fat rubber tyres of Formula One, yet the bodywork took the shape of the kiddy rides one might see outside an amusement arcade, moulded in fibreglass. Just visible above the curve of a steering wheel, hidden within a crash helmet, Wilson sensed determined drivers with their eyes fixed firmly on him. He could hear high-pitched, revving engines and the smell of burning oil made his nostrils sting.

It was at that moment, Wilson realised all the spectators had stopped cheering and were now craning their necks towards *his* end of the track. He watched the traffic light flick from red to amber and a second later shift abruptly to green. At the sight of green for go, the crowd reignited as the bizarre collection of toy cars came hurtling down the metal tracks like missiles locked on target. Evidently, we all possess an innate desire for self-preservation, because without thinking, Wilson started to run as fast as his legs could carry him.

Climb on those hay bales and you're safe.

As he propelled himself, arms pumping like pistons, in the most frantic race of his short life, Wilson became aware that his legs were not following with the same urgency. He looked down. His right foot was hidden inside a huge felt slipper with the face of Mickey Mouse looking up. His left foot was wearing Goofy, and neither character seemed able to move. The hard plastic of the racetrack was turning into a lumpy, clingy jelly. Mickey and Goofy were frowning helplessly as both slippers sank deeper into a treacle blancmange. Wilson looked up, the cars were still on a collision course. Eighty metres, fifty metres, ten metres away. His ankles were almost entirely consumed. Wilson braced himself for the inevitable. Then somebody shook the snow globe and a blizzard of white flakes swirled across the square. As the flakes began to settle, the cars, the cheering fans and the syrupy tarmac all melted away and a new stage set was unveiled.

Someone tapped Wilson on the shoulder. He turned and immediately jumped back. An astronaut in a bulky, white spacesuit stood towering over him. Wilson could see his spoon-face reflection in the smoky glass visor. The astronaut was holding the lead for what Wilson presumed to be a dog. He couldn't be certain, because the four-legged creature was also wearing a spacesuit.

"Do you know where I can find the Burger King, young man?" the astronaut asked.

Wilson was about to say, "to infinity and beyond," when an enormous giraffe with a pink felt tongue ambled into view and started licking the top of the rocket. A seam along the top of the giraffe's neck had split open and white stuffing was spilling out. Some ham-fisted infant had pulled one of its ears off.

"Ten seconds and counting," announced the astronaut.

Then as if to create a suitable canvas for the explosive spectacle of a lift-off, an 'eclipse effect' passed across the square and daylight was replaced by dusk.

As Wilson's eyes adjusted to the gloom, he was surprised to find The Market Square now totally empty. It had morphed once again. Ornate gaslights cast an eerie glow on the fascia of the butcher's, the baker's, the candlestick maker's. The astronaut and the giraffe had taken off, exit stage left.

Wilson heard a bell tinkle, then after a few moments, a door creaked open. He followed the sound to his left and saw a candle splutter to life in a room on the first floor of an imposing looking building that signage identified as 'The Bank'.

Carried in the still air, Wilson could detect the faintest of voices and then the silhouettes of two figures appeared, side by side, like shadow puppets framed by a window. One figure was short and round, the other tall and thin. Wilson shuddered as a flicker of candle light reflected from a pair of glaring eyes. Goosebumps rose on his arms and he felt a sinister chill in the air. The conversation between the figures continued with more whispering. All was fun before, but now Wilson was frightened. He didn't want to be taken by the child-catchers. The boy who gets eaten by the wolf. Cautiously, Wilson started taking small steps backwards, his eyes never moving from the two shadows.

Then he turned and ran.

The cloying darkness lifted as quickly as it had descended when a huge glowing moon rose in an indigo sky studded with planets patterned like glass marbles.

From somewhere behind Wilson, possibly to his left, but as often happens in a dream, from nowhere in truth, a party of schoolchildren walked past in a regimented single file. A stern faced lady, dressed in a matching tweed skirt and jacket brought up the rear. She was pushing a cast-iron bicycle with a basket overflowing with textbooks and appeared to be shepherding the children across the square.

The boys, who ranged in age from about five to fourteen, wore white trousers, white shirts and grey blazers with a large orange sun embroidered on the breast pocket. The girls wore pink pinafore dresses and hats in the shape of a Cornish pasty.

In the far corner of the square, to the right of the Clock Tower stood an elegant three-storey building, out of character with its neighbours. The walls were a creamy beige, while the window frames, louvre shutters and the entrance door were painted powder blue. The building resembled a small château. Window boxes were brimming with pansies and the letters wrought in a metal gate spelled 'L'École'. The singing children were being ushered in that direction, so with spirits restored, Wilson adjusted his stride to synchronise with the boy at the back and followed the class to school. He attended L'École for several nights and as a result, on the 29th October 2005, at 5.25 p.m., spoke his first sentence in French.

As you know, Wilson stopped speaking French in front of his parents after that extraordinary night in the family kitchen, but the visits to The Market Square continued. As a result, the contents of Alex Armitage's imaginary filing cabinet did indeed begin to grow. The second folder relates to an episode that occurred during Wilson's final year at junior school, during an art and craft lesson.

Chapter 4

The sunflowers

"Today children, you're going to recreate a truly amazing work of art."

Mrs Hope, Wilson's Art and English teacher, pulled back the dust sheet draped over a wooden easel to reveal a framed print of one of the world's most iconic images.

"I present to you, *Sunflowers.* Van Gogh's masterpiece of Post-Impressionism, painted in oils, shortly before the end of his tragic life."

Mrs Hope believed that when it came to art, the best way to acquire technique was to imitate the experts. So, if the class weren't making plasticine versions of the sculptures of Henry Moore they were challenged to forge a likeness of a Banksy or a Rothko – but in poster paint!

"I do hope you followed my request last week for home study on the style of the Post-Impressionists, because today children, it's time to put that knowledge to the test. Take note of the various textures and the balance of light in the composition. You have paper and brushes, so let's begin."

With that, Mrs Hope returned to her desk to mark a pile of poems handed in by Year Four the previous day.

It goes without saying, that a limited palette of school-grade paint was unlikely to facilitate even a passing resemblance to Van Gogh's *Sunflowers*, but in enthusiastic hands, the forging began.

Wilson was soon lost in his work. A mix of yellow with a

27

hint of brown made an exact-shade replica of the burnt ochre Van Gogh used to paint the sunflower pot. A little more red with a touch of yellow gave the pot a feeling of depth and a blend of blue with white and green made the perfect hue for outlining the pot – just as Van Gogh had done. Even to a trained eye, the developing composition was beginning to look like a masterly, school paint portrayal of the real thing.

With a sparsely bristled brush, Wilson moved on to re-creating the rich complexity of the sunflower heads and the tangle of spidery petals that surrounded them.

Half an hour later, an uncharacteristic stillness descended on the art room and perceiving the absence of the normal din as the unmistakable sign of mischief, Mrs Hope put down her green pen, lifted her eyes from the wretched poem she was marking and surveyed the scene.

For some reason, the entire class had decided to abandon their work and, more significantly, their desks and had converged in the vicinity of Wilson Armitage. Much jostling and pushing was accompanied by whispering:

"Come on, let me see."

"No, you move."

"It's incredible."

"Class, what the devil is going on?" Mrs Hope rose from her desk and strode towards the scrummage surrounding Wilson.

"Wilson, what on earth are you doing in there? Class, move back, at once!"

Just as the irate teacher was about to reach the hub of the slowly parting children, Wilson clumsily dropped his brush in a pot of water causing it to tumble and release a sea of milky-brown opaqueness all over his artwork. In a split second, all the detail in his masterpiece had been flushed away.

Had he not been so absorbed in the challenge of faithfully replicating the twists and turns of the sunflower stems, Wilson would have noticed the interest the entire class was expressing in his artwork. In which case, he would have released the localised flooding earlier. Unfortunately, the teacher came close enough to catch a glimpse and in the brief moment before the painting was obliterated, what she saw, left her almost speechless. As speechless as if Van Gogh himself had sat at Wilson's desk and improvised his own poster paint, post-impression.

Later that afternoon, as Wilson was walking home from school, a classmate, a stocky, ill-tempered lad who'd made it plain he didn't like Wilson, appeared on his left shoulder. The boy's elder brother appeared on the right. Wilson was expecting the usual stinging slap across the nape of his neck. But not the solid punch in the face that sent a front tooth deep into his top lip. Nor the elbow to the stomach that left him doubled-up in pain on the pavement.

"Smart arse freak" the classmate spat.

Wilson stumbled to his feet and watched them high five each other as they crossed the road, giving the 'V' sign to a driver who was forced to brake sharply to avoid an accident.

The punctured lip needed two stitches. Wilson told his mum he'd fallen and banged his mouth on the kerb.

This was not an isolated incident and questions were beginning to be asked in the Armitage household. The litany of torn school shirts, mud splattered sweaters, grazed knuckles, facial scratches and the missing kit bag could not simply be passed off as Wilson being clumsy, a growing lad or a bit of rough and tumble in the playground.

Two months later, at parents' evening, Mrs Hope spoke with Gloria and Alex.

"I have to be frank with you both, I am a little concerned about Wilson. From being one of our outstanding pupils, he seems to have regressed quite markedly in recent months. He used to be the first to raise his hand, always with the correct answer, always happy to contribute in class discussion, but now he seems more hesitant. His work no longer shines like it used to. It's as though he's content with not trying. A lack of confidence I suppose. I can't put my finger on it. Wilson certainly has super potential but seems not to want to apply it, or rather, he prefers to mask it. For example, he created a wonderful version of Van Gogh's *Sunflowers* and then seemed to intentionally destroy his work by knocking a water pot over it. It was a superb piece for anyone, let alone a ten-year-old, quite incredible and I would like to see more of that from Wilson."

Alex agreed with Mrs Hope that Wilson, "does indeed have hidden potential that occasionally bubbles to the surface."

As the words left his mouth, he'd already started to open the filing cabinet. Behind a folder tabbed with the words 'Speaking French', he inserted a second folder labelled, 'Painting like Van Gogh'.

Chapter 5

Three years later

It was the move up to secondary school that enabled Wilson to escape the 'freak weirdo' tag and bullying that dogged his junior years. By the age of thirteen, he had become a fully fledged chameleon, effortlessly adept at blending in, with the pendulum of his overt potential never swinging far from the median. And his camouflage had been perfect, until the day Gloria declared it was time to visit the charity shop.

"Girls, you have so much old stuff cluttering up your bedrooms. Those Bratz dolls have more clothes than Topshop and you don't play with them anymore – they need to be adopted by a new family. And that applies to you Wilson. It's time for Action Man and his Duplo pals to pack up and move out. Time for a tidy up in other words."

Wilson and his sisters followed orders and an hour later, after foraging under beds and delving in cupboards, all the forsaken were stacked in the hallway.

Alex returned home from shopping duties and promptly declared that he also had a loft full of old CDs, clothes and other bits and bobs.

"Ideal charity shop fodder Wilson, give me a hand with the ladders and I'll pass it all down." With that Alex bounded upstairs beckoning Wilson to get a move on.

As Wilson shuttled up and down the stairs, something half-hidden in a cardboard box caught his eye. He'd seen a boy playing with the same thing in L'École, a year or so earlier.

"What's this Dad?" Wilson held aloft the multi-coloured plastic brick. It was a cube measuring about six centimetres and each face was divided into smaller squares of different colours.

Alex's head poked out from the loft like a tortoise emerging from its shell. He smiled on recognising the object in Wilson's hand.

"Goodness me, I'd forgotten about that. It's a Rubik's Cube; the best toy ever invented. You don't see them around nowadays, but years ago they were more popular than Pokemon."

Wilson looked questioningly at the lifeless block in his hand as his father continued.

"The Rubik's Cube has six sides. You spin round the different sides, from left to right, and . . . here, throw it to me. It'll be quicker to show you."

Wilson tossed the cube up to his dad.

"At the moment all the squares on each face are mixed up. What you have to do is twist it, until you get all the same colours together. So all the small green squares are together, all the red, all the white and so on."

The verbal explanation was illustrated with much swivelling and rotating. Alex threw the cube back to Wilson.

"But what's the point Dad?"

"Well, the first point is to solve the puzzle, so that all six faces show the same colour. The second point is to do it as fast as you can. My best time was just under a minute but it took me months to be that good. The world record is six seconds."

Alex disappeared back into the loft.

"Be down in a minute. Think I've just about unearthed everything."

Wilson sat on a stair and studied the cube.

All the colours must be the same on each side.

He rotated the top face ninety degrees and followed a yellow square as it vacated its position for a blue square. A bewitching sensation, as if Wilson already knew the next move, in fact, how to complete the entire puzzle, then shimmered through his mind. He turned away from the cube and by some inexplicable mental alchemy, an instinct, an intuition, was creating, unearthing, a step by step guide for his fingers to follow. Wilson looked back down to the cube and began twisting the sides two at a time, just as the boy in L'École had done. His fingers were lost in a blur of motion as they followed the stream of instructions being transmitted down to his hands. Nine-seconds later, the sorcery ended with a final twist and sitting in his palm was the puzzle, all correct and solved, with six uniform sides.

"Wilson, just hold those ladders steady for me. I can't find anything else the charity shop will be interested in."

Wilson's wonderment at correcting the cube so quickly dissolved as an outstretched leg began searching for a foothold. He threw the toy into the box and shifted the stepladders to the required position. With both feet safely on the floor, Alex tucked the ladders under his arm and headed for the garage.

"Bring that last box down will you son. I'm taking everything to the charity shop this afternoon."

"Lunch is ready!" Gloria called from the foot of the stairs.

The door to Megan and Kate's bedroom flew open and Wilson stepped to one side as the girls barged past.

"Wilson, you've got to leave for football soon and you need to pack your bag. Muddy boots are by the boiler where you left them. Clean socks and shorts in the drawer. Can you also bring down any clothes that need washing."

As a result, Wilson forgot to carry that final box downstairs for his father, which meant he also failed to undo his handiwork.

Three hours later, Alex was opening the door to leave the Oxfam shop when he heard one of the ladies behind the counter say to a colleague, "and look at this, a Rubik's Cube, with all the squares in the right place. That chap must be ever so clever."

Alex didn't turn around; he didn't need to. The cube was all mixed-up when he threw it back to Wilson and somehow he'd managed to solve it without any apparent need for practise.

A folder labelled 'Rubik's Cube' was filed away.

Chapter 6

The youth club incident

At the age of sixteen, Wilson had two best mates and their nicknames were Hoover and Teapot.

Hoover was very tall for his age and as a consequence, very skinny. He had fine, jet-black hair that couldn't be coaxed into any style other than the flat, straight look. His eyes shone mischievously and a semi-permanent grin would stretch to laughter at the slightest comedic prompt. His gangling arms and legs looked out of proportion with the rest of his body and his coordination was terrible; as though he was breaking-in his limbs for somebody else.

Inexplicably, Hoover was a musical wizard when it came to playing the drums. His oversized hands struggled to control a knife and fork, (his nickname came from an ability to vacuum-up food without much need for cutlery), but give him a pair of drumsticks and he'd turn them into magic wands.

Teapot was also into music. He played electric guitar with the same enthusiasm Hoover had for drums and two nights a week they would rehearse in Wilson's garage with the other members of The Girl Guides. Nick Storey was lead vocalist and Tom Archer played bass. Wilson felt sorry for Teapot for two reasons. The first, his nickname and the second, his mum.

Teapot was really called Graham Clarke and the nickname was a self-inflicted injury.

One afternoon, a few mates were gathered in Wilson's bedroom playing *FIFA World Cup* on the PlayStation when

Graham Clarke declared that he wanted a nickname.

"What do you want a nickname for?"

"Cos it's boring being called Gray all the time."

"So what nickname do you want then?"

Hoover had little interest in the reply. Both eyes were glued to the TV screen and his clumsy hands were furiously rotating the toggle of a PlayStation controller. No matter what move he tried to make, the players either ran in the wrong direction or ran off the pitch. His man management skills were hilarious.

Graham considered the nickname question.

"I don't know. Something different. Could even be totally random."

Hoover was pressing every button in an attempt to stop his striker scoring an own goal, and so Wilson, transfixed by the comedy of unforced errors, wasn't really thinking when he said, "What? Like err, I dunno . . . Teapot?"

And before Graham had a chance to tell Wilson to stop being bloody stupid, Hoover rubber stamped it: "Yeah, that's excellent. Let's call him Teapot!" The naming ceremony was over and from that moment onwards, much to his annoyance, Graham Clarke was referred to as 'Teapot', or informally, as 'Teaps'.

The real reason Wilson felt sorry for Teaps however, was because of his mum. She went missing when he was a baby and Wilson didn't know the full story. Apparently, Vanessa Clarke, Teapot's mum, had been a successful business women and happily married. Then soon after giving birth to Teaps, she went to a meeting in London and never came home. Teapot's father, Michael, never understood what he'd done to drive his wife away and over the years the guilt took a toll on his well-being; to the extent that his landscape gardening business collapsed and he turned to alcohol for solace. Teapot and his dad lived in a small flat in the centre of Stockport and survived on Jobseekers' Allowance and Teapot's part-time work, stacking shelves in a supermarket.

Not that you'd think Teapot's life had been touched by ill fate.

He was good looking, popular on social media, wore his hair tied in a trendy ponytail and was forever flitting from one girlfriend to another. Gloria Armitage thought Teapot had a permanent air of sadness about him though. "The sparkle seems to be missing from his eyes," she would say, and be overly fussy whenever he called round.

At the time of the youth club incident, the academic year was over and a "summer of football and *fräuleins*," as Hoover put it, was on the cards. To celebrate the end of term, Bramhall Youth Club was throwing a Leavers' Ball and The Girl Guides had been booked to play.

The Youth Club booking was the band's first performance in front of an audience and the day was spent rehearsing and sound checking, plus order-taking and general roadying for Wilson.

Twenty minutes before they were due on stage, Nick Storey took a call on his mobile. Wilson and Teapot were standing at the back watching a boisterous audience stream through the entrance doors.

"Bloody hell," said Wilson, "there's about forty people here so far. The rugby lads are in and that girl Hoover fancies is over there with her mate. My sisters are here as well. Don't bottle it Teaps or this could be very embarrassing."

Storey had walked to a far corner of the stage so none of the group could hear his conversation. When the call ended, the look on his face said it hadn't been good news.

"Archer's cried off."

"What?" They shouted in unison.

"What do you mean he's cried off?" Teaps asked.

"He said he doesn't think he's good enough to play. He's totally stressed and he feels sick."

There was a moment's silence as the news sank in.

"So, does that mean he's not coming . . . now, in a few minutes?"

"Yeah, that's exactly what it means Hoover you muppet!"

The audience, which had swelled to over sixty, was getting restless. Egged on by those who'd managed to get served in the pub across the road, the crowd now began singing their *own* songs."

It was all going disaster shaped.

Storey was about to tell the club manager the performance would have to be cancelled when Wilson turned his camouflage down a notch.

"Hoover, silly question, but is the bass player really essential? I mean, can't the band play as a three piece rather than four?"

Hoover gave him a look that said, "you haven't got a clue what you're banging on about."

"Alright then, look, Archer's guitar's there, so I'll stand in for him. You can't cancel your first ever gig. Come on, we don't have any other options."

Teaps turned to Wilson.

"What do you mean, stand in for Archer? You've never played a guitar in your life. You think you can just pick up a bass and bang out a tune? Sorry Wilson, there's no chance."

"Okay, okay. I confess. I was keeping it a secret, but I've been having lessons on the quiet; it was hacking me off not being able to play with you lot."

Teaps thought Wilson was joking.

"Are you any good?" Hoover asked, knowing the question was open to interpretation.

"I'm okay. Well, I'm not as good as Archer, but I know all the songs, I've heard you cock them up enough times. Besides, the rugby lot look like they're about to kick off if something doesn't happen soon."

Given the lack of alternatives, Hoover persuaded Storey to give it a try "It's either play with Wilson or we do a runner, and that won't be easy, since I'm the one with a drum kit."

As Wilson strapped the bass over his shoulder and checked the tuning, the club manager apologised for the delay and the change of line-up, which now included the last-minute stand-in, Armitage Wilson!

The hall lights went out, the stage lights came on. "One-two-three" yelled Hoover and The Girl Guides launched into their set.

Although Wilson's ability was equal to that of Tom Archer, he made a point of playing a few duff notes in each song. His offer to stand-in was the only option to keep the gig alive and he knew better than to steal the limelight. But for that one night, he took a chance and enjoyed it. Those hours spent jamming in the music room of L'École had paid a dividend.

The next morning, Kate and Megan shared the news over breakfast, but for some reason, Dad didn't seem at all surprised by the revelation his son was a budding rock star.

Chapter 7

What's going on?

While those of a cynical disposition could dismiss the *'incidents'* on the previous pages as nothing more than snapshots of innate talent; like a mathematical genius performing long division in their head or an opera singer always hitting the right note. Wilson however, was not born with the innate talent for saving the lives of car crash victims. His extraordinary abilities were not a genetic windfall or a quirk of nature. The *'incidents'* were actually mistakes. Careless mistakes, made on the handful of occasions when he dropped his guard and allowed a divine light, albeit fleetingly, to shine through the fog of everyday life.

Over the course of twelve years, from speaking French at the age of five, Wilson visited The Market Square at least once a week, sometimes for three or four nights in a row.

In the early years, he was drawn to L'École and behind a desk in Class 6a, wearing a blazer with a flaming orange sun embroidered on the pocket, he was introduced to number of languages in which he quickly became adept. It was as though in the course of a dream, Wilson could soak up the steady drip-drip of foreign words and then in daylight hours, trace the leak back to a full reservoir of vocabulary and grammar. Having dreamed a little, it seemed Wilson knew where to find the lot. In the same way, Wilson mastered a wide variety of other subjects on L'École timetable. By clutching a twig of information during the night, he found it was connected to an entire tree of knowledge when he woke the next day.

One night, having fallen asleep reading a school textbook about the Battle of Britain, Wilson found himself dreaming about Winston Churchill and how the country would 'never surrender.' When he woke the next morning, he was not only able to recall a great deal of historical fact from the summer of 1940, he could remember – no, more accurately, he had access to the broader story of Winston Churchill himself. Everything experienced by Churchill around that time became a sort of flicker book that Wilson could refer to during waking hours and open on whichever page he chose.

As Wilson grew older, his appetite for nocturnal experiences graduated to the full smörgåsbord available in The Market Square. Martial arts, skateboarding, scuba diving, sailing, flying lessons, lion taming, every pursuit and pastime that could be dreamed up, was on the menu. Two activities were listed as 'compulsory' on the syllabus for Wilson, and those were motorcycle maintenance and the paramedic training course.

Now you'd think living a schizophrenic double life, with all that information crammed inside your head, not to mention the paranoia, self-doubt and self-identity issues, would drive you crazy. And why bother going to college when you can learn more at night school?

Well, one reason Wilson was able to maintain an even keel, was because the knowledge acquired during his dreams wasn't actually stored in his memory; only the links to it. It was as though once Wilson had been given the taster for a particular experience or topic, *(the drip-drip)*, the entire subject matter, (*the reservoir of knowledge*), was held on file in the equivalent of a data server, a 'cloud computer', somewhere beyond the realms of his consciousness. When not logged in to his cloud account, Wilson could concentrate on being himself, with no distractions. But when the need arose, as was the case with the rescue of Sally Bennett, he could tap a key to recall a first aid lesson and thereafter, access an entire Wikipedia of paramedic skills.

The second reason for the level-headedness was the fact that although Wilson knew he was *abnormal*, as a teenager, he had no intention of being seen as anything other than *completely normal*. So the self-questioning was always put to one side, ignored, avoided, left for on another day, when no doubt the psychiatrist would be called.

There's much to be explained and all will be revealed, but right now, we have to catch up with Wilson, as he is today, almost eighteen and just a few hours away from an unlikely rendezvous and a potentially 'game changing' event.

Chapter 8

Wilson has a dilemma

Thirteen years have passed since Wilson first arrived in The Market Square. The 'peas in a pod' are in the final year of their fashion course at Central St Martins. Broadband infrastructure now interlaces the country, so Alex spends his working week determining where the information superhighway will go next. With her three children *almost* flown from the nest, Gloria has time to run a local charity shop, enjoy twice weekly yoga classes and fight a losing battle with the bathroom scales and the advance of grey hair. Bifocals are never far from the tip of her nose.

"Don't worry Mum, you've still got it" Wilson would observe whenever Gloria complained about her jeans stretching a seam. But that also meant Wilson was probably after something; like a lift into town or his mobile phone topping up.

As for Wilson, he went from junior school to Davenport Secondary and then to Stockport College where he's currently studying for A levels in English, Maths and Biology. He's the goalkeeper for a college football team and Hoover and Teapot are still his best friends. He likes the music of Radiohead and Coldplay; and has never had a steady girlfriend, just a few unsteady ones.

As this chapter unfolds, we find Wilson lying on his unmade bed. He's just finished scraping dried blood from his fingernails with a nail file. The blood was from a girl in a car accident earlier that afternoon. Wilson was pleased, because a call to the hospital confirmed that Sally Bennett was going to be okay.

Empty crisp packets, crushed Pringles tubes, Coke cans, all the detritus of a teenage lad litters the floor, including wet towels and odd socks. On the wall facing Wilson's bed, a flat-screen TV is connected to a PlayStation and although the signal to the TV is on pause and the image blurred, it clearly shows the cockpit of a helicopter. Wilson is staring up at the ceiling with a perplexed look on his face. There's something he can't quite figure out. He has a dilemma.

The previous night, he'd arrived in The Market Square with the intention of seeking Mark Sampson's advice on the best winter tyres for his Vespa scooter. A travelling circus was snaking through the Square and Wilson had to weave through a nose-to-tail convoy of animals and a troupe of acrobats. En route, a mime artist all in black with white face paint, gesticulated towards his unicycle. Wilson soon got the hang of it and even managed a few words in sign language. Moving on through the melee, a clown in a baggy, striped suit taught him to juggle with five skittles and a magician showed him how to conjure a white dove from a wine bottle.

As Wilson stepped onto the pavement in front of Sampson's Motorcycle Workshop, two chimpanzees, walking upright and looking very business-like in pinstripe suits, sauntered past smoking bananas.

"I'm sure I saw Uncle Bill on Nat Geo Wild last night," said one.

"Who – uh, uh?" questioned the other, chimpishly.

Wilson ignored the monkey business, pushed open the

door and stepped inside the shop.

It smelled of grease and spray paint and an impressive line-up of motorbikes and scooters with lots of gleaming chrome ran the length of the workshop. At the far end, sitting on a work bench, was Mark himself. He was wearing oil-stained overalls, a torque wrench was protruding from a grimy fist and he was talking to someone.

Wilson closed the shop door, Mark looked up, smiled and beckoned him over.

"Hey Wilson, how's it going my friend? Haven't seen you for a while. Speak of the devil and the devil walks in. Was just chatting about your problems restoring that old Vespa with . . . erm . . . "

'Erm' was leaning against the seat of a Harley Davidson with their back to Wilson. Wilson had been too busy acknowledging Sampson to notice whether 'erm' was a him or a her, but as the customer turned to Wilson, the swish of a ponytail followed by a pretty face confirmed the 'erm' was definitely a her.

"Hi, I'm Daisy, Daisy Meadowcroft."

She extended her hand.

For quite a few seconds nothing happened following the proffered handshake. It was as though Wilson's mental faculties had all scarpered and were peeking from behind a sofa somewhere waiting to see what happens next. Wilson came to his senses and realised he was thunderstruck.

thunderstruck
adjective
    1.   completely taken aback; amazed or shocked
    2.   (rare) struck by lightning

And Wilson had been hit by the *(rare)* version.

Daisy Meadowcroft was quite simply the most beautiful girl he'd ever seen. He was face-to-face with his dream girl and couldn't shake her hand, because his palms were too clammy. So for some reason, he stood on the balls of his feet to make himself look taller.

"Hi. I'm Wilson. Wilson Armitage."

"So I can't help you then?" Mark Sampson asked. He had an odd smile on his face as he headed off to a partitioned corner that stood for an office.

Wilson descended to normal height. Daisy really was lovely. She had chestnut highlights in the satin sheen, auburn hair that Wilson guessed would reach her shoulders but for the ponytail. She had a perfectly proportioned face, with a soft roundness rather than a point to her nose and her olive skin had the sheen of a Mediterranean tan. No, even better, her silky-smooth skin was a shade of creamy butterscotch. Her lips and mouth were a work of art. She was slim and above average height; in fact, only a few inches shorter than Wilson, which may explain why he thought it necessary to try and look taller. She was wearing a cropped white t-shirt with the word 'HOAX' printed on the front, burgundy jogging pants and a pair of hi-top trainers. An assortment of bangles and bracelets jangled as she held out her hand.

"Hi, like I said, I'm Daisy Meadowcroft."

This time, Wilson took the outstretched hand. It was warm and soft and firm all at the same time. Then something like pins and needles ran the length of his arm. Wilson instinctively pulled his hand free.

"Whoa, what was that?" He shook the charge out from the tips of his fingers.

"Thought so," said Daisy. "I know you!"

"You know me?"

"Yes, I remember you from the school, L'École – you know, in the bottom corner of the square, behind the Clock Tower? It was a few years ago. We sat next to each other in French class. Didier had the desk on your left and I was on the right. We were only young. But I definitely remember you."

"Well, that's going back a bit. Sorry for not remembering you." Wilson paused and waited for an interesting follow-up sentence to enter his head.

"You've probably changed since then?"

This was not only, *not*, an interesting follow-up sentence, it made him feel as though he was still in infant school. Daisy smiled, then replied.

"Yeah, of course I've changed, I'm not five anymore! Everything looks different as you get older. Even The Market Square. You've been coming here as long as I have, so you must have seen the way it can alter?"

She paused for a moment.

"And you must've learned lots of neat things from this place?" Daisy raised both eyebrows questioningly.

Wilson wasn't certain if Daisy was hinting that she knew the secrets of The Market Square.

"Oh yes, I know what happens here. More than you'd think."

There was a moment of uncomfortable silence but then the penny dropped and Wilson admonished himself for being overawed.

"Of course you know about The Market Square, because you're in my dream. My subconscious brought you here, invented you I guess and decided to call you Daisy – you're just a figment of my imagination!"

Wilson waited for his brain to instruct Daisy to praise his subconscious powers but she just laughed at him. The richest, syrupy sweet laugh imaginable.

"That's a hell of a theory Wilson."

Her look of bemusement then became tempered with pity.

"So what do you call someone who invents a girl just to meet them in a dream? Desperate? A sad loser?"

Daisy was now grinning and Wilson could see from her dancing eyes there was more to come.

"So that means, if I'm your invention, I can jump around and do crazy things, because really it's you in control of all the jumping. And if I do this," – Daisy stepped forward and flicked the tip of Wilson's nose – "it's self-inflicted. Stop it Wilson. That's painful. You'll get a nosebleed."

Daisy was enjoying the moment.

"Wilson, why did you make me do that? No, why did you do that to yourself? Oh heck, it's complicated, this dreaming stuff."

Wilson's nose was definitely stinging, with real pain. He was bewildered and on the verge of trying to banish Daisy from the dream in order to prove that he was fully in charge of what happened in *his* Market Square. Yet, at the same time, he wanted Daisy to stay right there. In fact, a parallel line of thought was trying to fathom out what he'd done to bring Daisy to Sampson's workshop in the first place, how he'd been able to create her to look the way she did, and how to do it again in the future!

"You're thinking of how to block me from this dream, aren't you?" Daisy asked, laughing at the same time. "But you can't seem to get rid of me. Even though I've been created by you."

More laughter flowed until Daisy finally took a deep breath and composed herself.

"Do you know why?"

Wilson had no answer and stood there entranced.

"Well, I'll tell you why. Because this dream is also mine. Well, it's shared actually."

"What do you mean, this isn't my dream? Of course it's my flipping dream."

Wilson was getting flustered and once again stood on the balls of his feet. But this time it didn't make him look taller, just a bit of a plonker.

"Do you remember a few moments ago, when you entered the shop and we shook hands? Did you feel a sensation, like an electric current running up your arm, just for a split second?"

"Yeah, 'course I remember. That's the first time that's happened – and I have some pretty vivid dreams."

"Good for you. But what was really happening at that moment Wilson, was you and me, crashing. My grandmother told me about it but I don't remember all the details; I was young at the time. Anyway, here in The Market Square it's possible. If you're a special person . . . "

Daisy began twirling round, making spidery movements with her hands, " . . . and have special powers."

Wilson's blank expression confirmed he was utterly lost.

"Okay Wilson, how can I put this? People like us find it easy to crash into dreams. It's like, it's like hijacking someone's thoughts while they're asleep."

Mark Sampson poked his head out from his office and considered correcting Daisy's explanation, but then thought better of it.

"So in theory then," said Wilson, trying to rationalise

49

things, "although this is just a dream, I know that when I wake up tomorrow morning, I'll be in bed in Stockport and if I stick a pin in my thumb the blood will prove I'm real!"

He peered intently at Daisy, enjoying the moment before his checkmate move.

"So, the question is this. If you and I meeting here tonight, is also your dream, that means there should be a real Daisy Meadowcroft, sleeping in a real bed in a real house somewhere?"

Daisy removed her bobble, tilted her head back to shake her tresses free, then she gathered them all together in one swift movement, twisted the bobble and pulled the new ponytail tight.

"I live in Macclesfield, it's about twenty minutes on the train from Stockport, and when I wake up tomorrow, I'll stick a pin in my thumb if you like!"

Daisy held up her thumb and pretended to lick the blood, then she added.

"Want to meet for a coffee in Starbucks tomorrow night? The one on Deansgate, in Manchester. My pottery class finishes at five so we could meet at seven. What do you think?"

Wilson's attention was lagging quite a distance behind.

"Wilson!" Daisy stepped forward to give his shoulder a gentle prod. "What do you think? Meet tomorrow? Coffee?"

To describe Wilson as in shock is possibly going a bit far, but he was certainly not all there.

"Err, yeah, 'course, Starbucks, at seven," he mumbled.

And that's why Wilson was in a dilemma. He was troubled by the concept of creating the perfect dream girl, only to then be invited, to meet her in real life. It was surreal. Like sending a personal invitation to meet yourself.

He rolled off the bed, clicked 'play' on the PlayStation and with expert thumbs and fingers, proceeded to put the world's most advanced attack helicopter through its paces.

Chapter 9

Teapot's mum

After half an hour, Wilson paused the game for a second time when Teapot barged through the door shouting, "Black Hawk Down, Black Hawk Down." Teaps then proceeded to career around the bedroom imitating a stricken helicopter and rotating his arms to a 'pffuh, pffuh, pffuh' sound effect before crash landing on Wilson's bed. The amateur dramatics ended as he wrestled with an unresponsive joystick and declared, "I ain't gonna make it this time," then sat up and threw a pillow at Wilson.

"Apache Pilot Pro," Teaps said, nodding at the screen. "Awesome. And you've got your captain's wings. They reckon if you get to that level you could fly the real thing. I'm impressed."

Wilson's blank expression said everything he was going to say on the subject.

"But thinking about it, it's your love life that needs to take off Wilson, not a helicopter. You need to get yourself a girlfriend."

Teaps laughed.

"Seriously Wilson, there's loads of babes on that media course. Put yourself in the shop window. Let 'em know you're available. Hey, here's an idea. I could design a sign for you to wear around your neck at college, saying something like . . . "

"I strangled Teaps cos he was winding me up?" Wilson was not amused.

But Teaps was, and he had a fit of the giggles as he suggested a variety of messages that could be written on Wilson's, 'Sign of Love'.

Wilson wasn't in the mood for joking around, given his dilemma and besides, there was something else, another matter, he wanted to broach.

Perhaps now is the moment?

"Teaps, can I ask you a question? It's kind of personal. And I don't want to make you feel uncomfortable"

"Sure. Fire away."

Wilson placed the PlayStation controller on his desk.

"Do you ever think about what happened to your mum?"

A shadow crossed his friend's face.

"I know she disappeared – and I've always wanted to say I'm sorry for that – but it seems false, cos, I don't really know what happened."

"It's alright. I don't mind. It would be good to get it out in the open for once, to talk about, 'she who can't be named'." Teaps made the paraphrasing actions with his fingers. "To be honest, no-one ever asks me about her. They think it's too delicate a subject. It happened so long ago though and I was just a baby, I don't remember my mum."

Teaps deliberated over his next words.

"I only know life with Dad. I can remember our old house, when he still had the gardening business, bringing me up by himself, finding the money for after school care and all that. But then the depression and the drinking started. There's nothing I can do to change things. I can't bring her back. If that was possible, Dad would have done it ages ago." Teaps took a deep breath and shrugged his shoulders. "It would be good to get my old dad back though. He's never given up hope she'll come back one day."

"Teaps, I don't want you to think I'm being nosey about what happened. I suppose what I'm trying to say is, I'm really sorry for how your life has been. I feel guilty mine has been so easy compared to yours and I never . . . "

Teapot was not listening. His eyes were looking straight ahead, fixed on some dim memory in the archives of the past.

"My dad keeps a scrapbook filled with old family photos. I flick through it sometimes to remind myself I did have a mum once. She was a babe, even if she was my mum. She was half-Italian and met Dad when he was the gardener at her uni. Built her own recruitment business from scratch."

He turned to Wilson and a sad, grudging smile stretched his lips.

"She'd had enough of domestic life with Dad I guess. Or maybe it was postnatal depression. I was an awful baby apparently, crying all night, giving her no sleep. But Dad said it was only because I had colic.

"I blamed myself for a time. You know, 'cause she'd run off. But Dad said she never complained and would cancel a meeting if I'd had a bad night and stay at home to make sure I was okay."

Teaps hesitated.

"Then one day she didn't come home. She went to a meeting in London, won a new contract, had lunch to celebrate then left to catch the train back. The clients said she was in a great mood. But she never came home."

Teaps was sitting cross-legged on Wilson's bed, head stooped, peering down at his hands.

"It's one helluva mystery Wilson."

"But Teaps, surely there must have been an investigation;

the police must have been involved?"

"Yeah, one of Mum's competitors told the police she was having an affair with the new client, and that was how she'd managed to win the contract in the first place. Blackmail was mentioned. When the police investigated, they discovered she'd used her credit card to take cash from her business account the day she disappeared and a few days later in Dover, at the ferry terminal.

"But after a month, they were no further on, so they changed tack and started searching for Mum as a missing person rather than a criminal on the run. But the newspapers weren't interested in a missing mum story, she'd had her fifteen minutes of fame. They preferred the headline 'shady businesswoman runs off with cash' rather than 'where's Mrs Clarke, loving wife and mother?'.

"Dad said the police also cocked things up. The case was passed over to some useless detective who used an old photo of Mum from her student days. So everyone was looking for a young hippy with short curly hair and not a businesswoman with long straight hair.

"The duff copper lost some of the surveillance camera images from the train station. Then Dad found out that a lot of street cameras were out of order. The police dredged the canals, searched empty buildings near the train station, rang the hospitals, but she was never found.

"In the end, the whole thing ruined Dad's life and I guess kind of ruined mine, compared to what it might have been. I'm sure things would have been much better for me and Dad if she'd been around all these years."

"I can't imagine what you've had to go through Teaps, it's just terrible" said Wilson, placing a hand on his friend's shoulder, "but things will get better, I'm sure."

"Yeah, I hope so mate, I really do."

They sat in silence for a minute or so until Wilson glanced at his watch and then leapt to his feet.

"Whoa, Teaps, sorry, don't want you to think I'm being insensitive, but I've got to go in fifteen minutes."

Wilson grabbed a clean white polo shirt from a shelf and fresh jeans from a hanger in his wardrobe.

"Why, what're you up to?"

"Contrary to my single man status, a flame of passion has been lit. Well, it's more of a spark really – I'm going to meet someone in Manchester for a coffee."

"You mean a date? With a real girl?"

"No Teaps, a real rabbit!"

"Excellent, come on then, spill the beans."

"Yeah, I met her in a dream and we . . . "

Wilson blinked and his cheeks erupted in a red flush.

"I mean, a drama class, a drama class about dreams, that's where we first met."

"What?" Teapot looked understandably confused.

"Yeah, I met her in a drama class. A workshop actually, at a college in Macclesfield, that I went to . . . last summer. We had to act out this story that was all about a dream, that's where we first met. She gave me her number in the canteen afterwards and we kept in touch. She lives in Macclesfield. Probably won't come to anything."

Teapot wasn't convinced. He was also a little disappointed with Wilson's gibberish, particularly after revealing the heartfelt story about his mum.

Wilson felt the rift and decided to dilute the damage by playing the village idiot. So he jumped up and did a couple of awkward looking karate kicks and hand chops.

"As from tonight, I'm in the game my man. I'm making my move Teaps, I'm making ma moves."

Teaps was a hundred per cent certain that Wilson was winding him up, but couldn't see the point in questioning his ridiculous story so let it pass.

"We're meeting for coffee in Starbucks on Deansgate at seven," said Wilson. "She's called Daisy, as in daisy the flower."

"Well, I didn't think it would be Daisy, as in Daisy the cow! Nevertheless, I'm sure love will blossom – kerrrching."

They both laughed.

"Anyway, good luck mate," said Teaps, "gotta shoot; working the late shift and then gonna eat with Dad. Tell me about it tomorrow. And thanks for listening about, err, you know who. Appreciate it."

With that, Teaps left Wilson's room, bounced down the stairs two at a time, shouted "See ya, Wilson's mum" to Wilson's mum and slammed the front door behind him. Wilson released a sigh of relief.

Chapter 10

In the mirror

Wilson took a quick shower, double-brushed his teeth and stood for a moment in front of the bathroom mirror.

"Like a blonde version of Ed Sheeran but without the tattoos," is how his mum had once described him. Wilson wasn't sure if that was a compliment. However, as he studied his reflection, he wasn't inspecting the unruly cropped hair, stubby nose, green eyes or the sparse presence of sprouting bristles; he was looking beneath the surface and facing up to something much deeper than a mirror's superficial reflection. Wilson was trying to see inside himself, to garner a true impression of the person staring back.

For too long, Wilson had failed to admit to himself what he was capable of; believing that if he ignored the strange gifts, they would go away and the whole dream thing would eventually stop happening. The phrase 'I'll grow out of it' had been a comfort blanket for far too long. Now, after the heroics beneath the car, there was no escaping a confrontation with his adult self. It had all come to a head. He was nearly eighteen-years-old, physically mature, yet still demonstrating the inexplicable ability to learn from a dream and carry the knowledge back to waking life. He was certainly *not* growing out of it.

You're going to have to get to grips with this. What you do is nothing about being clever or a child prodigy; it's actually a miracle, plain and simple. It defies explanation – and it's not going away.

He continued to silently question the person in the mirror.

Plus, if Daisy does turn up, it will be the equivalent of a ghost being captured and interviewed on TV. There's no law of nature able to explain how you can meet a stranger in a dream and then meet in real life. 'A-squared plus B-squared equals C-squared' won't matter, because there'll be a new, top trump law in town. If she turns up, it will be the tipping point, the point at which you'll finally have to confront this dream phenomenon and find an explanation for what exactly is going on.

As Wilson brushed his teeth for the third time, fifty per cent of him hoped Daisy would show, fifty per cent hoped she wouldn't and a further fifty per cent thought he was going mad.

Intrigued by the implications of *'possibly'* seeing Daisy again, he grabbed the scooter keys and zipped up his parka.

"Mum, just off into town. Need a book for college. I'll see you later."

"But Wilson, what about something to eat?"

"I'll get a McDonald's or a Subway."

"Wilson, you know that food's not healthy."

"I know. I'll ask for extra lettuce. See you later."

"Be careful love, on that scooter. It's rush hour."

"I will, don't worry."

Wilson pulled up the garage door to reveal a fully restored, 1959 Vespa GS 150 – a classic 'mod' scooter complete with the essential stack of mirrors, multiple headlamps and bodywork painted like a Union Jack. The Vespa was Wilson's pride and joy.

With one kick the scooter fired up and ten minutes later Wilson was navigating his way through Davenport village, on his way to Starbucks in Manchester, with a seemingly zero per cent chance of meeting a figment of his imagination by the name of Daisy Meadowcroft.

Chapter 11

A pause, for background on the Vespa

Wilson first noticed the abandoned scooter from the top deck of a bus. He'd just turned sixteen and for six months watched it continue to disintegrate, day by day, rusting and neglected on someone's driveway.

At the time, he had no interest, in fact, no awareness of the world of scooters. However, a plaintiff cry must have been heard, because Wilson spent several nights pottering about with Mark Sampson in his motorcycle workshop and not only acquired access to the skills of a competent mechanic but also a love of Vespas. With his newfound interest in two-wheelers, Wilson plucked up the courage to knock on the owner's door and ask if the machine could be salvaged.

"It belonged to my son," said the elderly lady as she tapped the rusting carcass of metal and chrome with the side of her foot. "He emigrated to Australia about ten years ago and though he promised to ship the scooter over, he never did. I'm surprised, because he loved his Vespa. He was obsessed with everything about the sixties and looking like one of those mods. Dressing like a mod with the special hair cut, his black suits, the music, and of course the scooter was essential. Not that it looks like much now. I remember him going to Blackpool on it once, with all his pals, for some kind of Sixties revival thing."

Wilson knelt beside the decaying icon and pictured the machine in its heyday with all the headlights and mirrors.

I can bring this back to life, he convinced himself.

Three weeks later, following a conversation with her son, the elderly lady offered Wilson the Vespa free of charge, in return for removing the eyesore from the side of her house and she wished him luck with the restoration.

Wilson nursed the scooter the two-mile walk home and as he wearily pushed seized wheel bearings and two flat tyres up the driveway, Kate blocked his path.

"Are you starting a scrap metal business Wilson? Cos there's no way you're gonna be able to fix that. Dad will have a fit when he sees what you've brought home."

Using the last of his strength, Wilson eased the Vespa into the garage like a hospital porter pushing a patient into surgery. He gently laid it to rest on its side before bringing the garage door down on the face of his grinning sister.

"Well, see you in a few years then," he heard Kate shout.

As Wilson surveyed the pile of dented and corroded metal, seized components and smashed headlights lying on the concrete floor, he couldn't help but think Kate may have had a point; perhaps he had bitten off more than he could chew?

From the day the Armitage family moved into 7 Midland Drive, the garage had been a dumping ground for items that were either broken or no longer loved. Scanning the garage, Wilson could see an old pine table and four matching chairs, a stained mattress, plastic storage baskets filled with junk, a pair of step ladders and stacks of old paint tins. This was all piled strategically in front of the window at the back of the garage. The last thing he needed was his sisters snooping around and reporting back to Dad.

It took Wilson a day or so to dismantle the scooter into its component parts. He then spread these across the garage floor like a one-to-one scale 'build your own knackered Vespa' kit. He bought a book about rebuilding classic scooters, a couple of enthusiast magazines and printed off a bundle of pages relating to the technical aspects of scooter restoration from various sites on the web. Wilson then left this assortment of literature lying around the house to convince his dad that the restoration was being done in the old-fashioned way, with oil under fingernails and learning from mistakes. Questions like "Megan, have you seen this month's copy of *Scootering* magazine?" and "Mum, has the vinyl material for my scooter seat arrived from Amazon yet?" provided Wilson with the necessary smokescreen.

To say that Wilson enjoyed the project would be an understatement. Hidden from the prying eyes of Kate and Megan, he dedicated every spare hour to the reincarnation of the fifty-year-old Vespa. Mark Sampson's tutoring in the basics of engine rebuilding, panel beating, spray painting and welding seemed to be amplified the moment Wilson pulled the roller door down on the garage. From knowing just a little, it seemed, he knew where to find the lot. As though a workshop manual, a step-by-step guide to restoring scooters, was stored, or retrievable, in flicker book format in his brain. Plus, he had a genuine flair for the work involved.

Wilson's dad inadvertently caught sight of the Vespa halfway through the restoration (as bad luck would have it, on a night Wilson had forgotten to lock the garage door) and was amazed, not only by the work in progress but also by the sight of his sixteen-year-old son stretch-forming a side protection bar from a length of chromed steel tube. Though that was nothing compared to the afternoon Wilson wheeled the scooter out and asked his parents to open their eyes. Gloria gasped and grabbed Alex to help support her jelly legs. She was looking at something brand new, very shiny and straight from a showroom.

"It's just beautiful Wilson, just incredible. I can't believe you did all that by yourself. It's . . . it's . . . " She was lost for words. "It's like a miracle on wheels."

Gloria was not wrong.

At the sound of the commotion, Kate stepped out of the front door, took one look at the scooter and declared, "Wilson, there's no way you made that!"

She then turned on her heel, took one step back inside the house and shouted, "Megan, I was right. Wilson did throw that pile of scrap away and he's bought a new one with his meatpie money."

Alex Armitage had to pretend to his incredulous wife that there was nothing remarkable about Wilson restoring an old scooter.

"I did exactly the same thing myself," he said, with fingers firmly crossed behind his back. "They look more complicated than they are. You see, you start with Lego, then move up to Meccano and soon after you have all the skills to rebuild a motorbike. It's a rite of passage for a growing lad, like your voice breaking."

"Wilson, it's just . . . wonderful," said his mum, who wasn't really listening to her rambling husband. Then she wiped a tear from her cheek with the back of her hand and tried to say, "I'm so proud of you," but it came out mixed with a sob, which only other proud mums can fully understand, so she simply turned round and went back inside the house.

Wilson on the other hand, *had* been listening to his father;

in fact, he'd made a point of watching his dad's reactions very closely.

He did the same thing after playing with Meccano. What's all that about?

Though his dad knew zip about scooters, he did seem to know how to protect his son from a mother who would need a straitjacket if she'd understood the full implications of what she'd seen.

"Wilson, I don't need to tell you how impressed I am at what you've done here," Alex said when they were alone. "It's incredible. But I think you and I need to have a little chat, because it's *too* incredible."

They pushed the scooter back into the garage and returned to the house for their 'little chat'.

With two cups of coffee for company, Alex closed the lounge door and they sat on the sofa.

Wilson sipped his drink and waited.

"Son," began his father. Alex then scratched the back of his neck and sipped his drink. "What I said about building bikes being part of growing up was true. There's nothing remarkable about teenagers messing with scooters, dismantling them, tuning engines, doing them up. In fact, I had a mate at school, Charlie Smith, whose dad had a business renting out tractors and diggers and all kinds of . . ." Alex paused to reorder his words and to take another sip of his coffee.

"What I'm trying to say is that Charlie was messing around with machinery before he could walk. He worked with the mechanics who fixed JCBs and got involved in stripping down these huge great engines. The point is, at sixteen, he'd been brought up doing mechanical stuff like that and one summer I helped him renovate a scrambler bike. His dad's workshop had all the tools and do you know what? Our project ended up a disaster! The engine constantly misfired, the gearbox rattled like it was full of rocks and after five minutes bouncing round a muddy field the back wheel fell off. Seriously."

Wilson was laughing.

"The point is, the best we could do at your kind of age turned out to be a complete dog's breakfast. But starting with a pile of rusty old scrap – in fact, an infinitely more knackered starting point than Charlie's bike – you've built that!" Alex nodded in the general direction of the garage. "A bloody jaw-dropping, retro perfection. And ignore Kate; I know you did it all by yourself because I saw you working away that night."

Wilson got the point. "Yeah, but you know I can be a bit of a perfectionist, and I had the magazines and internet for help. I bet Charlie Smith didn't have access to bike blogs in the 1920s."

"No, he didn't," replied Alex, too absorbed in thought to notice the dig, "and I agree, you can order parts and ask questions online. But you can't download expertise and bloody skill Wilson. You'd have to be a fully trained mechanic to do what you've done. Plus a welder and spray shop expert and Christ knows what else."

Wilson's father seldom swore, so to say the bloody word twice and now the 'C' word meant he was building up a head of steam.

"So are you going to give me some answers or do I accept my son is a genius and call Mensa?"

Wilson finished the last of his coffee and put the cup down.

"Alright Dad, I'll tell you everything, but you've jumped to the conclusion I did it all by myself. Yeah, I made the Florida bars when you saw me that night, but bending steel pipe isn't that difficult. The truth is, I bought most of it. The original scooter was too badly rusted and bits were missing and I couldn't understand a lot of the expert advice on the internet. I bought most of the parts and a mate of Hoover's brother, who's a mechanic and into all the mod scooter stuff, did a lot of the work in his workshop and quite a bit here in our garage, when you were working away."

Alex Armitage sat back on the sofa, unconvinced.

Wilson hated lying and contemplated telling his father the real truth. Yes, he'd bought some of the parts – after all, he wasn't about to buy a lathe and start turning engine pistons from aluminium block, though he probably could have done – but the rest of it was all his own work. Then he did a quick mental run-through of how the 'tell the truth' story would conclude:

"So how do you like that for an explanation, Dad? I knew how to do it, because I dreamt I could do it. All of it: rebuilding the engine, fitting new brakes, the electrics, spray painting. No, I don't believe it either, but since it's the truth, you'll just have to accept it."

Wilson felt his bottom lip drop as he admonished himself for letting those stupid dreams once again get him into a stupid mess with no explanation as to why he was a goddam sleep freak. But he composed himself and stuck to the story.

"Yeah, it's the truth Dad."

Alex scratched the back of his head and darted to a different line of questioning.

"So where did the money come from then? That Vespa's not a pocket-money-sized project. How did you pay for it all?"

66

He folded his arms as if to say, "now let's see you wriggle out of that one then."

"I earned it from my internet business," came Wilson's robust reply.

There was a pregnant pause, quickly followed by Alex giving birth to a howl of laughter.

"What? You earn money from an internet business? Based where? In your bedroom? In the garage? Wilson, you are incredible!"

"No Dad, it's the truth, straight up – and you'll be impressed with this."

And for the next twenty minutes, over a second cup of coffee, Wilson explained to his father how he had set up a website called Meatpie.com, basically a spoof search engine. The tag line was: 'Ask a silly question, get an even sillier answer!'

"We get loads of daft questions, me, Teaps, Hoover and a few others, and we reply to them with even dafter answers and post them all on Facebook. As some of them are really funny, we get lots of likes and referrals. And here's the crunch – we carry links to boys' toys and gadgets, the stuff lads buy online, and when they do, we get paid a commission. We made nearly three hundred quid last week."

In his office the following day, Alex checked out Wilson's website story and found that although his son's revenues from e-commerce weren't likely to worry the accountants at Amazon, they were more than sufficient to fund a scooter restoration.

Wilson was off the hook for his fundraising talents. However, the source of the skills required to restore a Vespa remained in question, a question that led Alex to the filing cabinet with yet another folder, this one entitled 'Vespa Restoration!'

Chapter 12

Back to the journey to Starbucks

Wilson was scootering along the A6 and about to pass Stockport Infirmary, or to be more accurate, the still standing Victorian wing with the frontage on the A6, when he felt the all too familiar sensation of déjà vu. That short-lived perception of having experienced a particular moment on a previous occasion. It was not uncommon for Wilson to have two or three such episodes a week. But this time the feeling was stronger and more substantial. As though he'd made this stage of his journey before: in the same place, same clothes, in heavy traffic with the hospital on the left. And this wasn't the usual sensation that dissipated in a second. This was a prolonged déjà vu that dragged its heels, refused to vacate its time and place and was accompanied by a throbbing, migraine headache and blurred vision. Wilson was trying to steer his scooter while looking through a crash helmet visor made from 3D vision glasses. With his sense of balance about to topple over, Wilson managed to aim the scooter at the kerb where it came to halt with a front tyre perched on the pavement.

He took a deep breath then unclipped and removed his helmet. His forehead carried a film of sweat and a fine mist fogged the inside of the perspex visor. Wilson peered back over his shoulder along the route he'd just taken, to the point where the déjà vu had started. Traffic and pedestrians hurried by oblivious to his discomfort. Then gradually, like a compass needle settling on the North, Wilson's eyes were drawn towards a huge, mullioned window set between two ornately carved sandstone columns. It was the central feature, a focal point, that dominated the facade of the old part of the hospital building. The sun was low in the sky and although its rays defined the ornate brickwork of the Victorian architecture, the window was a dull plate of non-reflective blackness, as though Teflon coated. Reflections didn't seem able to stick to it. As Wilson contemplated this strange, 'trick of the light,' the headache increased in intensity making him feel nauseous. A sixth sense was telling Wilson that someone was observing him *from the other side of that window* and they were not wishing a good afternoon. Malevolent thoughts were being projected and a message of ill-will filled his head like a telepathic warning. Wilson tried to decrypt the code. Was he being threatened? Warned to stay away? Warned against doing something? The full translation wouldn't come. The subliminal communication continued to mesmerise for a few seconds more and then abruptly stopped. The black hole of window imploded with a burst of brilliant sunlight as the driver of the number thirty-seven bus beeped impatiently at the trespasser in the bus lane blocking his path.

Wilson shook his head in an attempt to bring order to confusion, pulled on his helmet, pushed his scooter from the kerb and steered the Vespa back into the throng of early-evening traffic. As he headed to the centre of Manchester, trying not to dwell on what had just happened, the headache abated, his self-composure returned, then came the fluttering of butterflies in his stomach. The moment of truth was less than five miles away.

Chapter 13

Starbucks on Deansgate

Darkness had fallen as Wilson stood face to face with the cube of concrete and glass, home to Starbucks on Deansgate. It was 6.55 p.m. and he was five minutes early. Reflections from streetlights and headlamps made it difficult to appraise the interior. Wilson cupped both hands against the tinted glass of a window and peered inside like a submariner scanning the horizon through a periscope.

Is it wise to surface and reveal one's self?

He couldn't see anyone who resembled Daisy.

The coast is clear, she hasn't arrived yet.

The usual menagerie of shoppers, students and office workers, sat relaxing at booths and tables, chatting over cappuccinos and carrot cake, while others stood in line, texting and Facebooking and waiting for their peppermint teas and macchiatos.

What will I say if she does actually turn up?

It was at that moment Wilson realised how totally unprepared he was for such a conversation. Butterflies were still flapping deep inside his stomach, his mouth was parched and he had the urge to run – very quickly indeed. To submerge and dive back into the night.

What the hell am I doing? This is totally stupid. I'm going mad. Believing that someone I invented in a dream might actually be alive. A real person. That something I dreamt, could influence the future.

That final, emphatic appreciation of the impossibility of being able to meet Daisy – in fact, the impossibility of Daisy existing at all – settled Wilson's nerves.

He pushed open the door and entered.

Usually, by 7.00 p.m., most Mancunians would be making their way out of the city centre, but on this occasion Starbucks was still busy. Wilson queued patiently and considered the etiquette of only ordering for himself prior to Daisy's arrival.

Should I wait? Order for two?

He wasn't aware of a protocol for his particular situation. Surveying the crowded room, he also realised there would be nowhere to sit if Daisy did actually arrive.

Which isn't going to happen of course.

But just in case, I need to find somewhere quiet. We don't want people overhearing our conversation, so we can't share a table!

Dr Jeckyll continued debating with Mr Hyde.

Perhaps over there would be best? Oh no, someone's taking those seats.

Wilson, does something so ordinary as choosing somewhere to sit really matter in the face of something so extraordinary as Daisy walking through the door?

Wilson's existential debate with himself would have made an excellent thesis topic for a philosophy student.

One of the baristas called Wilson's attention.

"Can I help you?" The girl spoke with a Dutch accent.

"Caffè latte please, with an extra shot."

"Medium or large?"

"Middel tevreden," confirmed Wilson, his mind elsewhere. He handed over four pound coins. *"En hod de verandering."*

The face of the barista lit up. He smiled in return and was

about to continue the conversation when a shutter slammed down.

"Err, sorry. I mean, keep the change."

"Hey, but you speak Dutch. Great, you're my first Dutch speaking customer. I've only been here a month though."

"Um, no, I don't really," stammered Wilson, "in fact, not at all — just got lucky with that. Probably heard it on TV, in a Heineken advert; that's made in Holland, you know."

Head down and blushing, Wilson took his coffee cup and made for the sugar counter where he mentally kicked himself. It wasn't often he slipped up like that. First Teaps, now this. Daisy had him totally on edge.

He noticed two vacant stools by a small round table toward the back of the coffee shop. They would offer a good view of who was coming in and some privacy when, *if*, Daisy arrived.

Wilson sat down and checked his watch. Five past seven.

He poured out the contents of a sugar sachet and watched it slowly sink into creamy froth.

Will she, won't she?

He gave the coffee a stir and took a sip. Then he studied his reflection in an adjacent window. The crash helmet had not crushed his hair too much. He inspected his fingernails. Then checked the tip of his nose for coffee froth. Then discreetly sniffed his armpits.

All good.

Wilson checked the time on his phone: 7.10 p.m.

There was a missed call from Hoover and an accompanying voice mail from an hour earlier. He clicked 'play'.

"Wilson, it's Hoover. Teaps told me you're all loved up. So just a quick call to say I hope the date's going well and ask if she's got a fit friend for me?"

Minutes ticked by.

Sixty seconds followed by sixty even slower seconds.

The next fifteen minutes dragged.

Wilson sipped the lukewarm dregs of his coffee and kept an eye on the comings and not comings.

7.30 p.m. Only grounds remained in his cup. Apparently, like tea leaves, they can also predict the future; but Wilson couldn't see any portents in the sticky patina staining the bottom of his cup; only a shape vaguely resembling Australia.

Starbucks was virtually empty and Daisy was half an hour late.

Guess that's normal with girls. Treat 'em mean and all that. I'll give it a bit longer. Perhaps she's stuck in traffic.

7.35 p.m. During those last five minutes, Wilson had checked his watch and phone twice.

7.40 p.m. The barista asked Wilson if he would like a top-up on the house? He said thanks but no thanks and seemed so lost in his own world, she decided further questioning on the origin of his Dutch would be futile.

At 7.45 p.m. Wilson finally admitted that Daisy wasn't going to make an earth-shattering appearance. The whole notion had been ridiculous in the first place. He felt totally stupid for misleading himself, for even half-believing a meeting could have been possible.

Though not as foolish as the moment Hoover and two equally unwelcome mates, Denver and Sam, piled through the door.

"Well, well, well, look who's having a cosy bit of me time?"

Hoover could see from Wilson's woebegone expression and the single coffee cup that his date had stood him up.

"You're such a loser mate. I'm obviously gonna have to give you a few lessons regarding playing the ladies. You're letting the side down man."

Hoover locked his long arm playfully round Wilson's neck and messed up his hair.

"Come on, get your hand in your pocket. You can buy us a brew and then tell us all about it."

So at 7.50 p.m., fifty minutes after Daisy was meant to arrive, Hoover and his mates sat down and peppered Wilson with uncomfortable questions about the name and identity of the mystery girl, what would be his next move and which of the two Starbucks baristas was the best looking. Daisy Meadowcroft never arrived to join the conversation.

An hour later, as Wilson made the return journey home, (which included a detour to avoid passing the hospital), he detected an abnormal clicking noise coming from the Vespa's engine. He disengaged the clutch and let the scooter freewheel. After knocking the scooter back into gear, the tapping returned. Wilson knew exactly what it was. One of the nuts holding the clutch plate had come loose and was rattling around inside the housing. To open the engine and access the clutch, he would need the special spanner that only Vespa dealers were officially supplied with. Fortunately, he had fashioned one from an old wood chisel during the restoration, which meant the repair would only take ten minutes. Wilson nursed the Vespa through the last few miles, jacked the scooter on its stand and locked the garage door. He stood in the fresh, evening air and shook his head.

Meeting Daisy was never going to happen!

It was only 9.20 p.m., but Wilson was tired. And he knew why. Although he got plenty of sleep, eight hours at least most nights, he didn't actually get much *proper* sleep. Certainly not the kind that made you feel refreshed and recharged. The ever-present shadows under his eyes told as much. His personal trademark. Gloria greeted him from the kitchen door.

"You're back late love. I was getting a bit worried. Have you eaten?"

"Yeah, had a Subway, with Hoover and the boys in town."

"The girls are back for the weekend; your dad's gone to pick them up from the station. There's a bowl of chilli in the oven if you want it?"

"No Mum, I'm good, really. I've got a problem with the scooter and need to get on the internet to find a fix."

"Okay, I'll bring you up a cup of tea later."

Gloria returned to the kitchen and left Wilson to climb the stairs, leaden footed. His bedroom was in semi-darkness and the soft luminous glow from the grinning face on his alarm clock was reassuringly normal, exactly what he needed after an evening spent anticipating the decidedly abnormal. Wilson negotiated a path to his bed and flopped, deflated, on his duvet.

What an idiot. What a bloody idiot. Why on earth did I think for one minute she'd turn up?

Chapter 14

Words of wisdom

Twenty minutes later, as Wilson lay on his bed thinking about the grief Hoover and Co. would be giving him the next day, his father popped his head round the door.

"Hey stranger. Fancy a brew? Room service has sent up a cuppa and custard creams."

Wilson sat up, switched on his bedside lamp and took the mug and plate.

"Cheers Dad, just the job."

He took a couple of sips and dunked a biscuit.

"Got a minute?" Alex pointed at the stool by Wilson's desk.

"Grow florit," replied Wilson, trying to retain a mouthful of tea-and-biscuit mush.

"Haven't seen much of you recently son, so I thought maybe we could meet for breakfast tomorrow morning?"

"Sounds like a plan."

Alex picked up the *'Making a Mint on eBay'* magazine on Wilson's desk.

"So how's the online empire looking?"

"Pays the bills Dad. Keeps me in Vans, the Vespa on the road – you know how it is, with all the sundries."

"Yep, those ice cream sundries can certainly add up." Alex quipped.

Wilson forced a laugh, as though instructed to do so on a TV studio cue card. He wasn't in much of a mood for dad jokes.

"It's all going okay dad."

"Good son, that's good."

Wilson had an easy relationship with his father and though the subject had never been formally raised, he half suspected his dad retained a memory bank of 'questionable' incidents relating to inexplicably precocious abilities. Speaking French at the age of five would have been the first deposit. Sure, over the years he'd faced the occasional lightweight probing, but nothing more. Deep down however, Wilson knew his dad would never draw a line under the matter without at least one earnest interrogation. Perhaps the moment had arrived.

"You seem to be pretty busy at work Dad. Mum says you're being promoted to more of a consultancy role mixed in with research stuff, meetings in London, advising the government. Sounds pretty good."

"Well, I wouldn't call it a promotion as such. It's just that my old job has moved on. Everything is wireless nowadays with computers and routers talking to each other through thin air."

"The never ending march of progress, eh?"

"It is, and part of my new role is to try to work out where we go next, how the internet can be developed further. Web access for the third world from solar powered satellites for example. More importantly, I have to figure out if all this new technology is good for us."

Alex remembered an apt line from *Jurassic Park*.

"Our scientists were so preoccupied with whether or not they could, they didn't stop to think if they should."

Wilson laughed.

Alex paused for a moment.

"Take this new charging technology for example. You

know, how you can put your mobile phone on, well, basically a metal plate and current flows through the plate to charge the phone's battery, with no wires? It's mind-blowing. But the problem is, it could quite literally be mind-blowing. In the old days, the internet flowed through insulated wires, like water in a pipe. But now it's all around us in WiFi networks in the air."

Alex pointed to the flashing router on the wall beside Wilson's desk.

"Data billows out of that thing like smoke signals from a campfire and we have no control over where it goes. Your laptop can read the smoke signals, but the problem is, the smoke sometimes gets blown around by the wind. And I don't mean wind, as in a windy day, I mean energy fields that act like a wind to disrupt the WiFi. How many times have you told me the internet is slow today? Well, quite often it's because energy fields are blowing the smoke around so much that your computer can't grab the signal. We have no idea where WiFi signals go once they're out there, nor how they react with other energy fields, such as solar or magnetism."

Wilson was intrigued. He knew his dad's little lecture was going someplace and he was curious to find out where.

"But what's really worrying Wilson, is the fact that this new wireless charging technology will soon be used to charge huge batteries in cars and lorries. Think about that. We're using magnetism to transmit energy to charge batteries without a cable or a tube. So, what if some of that electrical energy doesn't make it to the phone and gets sidetracked and mixed up with smoke signals from that internet router? Plus, there may be other energy fields yet to be discovered. What happens when they all starting mixing together, in thin air?

I'm not sure all that smoke is going to be good for our lungs, could even be mind-blowing, so my new responsibility is to set up various research programmes to try and find out. Then I have to report back to a government committee with a heads-up every now and again. No smoke without fire, as they say."

Alex leant forward to address his son, face-to-face.

"What I'm trying to say is that sometimes strange things happen and it's best to keep an open mind until we fully understand exactly what's going on."

With that, Alex stood up, picked up the empty mugs and headed out of the room. As he reached the door, he stopped and turned.

"And here's the funny thing Wilson. The name for one of the new open standards for wireless charging is pronounced 'Chee'. It's a Chinese word that refers to the life energy that exists in all living things. Life energy, charging batteries – interesting, eh? We can talk whenever you want son, I get this stuff."

Wilson lay back on the bed and slowly exhaled the air from his lungs.

Boy, that was cryptic. Life energy and no smoke without fire!

As he lay mulling things over, Wilson reached the conclusion that his day had been one helluva day. He didn't visit The Market Square that night or for the next few nights. The Market Square didn't seem to be open. That sometimes happened and in a way Wilson was pleased. He still hadn't got his head round the whole 'meet in a dream and meet in real life' conundrum.

Chapter 15

The supply teacher

A week after the chat with dad and no further encounters with Daisy, Wilson arrived at the freshly inscribed milestone of his eighteenth birthday. It was the 18th October 2017. Wilson slid behind his usual desk at the back of Lab 2, opened his textbook and waited for the biology lesson to start.

At 9.40 a.m., as the class grew boisterous, an unfamiliar man strode purposefully through the door and announced that he was Mr Catlow, a supply teacher. The lesson that morning was being given by him because, funnily enough, Mr Edwards, their usual teacher, was having a wisdom tooth removed. A couple of quick-witted students laughed at the irony.

Mr Catlow was only a few years older than Wilson. He had spiky, bleached blonde hair, wore flared jeans, a Nirvana t-shirt and had an ear piercing.

"Now," he said, chalking out a long and complicated-looking mathematical equation on the board. "I thought this morning we would start by going through the maths underlying the genetic code for the human genome."

The same two students laughed for a second time, the others just groaned.

"Okay, I'll take that as a no shall I? Shame, because the way you solve the complicated bit just here is really ingenious." Mr Catlow pointed to a hieroglyphic like symbol in the middle of the equation.

More groans.

"Okay, only joking. I think Mr Edwards should be back tomorrow, so they've drafted me in just for today to give you a different viewpoint. A bit of thinking outside the conker shell. Things we can't explain."

Wilson adjusted his seating position.

Think my dad gave me this lecture last night.

There was another minute of preamble before Mr Catlow drew the basic outline of a fish, a blob with a beak that could have been a bird and squiggles that vaguely resembled a spider. He turned to the class.

"The natural world, the world of biology and plants and animals is a strange world indeed. Take this spider for example."

Mr Catlow pointed to the eight-legged squiggle by way of illustration.

"How does this baby spider know how to build a web within hours of being born? Anybody know? Anybody?"

Hoover raised his hand.

"It has a knitting lesson from its mum, sir?"

Mr Catlow waited for the ripple of laughter to end.

"Good point, my learned friend. But when baby spiders hatch from eggs they are completely alone. Mum's not around to give knitting lessons and tiny spiders don't really have a brain, as such. Yet a one-day-old spider can build the most delicate and complex structure with which to catch its prey, from the word go. And the spider doesn't even need to practise. It doesn't have a few efforts and declare, 'Mmmm, that's not so good, let me try another one'. No, it builds an amazingly intricate web, perfectly, with its very first attempt."

Mr Catlow paused and surveyed the class.

"So the question is, where does the information come

from? Where's the blueprint stored? Where's the instruction manual? It's like you my learned friend," he said, pointing to Hoover, "being able to make a trap to catch a rabbit the day after you were born."

Mr Catlow then tapped his finger on the fish shape.

"And what about the salmon? Salmon are born in rivers and when they're about five inches long they get this sudden urge to swim out to sea, to feast on scampi. A year later, when they get the other urge – you know, to start a little salmon family – they find their way back to the very same river in which they were born. I get lost driving to the supermarket, so how can a salmon find its way halfway across the Atlantic Ocean and back home again? Only to swim down the river after spawning and start the process all over again. How? How is it able to do that? Where does the GPS come from?"

The puzzled-looking Mr Catlow gazed at the students, who sent his question back without reply.

"Finally, and even more interesting, is the cuckoo. Did you know the cuckoo is the only bird that doesn't build a nesting place? What mother cuckoo does is lay an egg in the nest of another bird, such as a blue tit or a robin. Robins are way smaller than cuckoos, yet they soldier on feeding the greedy cuckoo chick. And you know what happens then?"

The class had no idea.

"Well, once the mother cuckoo has laid the egg, she flies to somewhere warm for a break. Then – and this is the good bit – when the baby cuckoo is big enough to leave home, it also flies off to join its real Mum in Mallorca or Marbella for a family holiday. Then, a few months later, they all fly back to England and start the process all over again.

"The big question is, how does the baby cuckoo know

where Mum and Dad have gone? They didn't leave a forwarding address. No tweets. Yet each year, young cuckoos fly thousands of miles with no sat nav to meet up with their parents. It's incredible. Almost like there's a network of instructions the cuckoo, salmon and spider can access, like a kind of naturally occurring WiFi."

Wilson gulped audibly as Mr Catlow continued.

"A WiFi of nature, an internet of past behaviours that animals can log into to understand what to do in the future."

"Sir," said Hoover, raising his hand, "when the spider learns to catch a fly, does it log in to the world wide spiderweb?"

"Yes, yes, very amusing and not far off the mark."

Mr Catlow didn't allow the wave of laughter to drown out his next point.

"Professor Rupert Sheldrake, a famous biochemist from Cambridge University has an interesting theory about this. Simly put, Sheldrake believes the information a baby spider needs to build a web is readily available at birth, but not in a genetic inheritance way, from its parents, he believes the information is stored elsewhere, in the 'WiFi of nature', in what he calls a Morphic Field. The young spider is able to tune into a Morphic Field that exists specifically for spiders and download all the instructions it needs to build a web."

It was a Eureka moment as the apple of Morphic Fields landed with a thud.

Wilson stopped listening to Mr Catlow's lecture and his thoughts began branching out to join the dots between spiders, cuckoos, inexplicable abilities and himself. Mr Catlow's open window on phenomenal behaviours in the natural world had just provided Wilson with a starting point for an insight into his own extraordinary powers.

Could it be that in his sleep he was also able to access a Morphic Field, the Morphic Field of dreams? And then download and acquire experience and skills like a spider accessing the knowledge to build a web. On the face of it, the notion was little more than a pairing of ill-fitting ideas, like wearing red trousers with a green shirt. However, if a Cambridge University professor was sold on the shirt, Wilson was prepared to try the trousers.

Though the word 'explanation' sounded insufficient for the task, too flimsy for the heavy lifting required, there had to be an 'explanation' for an ability to speak French at the age of five without tuition, not to mention all the other miraculously acquired, competences. The 'WiFi of dreams' glowed like a single bulb in the darker recesses of Wilson's mind. A path that once looked impenetrable, with no obvious starting point, was now illuminated and had its first signpost.

Half an hour later, as a bell rang to signal the end of the lesson and students scooped up books and bags and trooped off to their next class, Wilson wrote 'Morphic Fields' and 'Sheldrake' on the back of his hand and headed for the college library.

Chapter 16

Wilson. In the library. With a computer.

The library was always quiet mid-morning so Wilson had no difficulty in finding an empty booth. He opened his laptop, checked to make sure Hoover wasn't going to suddenly peer over his shoulder, logged in to the college WiFi and typed the words 'Morphic Fields'. Moments later the results came back.

'You are not connected to the internet. This page cannot be displayed because your computer is currently offline.'

"Not again," he sighed. "That's the third time the network's been down this week."

Wilson pushed back on his chair and considered complaining to the librarians idly chatting at the front desk, but he knew from past experience that banging his head against a wall would achieve the same result. So since he was in a library, the fount of all knowledge for the pre-internet age, he'd just have to go old-school, and leaf through some books instead.

A search through index cards for anything by author 'Rupert Sheldrake' or the subject of 'Morphic Fields' came up blank, so Wilson walked over to the Science section and scanned book titles one by one. From a shelf labelled 'Psychology', he selected *Dreams Explained* by James Charlton. It was a thick, well thumbed paperback and fell open on an earmarked page that at first glance appeared to be describing an experiment. Wilson found a chair and started reading.

'In 2008, a research team at Johns Hopkins University School of Medicine monitored the REM sleep of eleven healthy participants in conjunction with images of their brain activity. The researchers found, that even when we dream, activity still occurs in the areas of the brain responsible for sight, hearing and movement.'

The text was accompanied by images of cross sections of a brain with hot spots picked out in orange. On the following page, the results of the experiment were summarised by the book's author in easy to grasp terms.

'In other words, if someone dreams of climbing a mountain, the brain behaves like they really are climbing that mountain. In real life, the brain sends messages, using lots of electrical energy, to move that hand, put a foot there and make sure you don't slip. But none of that happens in bed. You're not clinging to a rope. You're fast asleep. So here's an interesting question; we know where the energy goes when we really climb a mountain, but what if we only climb that mountain in a dream? Where does all the energy go then? For the person dreaming, the dream is as real as their perception when wide awake ... '

Flicking quickly through the chapters, Wilson was intrigued and fascinated. Here was a textbook talking seriously about dreams, with scientific facts, experiments and research findings. He couldn't find a specific reference to 'learning from dreams', but in the A-Z at the back, under the letter D, he stumbled on 'déjà vu. p. 62'. It was a surprise to find the subject included in a book about dreams.

He gave an approving nod to the definition of déjà vu.

'An unsettling feeling that a time or place is familiar, as if

one had been there before, or that a new experience had been experienced before.'

But it was the following paragraph that really caught his attention.

'Other explanations propose the idea of a collective consciousness through which one is in touch with the universal experience of the human race.'

Wilson was taken by the notion of a collective consciousness and that somehow, déjà vu could be connected to what he'd heard earlier, in Mr Catlow's lesson, about Morphic Fields.

'It has been postulated that some déjà vu experiences are indistinct memories of past lifetimes. Another view, is that déjà vu is a psychic episode based on dream experiences that surface with the prompting of a situation or place when awake.'

Startled, Wilson read that last sentence a second time.

Although he couldn't fully grasp the implications of what he was reading, he felt certain his déjà vu moments were in some way connected to his dreams. But more importantly, a scholarly textbook was giving a stamp of recognition to dreams as a subject worthy of serious, scientific study. A second signpost perhaps?

"Old-school is so cool" he announced to the startled librarians as he left the library with a spring in his step.

The rest of the morning was taken by a double period of English and an afternoon of sport followed. Wilson was the first-choice goalkeeper for the college second eleven and as he walked across the muddy pitch, the team were gathering in a circle around their PE teacher, George Daley.

"It's the big one this weekend, lads. St Bede's away –

as tough as it gets. So I want to put in a good session this afternoon. There'll be no point in playing a two-touch passing game. Their midfield general, the Grundy lad who plays in County's reserve team could probably beat us by himself, so our tactic on Saturday is to take him out of the equation. It won't be pretty, but our best chance is to fire in long balls and use Hoover's height to cause havoc in their defence."

Mr Daley paused for a moment as he sought the kingpin in his masterplan. Then his jaw dropped.

"Hoover, what on earth are you wearing?"

All eyes turned to the lanky figure of Hoover. While most of the squad were wearing tracksuit tops to keep out the cold wind, Hoover stood head and shoulders above them all in what appeared to be his mum's fur coat. It was like a cream-coloured, fluffy bomber jacket. Eight inches of hairy forearm protruded from each sleeve and it was zipped up from somewhere near his belly button.

"What have you got on?" Daley exclaimed incredulously. "You look like a bloody ostrich Hoover. We're supposed to be playing football not going to a fancy dress party."

"I know sir, but I couldn't find my trackie top and I wanted to make sure I kept warm and, err, you know, I don't want to pull anything, like a muscle."

An outbreak of laughter was getting infectious.

"Not pull anything, not pull anything, you, you . . . "

Mr Daley was temporarily lost for words.

"Hoover, the only thing you'll pull dressed like that is Big Bird from *Sesame Street*. And what's with the odd socks?"

The team kit was all black. Black shirt, black shorts and long black football socks. Hoover was wearing one long black football sock and on the other foot, a short, thin, light-grey business sock. Half a shin pad was sticking out of the top.

"It's all to do with my sock drawer sir, and my mum. All my socks keep going missing. Seriously. I can't find my other football sock. Mum said she'd definitely put two in the wash but then only one came out. She searched everywhere but it just disappeared. So I borrowed a sock from my brother. He doesn't do any sport, he's a solicitor and this was as close as I could get."

It took about five minutes for Mr Daley to retake full control of the Under-18s' 2nd XI and for the laughter to finally subside.

"Hoover, in the words of Roy Keane, 'fail to prepare, prepare to fail'. Now, take that stupid fluffy coat off and let's get started. Two circuits of the pitch to warm up."

Ninety minutes later, ruddy cheeked and mud-splattered, Wilson and company sat in the warmth of the changing room picking lumps of earth from the studs of their boots.

"If it's any consolation Hoover," Teaps confided, "my sock drawer is full of odd socks as well."

"Mine too," said Denver.

"And mine," said Wilson.

"I'm gonna get to the bottom of this," said Hoover.

"Wearing your mum's fur coat for training. That's so not right," said Iqbal, shaking his head.

Chapter 17

Coming of age

Wednesday 18th October 2017

Kate and Megan were home on a flying visit (something to do with a student fashion conference in Preston but more likely because Gloria pressed them to be back for Wilson's eighteenth birthday). So that evening, when Wilson arrived home from football training, Alex announced a plan to visit their favourite Chinese restaurant in order to celebrate the coming of age of his number-one son.

Wilson would have preferred to stay at home and continue investigating Morphic Fields but he could see his mum had been to the hairdresser's specially for the occasion and his dad was even wearing a suit! Plus, four or five gift-wrapped presents and a handful of cards were stacked in the hallway waiting for the trip.

The restaurant was busy, the atmosphere great and the food, top nosh. Table talk was dominated by Kate and Megan's gossip and Alex told a couple of jokes, including the completely inappropriate one about the Chinese restaurant and the steak being rubbery.

Gloria had a gin and tonic too many and started waving at a well-known actress, who was with a male friend and trying to be incognito. Wilson prayed they wouldn't dim the lights and bring him a candlelit cake while the entire restaurant sang 'Happy Birthday'. Gloria was certainly in that sort of mood.

The dinner had just reached coffee stage when Megan lifted the carrier bag onto the table and declared, "now it's time for the presents."

Wilson opened the birthday cards. The first one was very amusing and not just because it said, 'Now you are 14' on the front. The card was from Auntie Melinda, Alex's elder sister and his only sibling. Melinda was completely eccentric but somehow managed to hold down a top job as an editor at *The Sunday Times*. Inside the card was a book voucher for twenty pounds and a message that simply said, 'Happy Birthday William'.

After the cards, Wilson opened the presents which included his first electric shaver, an excellent drip-feed battery charger for the Vespa, two pairs of boxer shorts, a mint-scented shower gel and a set of three super-strong Belgian beers.

"Cheers," he said, "just the job. Thanks a lot everyone."

Wilson put the gifts and cards back in the bag ready for the return journey.

"So have you enjoyed your night then?" Gloria asked.

"Yeah, it's been great Mum, really good. Also had a very interesting day at college."

"Why, did they give you a balloon or something?"

Megan had obviously had a bit too much bubbly.

"No Megan, they didn't give me a balloon. And before you ask Kate, they didn't make me stand on the stage during assembly either. It was interesting because we had this temporary teacher for Biology, some young boffin full of crazy ideas. He didn't bother with the textbook, told us all about strange phenomena in the natural world – how baby spiders can build webs, how salmon go back to the same river to spawn. He said that nobody could really explain how they do it. Has anyone heard about Morphic Fields?"

Kate and Megan turned to Alex for help.

"That's an interesting question son."

This was permission for Wilson to continue.

"Seriously, he told us about the possibility of this kind of natural WiFi that animals log in to for guidance on how to do stuff, rather than being born with it or taught by their parents. You know, like how to build a spider's web. A baby spider isn't born with the instructions. It doesn't have a brain really. So it downloads them from what he called a Morphic Field. It was pretty cool."

Wilson was playing a game. He knew his mum and sisters wouldn't have a clue what he was going on about, but would his dad? After all, he was an expert in networks and WiFi. Talking to his dad directly would raise an eyebrow, but under the cover of a family meal and his feigned wonder at the subject of the lesson, maybe Wilson had a chance to tempt his dad into spilling what he knew.

"Wilson, has this anything to do with your potato pie website?" asked Kate.

"Definitely sounds like something to do with Hoover," added Megan.

"Are you referring to Professor Sheldrake?" Alex asked.

Wilson gulped audibly for the second time that day.

"Yeah, I think that's the name he mentioned."

"Yes, I'm familiar with the work of Rupert Sheldrake. He's a really interesting fella. Treated as a maverick by some in the scientific community, but his ideas are . . . well, challenging and different, to say the least. Some people even think of him as a prophet. I once delved into his concepts as part of my doctoral research. Strange you should latch on to him Wilson."

"Wilson I think you're just winding dad up," suggested Megan.

"That's enough Megan, Kate, if you don't mind," said Gloria, "we're here for a pleasant family meal, no need for you two to gang up on your brother on his birthday. It's nice that he's curious about the wider world, rather than who's wearing what and what's in and what's not. Hey, it seems I am a poet and I didn't even know it."

Alex rolled his eyes and checked his watch.

"Come on Gloria, I think it's time to get the bill; it's getting late and we've all got an early start in the morning."

But before calling over a waiter, Alex kept his eyes fixed on Wilson for a moment longer than could be considered polite and that said everything about the importance of Morphic Fields.

Chapter 18

The Gateway

Wednesday 18th October into Thursday 19th October 2017

Later that evening, around 11.50 p.m., Wilson arrived at a Market Square hidden within a dense bank of fog. The corner of a flower bed and the base of the Clock Tower were the only tell-tale points of reference. The smell of gunpowder, like spent fireworks the morning after bonfire night, flavoured the air. The thump of an explosion, muffled by distance, confirmed the peasouper was the result of smoke and not fog.

Okay, interesting, so what's this all about then?

As Wilson considered his next move, a breeze ran across the square shepherding woolly blankets of white smoke in the direction of L'École. Moments later, as the swirling curlicues shifted and thinned to expose an avenue of clear space, Wilson caught sight of a far corner of The Market Square and it had quite literally been blown to pieces. A terrace of four pretty cottages and a bow-windowed shop had all been reduced to a pile of rubble, like a desecrated graveyard from which the stumps of wooden beams and maimed furniture jutted out. An adjacent property was still standing, but the front fascia had been ripped away to expose a pristine interior resembling the inside of a giant doll's house. The air was clearing fast as a World War II tank flying an American flag trundled into view. The double bass of its mighty engine reverberated around the square and the steel tracks spat sparks as they grated over stone cobbles. A platoon of soldiers in camouflage uniform emerged from the ruins of Sampson's workshop and following a hand signal, sprinted to the rear of the tank. They grouped together for cover and scanned the square nervously, as though expecting sniper fire at any moment. Two cameramen and a girl with a fur covered microphone clamped to the end of a three metre boom, followed the sound and action.

"And cut," shouted the director, through a loudhailer, "at ease men."

Wilson was on a film set.

The soldiers dropped their weapons and started chatting and sharing cigarettes. The director began a conversation with the leading man – the hero sergeant in Wilson's favourite war film. Then a new curtain of smoke passed across that scene, exposing a different, though equally bizarre spectacle to Wilson's left.

In front of the bank building, mobile catering trailers were serving street food and refreshments to film crew and actors in a variety of familiar outfits and identities. There was a fuss at the food van closest to Wilson, where a sickly looking youth with scars and nicks all over his pale face was having difficulty eating a hot dog. This was not surprising, for his fingers had been replaced with knives and scissors and a sausage was skewered on the blade of his thumb. A broad-shouldered man in a black cape and a skull cap with triangular flaps for ears, had sliced his finger open trying to remove it. Wilson grinned when the caped crusader turned to a cocky looking pirate with dreadlocks and black eyeliner and asked for a sticky plaster. A second superhero, in red Lycra with a spider motif on his chest, was sitting on the floor. Black sticky goo was seeping from knife cuts to each sleeve and as a result, his wrists were handcuffed with stringy elastic webbing.

Wilson was tickled by the sheer nonsense of it all.

What an excellent start to a dream.

Cameras were still rolling as the show continued.

A red sports car accelerated across the square and with a squeal of tyres, skidded through ninety degrees and roared off down a lane on the far side of L'École. It was followed by a speeding black and white, NYPD cruiser with a siren blaring and its roof lights flashing. A policeman was hanging out of the window firing a gun at the moving target.

Then a call came over a tannoy somewhere.

"Last call for Wilson Armitage. Remake of *Ferris Bueller*, Set Three."

Wilson ignored the message. This was The Market Square in glorious technicolour inviting him to acting lessons. He couldn't help but smile.

An excellent day and now an excellent birthday night.

For some reason, Wilson's focus shifted back to L'École and the unfamiliar thoroughfare the cars had driven down moments earlier.

Haven't seen that there before, I wonder where it leads to?

Skirting round the back of the Clock Tower, Wilson reached the far right corner of the square and stopped. To his surprise, the lane was less than a metre wide, more of an alleyway, and certainly not wide enough for a police car. Confused, he turned to the Clock Tower to check his bearings. He was in the right place.

The alley consisted of red brick walls running in parallel and towering six metres or more in height. They formed a narrow tunnel, at least eighty metres in length and starved of light. At the far end, Wilson perceived a thin, vertical strip of ill-defined colour, open countryside perhaps. Ignoring the feeling of claustrophobia, he began walking down the passageway; a white mouse scurrying through a maze, conditioned by The Market Square to respond with the expected behaviour. A final stride led to clear, open daylight and liberation, in a field full of poppies.

The top heavy flowers, like red teacups balancing on slender green stems, were swaying in a summer's breeze, in every direction, for as far as the eye could see. Wilson gathered a crown of petals in his hand, it felt soft yet brittle, like velvety egg shell. A startled bee hovered out like a micro-drone, buzzed angrily and zoomed away. Wilson followed the flight path for a few moments, until his gaze landed on something far more significant and he was forced to squint into the glare of the sun.

Floating like a mirage on the horizon was the shimmering facade of a truly enormous building. It was some kind of palace or a magnificent hotel, with great stone pillars, a central colonnade and wings either side filled with rows of windows. Wilson was certain the colossal structure had to be the intended venue for the next sequence of his dream. It was too far away and too indistinct to establish more by way of detail, so he decided to walk through the poppy field and move on to the next scene. Strangely though, as Wilson took his first stride, the edifice also seemed to advance towards him, to bridge the distance, as if impatient for his arrival. So as a result, after taking fewer than ten paces, Wilson found himself confronted by the monumental building.

Broad stone steps led up to a vast portico supported on two rows of white marble columns. This central section reminded Wilson of the entrance to the British Museum in London, but on a much grander scale. The stone columns towered more than twenty metres above his head. The two wings, eight storeys high, featured row upon row of evenly spaced Georgian-style windows curving away to the horizon on the left and right. Craning his neck upwards, Wilson contemplated the battle scene sculpted into the triangular shaped pediment. It seemed a one-sided fight. Human warriors dressed in ancient battle dress were firing arrows into the air as fantastical winged creatures retaliated with bolts of lightning. In the centre of the carnage, on a raised panel of smooth stone, a mason had chiselled the words, 'The Gateway.' The deep impression of each letter was inlaid with gold leaf. More than intrigued, Wilson was keen to investigate further.

Taking each step with two strides, he reached the top of the stairway and paused to take a breath in the cool, shaded area beneath the portico. It was the size of an Italian piazza. Wilson expected the building to have the grandiose, revolving entrance of a luxury hotel, but was disappointed to be confronted by a pair of tall, featureless doors. They were painted a nondescript matt grey and appeared firmly shut with no handles or doorbell and no archetypal brass knockers, the least one might have expected on such a distinctive building.

Wilson stepped back and peered upwards. Fixed to the wall above each door was a tarnished brass plaque inscribed with feint lettering. He could just about read the words.

The plaque on the left stated: 'The Gateway. Visitors Only'.

The plaque on the right: 'The Gateway. Residents Only'.

Wilson stepped up to the door on the left and pushed. It opened a few inches. He then applied his full weight and the door yielded more ground.

It's my dream and I can't get prosecuted for trespassing in my own dream, can I?

Wilson squeezed through the gap – and into the most astonishingly, cavernous room imaginable. It resembled the interior of a vast cathedral, but twenty times the scale and built on a marked incline, so he had the impression of standing at a vantage point looking down as the floor sloped away. High above, shafts of sunlight poured through the kaleidoscopic colours of stained glass set in stone mullioned windows. Particles of dancing dust created a rainbow of sparkling mist. The vaulted ceiling, forty metres above Wilson's head, rested on a phalanx of interlocking, white stone arches, like the ribcage of a whale, aggregating to the size of a pinhead at the limit of Wilson's vision.

Wilson couldn't see much of the red marble floor because almost every inch was covered by enormous mounds of what appeared to be golden jewellery – wrist bracelets to be exact. Undulating dunes of gleaming, gold bangles completely filled the vast interior like a desert of dazzling, burnished metal. At regularly spaced intervals, white banners bearing a four-digit number were fixed to cables hanging down from somewhere high in the firmament. A 2017 banner was followed by 2016 and they continued back in numerical order until Wilson could just about read the banner for 1967. After that, the years became indistinct.

The quantity of bangles stockpiled for 2017 was the smallest, but nevertheless, they were still spilling all over the floor around Wilson's feet. He bent down to pick one up. It was lustrous and heavy, and Wilson was certain it was solid gold. He turned the bangle over in his palm. It had a smooth, rounded profile but the inside face was flat and bore an inscription of some kind. His eyes strained to read the fine lettering.

Mavis Moss. Nineteen forty-seven, to, two thousand and seventeen

"That's a fresh one."

Wilson jumped at the sound of the high-pitched, childlike voice.

"Yes, freshly minted today," said a lower-pitched, though equally childlike voice.

Wilson turned to face the direction of the voices and as he did so, the bangle slipped through his fingers and fell to the floor. He followed its progress as it bounced twice and rolled away, before coming to rest against a pair of highly polished black shoes.

"Tut, tut, that was careless."

A second pair of highly polished black shoes appeared beside the first.

"Yes, yes, very inconsiderate."

Wilson's eyes then followed the trail of matching pairs of black worsted trousers, black snakeskin belts, crisp white shirts, black silk ties, black leather jackets and arrived at two bald heads; one round, the other long and thin.

"Welcome to The Gateway" proclaimed round head, in the high-pitched, childlike voice.

"Yes, welcome" said long head, in the lower pitch.

As Wilson studied the strange individuals, he experienced a feeling of familiarity, a déjà vu, that suggested he'd been in their presence before. Round Head was the shorter of the two. He was chubby and cherubic, a Tweedledum or Tweedledee. Long Head was taller and skinnier, a body double for the creepy butler in an old horror movie. His wax paper skin was

101

pulled taut over the sharp contours of his skull. There was something about the pair that made Wilson feel ill at ease. They seemed comical, yet menacing at the same time. Like a cruel joke.

"Do you work here?"

"Yes we do" said round head.

"Indeed we do" said long head.

There was no trace of emotion on their faces, and although their voices had a childlike quality, the words were delivered in a stiff, formal monotone. Wilson scratched his head, for time to think rather than to relieve an itch.

"Cool place man," he said, acknowledging the stunning interior and dazzling contents.

"This," said round head, "is The Gateway."

"The Gateway to what?"

"The Gateway to the Spirit World."

"And this," said long head, moving his outstretched arm in a slow arc to indicate the vast expanse of space around them, "is The Hall of Extinguished Spirits."

"Wow," declared Wilson, politely following the imperious hand movements, "and is all this jewellery, you know, these piles of bangles, is it all real gold?"

"Indeed it is."

"Awesome!"

A silent moment slipped past and led Wilson to suddenly remember his manners.

"I'm Wilson by the way, Wilson Armitage. Nice to meet you both."

"We know who you are Wilson. We've been watching you, we've seen your trace. You're a number eleven. Allow me to introduce myself. My name is Big Mac."

"And my name is Short Cake," said long head.

Are they having a laugh? The little guy's called Big Mac and the tall one's called Short Cake. Well, whatever!

"You're like one of our butterflies Wilson," said Big Mac, "when you flap your wings, the outcomes have repercussions."

"Indeed" added Short Cake.

"Yes," continued Big Mac, "your unpredictability makes life more interesting. The Powers That Be don't like everything to run like a clockwork train set, so they allow certain elevens to cock-up the timetable. Happy birthday Wilson."

That Chinese food, that's where all this is coming from.

"Okay, Mr Mac and err, Mr Cake, so what do you guys do then?"

"We are the Custodians of The Gateway," replied Big Mac, "the caretakers of this magnificent room, our Hall of Extinguished Spirits."

"Wow, that's quite a job, given the size of the place. And what's the story with the gold bangles? You've got millions of them."

"There are indeed millions Wilson, and each bangle represents an extinguished spirit."

"In other words, a dead person," added Short Cake.

It took a moment for Wilson to digest those last three words.

"So, no wonder it's so big then. It's like a Hall of Remembrance, but instead of a headstone you get a gold bangle?"

"Exactly," said Big Mac, "each bangle carries an inscription with the owner's name and relevant dates."

Wilson stepped forward to retrieve the bangle resting against Big Mac's shoe.

"So this bangle represents the extinguished spirit of, let me see, Mavis Moss, and she lived from nineteen forty-seven until two thousand and seventeen. So that's why it's fresh, right? Because her spirit was extinguished this year."

"She moved on earlier this afternoon," confirmed Big Mac.

Wilson picked up three more stray bangles from the floor.

"This one says 'Emily Winters'. And the date shows nineteen fifty-two to two thousand and seventeen."

"Moved on last Friday."

"What about this one? It says... 'David Ellis'. Two thousand and nine to two thousand and seventeen."

"Ah. Yes. Quite sad. Just a child."

"And this one? This says 'Eric Murphy', from eighteen sixty-six to . . . " Wilson looked up at Big Mac. "He was over one hundred and fifty years old?"

"Mmm, an excellent choice Wilson."

"Are you telling me these bangles represent people who've died, and their spirit has been extinguished and turned into gold?"

"Yes and no," replied Big Mac. "Yes, the bangles represent people who've died. But no, not all the spirit is extinguished. Only the outer layer, or Shell, which is kept as a golden memory of a life well lived. The Residual goes elsewhere."

"To the other side," added Short Cake, "to The Powers That Be."

It was entirely understandable that Wilson didn't understand a single word. Big Mac helped to clear up the confusion.

"We can never totally extinguish the Residual Wilson, because it's what you'd call, the soul. It's impossible to extinguish a person's soul. The soul goes on to eternity. But the protective layer of spirit, the Outer Shell, lasts only until it has just three ounces of energy left."

"I think of the Outer Shell as someone's 'will to live'," chirped Short Cake. "At the end of the three score and ten, when someone has *lost* their 'will to live', or, for the less fortunate, when the will to live has been taken prematurely, the Outer Shell delivers the Residual here. We extinguish the Outer Shell to release the Residual, and three ounces of Outer Shell are converted into three ounces of gold bangle bearing the owner's name. You see, spirit is energy and energy is spirit, and neither can be destroyed, only changed from one form to another."

"So, let me see if I've got this," said Wilson. "All the numbers, like nineteen ninety-nine and so on" – he pointed at the seemingly endless line of hanging banners – "are the years that the people died. The year part of their spirit, the protective Outer Shell, was extinguished and turned into a gold bangle?"

"Indeed," said Short Cake.

Wilson had no idea from where his brain had conjured the source material for his dream. And more specifically, the bizarre conversation. However, determined to get to the bottom of it, he continued.

"So how do the two parts of spirit find their way into here?"

"Through the Residents' Entrance," answered Big Mac, "the door that was on your right when you stood outside. You wouldn't have been able to open that door. After a person has died, the Outer Shell brings the Residual to that door, to us, the Custodians. Only the Outer Shell can open that door. Would you like to see the other doors?"

Before Wilson could answer, they shuffled off behind the steep slope of bangles from 2015 and into the shadows where two executive-style desks with matching chairs, were illuminated by two angle-poise lamps. Beyond the desks was a red-brick wall inset with three doors, similar to, but smaller than those at the entrance to The Gateway. A neon sign glowed above each door.

The first one read: 'Exit to The Market Square.'

The second: 'Exit to Ghost World. Non-Extinguished Spirits Only.'

The third sign read: 'Exit to Eternity. Residual Spirits Only.'

To the right of the three doors, about twenty metres further along the wall, Wilson could also see a hole, the size of a serving hatch, roughly knocked through. Voices could be heard echoing up through the hole, as if workmen were busy a few floors below. On cue, somebody yelled in pain, as though they'd hit themselves on the thumb with a hammer. Even further along was another door, partly obscured by a ridge of bangles, with a white box light mounted above. Wilson presumed it had the words 'Fire Exit' printed on the front; it was too far away to see.

Referring back to the three doors Wilson considered the possible meanings of the neon signs. Big Mac offered guidance.

"When an Outer Shell is extinguished, the Residual is released and goes through the door marked Exit to Eternity."

"So what happens with the middle door then? Who goes through the Exit to the Ghost World?"

"Spirits that are overweight, because they've arrived before their time."

"Simply put," interjected Short Cake, "when a new arrival

has not completely lost the will to live but is nevertheless, dead, they must go back to where they came from, through that door, as a ghost."

"A phantom," said Big Mac, "a thing that goes bump in the night. Either way, they go back for as long as it takes for their Outer Shell to reduce its energy level to our management requirement of exactly three ounces. When the will to live is finally exhausted, they come back through the residents' entrance and we do our funky stuff. Extinguish and bangle."

"Indeed we do," nodded Short Cake, "and the more haunting they do, the quicker they're back. If they're happy to float like a shadow, wailing now and again, well, that won't burn up much energy, so they could be a spectre for hundreds of years. But banging on radiators with saucepans, slamming doors, active stuff – consumes lots of energy and they're back here sharpish."

"So," said Wilson, "the bangle for Eric Murphy, eighteen sixty-six to two thousand and seventeen, he went back to the Ghost World, didn't he? And then, when his Outer Shell, his will to live, was fully used up, he came back here?"

"You learn fast, Mr Armitage."

Big Mac turned to his companion.

"I think our work is finished for the day, don't you, Mr Cake?"

"Indeed I do."

"One question though," said Wilson, "who are The Powers That Be?"

Big Mac stepped forward to supply the answer.

"The Powers That Be know everything."

"Everything about The Gateway?"

"No, everything about everything."

"They like mischief and they love gambling," added Short Cake. "And they're watching you Wilson, and so are we. We've seen your trace."

"What do you mean, you've seen my . . . ?"

But before Wilson could finish the sentence, the distinctive 'tring' of a hotel service bell echoed around the hall. Big Mac and Short Cake rushed forward, grabbed Wilson by the elbows and, surprisingly powerfully, lifted him off his feet and carried him toward the door marked 'Exit to Market Square'.

"You have to leave right now Wilson. A new resident has arrived" stuttered Big Mac, red faced and straining.

"Oh, I do hope it's a returnee from the Ghost World. They have such fun stories," said Short Cake. "It's truly been a pleasure to meet you birthday boy, do call and see us again."

They left him at The Market Square exit and rushed off to prepare for the new arrival. Wilson was just about to leave when a thought stopped him in his tracks and he turned back. Big Mac was behind his desk and about to write something in a thick ledger book with a chubby fountain pen.

"Sorry to trouble you, err, Big Mac, but I have one last question."

Big Mac looked up. "Be very quick, young man."

"Can you tell me if you have a bangle for someone called Vanessa Clarke? Extinguished around nineteen ninety-nine?"

Big Mac peered over his reading glasses at Wilson. The light from the lamp cast a sinister shadow across his face.

"I checked the records earlier Wilson, in anticipation of this particular question. We have no bangle inscribed with the name of Vanessa Clarke from that year. Nor has the Vanessa Clarke you're referring to, gone through there."

Big Mac pointed his fountain pen at the Exit to the Ghost World.

"So I suggest you conduct further enquiries in The Market Square. Now please leave, immediately, we have company. Good day, sir!"

Chapter 19

Squaring the circle

Thursday 19th October 2017

At 7.30 a.m., Mickey Mouse announced the new day, by hammering his mallet against a silver bell in a frenzy of excitement. Wilson surfaced slowly from deep sleep and silenced the alarm with a well-aimed slap.

"Oooaaghh."

He combed his fingers through his hair, rubbed his face with both hands and slowly opened his eyes. The scenes and characters from last night's dream presented themselves like images on a carousel projector. Big Mac, The Gateway, gold bangles, Eric Murphy, poppy fields, Ferris Bueller.

What a night. Where the hell did all that come from?

Wilson dressed, splashed water on his face and caught his reflection in the bathroom mirror. The bags under his eyes carried the shadows of someone who'd been up all night.

He made a plodding descent downstairs and trudged into the kitchen where Alex was hidden behind a newspaper and Kate and Megan were eating boiled eggs.

"Morning everyone," he mumbled, flopping onto a chair.

"Morning love. Sleep well?"

Gloria was stirring something on the hob with her back to Wilson.

"No, not at all. Had this really strange, intense dream."

The yawn came without warning. "I feel like I've not slept all night. Don't think that Chinese food agreed with me."

"Oh, what a shame. – and after such a lovely evening. Well don't worry. A strong milky coffee will clear your head and porridge will settle your stomach. A good healthy start to the day."

Gloria carried a bowl over to the table and when Wilson turned to say thanks, she saw his face .

"Gosh, you're right, you do look a bit under the weather. I think you must be coming down with something?"

She placed her palm on his forehead and held it there for a few seconds.

"Mmm, well you don't seem to have a temperature, so it's probably nothing a restful day won't fix. I'll call college and tell them you've got a stomach bug."

"Nah, I'm okay Mum. I've got loads on. Plus, the Vespa's not firing properly and I need to sort it before an exam at ten."

"In that case, take it easy, drink lots of water and early to bed tonight."

Gloria turned to her daughters.

"Girls, how are you getting on with those eggs? Would you like some soldiers?"

"Gloria, I'm sure the girls don't need any help to eat an egg." The newspaper shook as Alex chuckled away.

"Yeah, please mum," said Megan, "but not for Kate. She's modelling my outfits in the show next week and I don't want all the buttons popping off."

Kate was laughing as she knocked the helmet off a second egg.

"You know what they say about dreams Wilson?" The voice came from the other side of the *Financial Times*.

111

"No Dad, what do they say?"

"They say dreams are the gateway to another world."

Wilson thought there was extra emphasis on the word 'gateway' but perhaps he was just being neurotic; either way he lost his appetite and pushed the bowl of porridge to one side. He didn't want the conversation with his dad to proceed a single word further.

"Gotta go folks, running late."

"But Wilson, you've not finished your breakfast . . . "

"Gotta scoot, to fix the scoot. Catch you later family."

He grabbed his jacket and rucksack and made for the garage.

Wilson soon had the two stroke engine drumming like Hoover and set off for college in good time for the English exam. Gloria was looking down from her bedroom window and saw him ride off.

I do worry about that boy sometimes. He seems to live in his own little world.

Following the exam and after lunch, Wilson headed to the library where he presumed the internet would now be up and running. At an empty cubicle, he took a pen and paper from his rucksack and shifted his brain into first gear.

If you're looking for buried treasure, you need to have a map.

At the top of a blank page, he wrote the words 'Morphic Fields'. As a concept, it sounded so similar to his dream experiences; the WiFi of nature had to be worth exploring.

So what's my hypothesis then?

He chewed the end of his biro, sat back and mulled over

the question. A minute later, he leant forward and wrote the words 'Dream Fields' on his pad and circled them.

My hypothesis is that Morphic Fields and Dream Fields are the same kind of thing. A Morphic Field holds the instructions to create a spider's web. A Dream Field holds the instructions to restore a Vespa.

He drew a curved arrow to connect the two terms. It wasn't a revelation, but it was a start. And for the next five minutes Wilson stared at the words as the start, refused to get fully started. The cogs inside his head were turning, but idling in neutral. His flow diagram was frozen.

Come on Wilson, think. What other types of fields are there? Magnetic? Electrical? Gravitational? Yeah, energy fields.

Now a thaw was setting in.

Exactly, they're all energy fields! And so Morphic Fields and Dream Fields could also be types of energy field!

The evolving clock face now looked something like this: 'Morphic Fields' at twelve, connected to 'Dream Fields' at three, connected to 'Energy Fields' at six.

Now, what will square the circle? Where's my nine o'clock?

Wilson pulled the laptop from his rucksack and asked Google to search on the phrase 'Morphic Fields'.

The results came back and as expected, all the information centred on Rupert Sheldrake. Wilson scanned down the links until a word in the following paragraph grabbed him by the collar and told him to sit up straight.

'Sheldrake's morphic resonance hypothesis states that 'memory is inherent in nature' and that all natural systems, from spiders to orchid plants, inherit a collective memory from all previous things of their kind.'

Wilson began playing tag with the word memory.

Memory is connected to Morphic Fields, and memory is about what's happened in the past. Dreams involve memories too. The past is measured by time and we collect memories over time. So Morphic Fields and Dream Fields have something to do with things that have happened in the past.

It wasn't exactly another Eureka moment, but the notion of 'time,' like the new kid whose folks just bought the sweetshop, seemed to warrant membership of the gang.

Wilson wrote the word 'Time' in the 9.00 p.m. position, put down his pen and studied the diagram. Not fully satisfied, he then added a new arrow, curving away from 'Time' at 9.00 p.m., pointing to the words 'déjà vu', which he underlined, before once more placing the pen back on the desk and folding his arms.

Now that's what you call thinking outside the box, and it's all about time and dreams and fields and ... energy. Energy!

He toyed around with the word like a kitten with a ball of wool and then pounced.

What was it that Short Cake character said about energy last night?

He scanned the vivid memories of his Gateway dream and found the scene with Short Cake's dialogue.

"Spirit is energy and energy is spirit, and neither can be destroyed, only changed from one form to another."

Does that actually mean anything?

Wilson Googled 'energy can't be destroyed, only changed' and was truly flabbergasted when the results came back.

"What the ... !"

The words invented in his dream were a true fact. A famous saying that existed. As quoted by Albert Einstein no less.

'Energy can neither be created nor destroyed, only conserved or changed from one form to another'.

How the hell did I know that, in order to dream it?

Wilson stared at his laptop screen in disbelief. Things were getting curiouser and curiouser.

At the centre of the circle he wrote the words 'Conserved and Changed'.

Wilson tried to fathom out how he could know, unknowingly, Einstein's theory of energy conservation and came to the conclusion that it had to be similar to knowing, unknowingly, how to speak French.

It was all connected somehow?

A spider logs in to the memory of the natural world for instructions to build a web. Just as I log in to the memory of the dream world for instructions to speak French. Or the language of Einstein.

Feeling he was on to something, Wilson once again reviewed the previous night's dream from the beginning, perhaps there were more hidden messages. His mind's eye zoomed in when the first gold bangle came into frame.

What does it say again? Mavis Moss. 1947-2017. What if I . . . ?

He keyed the name and dates into his laptop and pressed 'search'.

It took a few minutes for Wilson to review every Mavis Moss in the list of results, but there didn't appear to be anyone who'd lived from 1947-2017. Searches for Emily Winters, David Ellis and Eric Murphy, also drew a blank. In fact, the Eric Murphy search returned absolutely nothing. Then it dawned on Wilson that there couldn't be any results for 'Eric Murphy, 1866-2017', because nobody lived to be one hundred and fifty years old. The only reason the spirit of Eric Murphy was extinguished in 2017 was because he'd supposedly been pottering around as a ghost for the majority of his years. Wilson deleted his search for 'Eric Murphy, 1866-2017' and quickly replaced it with 'The ghost of Eric Murphy, 1866'.

Google paused for a second, as though afraid to bring back the skeleton it had unearthed. And no wonder, given the brief summary in the search result.

'Cleaning lady at Bramhall Hall reports yet another sighting of the ghost of Eric Murphy. Stockport Advertiser. June 2010.'

It was one thing to learn to speak French in your dreams, but being introduced to the extinguished spirit of the dead – that was taking things to a whole new level. Wilson's index finger trembled slightly as he clicked the link and opened the full article.

'Eric Murphy, the genial ghost in residence at Bramhall's historic seventeenth-century hall, has once again made his presence felt. According to records preserved at Manchester's John Rylands Library, Eric Murphy, the son of a blacksmith, was born in a worker's cottage on Lord Bramhall's estate in July of 1866 and died of tuberculosis in 1899.

So frequent are the sightings of his ghostly apparition that Eric has become Bramhall Hall's most popular tourist attraction, particularly with Japanese ghost hunters, who . . . .

The article continued, but Wilson had read enough.

"Jesus H Christ," he mumbled, folding his laptop away, "what's going on?"

Looking up, he saw Teaps enter the library, wave, and then head in his direction.

"Hey Wilson. Hoover said you'd be here. What're you up to?"

Teaps grabbed a neighbouring chair and sat down. For some reason he was wearing sunglasses.

"Nothing much. I was just trying to solve a puzzle."

"What kind of puzzle?"

"Errr, a kind of biology-slash-maths puzzle. A brainteaser involving energy."

"Need some help?"

"But you don't do maths, *or* biology."

"I know, but I like puzzles."

Teaps removed his sunglasses.

"Whoa Mate. How did you get the black eye? Jeeez, let me see."

It was a textbook shiner. All red and swollen with purple and yellow eyeliner to complete the effect.

"That. Is. A. Beauty! Girl trouble?"

"Long story."

"I'm listening."

"It was that 'b' word, Blamire. Warren Blamire."

Teaps kicked the desk angrily, disturbing the peace and quiet of the library.

"He has that gold dealer and pawnshop place in town. He's Stockport's drug lord, general thug and unfortunately, the landlord of our flat. We fell behind with last month's rent so yesterday he comes round havin' a go at Dad; calling him a waste of space, and threatening to throw us out. So I flipped and it kicked off big time and I came off worse. He's a total nut job. Threatened to call the bailiffs in if we don't pay double, and interest, by the end of the month. Dad's been drinking quite a bit since then. No idea what I'm gonna do."

"Jeeesus Teaps, I'm really sorry. Couldn't you call the police or something? Do him for assault or . . . "

"No, I was the one who started it. The only reason he's not pressing charges is because I came off worse, says he enjoyed it and wants to do it again in two weeks, when he throws us out on the street."

"What a lowlife! What're you gonna do?"

"Dunno. I checked the back of the sofa but we're skint mate. Was thinking of asking the council for temporary accommodation, or I'll look for a place for the homeless. I've no idea. Could try for another shift stacking shelves, but that's peanuts. Need to find nine hundred quid, like yesterday. Fancy robbing a bank?"

"Funny you should mention that Teaps, but no, I'm totally against crime. We could kill Blamire though."

"Now you're talking. What I could do with a pair of pliers and a hammer."

"Teaps, I've got some savings. I could let . . . "

"Forget it Wilson. I only told you because you asked me about my black eye. Thanks man, if I get really desperate, I'll let you know. I need to sort this by myself. No idea what we'll do if we're thrown out. It could be the last straw for Dad. He might do something he'd, we'd regret and . . . "

"Okay, stop; it won't come to that. I'm gonna help. We had good sales from the website last week, so I can give you all that. It's about three hundred quid."

"Thanks mate, it's good of you to offer, but I need a fair bit more."

Teaps grabbed his bag and pushed the chair back under the desk. "Gonna go and check on Dad. See you tomorrow."

"Yeah, see ya Teaps. And let me know if I can do anything to help."

Wilson tore the top sheet from his pad, folded his diagram,

zipped it safely in the side pocket of his rucksack and followed Teaps out of the library.

Chapter 20

The torn pocket

Thursday 19th October into Friday 20th October 2017

It was midnight and a funfair was in town. The Market Square was a merry-go-round of carnival rides and glowing neon light. Music from a Wurlitzer organ rose and fell with the rhythmic motion of the seats on a whirling carousel as visitors, drawn like moths to a candle flame, flitted between attractions, food vendors and 'try your luck' stalls.

The Clock Tower, masquerading as a poor man's *Eiffel Tower*, and at quarter scale, was bedecked with strings of giant fairy lights. One moment they were glistening like ice crystals, the next, they were racing round latticed steelwork with red pulse, chasing green, chasing blue. Tubular beams from searchlights swept lazy arcs over the heads of the crowds. Fleetingly, they would illuminate the random, jerky flight path of what appeared to be a giant bat camouflaged against the sooty black sky. The roving light show strained Wilson's eyes as he searched for another sighting and confirmation of the fact that . . .

"Head down sonny!"

The instruction, in ultra-sound, was felt rather than heard and Wilson instinctively ducked, as an articulated wing of school satchel leather flapped inches above his head. The creature changed direction with a sharp crack, as though a freshly laundered bed sheet had been shaken.

Yeah, that's definitely a bat; with bat ears and a bat body – but a bat the size of an elephant!

The bat was on a leash, anchored to the Clock Tower on a steel cable and a roller-coaster style carriage was saddled on its back. The cargo of passengers, all holding on for dear life, shrieked with laughter as the bat buckaroo'd haphazardly and flew off into the night.

Health and safety would have a field day with this.

Wilson's eyes followed the stomach churning spectacle until the darting and diving became less extreme and the bat eventually folded its wings and settled upside down on the statue of Mr Ludlow (or possibly Mr Abingdon). Dizzy, grinning passengers pushed away their padded restrainers and stepped, somewhat unsteadily, back on to solid ground.

A neon sign read: 'The Bucking Bronco Bat Ride. You gotta be batty to try it.'

Awesome.

Someone tapped Wilson on the shoulder. A circus ringmaster in top hat and tails, striped waistcoat, white breeches and knee-length black boots, was grinning beneath his handlebar moustache.

"Care to trunk-wrestle the elephant my friend?"

The sweep of his arm and a wink drew Wilson's attention to a baby elephant sitting on a three-legged stool behind a round wooden table. The elephant raised its trunk and trumpeted as if to amplify the challenge.

"Trunk-wrestle? What exactly does that mean?" Wilson was confused by the word pairing.

"It's the same as arm wrestling, but the elephant has to use its trunk, because clearly it doesn't have any arms."

The indignant ringmaster was stating what he believed to

121

be the blindingly obvious.

Wilson released a burst of laughter.

"Oh, that seems fair enough then."

"It's only a pound and if you win, you get fifty quid back. Good odds, eh?"

Wilson was struggling to maintain a straight face.

"Has the elephant ever lost?"

"God no. Never."

"Mmm, that doesn't come as surprise, so you must make a lot of money from this . . . attraction?"

"Oh yes, a small fortune!"

Wilson wasn't sure if it was all a spoof, a set-up and a hidden camera was following for TV entertainment. He compared his outstretched arm with an elephant's trunk that was thicker than his leg.

"Well?" asked the ringmaster, impatiently.

"Maybe later," said Wilson, having reached the conclusion that there could never be a positive outcome from wrestling with an elephant. He began to take steps back.

"Just gonna check out the flying bat ride, over there, so half an hour and . . . "

Those last words didn't register, because the ringmaster was now pitching his challenge to three teenage girls eating candyfloss.

As Wilson turned and headed off towards the Clock Tower, a subliminal thought he'd left behind, came running up and prodded him in the back. Wilson stopped in his tracks and looked over his shoulder.

The three girls talking to the ringmaster were identical triplets. Same eyes, nose, mouth – all their facial features were exactly the same. However, one girl was tall, one was short and the other had red hair. Stranger still, Wilson couldn't be certain they were girls. Sure, they were dressed like girls, but they appeared to be genderless; and possibly not even teenagers, maybe much older. The more Wilson studied their faces the less he could pigeonhole them as this age or that, boy or girl. As Wilson looked on, a man and a woman also stopped to listen to the ringmaster's pitch.

Hold on a minute, those two are identical as well.

That observation was then followed by something far more seismic, as it dawned on Wilson that the matching pair 'snapped' with the trio.

Five identical faces?

Wilson scanned the crowd and a shiver ran through his entire body.

"Whoaaaa."

Everyone was a twin of somebody else and vice versa.

A child in a buggy wore exactly the same facial features as the parents, who in turn looked like each of the five teenage lads to their left. The only clues as to their age and gender were the clothes they were wearing and their physical size. Though surprising, the phenomenon wasn't disturbing; the carnival atmosphere dispelled any feeling of unease, so Wilson quickly overcame his initial shock and continued moving in the direction of the Bucking Bronco Bat ride.

You gotta be batty to try it. Sounds about right.

As the crowds became congested, Wilson was forced to stand to one side to allow a daughter, sized about seven-years old, and her parents, sized about thirty-years-old, the right of way.

The girl was carrying a fluffy bear her father had won. The

Koala shook Wilson's hand with a lifelike paw and said "G'day mate"as the family brushed past.

"Well you certainly stand out in a crowd," chimed a familiar voice.

Wilson turned to locate the source and the unmistakable presence of Daisy Meadowcroft, with a beaming smile on her lovely, *could only ever be one*, Daisy Meadowcroft face was standing a metre away.

The strongman with a mallet hit the sweet spot and Wilson's heart went 'kerching'.

"Wow. Daisy. Is that really you?"

"Yes Wilson, it really is me. But let's not start the 'whose dream is it' debate again."

Daisy reached for his hand. "Come on, we need to talk."

She navigated a course through the sea of same faces, tugging Wilson in her wake, and pulled up at the ticket booth for the 'Catapult Gliders'.

"Well, hallelujah," she said, "found you at last. How are you enjoying all the fun of the fair?"

Wilson struggled to reply. Daisy had returned to his dream, he was surrounded by hundreds of people with identical faces, a gigantic bat was flying all over the show and he'd just turned down the offer to arm-wrestle with an elephant!

"Err, I think I'm good," not really certain if that was true. "I really wasn't expecting to see you again."

"Why not? I was sure I'd meet you. It was inevitable."

"Well, you know, I'm still not convinced that you're not just a figment of my imagination."

"Wilson, you've got to stop with that. I told you, when we first met, I have special talents and . . . "

Daisy made spidery movements with her fingers.

". . . magical powers. Remember our last conversation? Duhhh?"

"How could I forget?" Wilson was still questioning the reality status of the girl standing in front of him.

Daisy was wearing denim dungarees over a white t-shirt, cream coloured trainers and Wilson had to admit;

she looks fantastic with the same chestnut coloured hair deep brown eyes, a perfect nose, perfect lips and butterscotch skin. And tonight . . . she's even more perfect!

He snapped out of the trance.

"I've thought about the night we met every day. I went to Starbucks like we agreed and I waited for ages. I felt a total idiot when you didn't show up."

Daisy frowned. "I know. It wasn't my fault though. It's a long story. But hey, I've got all night to explain."

She looked over her shoulder at the ticket booth for the Catapult Gliders. An old man with a gurning face sat hunched inside counting ticket stubs.

"Have you tried this ride? It's better than anything at Alton Towers."

Wilson hadn't really taken in his surroundings, he'd been too preoccupied taking in Daisy, but as she spoke, he tried to fathom out the appeal of the Catapult Gliders. Beyond a barrier fence, Wilson could see a slowly advancing line of 'carriages'. Each was about four metres long and represented, in a simplistic way, a jet plane, with an open cockpit, a cigar-shaped body, broad delta wings and a stumpy tail. They reminded Wilson of the toy glider his Dad bought him once on holiday. A little plastic plane that he launched with an elastic band. A red one, that always crashed nose first in the sand after a series of loop-the-loops.

Beyond the creeping line of glider carriages was a rudimentary launch strip, like the short runway on an aircraft carrier.

"Come on," said Daisy, pulling Wilson along by the arm, "there's no queue. I'll explain on the plane."

The man waved them through the turnstile without looking up and mumbled that they should "take that next red one." They climbed the steps onto a wooden platform and followed the red glider as it inched along. Wilson jumped down into the cockpit, offered a steadying hand to help Daisy on board, and pulled down a padded restrainer to hold them securely in their seats. The plane had no instrument panel or controls.

"Prepare for take-off," announced a tinny voice from a speaker in the footwell.

The glider continued taxiing towards the end of the platform where it slowly juddered through a ninety-degree turn, lurched forward and then stopped, dead centre, at the start of the runway. A series of heavy mechanical clunks then shook the carriage, as though something was locking itself on the nose of the plane. The stretching creak of tension being applied then followed. In the distance, the runway rose to the height of a three-storey building and abruptly stopped, like the end of a ski jump.

"How do we fly this thing?"

"Wilson, it's not a real plane, it's a fairground ride. It's in your dream. Nothing bad can happen. You're still going to wake up safe and sound in the morning, even if we crash. Anyway, I've been on this one before, it's wicked."

Daisy patted Wilson's knee then gripped the handholds on the restraining bar. "You're so going to enjoy this."

Then, as the word 'this' was released into the indigo expanse of the night, Wilson was catapulted into said, indigo expanse, at approximately seven hundred miles per hour.

For a few seconds Wilson wasn't able to breathe. He couldn't do anything actually. Couldn't move, couldn't see, couldn't think, couldn't even couldn't. He was aware of the sensation of moving forward, like entering a tunnel on a rocket-propelled train, then zooming upwards even faster and his sight all blurred and he was upside down then back to front and speeding like a bullet.

Daisy was laughing and shrieking and punching his arm, then jerking forward and laughing some more, then banging her feet on the floor.

"Oh my God, oh my God, what an adrenaline rush. Wilson! How . . . good . . . was . . . THAT?"

Wilson didn't fully understand what the 'that' was. His hands were superglued to the grips on the sides of his seat and his knuckles were white. He tried to reply, but his mouth was no longer where it used to be and his brain was all mashed like Mr Potato Head.

"What . . . the . . . hell . . . " he stammered.

Daisy threw her head back against the cushioned headrest and cried with laughter. Just like the night they met in the motorcycle workshop.

"Daisy, that, that was . . . "

Wilson's faculties slowly returned and he loosened his grip to let blood flow into his hands.

" . . . that was the best thing ever! I mean, how incredible was that? Just unbelievable. Totally awesome. Err. Where are we?"

Wilson looked over the side of the glider and down into a

void of clear air. Far below he could make out the glowing neon of The Market Square and roving lights sweeping around the Clock Tower searching for a bat on the run.

"Daisy, we're about a mile above the ground and we're flying in a plane with no controls or parachutes."

Daisy's head bounced back off the headrest for a second time.

"No Wilson, we're not flying, we're gliding. We've been fired from a catapult and now we're slowly gliding back down. Incredible, isn't it?"

"Yeah, I guess so" he said. "It's really, just ... indescribable."

They sat in silence as warm air ruffled their clothes and hair and the glider descended in a gentle curve.

"The loop-the-loop bit was the best."

"What?" Wilson exclaimed. "We looped the loop?"

"Yeah, immediately after we launched. It's the first thing that happens."

"If you say so, I don't remember too much about it. One moment I was down there and the next, I was up here. Phenomenal."

After shaking his head in disbelief for a final time, Wilson began to relax and fully enjoy the experience. Best of all, he was in the company of his dream girl.

"Daisy, this is incredible. And whether it's my dream or your dream, who cares? I wish we could do this all the time. When I said that I'd been thinking about the first night we met, every day, what I really meant was, I've been thinking about you every day, since we met. If that makes sense?"

Wilson turned away as a hollow feeling, a reality bite, snapped at the heels of his hopes.

This is stupid! She's not real. Not flesh and blood. Not

going to be around tomorrow morning when I wake up. This is all a dream.

Daisy placed her hand on his.

"Wilson, I know you're a real person, in real life I mean. That you have a family, and a job, or you go to college, or whatever. The point is, you have to believe me when I say that I'm also a real person, just like you. I do live in Macclesfield. My dad's a painter and decorator and so is my brother. My mum's a nurse and sings in a choir."

The glider continued its slow descent and as the hubbub from the funfair rose in volume, Wilson caught a whiff of hotdogs and burgers.

"Okay Daisy, so if what you say is true, and you *do* exist, then why did I spend an hour hanging around Starbucks looking like a fool in front of my mates?"

"That's what I wanted to tell you Wilson. It wasn't my fault. I left college and caught the ten past six train, but it broke down after ten minutes and they had to send a bus to take us back to Macclesfield and . . . anyway, it was eight o'clock before the new train arrived. I had no phone number, no way to get hold of you. I rang Starbucks but they didn't answer. I'm sorry. I've been looking for you in The Market Square ever since."

"Well, you've found me now. So I guess I'll get over it."

"That's the spirit," said Daisy. "What doesn't kill us can only make us stronger. Speaking of imminent death, how far from the ground are we?"

"About twenty miles."

"Wilson you liar." Daisy checked for herself. "Three minutes to touchdown."

There was a brief silence and then Daisy asked, "Were you

here *waiting for me*, you know, on those nights I was *trying to find you*?"

"No, I haven't been back here since that night. Well, apart from last night, when I met these two weird guys who told me all this stuff about energy and spirits and ghosts; all of which turned out to be true. We were in this like, huge cathedral building called The Gateway. Search me what it all meant, but there was something about the whole thing that ..."

There was a terrifically loud bang, the screech of metal on metal and a bone shaking judder as the glider came to a sudden halt and then began inching its way back along the platform. The restraining bar lifted automatically and the tinny voice from the speaker announced, "thank you for flying with the Catapult Gliders today. Have a safe onward journey and do fly with us again."

As they passed the ticket booth, Daisy complained to the man inside about the lack of a drinks service on the flight.

"What's next?"

"Well," said Daisy, "since the dream is still young, why don't you go and win a cuddly toy for me?"

"Err, not a good idea Daisy. I think the fluffy bears might bite. But what the hell, yeah, let's check out the other rides. If there's anything half as good as the gliders, I'm going for it."

"Make sure you don't lose me in the crowd though," said Daisy.

"Oh very funny. Hey, did you ever see that video with George Michael and Mary J. Blige?"

"No, why?"

"It's exactly like this dream, where everyone looks the same. I think that's where it's coming from."

Wilson smiled foolishly and gave Daisy a clumsy hug. He wanted to find out if she was solid and warm and full of real bones. And she was.

They linked arms and paused in front of the 'Dart Birds Game'. This appeared to involve adjusting the wings of a bird with a pointed beak before launching it at a moving target of floating balloons. Wilson presumed the aim was to pop a balloon and win a bear. He could see koalas eating leaves in the branches of a tree.

At the next stall, the mallards recruited for 'Hook the Ducks' didn't seem all that keen on being 'hooked' with a metal pole. They quacked and flapped and kicked up all kinds of fuss.

'Pin the Tail on the Donkey' was equally cruel, given that the donkey was alive and a blindfolded size-nine-year-old was attempting to pin the tail in the donkey's eye.

In the distance, a gigantic Ferris wheel was slowly turning beneath umbrellas of exploding fireworks.

"Fancy a go on that?"

"Sure do," said Daisy. "But first, we've definitely gotta check this one out."

Daisy pointed to a rickety, metal staircase spiralling round a huge cylinder panelled with wood planks. It resembled a four storey barrel. The ticket booth was unattended so they forced the turnstile and raced each other up the creaking iron stairs that led to the 'The Ten-Mile Drop'.

At the top, the stairway opened out onto a metal-plate platform with safety rails and a bird's-eye view over the funfair. A red door was the only possible entrance to The Ten-Mile Drop so Wilson gave it a push.

The door swung open to reveal a dark, circular room with

a clear glass floor and a ceiling studded with twinkling star-lights. They searched each other's faces for a suggestion of what to do next. Daisy took the initiative and shoved Wilson over the threshold.

"It's only a dream. Be a man, you scaredy-cat."

Wilson edged gingerly out onto the glass, looked down, and leapt back to safety.

"Well, that wasn't much of a ride, was it?"

"Daisy, do you know what you see if you walk out onto that bloody glass?"

"Err, a ten-mile drop maybe?"

"Exactly, a ten-mile drop. Straight down. Whooosh. Ten miles."

"Yeh, I know Wilson. I get it. And I presume that's why they call it the Ten-Mile Drop; so you get the idea in advance."

Daisy followed Wilson, a small step at a time, out onto the glass.

"Whooaaa," said Wilson.

"That is a long – way – down," said Daisy.

Wilson felt his knees about to buckle so they gazed down through the glass floor on hands and knees.

Far below, a battenberg of green, gold and brown was dappled with shadow and sunlight.

"They're fields," said Wilson.

Around the circumference of the glass they could see the earth curving away and jagged outlines of snow-capped mountains. Wisps of cloud were drifting by as though a steam train was passing beneath their feet. Then someone pulled a lever and the glass floor wasn't there anymore.

"Wilsonnn!" Daisy was yelling. "Wilsonnn. This is so great."

She was almost within touching distance as they hurtled earth bound at breakneck, break-leg, break-everything speed. Wilson reached for Daisy's hand, then an arm, both arms and then they were facing each other – locked together in freefall, like skydivers. The air drumming their clothing was louder than a loose tent flap in a hurricane.

"Is this supposed to be happening?" Wilson yelled, as they plunged headlong towards terra firma.

"Yeah. That's why it's called the Ten-Mile Drop."

"But I thought we'd just look at the ten-mile drop."

"So did I. But this is ten miles better, don't you think?"

Despite the blast of rushing air, Wilson noticed that Daisy's mouth and cheeks weren't stretched and rippling – as might have been expected.

"It's just a dream Daisy," he yelled.

"I know, Enjoyyyyyy."

And with that, she released herself from Wilson's grasp and cartwheeled away.

"Yahoooo, I'm a bird, I can flyyyyyy." Wilson cried out, just because he could.

Minutes later, as the patchwork quilt of rectangular colour began to resemble crops and ploughed fields, their rate of descent declined.

The Ten-Mile Drop ended with a cushioned landing on a conveniently placed haystack. Daisy was engulfed by the hay and it took a few minutes of giggling and pulling to get her feet back on solid ground.

"Bet they don't have that one at Alton Towers either" said Wilson.

"Thank goodness," said Daisy, pulling stalks of straw from

her hair. "I'd live there if they did."

"Phenomenal ride," said Wilson, looking directly above. All he could see was blue sky and wispy clouds; no evidence of a glass ceiling.

"How do you beat that?"

"Don't know Wilson, but I think we should try. We may never get the chance to dream here again. Come on."

A plastic banner with the word 'EXIT' had been tied to a hay bale and beneath it a red arrow pointed to a door half-camouflaged in the straw. Daisy pushed the door open and they stepped back into the buzz and spectacle of a funfair at night.

Firework rockets were still exploding above the Ferris wheel at the top of the square. Wilson plucked the last stalk from Daisy's hair and tentatively put his arm around her shoulders. Daisy hooked her thumb in the back pocket of his jeans. A few stitches along the side seam gave way and left a ragged flap hanging down.

"I don't want this dream to end" said Wilson.

"Neither do I" said Daisy.

They walked along in silence, following the flow of the same faced crowd through the wafting aromas of fried onions and fresh popcorn, and eventually arrived at the Ferris wheel.

The ride was modelled on the London Eye, but on a smaller scale and without the pill-shaped passenger pods. Around the axis, the words 'Ferris the Catherine Wheel' shone with iridescent light. The white spokes of the wheel were gigantic, iron girders studded with rivet heads and bolts and inlaid with rows of light bulbs. Black tubes, the size of wheelie bins, were fixed to the circumference at two metre intervals. The wheel was rotating at walking pace.

Same-faced workers in yellow jackets were organising the boarding process. Some were buckling passengers into a combination of harness and rucksack while others were helping passengers clamber into the black cylinders. As the wheel crept forwards, black tube after black tube was being loaded, locked and lifted high into the sky.

"But nobody is getting off" Wilson pointed to a section of wheel approaching the loading platform. "Look, all those black tubes are coming down empty. Where are all the passengers? How did they get out?"

"I've no idea, but it's not much of a ride. All they get to do is see the inside of a black bin."

"Come on, let's go Daisy."

She stifled a yawn.

"Yep, I've had enough of this one."

They were about to turn away when a tinny, trumpet fanfare sounded and lights running the length of the enormous spokes of the wheel started to flash.

Scores of spectators standing three deep along the perimeter fence, hushed in anticipation of the ride commencing.

Daisy and Wilson felt subterranean vibrations throb with increasing power as the wheel slowly, but very visibly, started to pick up speed.

"Look, it's changing, I can feel it through my feet," said Daisy, "let's wait a minute and see what happens."

Black tubes glided ever faster past the empty loading platform Every now and again a hand would wave out from one of the tubes and give an indiscriminate thumbs up.

Wilson chuckled.

"How can they tell if they're waving at someone they

know? They can't see anything from inside those tubes and out here everybody looks the same — apart from me and you!"

"Wilson, shush." Daisy kicked his shin. "I'm watching, I think something's about to happen."

The wheel continued to spin faster and faster as the hum from underground motors intensified.

And then Wilson got it; the name of the ride: 'Ferris the Catherine Wheel.'

"Daisy," he whispered, "it's not a Ferris wheel. It's a Catherine wheel. Like the ones on Bonfire Night. You know, you nail them to a wooden post and then light them and they spin round spitting out sparks." By now, the wheel was revolving so quickly it had become a blur of concentric circles of light and colour.

"So what happens with the black tubes?"

"Well, I don't think this Catherine wheel spits out sparks. I think this one spits out . . . "

"The passengers!"

As Daisy spoke, a cannon fired somewhere above her head and instinctively, they both looked up.

High in the sky, each resounding boom was accompanied by an exploding firework rocket. The visual spectacle and the boom after boom, followed by another forty booms, left them both speechless. When the volley ended their ears were ringing.

The wheel slowed rapidly and within a minute it was back to rotating at snail's pace. Fine plumes of white smoke drifted out from the black tubes as they passed by at eye level.

Then, as though a conductor had tapped his baton for audience participation, the crowds pressed up against the perimeter fence erupted in a chorus of cheering and waving.

Daisy saw them first.

"Look Wilson, there." She was pointing upwards and jumping with excitement. "And there's another one over there, and there and there."

Wilson saw them too: one, three, five, a dozen, dozens of red parachutes all gently drifting back down to earth.

Then Wilson was cheering and high-fiving and hugging Daisy and it was just the best night ever.

It took a chaotic ten minutes for all the passengers to be repatriated with family and friends, a task made more complex by the fact they all looked alike.

"Fancy a go?"

"No, another time. I'm feeling a bit tired now."

"Daisy, you're in a dream, how can you be tired?"

"I don't know Wilson, but I am."

The last passenger to touchdown was a size-eleven-year-old who was instantly mobbed by proud parents. Then the lights all over the wheel went off and the glow from the illuminated lettering around the hub dimmed.

"Looks like the show's over Daisy. What shall we do now?"

"Wilson, I was just thinking about what you said, about being tired in my own dream."

"And?"

"Well, what if my being tired and yawning in a dream is a sign that I'm about to stop dreaming in real life? You know, like the opposite. If my sleep pattern changes, I can't be here anymore. I'll just disappear and be back in bed and you'll be here by yourself until you wake up, or stop dreaming, or whatever."

"Daisy, I've no idea. I don't know what's going on myself.

In fact, I'm still not sure if you're real."

Daisy reached out for Wilson's hand and slid her fingers through his.

"Meet me at Starbucks."

Wilson rolled his eyes and tried to pull away.

"Seriously, I want us to try again. One more time. The stuff I told you about with the train is true. You can check it out for yourself. It really did break down. From tomorrow I'm away on a geography field trip in Ambleside, but I'm back next week, and I'll be waiting for you in Starbucks on Deansgate at seven o'clock, next Friday."

"Daisy, I don't know. I'll have to think about it. I . . . "

She could sense Wilson's conflicting emotions and kissed him on the cheek.

"Did that feel like a figment of your imagination Wilson?"

"Mmm, not so sure. Can I try another one."

She pushed him away and scowled.

"You'd better be there next Friday or you'll be in . . . "

Daisy stopped mid-sentence as the colour began to drain from her face, her skin, her hair and her clothes; it was as though she'd been called back to another place and her body was departing in instalments. As Wilson watched, her very presence diminished, Daisy was being washed away, fading into a sepia-tint, a monotone hologram, a translucent shadow of her former self. And within moments, incredibly, she was no longer there. Daisy had departed from dream sleep right in front of Wilson's eyes.

He swept his hand through clear air; through the space she'd once occupied. Daisy had dissipated, evaporated, and been carried back to bed like a beautiful mist.

Wilson tried to stifle a yawn, but the yawn fought back. He

felt tired, increasingly tired, exhausted, being extinguished. As though at that moment, all the energy in his body was changing from one form into another.

Wilson said goodnight to The Market Square and was no longer a face, in a same face crowd.

Chapter 21

Hoover's crazy idea

Friday 20th October 2017

Wilson woke the next morning with the feeling that a lifetime's supply of Valentine's Days had all arrived at once. It was 7.30 a.m.

For twenty sumptuous minutes, like a child savouring every mouthful of a favourite dessert, he relived the dream of the funfair and the clear-as-day memories of Daisy Meadowcroft.

Warnings from Gloria of being 'late for college' and 'no time for breakfast' finally coaxed him from under his duvet. After a quick shower, he buttoned up a clean shirt, belted his jeans and tucked his wallet into a back pocket. He felt a tear in the side seam at the top and something nagged his memory like an unfinished task.

"Wilson, you're going to be so late. What are you doing up there?"

Fast forwarding through the dream he saw Daisy and himself emerge from The Ten-Mile Drop. He plucked stalks of straw from her hair. They strolled along for a few yards. Then he put his arm around Daisy's shoulders and she tugged at . . .

Daisy tore the pocket. In my dream. No. That's impossible!

Somewhat puzzled by the idea of real, physical damage being the consequence of an event in a dream, he flicked the frayed flap with his finger and went downstairs for breakfast.

Gloria was wiping down a worktop as Wilson entered the kitchen.

"Morning love. You'd better get a move on. Me too. I'm opening the shop this morning. What do you want for breakfast?"

"Nothing Mum. I'll grab something in the canteen. I'm not hungry."

His mother tutted by way of reply.

"Mum," he said, "you see these jeans I'm wearing, my old Levi's?"

"Yes love, I do. I can see them because you're wearing them."

"Yeah, sorry, I know. What I mean is, when did you last iron them?"

"Those jeans? About three days ago, no, the day before yesterday, I did the ironing in the afternoon. Why?"

"Can you remember if they had this tear in them?"

He showed her the torn ear on the pocket.

"No, they didn't, or I'd have put them to one side for stitching. You probably caught it on something. Don't worry, they can be repaired."

"Are you sure it wasn't there two days ago?"

"No Wilson, it definitely wasn't. Now will you at least eat some cereal and then get yourself off to college?"

The morning's classes passed uneventfully and at lunchtime Wilson made for the college canteen where he ordered chicken and chips, a slice of lemon meringue pie and a can of Fanta. He saw Hoover sitting at a table, head and shoulders hunched over some paperwork and Wilson went to join him.

141

"Alright mate," he said, sliding the food tray on the table. "How's it going?"

"Fair to middling," replied Hoover. He was sketching something on an A4 notepad and concentrating.

Wilson tucked into his lunch as brief snippets of gossip were exchanged regarding various posts on social media, the new girl in Hoover's geography group, the weekend's football fixtures and Teaps's black eye. But Hoover wasn't fully engaged in the chitchat. He was more focused on the diagrams spread out on the table.

"What're you doing there then?" Wilson asked, spearing chips with his fork.

"Designing a website mate."

"Excellent. For any particular reason?"

"Yeah. To find my missing football sock."

Wilson nearly choked on a chip and a shot of Fanta bubbled-up inside his nose.

"To do what? To find your missing sock?" he asked incredulously.

"Yeah, I'm gonna show know-all Daley that it's possible for socks to go missing with no explanation. Everyone knows it's true. And I'm designing a website to prove it."

Hoover looked up and brushed the curtain of hair away from his eyes.

"Wilson, how many single socks have you got in your sock drawer. You know, like, odd ones?"

"Quite a few I'd say."

"There you are then. My website will help you find all the missing halves of the pairs."

Hoover made a few more notes and doodles as Wilson polished off the lemon meringue pie.

"And I've already got the domain name."

"So what's the site called then?"

"Missingsock.co.uk."

"Hoover, you're having me on."

"No I'm bloody not."

Hoover peered indignantly at Wilson.

"Look mate, I've done my research and every lad I've spoken to in this college has told me he has missing socks. And some of the teachers too! Mr Lewin told me he has more single socks than pairs."

"So?"

"So, the interesting thing is this; all the lads told me they've also found socks that aren't even theirs. Imagine that. You lose a sock and you gain someone else's. That's not right, is it mate?"

"No, it certainly isn't mate," said Wilson, hoping nobody was listening in on the conversation.

"So my idea is that I help people find the sock they've lost, by taking a photo of the one that's left – they can't take a photo of the sock that's missing, cos it's gone missing. So they upload the photo of the partner of the missing sock, plus photos of any socks they've got that don't belong to them. And my website matches 'em up. And you get your lost sock back."

"Genius," said Wilson.

"I know," said Hoover. "My brother's doin' computer programming at uni and he said he'd build the site for me, no problem. That's why I'm working on the design and words."

"And where do you make money with this vital public service then?"

"I don't mate. It's the thought that counts – and proving a point!"

Hoover returned to his site plan and continued scribbling.

"Well, good luck with that then. Let me know when it goes live and I'll do some uploading."

"Yeah, no worries mate." Hoover didn't look up.

Wilson contemplated a parting comment but then shook his head, grabbed his bag and headed for the library. His next class was at 2.00 p.m., so he had exactly an hour to go digging.

The library was quiet and Wilson headed for a corner cubicle where he opened his laptop, typed 'Macclesfield Reporter' and tapped 'enter'. He clicked the link to the newspaper's home page and watched it load. There was a search box in the top-right corner and Wilson paused for a second before deciding on 'Macclesfield train disruption'. A moment later a handful of abbreviated results came back. The most recent was from three weeks earlier.

'Falling leaves disrupt Virgin train service from London.

The entry beneath was from six weeks prior.

'Virgin train service to Euston breaks speed record'.

Wilson leant forward and scanned down the entire page. There was nothing relevant. Daisy's story was a fabrication which *he'd* obviously made up, just as he'd made *her* up. The rip in his jeans was just a weird coincidence. It was probably something he'd done himself, unconsciously, during the day, only to be reminded of in a dream during the night.

"I'm going mad" he muttered.

Wilson pushed back on the swivel chair, put his hands behind his head and studied the library ceiling. An interlocking grid of suspended panels and row upon row of fluorescent lights hanging from thin steel cables.

"Wait a minute."

He jerked back to the laptop screen with a new line of

enquiry.

Maybe I need to be more specific?

Wilson clicked back to Google and typed in 'Bus service for broken down train, Macclesfield, October 2017' and tapped the return key. A flood of results flowed down the screen and still there was nothing relevant. He clicked 'next' to call up a second page of results, not expecting any kind of revelation, but then a single line caught his eye. It was an extract taken from an Instagram post by someone called Jessie Evans.

'Bus service replaces broken train. Another night of mayhem at Macclesfield train station.'

The photo of a broken-down train with an engineer inspecting the undercarriage was supported with a caption.

'Thanks to the muppets who run the Macclesfield train service I missed a concert last night. Waited hours in freezing cold in middle of nowhere. Fat Controller should be sacked.'

Goodness, she's not happy.

But Wilson was. He was bordering on ecstatic.

He grabbed his phone, opened Twitter and keyed in '#macclesfieldtrainmayhem' and other similar hashtags.

A flurry of tweets came back, all warbling about the problem with the train and how the breakdown had caused this difficulty or that disappointment. A tweet from the Stoke Sentinel newspaper blamed it on bad weather caused by Storm Ophelia.

Wilson blinked and stared at the screen of his phone in utter astonishment.

So Daisy was actually telling the truth.

Wilson struggled to contain his jubilation.

I couldn't have heard about the breakdown because it wasn't in the news. The train had actually broken down. I

couldn't have known about that, and it was just as she told me.
And Daisy tore my jeans, which means she's real. Daisy is real.
Daisy exists.

Forgetting his environment – and inhibitions, Wilson leapt to his feet and with a huge grin on his face made a proclamation.

"Daisy Meadowcroft is real. She lives in Macclesfield. And I proved it." Then he raised his outstretched arms up to the heavens and told the entire library. "She's got blood in her thumb, just like me."

Wilson was asked to leave the library after his unwarranted outburst, an instruction he was more than happy to follow. He spent the rest of the day in a state of enlightened bliss.

"You alright, Wilson?" Teaps popped the question as they sat together in an English class an hour later.

"Yeah, why?"

"Oh, no reason in particular."

Following the English lesson, as Wilson made his way down a corridor towards the biology lab, he heard someone behind him shout, "a Daisy lives in Macclesfield." This was followed by, "and she's got blood in her thumb."

Which in turn, led to more ribbing and banter.

Wilson didn't turn to face the culprits. Instead he leapt and punched the air, then raised a middle finger. He was in a great mood. He'd discovered a kindred spirit, a really pretty one at that, and together they were going to lay bare the mysteries of The Market Square.

Over a meal that evening, Wilson spent an hour catching up on the latest news and gossip with his mum. This included the story of how Mrs Abbott had asked her son to fit a new plug socket in the charity shop, only for Mrs Green to sell his toolkit for five pounds when he went for a sandwich.

How Cybil had discovered a rare Dickens hardback in the books section, which she sold on eBay for two hundred pounds *and* gave all the money back to the shop!

How Kate and Megan both had boyfriends who were law students and wouldn't it be weird if the boyfriends were also twins! Gloria also suggested that Alex was doing more swanking about in London and hobnobbing with MPs in the House of Commons, than actual work!

Gossip over, they launched into a ten-minute session of 'Film Quiz', which basically involved reciting a classic one-liner and then challenging the other to name the movie. Gloria was usually the amazing memory woman but Wilson's line from *Jurassic Park*, gleaned from his Dad, had her stumped. Wilson was leading by a single point at the end. An end that came with the same closing line.

"Now that is a tasty burger."

Wilson really didn't need to say, *"Pulp Fiction!"*

He rose from the kitchen table and gave his mother a hug. "Got some homework to do Mum. Thanks for tea."

He was walking out toward the hall when an inkling, a random thought, made him stop and turn. His mum was folding a tea towel and quietly humming to herself. The mum who had carried him for nine months and then delivered him into this world. A vivacious, lovely, middle-aged lady who ran a charity shop. That was Wilson's mum, and Teaps didn't have one.

"Mum, where was I born?"

"That's a strange question Wilson. Funnily enough, you were born in the same hospital, in fact, the same ward as your dad – here in Stockport, in the infirmary, Ward 3B. It still exists but it's an old people's ward now. Mrs Bushel, a lovely old lady from the shop was in there for a while, but she died a couple of weeks after they moved her to an old people's home. Why do you ask?"

"Oh, no reason. It's just that . . . ah, nothing important. Love you Mum."

Wilson pulled the kitchen door behind him and bounded up the stairs two at a time.

"Love you too," said Gloria.

Chapter 22

Questions need answers

Night of Friday 20th October 2017

As Wilson entered his bedroom, his mobile phone rang.

"Hi Hoover. How's it going?"

"Good man, good. Listen, can you do me a favour?"

"If I can."

"Can you send me photos of all your single socks? Remember, you said you had a few. I need to get them over to my brother; he's started to build the website."

Wilson paused for a second, slightly irritated at the stupidity of what he was being asked to do.

"Let me get this right Hoover, you want photos of all my odd socks, so that you can put them on your website and wait for someone to find a match, just to prove to George Daley that socks have the power to go missing all by themselves? Is that right?"

"Yeah, that's exactly it. Oh, and if you find a sock that isn't yours, you know, like you don't know where it came from, send me that as well. So send me two folders, one with your odd socks and one with other people's socks if you have any."

"Hoover, are you serious? I thought you were messing about."

"No, I'm deadly serious mate. This missing sock thing is a real mystery. Like a conspiracy theory. It's too big to ignore without trying to find an explanation."

"Well I can't do it now. It's late."

"Come on Wilson, my brother can only work on this at night and he's ready to start. I've sent him the words and some of my sock photos, but he needs more to test the search engine. Why, what else are you doing, texting that imaginary girlfriend?"

"Very funny," scowled Wilson. "Alright, give me half an hour and I'll send something over. But don't tell anyone I'm in on this – just helping out a mate with mental issues."

"Cheers man, soon as you can." Hoover rang off.

Wilson looked apologetically at his sock drawer.

I don't believe this!

Nevertheless, he spent ten minutes identifying mismatched and partnerless socks and taking photographs, which he then forwarded on to Hoover. In total, he had six orphaned socks, including a very smart green sock with a Ralph Lauren 'Polo' logo embroidered in red. Those socks had been a Christmas present that he'd only worn once, before half of them went awol. He was not expecting repatriation via Hoover's website. Wilson also discovered a blue-and-white-striped sock that absolutely didn't belong to him, so he took a picture and sent it to Hoover with a fingers-crossed emoji. Then he sat at his desk and his thoughts returned to Daisy.

The torn pocket of his jeans, the discovery that Daisy's train had really been delayed, the very fact she visited The Market Square, was already a chain of events so implausible that the next link, meeting Daisy in real life, well, why not? However, the torn pocket was also troubling because the tear was a sign of actual, physical damage. Somehow, during the course of a dream, in which Daisy's thumb had loosened a few stitches, the same thing had happened to the real Levi

150

jeans lying on his bedroom floor. The notion brought to mind a horror movie and *Paranormal Activity*, then an even more sinister possibility followed.

Perhaps his assumption that Daisy existed was all wrong and it was *he* who had made the tear! And had subconsciously heard about the train problem in Macclesfield and woven it into the dream with Daisy.

Maybe he had some kind of personality disorder, schizophrenic even?

It was a shattering possibility.

But then a split personality wouldn't explain how he'd been able to learn languages, fly a helicopter, play the bass, simply by dreaming about it. He certainly hadn't learned to speak French in the conventional way, for that would have required a teacher and lessons and there was no evidence of that. The truth was, he could speak French and he'd learned it in a dream. Full stop.

Which meant he wasn't schizophrenic and there had to be an alternate explanation for the torn pocket and the delayed train. An explanation involving a girl living in Macclesfield

This controlled, rational thinking about highly irrational events reassured Wilson and allowed him to consider a number of other related questions.

There was no golden bangle for Teaps's mum; did that mean she was still alive? And should he meet Daisy, how was the dream world connected to the real world. How was it possible to bridge the gap?

Perhaps his clock diagram held the answers? Wilson needed the hour and minute hands to point the way.

Chapter 23

Tick, tock

Morning of Saturday 21st October 2017

During a night of restless, dreamless sleep the questions on Wilson's mind continued to nag for answers and he woke the next morning with a headache. He tried to escape further self-interrogation by pulling his duvet over his head but Big Mac tracked him down. Thinking back to The Gateway dream, Wilson sensed something indefinable in the content that was markedly different to The Market Square's usual manifestations. With its comic characters and dark subject matter, The Gateway dream had felt more profound, portentous, ominous even, like a different species of dream.

Also, was it just a coincidence that it occurred on my birthday? Could my birthday, my eighteenth birthday, coming of age and all that, have had an influence?

Wilson reached for his phone and searched: 'Significance of 18th October 2017'.

The first result came from Wikipedia.

'October 18th is the 291st day of the year in the Gregorian calendar. There are 74 days remaining until the end of the year . . . '

Wilson skimmed through the rest of the article. Although October 18th had been significant over the centuries – famous battles, major earthquakes, Edison generated electricity in 1878, the BBC was founded in 1922 and so on – nothing in the listings gave any insight into Wilson's musing.

That's a daft idea, he told himself, tossing the phone to one side.

After a minute of further contemplation however, he came back with a new plan.

Maybe I should be looking at the day I was born, 18th October 1999, rather than the day I turned eighteen. My actual birthday!

He reached for the phone: 'Significance of 18th October 1999'.

Once again, Wikipedia failed to shed any light and pages one and two of Google results brought the same disappointment. However, on page three Wilson saw a link with the title: 'Mybirthday.ninja. October 18, 1999. Birthday facts.' Intrigued, he clicked the link.

The page loaded under the heading: '**Here are some snazzy birthday facts about 18th of October.**' The snazzy facts included Wilson's age in dog years, which celebrities shared his birthday and again, all the major events. But under the heading '**What does a birthday on October 18, 1999, mean?**' Wilson read the following.

'Your birthday numbers, 10, 18 and 1999, reveal your Life Path number as 11. It is a master number that represents intuition, idealism and invention. You have the potential to be a source of inspiration and illumination for people.'

Okay, that's more like it, now what the hell is a Life Path number? Google had the answer.

'The most important number in your 'numerology' chart. Your Life Path number reveals a broad outline of the opportunities, challenges and lessons you will encounter during this lifetime.'

Wilson double clicked 'numerology'.

'Numerology is a belief in the divine or mystical relationship between a number and one or more coinciding events. It is often associated with the paranormal, alongside astrology and similar divinatory arts.'

As Wilson's eyes moved over the words, his attention lagged some distance behind, still dwelling on the word 'paranormal'. It soon caught up however, as he read the following:

'Numerology... was the origin of the theories of electromagnetism, quantum mechanics and gravitation.'

In other words, energy fields.

He clicked a link to www.numerology.com:

'...the 11 symbolises the potential to push the limitations of the human experience into the stratosphere of the highest spiritual perception, the link between the mortal and the immortal, between man and spirit, between darkness and light, ignorance and enlightenment. This is the ultimate symbolic power of the 11.'

Then he followed his search steps back to the words 'divinatory arts'.

'Divination, from the Latin, divinaire, to foresee, to be inspired by God.'

Understandably, it took a while for Wilson to pull together the disparate threads of information he'd just read and weave them into a sensical narrative.

So my Life Path number, the number eleven, is a special number that links me to the paranormal, to divination, the spirit and is connected with energy fields. What the beeep?

Wilson grabbed his rucksack, unfolded the clock diagram and jotted down his thoughts. He then put the paper back in his rucksack. It was Saturday and that meant one thing, football.

After breakfast, Wilson cleaned his boots, prepared his kit bag and checked the time. He had an hour to kill and the number '11' had been implanted on his mind like the mark from a branding iron.

Back in his room he returned to the search history stored on his phone and read the following sentence twice, to make sure he had it clear in his head.

'...the 11 symbolises the potential to push the limitations of the human experience into the stratosphere of the highest spiritual perception, the link between the mortal and the immortal, between man and spirit, between darkness and light, ignorance and enlightenment.'

Is this telling me that I have that potential?

Wilson recalled The Gateway dream and fast-forwarded to the conversation in The Hall of Extinguished Spirits.

"The soul is the Residual spirit, it goes elsewhere."

"To the other side, to meet The Powers That Be."

There was an obvious connection between the supposed power of the number 11 and the script for the dream. 'From ignorance to enlightenment.' Wilson grabbed a pen and double-checked the formula for calculating a Life Path number.

No point in getting too excited if the sums are wrong.

My date of birth: 18th October 1999

Month

October is the 10th month of the year.

10 reduces to 1 plus 0, which equals 1.

Days

My day of birth is the 18th.

18 reduces to 1 plus 8, which equals 9.

Year

My year of birth is 1999.

1999 reduces to 1 plus 9 plus 9 plus 9, which equals 28.

28 reduces to 2 plus 8, which equals 10.

Then 10 reduces to 1 plus 0, which equals 1.

Now add the 1 and the 9 and the 1, and the result is 11.

The master number 11.

No question about that, I am a number eleven.

Wilson then performed the same calculation for Kate and Megan and his mum. His sisters were both eight and his mum, a six. He made the calculation for his dad.

Wilson wasn't surprised to find his father was a number eleven, a master number, just like himself. He'd left that birth date until last, for just that reason.

Dad was born in the same hospital as me; says strange things happen that can't be explained; he studies energy and information networks; knows about morphic fields and we're both connected by the number eleven.

The frivolous side of Wilson's imagination then raised the alarming possibility that his father might also have visited The Market Square.

Wilson laughed at the thought, but not for long, because

the disturbing recollection of something Big Mac had said, wiped the smile off his face.

"We know who you are Mr Wilson. We've been watching you. We've seen your trace. You're a number eleven."

Stop! No more. This is seriously freaking me out.

Wilson grabbed his bag, scooter keys and left for the football match.

Chapter 24

How time flies

In the build-up to a 'potential' rendezvous with Daisy Meadowcroft, Wilson avoided all further thoughts of numerology, energy fields and flow diagrams. He didn't visit The Market Square once that week; the last thing he needed to mess with his head were more cryptic revelations from the dynamic duo in The Gateway.

Alex was working away in London. His sisters were busy planning a final year fashion show and Mum was fully occupied with the charity shop. That meant Wilson could keep his head down and focus on being a textbook student.

Here are the main stories of the week.

Monday was taken up by an annual event called 'Getting Ready for Work'. This involved a morning of talks and presentations by an employment agency explaining how students should prepare for job interviews, what to wear, how to write a curriculum vitae and other issues along the same theme.

Monday afternoon was slightly more engaging and involved a Career Path Assessment; the purpose of which was to help Wilson choose a suitable vocation based on the answers he gave to a series of multiple choice questions. After Wilson's tick boxes had been processed, the results came back and the careers lady told Wilson that based on various metrics, his ideal job would be that of a physiotherapist or a plumber.

During a maths lesson on Tuesday, finding a mathematical proof for a quadratic equation led Wilson to contemplate a mathematical proof for Daisy; which then led to a daydream, about a Geography field trip in Ambleside and tramping across the fells searching for interlocking spurs and oxbow lakes.

The major highlight of Wednesday was the launch of a new and indispensable website with the eponymous domain name: Missingsock.co.uk. Hoover Facebooked and Tweeted everyone he knew and by 9.00 p.m. a collection of twenty-nine socks were looking for partners online. 'Where single socks find the perfect match' was Hoover's snappy strap line.

Iqbal managed to diversify the entire business plan by uploading a lost glove.

Thursday dragged by with nothing noteworthy to report, and then Friday finally arrived.

Chapter 25

D-day

Friday 27th October 2017

Hoover and Teaps were playing pool in the students' common room with Hoover's younger brother and Eddie Spinner. Spinner was a drug dealer and general lowlife; the lad whose name was never called when picking sides for basketball. Wilson was also in the common room, counting down the minutes. He'd gone there for peace and quiet, to steady his nerves in readiness for the journey to Manchester, but then Hoover and Teaps had barged in. The last thing he needed was to be challenged to a game of pool. Any refusal would require an explanation, and any explanation would have to steer way clear of Manchester city centre and another date with an invisible woman. The merest scent of a fib and Teaps would be all over it like a rash. Another certainty, was the likelihood of Spinner wandering over once the game had ended.

One night, at a party at Iqbal's house, Wilson smoked a joint for the first time. He'd drank too much cider and Spinner told him the weed would help him relax and be more confident with the girls.

"Everyone does it man. It'll help you chill."

So Wilson took the joint, inhaled, held his breath for a moment, exhaled, coughed, and then coughed some more. Whether it was the combination of drink and drugs or just the strong weed, Wilson had no idea. But he did know there was no relaxing and no chillin'. Instead, his head became a volcano trying to erupt with all kinds of strange ideas and memories and thoughts and minutes after taking that solitary puff, he passed out.

Two hours later he woke up on Iqbal's bed with his eyes firmly shut. The short-circuits triggered by the spliff were still causing havoc. A cartoon was playing on the inside of his eyelids. A cartoon with characters he'd never seen before. Wilson staggered downstairs and stumbled home, much to the amusement of everyone at the party.

So the general opinion was that Wilson was a lightweight when it came to 'extra-curricular activity', as Hoover put it; but Wilson knew the reality was more to do with the way his brain was wired. Wilson also knew that Spinner hadn't given him the joint to be friendly; he'd supplied with the unspoken understanding that Wilson would be buying weed from him in the future. It would only be a matter of minutes before the pool game was over and Spinner would come creeping over with his predictable, smarmy, "Hey, Wilson, amigo, qué pasa?"

Wilson grabbed his Vespa keys, helmet and parka and made for the door. He'd rather be early and sit in Albert Square watching the pigeons than deal with Spinner and Inspector Teaps.

"See you at footy tomorrow lads," he shouted. "Elvis has left the building."

"Hey Wilson, wait, we've finished, Hoover's just potted the black with his elbow. Where're you going?"

But Wilson was gone.

Chapter 26

Will she? Won't she?

As the A6 descended into Stockport, Wilson remembered to turn left early and take the detour around the back of the infirmary.

Tonight's not the night for any déjà voodoo.

He arrived in Manchester city centre at 6.30 p.m., parked his scooter in a bay on Bridge Street then walked across Deansgate and up to Albert Square. Fine rain was falling as he sat on a bench facing the town hall and double checked the time and date.

Correct, just as arranged. Twenty minutes to go.

Perhaps it was the drizzle dousing his fire, or a bipolar switch had been pressed; either way, Wilson's mood changed as though a coin had been tossed. He felt strangely deflated.

Twenty minutes to go to what? Twenty minutes to the possibility of crushing disappointment? Twenty minutes until the psychiatrist is called?

Yes, he had his family, friends and compared to so many others – Teaps, for example – he had a great life. But observing the people hurrying across the square with purpose, feeling the pulse of a major city at rush hour, Wilson suddenly felt lonely and lost. A stupid lad with crazy dreams, foolishly wishing for a miracle to happen; desperately needing someone, another tightrope walker, to help with his mental balancing and 'always walking on egg shells' existence.

Pent up feelings of insecurity and self-delusion wrestled

free and charged into his head like Orcs into battle.

You're going mental mate, goin' mad, losin' it.

The needle on the valve was touching red.

Conned yourself into thinking she's real.

The dam was about to burst its banks.

Pulled the wool over your own eyes.

The lid was coming off.

Shot down in flames with your own bullets.

Would Daisy be his salvation, a lifeline, his sanity? She had to exist, must exist, because now, there was no way for this high wire act to turn back.

Words from a favourite Coldplay song, 'The Scientist' came into Wilson's head. He silently sang them from beginning to end, surprised at how poignant and pertinent the lyrics were.

'I was just guessing, at numbers and figures, pulling the puzzle apart.'

Each line seemed to capture his predicament perfectly and in doing so, they had a calming effect and took the edge off his agitation.

Come on, pull yourself together you idiot.

He was going to be ten minutes early, but set off nevertheless.

Turning onto Deansgate, Wilson pulled up like a horse refusing a fence when he saw the Starbucks sign. With the finishing line just a few lengths away he was still skittish.

This is the crossroads. This is the tipping point.

He felt his face and mouth and nose for anything that shouldn't be there and took a deep breath to prepare for either of two possible outcomes.

This is it. Now or never!

The coffee shop was warm and welcoming and the alchemy of fresh coffee aroma mixed with the musk of damp clothing cast a pleasant spell. Wilson took off his parka and put the crash helmet on the floor between his feet

The place was busy, but not so busy that Wilson wasn't able to look around and see that Daisy hadn't arrived.

I can't see her sitting down anywhere.

A lady with a teenage son and a man wearing a raincoat were placing orders at the service counter.

And they're definitely not her. But who's that over there?

A female figure was standing at the milk and sugar dispenser with her back to him.

She was about Daisy's height, wearing a trench coat with a turned-up collar, ankle boots, bobble hat, and she was fixing a coffee or hot chocolate; Wilson couldn't tell. He kept the girl firmly in his sights. Whatever she was doing, she was certainly taking her time about it. A wooden stirrer was deposited in the bin. With mug in hand, she began to turn, to reveal flushed cheeks, pink lips, a button nose, then she looked for somewhere to sit and her brown eyes found Wilson. For a split second, time stood still as the coffee mug slipped through Daisy's fingers. Wilson kicked his crash helmet as he started to run. The helmet hit a table leg and bowled out someone's umbrella. But that didn't matter, nothing mattered, because Daisy was in his arms. Her bobble hat fell off, strands of chestnut hair were tickling his nose and he was intoxicated by the scent of fresh vanilla. They were laughing and hugging and Wilson was saying "we did it" and Daisy was replying "see, I told you I was real" and all the Orcs were fleeing left, right and centre and she was warm and full of bones with butterscotch skin and blood in her thumb and the girl in Wilson's dreams really did exist.

"Now there's two of us," he whispered into the soft pink shell of her ear.

It took a few minutes for Daisy to explain to the manageress that Wilson was a best friend whom she hadn't seen for years; that she was sorry for dropping the coffee mug and they would go and sit at the table in the corner with two fresh coffees and not cause any further fuss or trouble.

Wilson's eyes never moved from Daisy throughout the conversation.

"Bloody hell," said Wilson as they sat down. "Double bloody hell."

"I told you I'd be here Wilson. Absolutely no problems with the trains tonight."

Wilson gazed into Daisy's eyes; an even greater delight to behold in the brilliant light of real life. He placed his hand on hers.

"Sorry I doubted you, but I can't believe it," he said. "I mean, I really, really can't believe it. I don't know what I would've done, what would've happened, if you hadn't come here tonight. And then if I'd met you in The Market Square again! You really have saved me Daisy. Saved my sanity."

They sat in silence for the next minute, hand on hand. Wilson kept his head down, manfully trying to hide his tears.

"Wilson it's alright. I'm here, I'll always be here, always have been, in this real world." He released a single, body-shaking sob.

"Wilson, I think we were meant to find each other. Some weird magnetism has drawn us together, like it was planned to happen. My grandmother said this was possible and I never doubted it. No need to be sad. It's not a bad thing."

"I'm not sad Daisy, I'm happy — in ways I can't begin to describe. And I'm trying to come to terms with the fact that I met someone in one of my crazy dreams, who also shares those crazy dreams, the only person I know who does in fact, and she's flippin' sitting here next to me, now, in real life. That's where I am at the moment."

He brushed a tear from his cheek. "That's not a tear of joy, it's the tear of a miracle."

"Yeah, it is a miracle, and they actually do happen in our world. We have to accept The Market Square as something inexplicable, but also true and go on from there. Maybe someday we'll discover the how's and why's."

"I'm glad I've found you Daisy."

"Me too Wilson," she said, without having to think.

They spent the next hour talking about all the things a boy and girl usually reveal on a 'blind date'. Family, friends, phone numbers, birthdays, likes and dislikes favourite bands; all the boxes were ticked. It felt necessary to do this groundwork, to give the relationship a conventional footing. Though all the while, the main item on the menu, The Market Square, was simmering on a hot plate in the background.

Strangely however, they knew intuitively, without the need for words, that Starbucks was not the place to broach the subject. The Market Square was simply too big an issue to dissect in the open forum of a coffee shop. Besides, the four guys on the adjoining table kept listening in to their conversation.

Daisy cupped her mug with both hands.

"Do you ever think about dreams Wilson, you know, their meaning, their purpose? Because even the top scientists don't understand them, or even know which part of the brain is responsible."

Wilson got the message. They would cover some neutral ground.

"Yeah, I do, I think about them a lot. And what amazes me is how we can just invent a dream in our heads, like a movie, with characters and a story, all invented on the spot. The most powerful computer in the world could never do that, yet we do it every night with no problem."

"And, without a script."

"Exactly."

Daisy sipped her coffee and her eyelids fell forward in the process. The lashes were curved and blonde at the tip, like the fine hairs in a sable paint brush. Daisy placed the mug back on the table.

"Okay try this for size. Did you know we spend more time, in our lives dreaming, than we do eating? No, don't laugh Wilson, it's true. I read it in a book. The average person sleeps for eight hours, right?"

"Right."

"And during those eight hours, we spend a quarter of the time dreaming, which, when you multiply it all out, is the equivalent of six years for the average person living until they're seventy-five."

"And the point is? "

"The point is Wilson, that we spend six years of our lives dreaming, but only four years eating. So what does that tell you?"

"Err, that dreaming is more important than eating?"

"Correct Wilson. But if you go into a bookshop, the cookery or food section will occupy a full wall while the three books about dreams are hidden somewhere on the psychology shelf."

Wilson stretched out his legs, clasped his hands behind his head and sat back in the chair. He was finally relaxing and fully at ease with this amazing girl who had miraculously entered his life; a nocturnal soul mate, a like-minded companion, the living embodiment of his salvation. Daisy was giving a cameo performance and she was making him smile inside.

"And another thing Wilson, dreams have meaning!"

Daisy tapped a painted fingernail on the table top; as any girl insistent on her boyfriend hearing what she has to say might do.

"A snake in a dream can even have a *double* meaning, both good *and* bad. It all depends on the colour of the snake apparently!"

As Daisy entertained Wilson in Starbucks, in The Gateway, an entirely different conversation was taking place.

"Ah, I see our friends have finally crossed the Rubicon," said Big Mac.

"They certainly have," said Short Cake. "Do you think The Powers That Be are aware?"

"If they're not, they soon will be."

Chapter 27

After dinner chat

Wilson and Daisy were the last to leave Starbucks and as they made their way to Piccadilly Station, the voyage of discovery continued with animated chatter under the cover of Daisy's umbrella.

"Have you got a boyfriend Daisy?"

Wilson wanted a feel for the terrain. For where he stood. Would he be treading on anyone's toes?

Daisy smiled. "Just friends, nothing serious. And you?"

"Same situation. But I have been engaged three times. Still not found the right one yet."

"Yeah, my second divorce is just going through. I'll probably lose my vinyl record collection in the settlement."

They huddled together on a rain sodden platform, pock-marked with puddles, waiting for Daisy's train to Macclesfield.

"Be careful driving back Wilson; the roads will be slippery after all this rain. Don't want our friendship to end on the night it started."

"Don't worry, I'll make sure all my headlights are on. The Vespa had five the last time I counted, so I should be visible."

Wilson paused for a second, then continued.

"So where do we go from here then? I mean . . . "

Daisy inched closer, slipping her hands inside Wilson's coat pockets for warmth.

"Erm, I go that way on the train and you go that way to

get your scooter."

"Daisy yeah, I know. But seriously. I mean, what do we do now? I've spent the last few weeks hoping for this moment and now it's here I don't have a plan for part two."

"Look Wilson, what's happened to us is off-the-scale crazy. But it's happened nevertheless. I've got your mobile number and you've got mine. So we can meet in Starbucks every day if you want, forever. That's set in stone. We found each other in a dream and now we can share our strange secret together." Daisy flicked the tip of Wilson's cold wet nose.

"Remember that night we first met?"

Wilson smiled and nodded. How could he not remember.

Daisy continued.

"As for The Market Square, maybe it won't continue to happen, all the learning stuff; it could stop tomorrow. But I think we've been given a unique gift, a strange gift, and we should accept it for what it is and not think too much about what's happened, or why us, or try to rationalise it, cos then I think we'd both be sectioned. Let's go with the flow and see where it takes us.

"Whatever happens Wilson, I exist, you exist, and if The Market Square closes down, because they have to build a supermarket on it, then good; we found each other and we can lead our lives knowing we don't have to appear in some bizarre freak show at night. But for now, let's enjoy it. We may never get the chance again to do things nobody else can do – well, nobody I know. We may grow out of this whole, ability to interact with dreams thing, or a wormhole will close and we'll become the same as everyone else."

Daisy's train was pulling into the platform.

"Here's a thought," she said, not wanting the night with

Wilson to end, "let's try to reverse the dream and see if we can meet back in The Market Square again, later."

"Wow, that's a cool idea, I'm definitely up for that. My dream or yours?"

Daisy rolled her eyes. "I'll text you later." She turned to board the train.

"No, text me now. Text me now from the train. Just to double-check I've got the right number."

"Wilson, you've double-checked five times already. It's my number. Speak later."

Then Daisy was waving through a window, finding a seat, pretending to text, laughing and then waving again as the carriage moved away. Wilson stood watching it pick up speed. Daisy was leaving him. As the train curved round a bend and disappeared from view, Wilson once again felt vulnerable and alone, negativity was still marbling his belief. What if the entire night had been nothing more than a dream? His phone beeped with an incoming text: 'Drive carefully, Wilson. See you tonight, D.'

As a precaution, Wilson once again took the detour around the back of the hospital and arrived home at 9.40 p.m..

Alex and Gloria were finishing what appeared to have been a romantic dinner for two with wine and candles. Wilson entered the dining room, and not surprisingly, was in a buoyant mood.

"Well, this is all very cosy, you've not been discussing having more kids have you?"

Gloria giggled, her cheeks blooming a deeper shade of red at the very thought.

"But you're drinking wine Mum, so you can't be pregnant.

Hold on, I've got it; you're going to be a grandmother?"

Alex joined in the laughter and poured Wilson a glass of red.

"Have you been smoking something Wilson, you're unusually chipper this evening. Or did you find a tenner in your pocket?"

"No, I just wondered what was so important to bring the tablecloth out?"

"There's no special occasion and as far as I'm aware, your sisters aren't pregnant." Alex checked his watch. "However, it is Friday night and still early, so there's definitely time."

"Alex!" Gloria shrieked. "That's a terrible thing to say about your daughters."

She threw a napkin at him.

"I know, I know, what a terrible father," said Alex dropping his head in mock shame. His shoulders shook as he laughed in silence.

Gloria ignored him and turned to Wilson.

"Are you hungry love? I saved you some lasagne and garlic bread. It's in the oven, still hot."

"Yeah Mum, that'd be great. I'm really peckish."

Gloria cleared up two empty plates and left for the kitchen.

Alex sipped his wine.

"How was London?" Wilson asked.

"Errm, interesting, I guess. But those MPs and that committee are bloody clueless. How about you? How was your week?"

"Errm, interesting. But those teachers in that college are also bloody clueless."

They toasted each other with the clink of wine glasses. A liquid high five.

"Actually, it was a top week. I met a girl" said Wilson.

"I thought you had a girlfriend. Steff Green. Walter's daughter? The champion swimmer. Sorry, no, I get those two confused. I mean the sister, Natalie. The netball player. Or am I thinking of ... "

"What are you two gossiping about?" Gloria placed a dinner plate in front of Wilson.

"Wilson was just telling me about a new girl he's met."

"Oh, but what about Stephanie Green? I thought she was your ... "

"Mum, time out. You're as bad as Dad. Steff's family moved to Wales about six months ago."

"And Natalie?"

"Mummm, stop! Natalie was her younger sister and she had to move to Wales as well. Given that she was only fifteen!"

Wilson held a forkful of lasagne suspended in mid-air as he pictured Daisy waving goodbye from the train.

"No, this one's different Mum. But I don't want to say too much. Tonight was the first time I've really, err, spoken to her. Though on the other hand, it also feels like I've known her for ages. It's kind of weird. Anyway, we'll have to see where it goes. Let's just say I like her and we have a lot in common."

"Oh Wilson, that's so lovely. There's no need to rush into things. Let nature take its course."

Wilson continued with his meal and the glass of wine as his parents returned to their tête-à-tête on the latest news from the twins, the possibility of renting a flat in London and the revelations behind a cousin's divorce.

Soft-focus images of Daisy and Catapult Gliders and same-faced people descending on parachutes floated around his head. During a lull in the conversation and with a second glass of wine a motivating factor, Wilson asked his dad if he knew anything about numerology.

"I've been reading about it, the power of numbers and I discovered that you're a number eleven Dad. I mean your Life Path number is eleven, one of the master numbers."

"And if my memory serves me correctly Wilson, so is yours."

"What?" Gloria turned from husband to son. They'd lost her at the mention of the word numerology.

"Ah, it's nothing love," said Alex, placing his wine glass down. "Just more pseudo-science Wilson's picked up from college."

Alex abruptly stopped speaking, as though someone had whispered something troubling in his ear. Slowly and very deliberately, he began tracing his finger around the rim of his wine glass, enticing a high-pitched, wavering tone to float around the dining room.

"This could be the song of a siren, couldn't it? Hypnotic . . . enticing . . . impossible to resist . . . drawing you in. Yet at the same time, something dangerous . . . likely to end in disaster . . . luring the weak to be dashed against the rocks."

Alex looked up at his wife.

"This wine glass is singing to me Gloria. It's singing a warning, a beautiful, dark, enchanting message. It's saying, 'Alex . . . Alex . . . tell your missus to stop drinking so much red wine'."

Alex started laughing furiously, tickled not only by his tale of the unexpected but also by the response of an infuriated wife flicking a fully loaded tea towel. He had to excuse himself and went to the loo, chuckling away. Gloria went to make three mugs of coffee and when she returned, the conversation sobered up and Alex revived the earlier conversation.

"We suddenly seem to be having some interesting talks about unusual subjects Wilson. First Morphic Fields and now numerology?"

Alex paused.

"I can see how you arrived at Sheldrake's ideas from your biology class. Off-grid, for sure, but brightens up a dull day for a bored teacher. But how did you land on numerology? I mean, I can't see that being on any syllabus. Well, unless you've switched to an A level in the supernatural."

"What?" Gloria was lost again.

Wilson intervened. "It's okay Mum, nothing sinister, just that I . . . "

Fully aware that the wine was affecting his judgement, Wilson headed into uncharted territory. The sirens were calling after all.

"It's just that I had a dream the other night and it was mad, sort of eccentric and bizarre. It was on the night of my birthday. I told you. Probably caused by the Chinese food. But it was so vivid, as though being eighteen had something to do with it. Can't explain why. Anyway, the next day I searched on the internet to see if my eighteenth was a special or significant date. I don't know what I was thinking; just seemed there was a connection. And do you know what I found out?"

"What?" Asked Gloria, for the third and final time.

"Absolutely nothing. A few bits about famous battles and pop stars with the same birthday, nothing unusual. But then I did a search for my actual birth date. The day I was born. The search results threw out a load of amazing stuff about this 'power of numbers' theory called numerology. It said I was a Life Path number eleven and that this was a big deal.

So I checked the birth dates of the twins and you two, and guess what? Dad's a number eleven also, and he was born in the same hospital and in the same ward as me. Strange coincidence, don't you think, Mum?"

"Well love, I don't know what to think. Sounds like you've been at the Ouija board to me."

From the corner of his eye, Wilson sensed Alex was observing him and listening with profound interest, but he didn't return the attention.

"Don't worry about it," Gloria continued. "I'm sure it'll all come out in the wash. You can discover everything's connected on the internet one way or another. Anyway, I thought you were going to a birthday party at the rugby club tonight?"

"Nah Mum. It'll be a late one, with the inevitable Jaegerbomb drinking games and money for the taxi. Besides, I don't really fancy it. It's the big game tomorrow; Stockport Grammar at home. So gonna watch a bit of TV and have an early one. 'Night folks."

Wilson felt the glare from his father sear the back of his shirt as he left the dining room.

"I don't know what to make of Wilson sometimes," said Gloria, brushing garlic breadcrumbs from the tablecloth. "You know, I still think about that night he spoke French when he was little. He can . . . he . . . I really can't put my finger on it. He just seems different to other lads of his age, like being interested in this numberology nonsense."

"Oh it's nothing. I think he's just got an overactive imagination love."

"Yeah, I'm sure you're right. Funny that you already knew he was that number eleven though?"

Gloria was oblivious to the significance of her comment.

Chapter 28

Reversing the dream

Friday 27th into Saturday 28th October 2017

Wilson entered his bedroom and stood with his back pressed firmly against the door. What he'd just confessed to his parents probably wasn't that smart and his heart rate agreed. Under the influence of two glasses of wine, he'd linked The Gateway dream with numerology, brought his father into the equation and mentioned the existence of Daisy.

The latter point, the outing of Daisy, albeit fleetingly, had been a spur of the moment decision; completely unrehearsed, spontaneous and by definition therefore, a stupid mistake. A slip-up that normally would never have got through his internal censor; the sentry at the gate who'd monitored and tempered Wilson's behaviour since his junior school days.

Let's not draw any attention now Wilson, there's a good lad. Don't want to cause a scene with one of your episodes. Putting your head over the parapet. Upsetting everyone with those tricky talents of yours. Probably best not to mention Daisy either at this early stage in the relationship. It might not come to anything you know. She's not exactly the girl next door.

As Wilson's heartbeat returned to normal however, he realised he didn't actually care about the disclosures he'd made over dinner. For too long, any deviation from his behavioural norm had brought feelings of guilt. The mental equivalent of a self-administered slap across the legs for showing off.

Now, the straitjacket had been removed. Meeting Daisy was living proof he wasn't a castaway on his own crazy island and it brought the confidence and impetus to think he could finally get to the bottom of what was going on; and get off that bloody island. So if that meant ruffling his dad's feathers and kicking the apple bucket or whatever the phrase was, just because he'd spoken about numerology, then what the hell, he was going to do it.

Wilson opened his phone and scrolled to the new entry in contacts: 'Daisy Meadowcroft. 7 Cedars Lane, Macclesfield. SK10 13N.'

She said it was near The King's School.

A Street View search confirmed the house was there, exactly as described: the middle cottage in a row of five with a black door. Wilson entered the digits relating to Daisy's birth date into the calculator tool. Her eighteenth was only a few days away. He wasn't in the least bit surprised to find that her Life Path Number was an eleven.

If we do meet later, must remember to ask her where she was born.

He suspected he already knew the answer.

Brushing his teeth, Wilson wondered whether Daisy would be able to smell toothpaste on his breath. He couldn't begin to answer such an abstract question, but just to be safe, he sprayed a double helping of deodorant under both arms, checked his hair and climbed into bed.

It was only 10.25 p.m. Wilson switched on the TV and watched the local news. Then he tried to relax with a chapter of *The Count of Monte Cristo*. His phone beeped with a text from Daisy.

'Hope you made it home safe. Getting sleepy over here in

Macc'. See you in an hour or so. Fingers crossed. D. P.S. How will I recognise you?'

'I'll be waiting by the Clock Tower – with a box of chocolates.'

'Wilson, you're a KEEPER. See you there. 'Night.'

A minute later Daisy texted again.

'This is going to be so cool if we can do it!'

'Cooler than cool!'

Like an excited child on Christmas Eve, waiting for sleep to send the all-clear signal to Santa, Wilson couldn't seem to nod off either. He started thinking about the parallels between himself and Edmond, the main character in his book and the girl he travels the world to find. His mind wouldn't switch off. For two hours he tossed and turned. Then the 'what ifs' arrived. Questions came out of the darkness like film credits at the end of a movie.

What if The Market Square isn't there?

Or I can't find the real Daisy because everyone looks like her and it's a nightmare?

What if Daisy doesn't look like Daisy?

Or she doesn't recognise me? Or we see each other but we can't speak?

The more he tried to sleep, the more frustrated and wide awake Wilson became. He checked his phone. No more messages and it was 12.50 a.m.

She's been waiting for hours. Probably thinks I've stood her up. She could be searching for me and doesn't know I'm still wide awake in bed at home.

At last, as Mickey's gloved hands pointed to 1.25 a.m.,

Wilson's eyelids began to flutter and he finally arrived in The Market Square where a sporting event was in full swing.

The cobbled surface of The Market Square was overlaid with a layer of lush, green grass and reminiscent of a school playing field. A running track six lanes wide had been marked in white lime and covered the hundred metre distance from Sampson's Workshop top left corner, down to L'École, bottom right corner. Wilson was aware of athletes and spectators but didn't stop to take in the finer details. He could see the Clock Tower and sitting alone on a bench seat was Daisy. She'd been waiting from the moment Mickey pointed to 11.55 p.m.

Daisy waved as she saw Wilson make his way across The Market Square and ran to meet him halfway. They stopped a metre apart and Daisy pointed at something.

"Hey, you remembered."

Wilson felt the something in his hand and looked down. It was a box of Thornton's chocolates tied with a red ribbon. He looked up at Daisy, smiled and shrugged his shoulders.

"The thing is, I don't even know where the Thornton's toffee shop is. How crazy is that?"

They walked back to the bench seat where Daisy tore into the chocolates. She passed Wilson an Orange Cream and with a mouthful of Caramel Crunch declared that they tasted just like the real thing. Wilson was about to say, 'of course they taste like the real thing, why wouldn't they?' when he realised he was in a double dream, sharing chocolates and the only *real thing* was the fact he was fast asleep back in bed.

It was a glorious summer's day and honeybees murmured contentedly as they hoovered up nectar in patches of clover. Huge butterflies, species that Wilson knew with certainty would never be found in reference books, chased each other chaotically through the warm air. The Market Square was fielding an athletics meeting and the hub of activity appeared to be focused in the bottom-right corner, in front of L'École.

"It's a school sports day, but for big kids." Daisy confirmed.

In an area cordoned off with rope, directly in front of L'École, athletes in sports kit were stretching and warming up with short sprints, star jumps and bunny hops. Some were covering impressive distances jumping with both legs hidden in sacks. Others were twirling hula hoops around the waist.

Dispersed amongst the competitors Wilson also identified the other unmistakable sign of a sports day – the overly enthusiastic parents. Summer dresses and flat shoes for the mums and short-sleeved shirts and chinos for the dads. Some parents were holding hands with their children, doing their best to stop them running off.

These 'children', who appeared to be mature and accomplished athletes and certainly not school kids, were nevertheless, extremely excited.

Wilson and Daisy were looking on as a tall man with an impressive physique, wearing a tight-fitting, lycra running suit, sprinted powerfully away from L'École.

"Roger, come back this minute and do as you're told!"

The athlete, a doppelgänger for Usain Bolt, pulled up the moment he heard his name and jogged back.

"Sorry Mum."

As Roger came within striking distance, the petite lady in the flower patterned dress seized his arm and gave him two stinging slaps across the back of the legs.

"Stop running away." Her arm was fully raised but the accusing finger still stopped ten inches short of his nose.

Roger stamped his foot on the grass three times, folded his arms across his chest and looked as though he was about to cry.

"Oh it's definitely a sports day" said Daisy, giggling at the spectacle.

"Certainly is and I'm sorry I arrived so late. Took me absolutely ages to get to sleep. I was still awake at one."

"Really? I was only waiting for a few minutes."

Wilson paused for a moment, searching for an explanation.

"No idea how that works! But at least we reversed dream travel. We're clearing hurdles by the minute."

"And breaking all records" said Daisy.

They both laughed, at ease in their familiar, surreal world and developing friendship.

"Seriously though Daisy. Do you ever wonder what this place is, what it all means? Where we are exactly?"

"Funnily enough, I was thinking that exact same thing earlier, when I was lying in bed. I remembered what my grandma once told me."

Daisy hesitated for a second.

"Quite a few years back, Grandma was ill in hospital. We went to visit and a doctor asked Mum if they could speak in private. So when I was alone with Grandma, she beckoned me closer and started whispering. I think she was on medication because everything came in a bit of a jumble but she told me she knew I'd been to The Market Square and that she'd been as well. Which came as a bit of a shock, to say the least! She described The Market Square as a place through which dreams travel and said that people like us could absorb all the experiences and memories held in those dreams. Something called crashing was okay but straddling was more serious. It's helped me a lot to know that my grandma's been here."

Wilson sifted through the words like a prospector panning for gold. The references to crashing and straddling were valuable nuggets.

"Hey, do you want to see something really cool, it's like a trick I discovered?" Daisy had a mischievous look on her face. Wilson needn't answer, she was going to show him anyway.

"Listen, you arrived here with this sports day thing going on, but I don't think I created this dream just because I was here first. I think it was arranged in advance, for both of us. I don't think we control what happens here. It's preplanned somehow. Maybe all the people here are also in their own dream and The Market Square facilitates it. Do you get what I mean?"

"I think so. You're saying we don't control, through our dreams, or at the start of a dream, what The Market Square will be like when we arrive here?"

Wilson had certainly *got it* in terms of telling Daisy exactly what she'd just told him.

"Yeah, but here's the trick; I know how to influence what happens once we're here. So, to carry on with the sports day theme, my hockey teacher at college is called Gwen Burton, she's nearly six foot tall and has ginger hair always tied up in a bun. Can you see anyone here who looks like that?"

Wilson cast his eye over the sports field.

Roger the sprinter and five equally focused athletes had taken starting positions on the running track and were holding eggs balanced on spoons. Parents lined the length of the track baying encouragement.

Wilson couldn't see anyone that fitted the description of Gwen Burton, though he did notice someone remarkably like

Mo Farah warming-up for the wheelbarrow race.

"Nope, can't see your hockey teacher anywhere."

"Okay, well watch this."

Daisy scrunched her eyes shut tight, seemingly searching inside her head for something, then after twenty-seconds, they burst open. The flickering eyelids were just for showmanship.

"*Now* look. She's wearing a navy-blue tracksuit with the name 'Burton' in white letters on the back."

Wilson cast his eye over the sport's field for a second time. Roger had dropped his egg and his mum was delivering another slap. His gaze stretched the length of the running track and up at the far end, directly in front of a table laden with trophies and rosettes, he noticed the word 'Burton'. It was written in white letters on the back of a tracksuit worn by a tall lady with red hair tied in a bun, and she was carrying a hockey stick.

"There," pointed Wilson, "she's up there. Standing by the finishing line with her back to us."

"Yep, that's her. Always looks exactly the same."

Wilson turned to Daisy, amazed. "How did you do that?"

"I pulled her in. I closed my eyes, imagined how she looks, how I see her at college, concentrated really hard and then pulled her into my dream, this dream. I actually think that's what crashing is all about. Or straddling? Cool trick, huh?"

"Bit more than a cool trick."

Wilson studied Gwen Burton, who was now in conversation with a parent, then looked back at Daisy.

"Phenomenal!"

"Give it a go," said Daisy. "Pull someone in. Just close your eyes and imagine a person you know really well, one of your best friends, someone who stands out; imagine how they usually dress, how they normally look, how you remember them. Focus for a minute and see if you can bring them here. Try it."

Wilson, while not fully certain of what he was being instructed to do, gave it a go nevertheless. He thought of Hoover. Tall, awkward, hair drooping over his eyes, black hoodie, black skinny jeans. Wilson concentrated on the picture in his mind for a minute, then opened his eyes. Hoover was easy to spot.

"Is that him? That guy in the black hoodie, acting a bit like Basil Fawlty, he definitely stands out."

Wilson was highly amused by Daisy's observation, but she was right, Hoover was there, mimicking a stumbling athlete in a three-legged race.

"Daisy, that is so cool – let me try it again."

And before Daisy had chance to consider the ramifications of pulling three people into the same dream, Wilson had an image of Teapot in his head. Pony tail, medium height, good-looking, white t-shirt, denim jeans, white trainers. He concentrated, then opened his eyes. Teaps was standing directly in front of them, five metres away, picking a beanbag up from the ground.

"So who's this new visitor?"

"Another best mate. We call him Teaps."

"Ah, so that's Teapot, the friend you told me about in Starbucks. You're right, he is good-looking."

"Mmmphhh" scowled Wilson, playfully pinching Daisy's leg as he rose to his feet.

"Where're you going?" Daisy grabbed his arm.

"I just want to say hello."

Wilson slipped out of Daisy's grasp and walked over to

Teaps.

"Hey Teaps, welcome to The Market Square. How's it going?"

"Wilson, I'm not sure this is such a good idea. I never speak to the people I pull in."

Teaps replied as though they'd just bumped into each other in the supermarket.

"Hey Wilson, what are you doing here?"

"Teaps. Mate. Welcome to my dream." Wilson stepped forward to pat him on the shoulder.

Daisy cried out "No Wilson, I don't think you should touch him." And then stopped, open-mouthed, as the physical effect of something like the shock from an electric current jarred Wilson's arm.

All activity in The Market Square instantly came to a standstill as though a pause button had been pressed. A female athlete, in full stride, with both feet inches above the ground, was suspended in mid air – freeze framed in action. The vibrant hues of the sports day, the emerald green grass, the vivid lycra outfits were now masked by a yellow film. It was as though Daisy and Wilson were suddenly viewing The Market Square through the coloured cellophane of a toffee wrapper. Roundels of red, purple and green then flared across the yellow film like droplets of coloured oil landing on water. The translucent roundels started to float free, to grow in size, to become more distinct and three dimensional like giant baubles from a Christmas tree. And clearly visible on the convex surface of each orb, were moving pictures resembling home videos playing on TV.

A red bauble was running a clip of Teaps playing tag in a school playground. He was six year's old and being chased

186

by two girls. Then a teacher was blowing a whistle and Teaps was at the end of a line marching back to class with his arms swinging like a soldier on parade. The blue, pink, yellow baubles advancing close behind were revealing more scenes from the same time; Teaps climbing a rope ladder in the school gym; in class, copying the five times table into an exercise book. Wilson stayed with this bauble until it was level with his shoulder, where it popped without sound, like a soap bubble.

Fresh baubles were hatching from the surface of the yellow film, floating free, coming thick and fast, and all portrayed different moments in the picture diary of a life. Teapot through ages. Teaps with long hair. Teaps with short hair. Teaps swimming, running, singing in church, as a toddler learning to walk, a little older and playing Scalextric with his dad, and there, right there, as a baby, in the arms of his . . . mum!

Daisy had seen enough. "No. No, you have to stop." She tugged at Wilson's arm and pulled his hand free from Teapot's shoulder.

The baubles scattered and dissolved as if 'play' had been pressed and the sports day came back to life with full colour and motion.

Wilson seemed confused and in a daze as Daisy led him back to the bench like a patient coming round from anaesthetic, He wasn't in any pain, but his head felt strange, like pins and needles were rippling over the surface of his brain.

"Wilson, I've never touched or spoken to anyone I pulled in. What happened just then?"

"We saw his past Daisy. All the scenes from Teaps's life. Did you see them?"

"Yeah, I saw it all. But I don't think you should have

touched him."

"I saw Vanessa, his mum, carrying Teaps when he was just a baby. It was . . . she was so real. How did that happen, just from touching him?"

"I can't tell you, I've no idea. But it's a dream Wilson, just a dream."

Daisy started to yawn. A long, deep yawn.

"I think I'm leaving Wilson; feeling tired. I'm going back to bed. Text me tomorrow when you're up. Don't forget."

Daisy started to fade from view, the tint of her presence ever diminishing and when the sepia hologram dissolved into shadow, she was no longer there.

Wilson stood up, stretched out his arm and rotated his shoulder and wrist. There didn't seem to be any physical damage. No red marks on his hand. He turned full circle, but Teapot and Hoover and Gwen Burton were nowhere to be seen.

Wilson sat back on the bench seat and for some reason the words of Mrs Hope, his art teacher at junior school, came into his head.

"Before class next week, please conduct some home study on the style of the Post Impressionists."

His memory of a painting lesson in L'École was still as vivid as coloured oils on a palette. Had he pulled Van Gogh into that dream in the same way he'd made Hoover and Teaps appear? Winston Churchill too? Was that how knowledge was acquired in The Market Square? Was that crashing, or straddling?

Mickey's finger was pointing to 5.30 a.m. when a sudden, debilitating feeling of exhaustion poured through his very being, diluted his presence and washed him from the dream.

Two familiar faces had been amongst the spectators at the sports day and were thoroughly enjoying the comedic performances, that is, until Wilson Armitage discovered the 'pulling people in trick' and took it to a whole new level altogether.

Soon after Daisy and Wilson had departed, a brief conversation ensued.

"I think the portents have commenced" said Big Mac.

"Indeed they have" said Short Cake.

"Shall we?"

"We shall!" Short Cake confirmed.

Then the Custodians of The Gateway strode across The Hall of Extinguished Spirits to the door marked 'Exit to Eternity' and hurried through to consult with The Powers That Be.

Chapter 29

The big match

Saturday October 28th 2017

First thing next morning, Wilson sent Daisy a text.

'Need to talk about last night – don't understand what happened. I can come to Macclesfield later. How about pizza or KFC – you choose – 7.30 p.m.?'

He was in the kitchen eating toast when Gloria entered.

"Morning Wilson. Did you sleep well?"

"Morning Mum. Yeah, I'm good. I made fresh coffee and it should still be warm."

Gloria poured herself a mug and came back to the table.

"So what's your plan for the day? Your dad was up at the crack of dawn to go fishing. Said he was off to bag a salmon."

"Yeah, heard that one before, yet to see the evidence. I'm gonna have a lazy morning, tidy my room, football this afternoon and then I was thinking of going to see Daisy. You know, the girl I told you about last night."

"The girl you met yesterday from Macclesfield. Yes, I remember; I do listen to you occasionally."

"I invited her for a pizza or a KFC."

"Wilson, you didn't suggest fried chicken! It's not exactly the way to sweep a girl off her feet. Pizza sounds much better. There's a really nice restaurant on the road that runs past the train station in Macclesfield. Think it's called Fabio's. It's one of those proper Italian places, with all the recipes handed down through the family and a real oven where you can watch pizzas being baked. We went there last year for the shop's Christmas party. I ordered the . . . "

"Mum. I got it. Fabio's. Near the train station. Daisy's not even said if she can make it yet so it's just an idea for now."

"Have you got money?"

"Mum! There's no guarantee I'm going. And yes, I've got money. A meatpie transfer arrived yesterday, so I should be able to do some sweeping off the feet. I bet she prefers KFC though."

"Well, if your night's a success, why don't you invite her round for lunch tomorrow? I'd love to meet Daisy. It's the first time in ages you've spoken more than a few syllables about a girl."

"Yeah, she's different Mum, definitely different. Let's see how tonight goes though."

Wilson downed the last of his coffee and went upstairs to tidy his room. He'd just deposited a bag full of crisp packets, empty drinks cans and scooter magazines in the bin at the side of the house when Daisy texted back.

'Hey W. Yep, made it back to bed. Bit tired now though. Just finished playing hockey. Mum wants to go to the Trafford Centre. But yes – pizza tonight. Where? Fabio's? Fab place. KFC – no chance. 7.30 p.m. Fabio's. Opposite the train station.'

The message was signed off with a thumbs up emoji.

'Okay – see you there.'

Two thumbs up.

"Was that Daisy?" Gloria had been watching Wilson from the kitchen window.

"Mum, it's like living with Miss Marple. Yes, that was Daisy and yeah, you're right, absolutely no fried chicken. She recommends Fabio's."

"Ha ha – female intuition you see. I'm liking that girl more by the minute. In fact, do invite her round for lunch tomorrow. I think we'll have a lot in common. Could even teach her some of my surveillance skills to keep an eye on you."

"Alright Mum, let's see how it goes tonight."

Wilson put his phone in his pocket and went back to his room. There was an item on the agenda before the Stockport Grammar match.

He needed to go back to the early days of the internet and look for something that happened in 1999. He wasn't sure if Google even existed then.

'Vanessa Clarke. Missing person. Search'.

He needn't have worried, the story of Teapot's mum was online for all to see, archived on a number of national newspaper websites.

The Times and *Daily Telegraph* reported the story objectively.

'North West woman disappears after a meeting in Mayfair' read the headline from *The Times*.

'Mystery prevails after businesswoman disappears in London' from the *Daily Telegraph.*

Wilson read both articles and the story was just as Teaps had outlined:

Vanessa Clarke travels to London on an early morning train from Stockport. She has a meeting room booked at The May Fair Hotel and spends the morning in the hotel preparing. At 11.30 a.m. the prospective clients arrive. She wins a big recruitment contract reportedly worth over £140,000 a year and celebrates with champagne and sandwiches. At 2.30 p.m. she leaves to catch the return train – and is never seen again.

The Times carried a grainy picture of Vanessa and Michael with Teaps as a baby and a picture of Vanessa as a carefree student with short blonde hair.

He then read other articles from the tabloid newspapers, all of which featured the same poor-quality images and said pretty much the same thing, but with more sensational headlines.

From the *Daily Mirror*: 'Stockport **businesswoman accused of IBM bribery scam'**.

From *The Sun*: '**Blonde bombshell bribes client for £140,000 pay day'**.

One of the articles printed in the *Daily Mail*, referred to 'a police line of enquiry that had not ruled out a change of identity and a false passport'. Another, from the *News of the World,* referred to '£2,000 taken from a cashpoint in Dover by someone fitting Vanessa Clarke's description'.

The Dover cashpoint and the false passport angle was of significance to the police who, according to the *Daily Mirror,* 'were working closely with the Gendarmerie in northern France'. After a week or so of declining media coverage though, the investigation appears to reach a cul-de-sac and the story withers on the vine.

It's all exactly as Teaps explained it. It really is a complete mystery.

Wilson recalled the night of The Gateway dream.

Big Mac had said there was no bangle for Vanessa Clarke in The Hall of Extinguished Spirits and that nobody by that name had gone through the door to the spirit world.

Wilson continued adding links to his chain of thought.

So if Big Mac was telling the truth and there's no bangle for Vanessa Clarke, then it's possible she could still be alive? And Teaps still has a mum somewhere? I brought Teaps to The Market Square and witnessed episodes from his past life, so maybe I could also bring Teaps's mum to The Market Square and do the same thing. If she is still alive and I can see episodes from her past life, then maybe I can discover what happened to her!

Wilson had to acknowledge there was a weird, flaky logic to the chain and it did seem linked with a degree of sound reasoning, given the revelations of the night before. He closed the laptop and grabbed his kit bag.

It was a bright, mild, autumn afternoon and perfect for football as Wilson arrived at college for the local derby with Stockport Grammar. He caught up with Teaps and Hoover and other team-mates as they walked across the car park towards the changing room.

"Alright Wilson, you up for it?" Tom Kelly played in the left back position. Wilson fell into step.

"Yeah, I'm good. A bit knackered. Couldn't get to sleep last night, and when I did, had this mad dream about a school sports day."

"Oh yeah, did you win anything?" Hoover asked.

"No, it was really odd. There was an egg and spoon race and a wheelbarrow race, like from infant school, except it wasn't kids in the races – it was all these top athletes."

Hoover laughed at the picture forming in his head.

"And the winners were standing on a podium and being given paper rosettes and this sprinter, called Roger, who looked like Usain Bolt started crying cos his mum told him off for running away."

"Wilson, you're losing it mate," said Teaps.

"Mmm, you're probably right. Funnily enough Teaps, you were also in the dream, with Hoover. Don't you remember it? You were picking up beanbags."

Now they were all laughing at the idea.

"And what was Hoover doing?"

"Oh, I don't remember now. He was just there somewhere, out on the periphery, not doing anything in particular."

"Sounds exactly like Hoover."

Hoover aimed a kick at Tom, who kicked back.

"No Kelly, it sounds like your game plan for this afternoon; out on the periphery, not doing anything in particular."

Then Tom started chasing Hoover round the car park, trying to get another kick in, while Hoover pretended to be carrying an egg on an imaginary spoon.

Wilson seized his chance.

"Yep, that was a real crazy dream because it's kind of like . . . weird, when you see someone, like a best mate, in your dream and you talk to them. You know what I mean?"

Wilson studied Teaps to see if his friend recognised the underlying question, which was; *do you remember anything about being with me in a dream last night – the sports day, my hand on your shoulder, strange visions etcetera?*

Wilson's subterfuge wasn't necessary.

"No, I didn't dream about anything last night. In fact, don't think I ever dream of anything. Well, other than of torturing Blamire – now that would be my kind of dream."

Wilson was relieved. It made things a lot less complicated.

"Think we have a chance this afternoon?"

Wilson was more than happy to change the subject.

"Yeah, we beat them last year, three-nil I think, and it's gonna be another clean sheet today. Come on mate, changing room's open. Let's get ready and warmed up. We need to be focused."

Five minutes into the match, Wilson noticed something odd. Standing amongst the usual bunch of hardy perennial parents who supported the Second XI rain or shine, was a face he'd never seen on the touchline before, the face of his father!

What's he doing here? Mum said he'd gone fishing!

But there was Alex Armitage, watching the game from the sidelines, with his hands tucked in the pockets of his fishing jacket. When play was safely at the other end of the pitch, Wilson glanced over.

It's definitely him. Still got his wading jacket on. And wellies!

Moments later:

Now he's talking to Toby Renshaw's dad!

Then, after a fairly decent save that brought applause from the home fans:

He's just given me a thumbs-up.

Wilson didn't know what to make of it. He could count on the fingers of his muddy glove the number of times his dad had watched a match.

Something's up, was the only conclusion he could draw.

Wilson failed to save a penalty with ten minutes to go but when the final whistle blew, Stockport College 2nd XI deserved their two-one win against the local rivals.

There had been five soccer matches that afternoon and although the area around the entrance to the changing rooms was congested with parents and players, Wilson couldn't avoid noticing his father beckoning him over for a word.

"Hey, Wilson, what a match. That was bloody great. Shame about the penalty."

"Yeah, he sent me the wrong way. But we won, that's the main thing."

"I really enjoyed it. Might apply for a season ticket."

The bonhomie seemed false to Wilson.

"Well there's no waiting list Dad. Anyway, thought you'd gone fishing. Off to catch a salmon."

"Yeah I've been, but the river was too low so I decided to call it a day and come and watch the match." Alex paused for a moment. "Plus, I wanted to have a word. It's something I don't want your mum to be involved in. Meet you in the canteen when you're changed? It'll only take five minutes. What do you want, coffee or tea?"

"Err, tea Dad, two sugars. See you in there. What do you want to talk about, the one that got away? Cos that'll take more than five minutes."

"No, it's nothing to do with fishing son." Alex's mind was elsewhere.

Wilson was towelling his hair dry when Hoover, being Hoover, shared his thoughts with half of the changing room.

"Wilson, was that your dad watching us before? I've never seen him here, ever."

"Yeah, he was supposed to be fishing. But now he wants a quiet chat in the canteen about something he doesn't want Mum to know about."

"Bet he wants a divorce." Hoover was rummaging in his bag for deodorant, oblivious to the hand grenade he'd just lobbed on the floor.

Teaps was so startled he half thought he'd fully missed a joke.

"Bloody hell Hoover, that's a bit random, where did that come from?"

Hoover then tried to put the pin back in.

"Well, you know Wilson, your dad's away a lot. Just sayin', that's all. That'll be why he wants to speak to you away from your mum. It happens. My uncle John was always up to . . . "

"Hoover, it's alright mate. I get your point. I'll find out in a minute won't I, when I speak to him?"

Wilson took his time gathering his belongings, his mind elsewhere, because clearly he'd grabbed the wrong end of the stick. The very idea that his dad wanted to talk about divorce hadn't entered his head until Hoover had suggested it. Wilson had been anticipating an uncomfortable chat about the birds and the bees, probably at the behest of his mum. He'd told her about Daisy and how she was special, so his mum now wanted Alex to emphasise the need to wear a condom and all that nonsense. Thinking about it, Hoover's theory was far more likely.

The noisy canteen was full of ruddy cheeked lads drinking hot soup and eating pies and clusters of parents swapping gossip over tea and coffee. Wilson quickly spotted his father sitting alone at a table for two. He dropped his kit bag and crash helmet on an empty chair and sat down opposite.

"Cheers," he said, sipping the sweet tea, "just the job. Needed that sugar rush."

Wilson studied his father's face. The skin had that pasty, bloodless look of plucked chicken and his eyes carried the hangdog droop of a guilty man.

"So what's on your mind Dad?"

Alex placed his drink on the table and glanced over his shoulder. Wilson sensed his father was nervous and wary of being overheard.

"I might be about to make a terrible mistake here son, so forgive my reluctance to get to the point. I'm trying to convince myself I need to do this before I do it."

Alex paused.

Wilson waited for the inevitable. His stomach was churning and his mouth and lips were dry, despite the tea.

"I'm going to ask you something in a minute son, just a small question. If it means nothing to you, absolutely nothing, then I want this conversation to end right here, never to be discussed. Forget it ever happened. Okay?"

"Okay Dad, I can . . . "

"Just bear with me. But if what I'm about to say does mean something, then tell me with a simple yes or no. No need to think about it. The question is easy and you'll know if the answer is a yes or a no."

Things were moving too quickly for Wilson to work out how to respond. It was obvious the question related to where Wilson would live; yes to live with Dad, or no, because he preferred to stay with his mum. But what about his sisters?

"Dunno Dad. I'd have to think about it. It's not as clear-cut as a yes or no. You can't just spring this on me right now, here at college, away from Mum and Kate and Megan. We have to discuss this together, as a family. Does the other woman you've met live in London?"

Alex's jaw dropped.

"What are you blabbering on about Wilson? What other

woman in London?"

"The one you're divorcing Mum for."

Alex's face was a picture. Like the picture of a respectable, middle-aged man being confronted with the details of his secret life as a male stripper. Then he roared with laughter, so loudly in fact, that virtually every other conversation in the canteen abruptly stopped and all the students and parents turned to look. Alex waved sheepishly at everyone and then turned back to Wilson and whispered; "We're not getting divorced Wilson, you silly bugger. Why would you think that? I mean, who told you that?"

"You did Dad. The secrecy of this little chat here in the canteen, away from Mum; that you're about to make a terrible mistake; that I have to choose yes to live with you or no to live with Mum."

Alex kind of laughed. But it wasn't a real laugh, because this laugh also involved him covering his face with both hands before massaging his temples and breathing deeply down his nose. He brought his face close to Wilson's.

"No son, this is not a conversation about a divorce. It's something even more momentous. The answer is a simple yes or a simple no, and the question is: do you visit The Market Square?"

"Yes," said Wilson, without having to think.

Alex Armitage sat back in his chair, put his hands behind his head and looked up to the canteen ceiling. Wilson looked down to the canteen floor and gripped the sides of his chair to steady the tremor in his hands.

Though it was only a few seconds, it seemed an eternity had passed before Alex turned his attention back to Wilson.

"Thanks son. Thanks."

Wilson felt embarrassed by the confession, as though he'd owned up to a shocking crime.

"How did you know that, that I've been there Dad?"

Wilson then saw the flip side of the accusation, a chink in the prosecution's case and the weight of guilt lifted somewhat.

"More to the point Dad, how do *you* know about The Market Square?"

"It's part of a dream world. A place you only visit at night. Somewhere I suspect you've been exploring for a quite a while — I've had my suspicions over the years. I think you're old enough for us to have this conversation now, but away from your mum, she knows nothing about this. Don't worry, we're talking about the same thing."

"But Dad, this is incredible? Do you know how it works, do you ever go there, do you . . . ?"

"Shhh, keep your voice down." Alex checked over his shoulder again. "Wilson, we're not discussing a trip to Legoland. We're talking about a place that if people knew existed, what happens there, it would send most of them crazy."

"Jesus Dad, you knew all along. But why tell me now? Why didn't you say something when I was younger?"

"Yes, I could have done that, but I couldn't see any problems with your behaviour, or in your life. I suspected you visited The Market Square, I kept all the mental notes, but there didn't seem to be a need to let the cat out of the bag before now."

"Dad, it's more than letting a cat out of a bag don't you think?"

"What I'm trying to say is that . . . "

Alex paused for a moment.

"I discovered The Market Square when I was about fifteen. Those night classes were the reason I was able to get into Cambridge University in the first place. And in my final year I met a few other people who'd also been there. Like this Indian guy, Pavrel. We went to an air show for vintage aircraft one afternoon and there was a plane that wouldn't start. These anorak types had the engine in pieces and Pavrel went over and told them how to fix it. They thought he was some kind of prodigy. It was only when he said he was at Cambridge University studying aero-engineering they decided he was just some brainy student. He was actually studying Ancient Greek, but spent his nights flying old bi-planes in The Market Square. Anyway, we were at a party later that night and after a few beers the truth came out."

Wilson knew his face carried a look of utter amazement but there was nothing he could do to change it.

"But like I said Dad, you could have told me this when you were certain I visited The Market Square."

"Possibly. But I stopped going after my years at Cambridge. I got the gist of what it was; a funnel for the energy from dreams."

Wilson couldn't believe his ears.

"Look Wilson, I accept that The Market Square exists, but what is its purpose, its potential, I've no idea. We don't fully understand the workings of the brain. We know the areas for speech and hearing and so on, but it could be that some unmapped areas are also involved in processing unknown, yet to be discovered, forms of energy. Conserved electrical energy from dreams for example. I prefer to measure temperature with instruments and apply science rather than just diving into a swimming pool and saying, 'Yeah, it's bloody hot'."

Wilson ran a hand through his hair, confused by what he was hearing.

"Wilson, you've got to stop going there. That's what I came to tell you. The Market Square is not just some benign, inexplicable phenomenon and until we understand more – its power, how the place can exist, its purpose, the potential, the dangers – you have to block it out of your life. Stop looking for explanations that will only drag you further in. Morphic Fields, numerology – stop probing into all that stuff."

"But I met a girl there Dad."

"In The Market Square? And?"

"And I'm meeting her for a pizza in about an hour, in Macclesfield."

"You did what? You met a girl in a dream, in The Market Square and now you're meeting for pizza!"

"Yeah. It's the girl I told you about last night. She's called Daisy and she lives in Macclesfield."

Alex wasn't sure he'd heard correctly.

"You met a real girl in a dream, in The Market Square and then you met in real life, yesterday?"

"Yeah Dad, yeah, exactly that."

"Christ," said Alex shaking his head, "I need to think that through."

"But what does it mean? How is it possible?"

"I've no idea Wilson. I know that many number elevens can access dream energy but I thought that was just a passive acquisition process, I don't think, didn't think, what you've just told me was possible."

"Well it is Dad, because it happened."

Alex stood up.

"I honestly don't understand what you've done. Let me

think and we'll speak again. Nothing in front of your mum though. Love you."

"You too Dad."

Alex stood up, pushed his chair beneath the table and walked out of the canteen, acknowledging familiar faces en-route to his car. Wilson ordered another tea and sat contemplating the totally unexpected conversation he'd just had with his dad.

In the space of twenty four hours perspectives in his life had changed completely and it was definitely fate, not free will, that was dealing his cards.

Chapter 30

The Eager Beavers

Saturday October 28th 2017

Wilson found Fabio's without difficulty. Macclesfield train station was well signposted and the restaurant frontage glowed like a homing beacon in the dark. The interior of Fabio's was candle-lit and cosy and Daisy was waiting at a table for two in a corner towards the back.

She was wearing a burgundy, wool dress in a sleeveless style that revealed her slender arms to perfection. The polo neck accentuated her heart shaped face and the plum-shade lipstick. Her hair was fixed in a bun with long, ornately carved hairpins jutting out at all angles. She looked stunning, with the indefinable aura of the naturally charismatic.

"Wow" said Wilson, by way of a compliment. He was over-awed and couldn't take his eyes from Daisy.

"I like what you've done with your hair. I mean, I like how it's held in that shape, with all those chopsticks."

There was a delayed reaction to Wilson's admission, a second at most, and then Daisy fell into hysterics. She couldn't release the laughter though, because a sip of red wine was blocking the exit; so she covered her mouth with a napkin, released a strained, whimpering noise through her nose and then flapped her free hand as though it were sign language for laughing one's head off.

Wilson slipped his parka back on, used a finger as a

directional arrow and with a questioning look on his face mouthed "Should I go out and come back in again?" This caused Daisy to jump from her chair, shove Wilson to one side and leg it to the ladies.

It took Daisy a few minutes to regain her composure and apply fresh lipstick and mascara. She was still giggling as she walked back to the table looking like an off duty princess.

"How's a poor girl supposed to cope with you Wilson?" Daisy was fanning her face with a napkin as she slipped back into her seat. That's when Wilson became conscious of the fact he was dressed in the same clothes he'd worn to football. He hadn't 'upped his game' by remembering to pack a clean shirt.

"Sorry Daisy, didn't think to put smarter stuff in my bag. You look like a celebrity and I . . . "

" . . . wouldn't want you any other way. You look perfectly normal, but with a few cute differences."

So Wilson relaxed, ordered drinks and placed his hand on Daisy's, with the full and final acceptance of there being blood in her thumb.

"What a day! In the space of twenty-four hours I meet you in Starbucks, go back to The Market Square, where I meet you again. I pull Teaps into the same dream, see his past life and his mum, whom I've never seen before. Then my dad tells me he's a fully fledged number eleven and the cherry on top, we beat Stockport Grammar two-one."

"No one can accuse you of boring table talk Wilson."

"I mean, I should be in shock after all that. But the cherry on top of the other cherry is my dad also telling me he knows about The Market Square! I've been looking over my shoulder to see what's coming next."

"What?" Daisy exclaimed. "Your dad knows about The Market Square?" She cast an anxious glance round the restaurant, lowered her voice and leant forward to get closer to Wilson.

"Your dad's been to The Market Square?" The words were delivered with no spaces between and in record time. Wilson was about to explain when a party of middle-aged women wearing t-shirts with the words 'Eager Beavers' emblazoned on the front, lurched noisily into Fabio's to celebrate a hen night. The increase in background noise meant Wilson no longer had to concern himself with being overheard.

"Yeah, he came to watch the match, which is strange in itself. But then in the canteen, after a bit of a misunderstanding, he told me he knew about The Market Square. He said he stopped visiting after a while and I should do the same."

"Goodness me, what a revelation! That must have come as quite a shock."

"Just a bit! I think something I said to him last night over a glass of wine may have been the catalyst."

"Or maybe, it could be some weird hereditary thing. I mean, you and your dad, me and my grandma. Just imagine if we all meet in The Market Square?"

Daisy snapped a breadstick for the dramatic sound effect.

"My brain hurts enough trying to figure out what's going on when you and I meet there Daisy. I can't begin to contemplate a family night out. For all these years I've been completely alone with my strange secret and now I find out there's a gang of us, including my bloody dad. And I'm sure numerology is involved, but no idea how. What's your birth date again?"

"Eighth of November nineteen-ninety-nine. I'm eighteen

207

in just over a week. A bit younger than you. I like roses and my favourite colour's blue."

Wilson took out his phone and talked Daisy through the calculation then waved the result as if it was damning evidence and he was resting his case.

"See, look, you're an eleven."

"Actually, I'm an eight. But after pizza, I, err . . . "

"Daisy, this is serious. Where were you born?"

"Stockport Infirmary."

"Which ward?"

"Not a clue. Maternity ward I guess?"

"Ward 3B I bet."

"Rings a bell, but not for me, for Grandma. My uncle Derek who works for the NHS is trying to get her transferred to 3B. She's in a hospice in Bournemouth so it's better if she's closer to us, and my uncle says Ward 3B has the best record for caring for very sick, old people."

Two pizzas and a salad arrived and they ate in silence for a few minutes, chewing things over.

"You know," said Daisy, "if Gran has sat by that Clock Tower and also lived to her age, well, I don't think The Market Square can be such a bad place. Can it? And what's the big thing about being an eleven? In fact, what is an eleven?"

Daisy helped herself to a slice of pepperoni from Wilson's pizza.

"To be honest, I've no idea, but I've read about other things that sound relevant; like they could all be connected somehow."

Wilson then outlined the concept of Morphic Fields and the WiFi of nature and his idea of the equivalent for dreams and how the conservation of energy could make this possible.

"But this is also related to time, because in just a few days, even hours, we can learn how to do complicated stuff, like speaking French or flying a helicopter."

"Or driving monster trucks."

"Monster trucks. Really?"

"Yeah, and I learnt how to play jazz flute."

Wilson wasn't at all surprised.

"But this number eleven, how and where does that fit in?"

Daisy was munching on a strip of carrot dipped in mayonnaise.

"I stumbled upon it in a strange dream on the night of my birthday. It was like a dream from a different dimension, in an enormous building called The Gateway. Anyway, the next day, because the experience had been so intense, I checked the significance of my date of birth and came across numerology, which has connections with energy fields and spirituality. Most important was the Life Path number, and depending on when you were born, it can be super-powerful. How was it described?"

Wilson searched for the words.

"That's it! People with the number eleven have the potential to be a source of inspiration and illumination for others – and numerology also has links to the paranormal."

"So you think, that because the number eleven is a big deal in the numerology world; which is somehow connected with energy and the paranormal; and because it seems this Life Path number eleven also connects you and me and your dad, that means . . . what exactly?"

"I don't know! I just feel they're all connected somehow. I think all these puzzle pieces will eventually make a full picture. I just need to discover how to pull it all together, to join the dots."

Half an hour later the waiter came over to ask about dessert or coffee.

"I'm full thanks," said Daisy, "but I'd love a caffè latte."

"Just an espresso for me" said Wilson.

Then he remembered his gift.

"Oh I forgot. I bought you a present Daisy."

"Oh great. I love presents" she said, scrunching up her nose and clapping her hands in the manner of an excited infant.

"What is it, what is it?"

Daisy's delight caught the attention of a tipsy Eager Beaver who prodded a friend.

"Awww Chanelle. Look how young and in love they are. Me and Pete were like that once."

With all eyes focused in his direction, Wilson made a fuss of searching for something in his jacket pocket.

"He's a bit young to be popping the question if you ask me" said Chanelle. "He only looks about twelve."

"Daisy, when I said a present, what I meant was . . . "

"Get on with it love, or she'll be running off with your best mate" boomed Chanelle, thereby calling the attention of diners on *all* the neighbouring tables.

Daisy was enjoying Wilson's blushes and apparent discomfort.

"Look, it's no big deal Daisy. Just my way of showing" — he dropped his voice to a whisper — "my appreciation for you being here, you know, in my life."

"Bloody hell, we're all falling asleep, get on with it lad."

Wilson coughed nervously, reached for Daisy's hand and held it palm open, facing upwards. The Eager Beavers were open mouthed, hanging on to every word.

"Daisy, I just wanted to ask, if you'd share with me . . . "

He glanced over at Chanelle.

" . . . this packet of wine gums. I've bought them specially for you?"

The words, "the black ones are my favourite," were lost in the sound of Daisy's laughter and the groans from the Eager Beavers.

"This means something Daisy. So don't laugh! This is important, a milestone. I know for you that bag contains only wine gums, but to me, they're like tiny, moulded pieces of jelly friendship."

"Oh Wilson, they're beautiful. But wait a minute, aren't these . . . ?"

"Yeah, they are" said Wilson, knowing exactly where Daisy was heading with the lines to the Britney Spears song.

"But I thought the old lady dropped them in the skip when they passed the best before date?"

"Well baby, I dived in there and got them for you."

"Awww Wilson, you shouldn't have."

Daisy then sang the chorus.

"Oops, I did it again . . . "

The Eager Beavers, being familiar with the chorus and in that sort of mood, all joined in and at the end, having enjoyed it so much, they served up a second helping whether Fabio liked it or not.

Five minutes later, decorum had descended and Wilson was sipping his espresso as Daisy checked the time.

"Mum'll be here soon and there's something I want to speak to you about. I know you said your dad stopped going to The Market Square and thinks you should do the same,

211

well I kind of agree with him. We were lucky enough to meet there and if I never go back, I'm more than happy. Maybe we *should* close a door and put all this craziness behind us – have a normal future and lead ordinary lives.

Wilson could tell Daisy's pitch wasn't off the cuff. A considered opinion was behind what she was saying.

"There was a time, a few years ago, when I did loads of stupid things in The Market Square. I'd think about people I didn't like at school, girls who were bullying me – and I'd imagine them tied to a bench and inflict all sorts of punishment on them to get my own back. That's how I discovered how to pull people in. Other nights, I'd be a total hell-raiser. I once jumped off the Clock Tower because I knew I wouldn't be injured. What I'm trying to say is that we've been given this amazing gift and it can't be just to do daft things like that. Shouldn't we use it to do something good? What happened with your friend the other night, when we saw the baubles with scenes from his life – we could do that with people traffickers or drug dealers, or dodgy politicians. See the secrets in their lives and use what we discover in The Market Square to expose crime and help their victims? I don't know what exactly."

Daisy held Wilson's hand and locked her thumb around his.

"I don't care about Morphic Fields and magic numbers and explanations for what we do. I honestly think it would be good to try and ignore The Market Square and hope it goes away. But before that, let's use it to do something good. One memorable thing."

Daisy checked her watch again.

"Mum'll be outside and I have to go. I've had a lovely night Wilson, really great and thanks for the present. Think about what I've said won't you. I don't want to go to The Market Square tonight, so don't wait up for me."

She gave Wilson a hug and a kiss on the cheek.

"Oh Daisy, I nearly forgot. Mum's invited you round for lunch tomorrow. She wants to meet you."

"Okay, yeah! I'd love to. Text me in the morning with the address and I'll see if I can get a lift over."

Daisy said goodnight to the waiter, shared a joke with the Eager Beavers and left the restaurant after waving Wilson goodbye.

Chapter 31

The Gateway II

Saturday October 28th 2017

It was after 11.00 p.m. when Wilson arrived home. Gloria was in bed and a bead of light around the door to the box-room-cum-office said his father was working late.

"'Night Dad" he called tentatively.

Wilson waited on the landing but there was no answer. His father wasn't in the mood to be disturbed.

Lying in bed, Wilson reflected on the previous twenty-four hours and the revelatory events that had dispersed years of self-doubt in every direction. During the course of one day, he'd gone from the brink of a neurotic disorder to discovering an incredible, like-minded partner, a father who shared his secret plus the seeds of an explanation for their unique abilities. For the first time, Wilson was looking forward to sleeping without any apprehension or concern for what new revelation the next morning would bring. From now on, The Market Square could be acknowledged completely, unquestioningly and accepted for the phenomenon it was because Wilson was no longer alone. As he began to drift off, something Daisy had said earlier played on his mind like the words on a scratched record.

"Try to do something good. Help people if we can."

Two hours later, Wilson was standing in a field of bright-red poppies. The dream was dressed in the mantle of a hot summer's day and the hazy outline of The Gateway shimmered on the horizon. After taking no more than five or six paces, Wilson stood facing the colossal and majestic colonnade. He paused for a moment, to contemplate the medieval battle scene carved in the pediment high above his head, then made his way up the broad stone steps and into the shadow of the portico. The two nondescript doors resembled the emergency exits rather than the main entrance. Wilson selected 'Visitors Only' and let himself in.

Nothing had changed in The Hall of Extinguished Spirits. The rolling hillsides of gleaming bangles still stretched away seemingly for centuries and once again, the cavernous interior took Wilson's breath away. The ridge beneath the 2017 banner had risen a metre or so; more bangles had been acquired since his last visit.

Two familiar voices carried through the hall.

"Well, well. If it isn't our good friend Mr Armitage dropping by to say hello. Or the other way round, because coincidentally, we were waiting for *you*."

"You've been summonsed. We need to have a chinwag about your mischief young man."

The custodians of The Gateway then revealed themselves to Wilson's left. They were standing by the hillock of bangles designated as 2015, and exactly as he remembered, from their polished black shoes to their shiny, bald heads. On this second meeting though, their facial features seemed more sternly set, the reception cooler, as though they were irritated.

Wilson was prepared for the verbal joisting.

"Funnily enough" he said, "I was hoping I'd meet you

two again. I wanted to say thanks for telling me about the conservation of energy theory. It came in very handy."

"Mmm! Energy can never be destroyed and all that," said Big Mac, waving a hand dismissively.

"Yeh. Thanks for the insight."

"Well, you've been a busy boy Wilson. A very, busy boy." Short Cake's words were delivered in the stark tone of a headmaster ticking off a pupil.

"You can say that again, what with meeting Daisy and then coming back to The Market Square to meet her again and then the numerology stuff and Dad's confession; all a bit of a whirlwind really."

"Oh, beautifully put Wilson. As though a butterfly had flapped its wings and created a storm and then snow, cold white snow had fallen on the Amazon."

Big Mac dropped the humorous lilt and took three steps towards Wilson.

"But that's not right, is it? The Amazon's a rainforest. The Amazon doesn't want snow. It's unsettling. It disrupts our forward planning. What do we call this unsettling Mr Cake?"

"We call it mischief, Mr Mac."

"Exactly! So much so, we had to visit The Powers That Be. Through the Exit to Eternity. Where we were firmly reprimanded for being negligent!"

"Well, I'm sorry if I . . . flapped my wings too hard. But to be honest, I don't have a clue what you're wittering on about."

Wilson saw the opportunity for a tactical move. He'd gained an insight the last time he was in The Gateway – about the conservation of energy, so perhaps he could do the same again.

"So what does crashing and straddling mean?"

"Goodness me Wilson, they certainly threw away the mould when they made you."

Big Mac turned to Short Cake who nodded approval to continue.

"Crashing is when you trespass in a particular type of energy field and straddling is when you trespass in two or more – with a foot in both camps, so to speak. We've seen your trace Wilson and you're one of the most accomplished trespassers we've ever seen. That's why you still have your permit to enter The Market Square.

"The Powers That Be find you very entertaining Mr Armitage. However, we brought you here to pass on a warning. When the roulette wheel stops spinning and all the bets have been placed, outcomes and repercussions always end in tears.

"You really should cash in your chips while you still can" added Short Cake.

Wilson wanted to glean as much as he could from the dynamic duo before the dream ended, but while their comments made him sound enigmatic, he was struggling to make sense of their verbal nonsense.

Maybe when I revisit this conversation in the morning, perhaps everything will be clearer.

"What exactly do you mean when you say you've seen my trace?"

Big Mac paused before replying, as though calculating how much of a secret he was prepared to divulge.

"Wilson, all the things you've done, all the places you've been, all the things that have happened in your life, they all leave a trace and we can see them."

"Like watching a home movie of the complete life and works of Wilson Armitage. Farts and all" added Short Cake

217

with a knowing wink.

"What? You mean you can see everything I've ever done. Every conversation. See where I've been, what I've been doing. Everything?"

Wilson was startled by the notion.

"Everything" said Big Mac. "You leave a trace for us to follow. Everybody does. You just need to know where and how to look."

"In which camp to put your foot" said Short Cake.

"I, err, don't understand" said Wilson, blushing at the thought that what he'd just heard could actually be true.

Short Cake nodded at Big Mac, as if to give consent to continue with the divulging.

"So let me explain" said Big Mac. "Take this instant right now, with you standing there, us standing here and nobody moving. Let's call that a single moment. And let's say we seize that moment."

From behind his back, Short Cake produced a Polaroid camera and smartly took a picture of Wilson. He passed the instantly processed print to Big Mac.

"That" said Big Mac, passing the photo to Wilson, "is *your* here and now, captured forever. A parcel of light photons, a bundle of energy, captured in time. So if we take a second photo . . . "

Short Cake passed over to Big Mac a new Polaroid snapshot.

"This second image has captured the next moment. The next bundle of energy. And this is the third, this is the fourth, this is the fifth and sixth, seventh, eighth, fiftieth, two hundred thousand millionth. And if we put them all in a line, we would have this."

Wilson was directed to the floor where hundreds and hundreds of Polaroid prints stood on edge, about a centimetre apart, snaking around the piles of bangles – like thin white dominoes about to fall forwards and knock each other over.

Wilson bent down to pick one up. It was the same as the first picture Short Cake had taken. He picked up another, then another. They were all the same, apart from miniscule differences. In one picture Wilson's mouth was very slightly open; in the next it was closing; after that it was closed.

"That" said Big Mac, gesturing to the meandering line, "is your trace. The first one always exists and the last one always exists, because each moment is made of energy and energy can never be destroyed, so it is always there. Any moment from the present always exists in the past."

Short Cake bent down to pick up a photo and threw it in the air.

"That one is out there."

Then he picked up another and threw that one in the air.

"And that one's out there. And that one. And that one."

And in seconds the air was filled with a blizzard of Polaroid pictures.

"An ever-growing album of your life is out there. There's a trace for everything and everyone. An energy field of your own personal history."

Big Mac snatched a Polaroid as it flew past his nose then the photos all fluttered to the floor and evaporated as the hall reverted to its solemn, silent self. Big Mac passed the Polaroid to Wilson without looking at it. It portrayed him standing between two jumper-goalposts on the playing field at junior school.

"All your past life is out there Wilson, every second of it, in tiny bundles of time energy that will never be lost"

"So when we saw you meet Miss Meadowcroft at Starbucks," said Short Cake, "and then watched you conjure Mr Teaps and the traces of his life, well, we were obliged to inform The Powers That Be."

"They don't usually like their butterflies flapping so well" explained Big Mac "creates too much of a storm. But for some reason they like you Wilson. They're excited to see where you're heading with this. So we brought you here to warn you, in the strongest possible terms, against further mischief, but also, paradoxically, to give you permission to continue."

"Game on" said Short Cake, rubbing his hands with glee.

Big Mac interlocked his fingers and cracked all his knuckles.

"I think that's all the issues resolved" he said, turning to go back to his desk.

"Indeed" said Short Cake. "Come, The Market Square is this way."

They beckoned Wilson to follow and he remembered just how physically persuasive they could be.

"Wait, wait just one second. Sorry."

Wilson wanted to glean more, to stay in the narrative of the dream for just a few seconds longer.

"So what is déjà vu? I mean, how does it work?"

"Well give that man a coconut!" exclaimed Short Cake. Big Mac nudged him in the ribs.

"That's a very good question Wilson. Very good. And easy to explain, because this . . . this is déjà vu."

For a second time, Wilson's 'life in photos' assembled itself on the floor in a long curling column, like the ribs of a paper snake.

"Look at your time trace Wilson," said Big Mac pointing to the Polaroid at the head of the snake. "This snapshot at the very front represents the instant reality of the here and the right now. But see what happens when a wind blows – and by wind, I don't mean a summer's breeze: I mean the wind caused by energy fields."

"Smoke, as your father describes it" added Short Cake.

"Here's what happens" said Big Mac.

Wilson watched, transfixed, as an imaginary breeze caught hold of a tight loop of Polaroids lined up a short distance behind the very first one, and in doing so brought photos from the past to a new position, ahead of the front. Like the leading coil of a sidewinder snake slithering forward and for a moment being fractionally in advance of itself.

"So the past is blown in front of the future" said Wilson, understanding the visual analogy. "We experience the feeling of déjà vu because the reality of the here and now is briefly overtaken by a moment from the past. So we sense something that has already happened. We experience the same moment twice."

"Indeed" said Short Cake, "but only for a fraction of a second when the wind is blowing in the right direction. That is déjà vu. Question answered. Time for you to go now."

With the same brevity and strength demonstrated on his first visit, Big Mac and Short Cake then transported Wilson, feet dangling, past two executive desks and two angle-poise lamps and out through the exit to The Market Square.

"Do heed our warnings Mr Armitage, our retribution can be swift and brutal."

Wilson sat gathering his thoughts on a bench seat by the

Clock Tower.

Neat explanation for déjà vu, but why the contradictory message?

Looking across the empty Market Square with fluttering photos still flying around his head, Wilson's thoughts turned to Teaps and the coloured bauble that portrayed a moment in time with his mother.

I wonder if I can do it without Daisy here to help?

Wilson closed his eyes and once again set to work building a clone of Teaps; with the same swept-back-hair and ponytail, the dark eyes beneath thick eyebrows, wearing jeans and trainers and rehearsing with the band in the garage. When Wilson's mental rendering was complete, he studied the body-double for flaws like an exhibit in Madame Tussauds, and opened his eyes.

Teaps was sitting on the bench seat opposite playing his guitar.

Wilson half expected an audience to be applauding or a brass band to march past in celebration.

Bloody hell. It really works and I can do it without Daisy.

He walked across to his friend and knelt on one knee.

"Hey mate, it's me, Wilson. How's it going?"

Teaps was strumming chords for the song 'Wonderwall'.

"It's good Wilson. It's all cool man."

Wilson sat on the bench seat to steady himself then reached forward and placed his hand on Teaps's shoulder. A jolt of energy once more surged along his arm as The Market Square paused on freeze-frame behind a yellow cellophane wrap. Coloured baubles began to appear, each one reflecting traces of Teaps's past life. Wilson focused on a bauble in the middle ground depicting a toddler playing football on the beach with his dad, and as it drew within touching distance, Wilson noticed that something peculiar happened. The images on the surrounding baubles and those coming up behind, all changed to portray a different scene, from the same holiday – as though they'd all switched to the same channel. There was Teaps building a sandcastle, flying a kite, Teaps wearing armbands and paddling in the sea. It seemed that by selecting one specific moment in Teaps's life, neighbouring baubles would then be instructed to tune-in to the same time frame. Not unlike a flicker book in some ways.

Wilson scanned each bauble as they glided by.

Teaps at school. *No, too recent.*

Camping two years ago. *The same.*

As a Cub Scout. *No.*

Teaps in the arms of his dad. *Yes.*

Wilson stayed with this latter bauble then turned to those on either side, drilling down into a very specific period of time.

Teaps in a highchair being fed by his dad.

Being bathed in the kitchen sink.

Crying in his cradle and his mum picking him up.

That's the one. Stay with that.

The baubles seemed to understand what was required and closed ranks on the most specific of memories.

Teaps being bottlefed by his mum.

Being christened with his mum and dad.

Teaps with his mum on a bed.

With his mum, laughing.

In each image, Vanessa was wearing her long blonde hair loose or fixed up with clips. Wearing lipstick or no lipstick. Always a pretty, smiling face. But the pictures were fuzzy and indistinct. Wilson was acquiring only a rough impression of

223

Vanessa. Would it be enough?

He lifted his hand from Teaps's shoulder who was oblivious to what had just happened and continued strumming the guitar. The Market Square emerged from behind its yellow mask. Wilson closed his eyes and tried to picture Vanessa, but it was difficult; he didn't have a strong image on which to focus and the most memorable, with Vanessa bottle feeding, wasn't sharp. Mentally retouching made no difference. After several unsuccessful attempts to bring Vanessa Clarke to The Market Square, Wilson was demoralised, his plan a failure, and Teaps's mum was nowhere to be seen. He sat for a while, listening to his best friend playing a medley of Oasis songs until he dissipated into a diminishing shadow and made his way back to bed.

Chapter 32

The wedding photo

Sunday 29th October 2017

"Are you hibernating in there Wilson?"

Wilson was dragged from the depths of sleep by his mother calling from the foot of the stairs.

"Why? What time is it?"

"It's half past ten. I know it's Sunday and you're allowed a lie-in, but I wanted to know if you spoke to Daisy about coming for lunch? If it's not too much trouble, can you tell me in the next half hour? We're having roast lamb."

Wilson reached for his phone on the bedside table: 10.37 a.m. He'd been out for the count and missed three texts and a call from Daisy.

He sat up, rubbed his eyes and opened the text messages.

'Morning. Am I still invited to meet your folks?' That was at 9.20 a.m.

'Wilson, sorry to trouble you, but an answer anytime soon would be good. My mum said she can give me a lift, but I need to confirm.' That was at 9.55 a.m.

'Wilson, you're not really creating a good impression here in the Meadowcroft household – text me – NOW.' That was 10.15 a.m.

"Jesus."

He threw back the duvet, texting at the same time.

"Mum, yeah, she's coming," he yelled down the stairs.

"What time's good?"

The simultaneous text read: 'Daisy sorry, yes, – come, 7 midland drive, stockport, sk7 6tf. Blue garage door. Text back.'

"About one o'clock if that's okay, I hope she's not a vegetarian."

"No Mum, she'll be fine. Roast lamb will be good."

Wilson hurriedly dressed, sent another text to confirm the time and popped his head round the kitchen door on his way out.

"Mum, gotta dash out for an hour. Daisy's mum's dropping her off about one-ish. I'll be back, but I need to see Teaps."

"What, right now?"

Gloria was peeling potatoes.

"Yeah, I've gotta see him about something – an English textbook I need. Won't be long."

"Well make sure you're not late love. I've told your dad to be back from fishing early. He says he's really keen to meet Daisy."

"Yeah, I'm sure they'll have loads in common. Mum I have to go."

"But you've had no breakfast Wilson."

"Mum, I'm good. Be back as soon as I can."

Wilson didn't have long to organise his plan. If you could actually call what was racing through his mind a plan. As the door to the garage rolled up, his phone bleeped.

'Don't know what's happening with you. Will be there for 1.00 p.m. Expecting more than a bag of wine gums – sports mixture might do it. Luv D.'

'Great' was all he had time for by way of reply. Five minutes later, the scooter was on full throttle as Wilson headed down the A6 towards Stockport town centre. He braked as the red-brick wall and the cast-iron railings of the hospital grounds came into view. Wilson pulled into a side street, jacked up the scooter and took off his helmet. He then walked back to the A6 and followed it for a further fifty metres until he reached the perimeter of the hospital.

The second Wilson arrived at the wall, his head started to ache. He continued walking, the pain steadily increasing, until he stood beneath the huge window that dominated the front of the original part of the building. A prolonged sensation of déjà vu swept over him, just as it had during that first trip to meet Daisy. The throbbing migraine intensified, his vision became distorted and blurred. Dizzy with pain, Wilson grabbed the railings for support and forced himself to continue peering up at the window. Like trying to focus on land from a pitching boat, his eyes were failing to lock on the shifting target. The glass carried a slate grey tint and seemed to swallow light rather than reflect it. The odious feeling of familiarity with something unpleasant, something he couldn't identify, made Wilson nauseous. Then two dark shapes, like back-lit shadows in a puppet show passed across the window. One figure was small and round, the other, tall and thin. Wilson managed a weak smile, his intuition confirmed.

I knew it. I knew that's where they lived.

Wilson's legs finally gave way and he slumped down with his back against the wall. The sickening ache in his head made him retch. A string of spittle stretched down from his mouth and coiled on his crash helmet. Wilson took a huge breath and forced himself to stand upright. He pushed away from the railings and staggered back up the pavement to his scooter. As the headache eased, he turned with a grin of satisfaction and a thumbs-up for the two characters still watching him from on high.

Wilson sat recovering on his scooter for a full twenty minutes. He wiped clean his mouth and helmet then turned the scooter away from the hospital and followed the back streets down to Mersey Square and the centre of Stockport. Teaps lived in a flat opposite a pub and he had a good idea of where it was.

After parking the scooter opposite The Sun and Unicorn, Wilson checked his phone. It was 11.20 a.m. He didn't have long and he wasn't certain he was in the right place. He dialled Teaps's number.

"Hey, it's me, Wilson."

"Yeh mate I know, my phone tells me. How are you pal? All okay?"

"Yeah, I think so. But listen. Sorry for calling you a bit random like, I've got a slight problem."

"Go on then," said Teaps, "hit me with it."

"I left my English Lit text book in my locker on Friday and I've gotta answer those three questions on the war poets for Monday morning or I'll get a major bollocking. Wanted to know if I could borrow yours?"

"Yeah, 'course you can. I've just finished with it. The one on Sassoon is tough, but yeah, the book's here. I'll text the questions to you if you want, or screen grab the page and WhatsApp it."

"Actually, I was gonna call round and collect it. I'm in Stockport anyway – just passing your flat in fact, I think."

"You're what?"

"Yeah, had to buy some, err, weedkiller for my dad, from the garden centre. So just on my way back; I'm near where you live, so I could grab the textbook, like now and then scarper. Only take two minutes."

"But Wilson, I, err . . . "

"I'm already here, outside the pub."

"Outside the Sun and Unicorn?"

"Yeah, I'm looking at it."

"Wilson, it's really not the ideal time."

Wilson sensed all was not right, but he had a plan to help his best mate and that sometimes required cruel love.

"Teaps, come on, help me out here. Just let me borrow the book. I can't work from WhatsApp; wouldn't be authentic."

Teaps went silent for a moment, then gave up on further protest.

"Okay Wilson. Shabby, dark green door, just opposite the pub. Looks like it's been kicked in a bit. Ring the bell and I'll let you in. But Wilson, Dad's not good right now so it'll have to be quick."

"Okay mate, fully understood. In and out, no worries. Be there in a mo'. In fact, I think I can see the green door."

Wilson crossed the road and pressed the cracked plastic buzzer. After ten seconds, he heard footsteps and an ill-fitting door scraped open.

"Cheers mate, I appreciate your help."

"No worries." Teaps looked stressed, his features pinched and drawn. "Dad's in there, I think" – he motioned to the pub – "topping up last night's bender and my shift starts in an hour. Don't really want you to meet him, so need to be quick. I'll show you what I've written."

Wilson followed him up the bare, wooden steps of a creaking stairway and into a dingy flat.

"Sorry mate, not much to look at, but it's okay for Dad and me."

The lounge-cum-kitchen had a tiny sink with a single tap,

a small oven with a two plate hob connected to a Calor Gas bottle and a rickety-looking table teamed with two odd chairs. There was no fridge and a carton of milk stood in water in the sink. The lounge area was furnished with two threadbare armchairs parked in front of a bulky old TV. Faded wallpaper was peeling from dark patches of damp and in a corner of the room, a fold-out bed was freshly made beside a small desk with a lamp shining on an open textbook.

"We call it the Blamire Hotel."

"Ah, it's not so bad. You've seen my room, it's not much better. And Megan's . . . well, wipe your feet as you leave."

"Does the job, I guess. We're waiting for a council flat. Told them what a health hazard this place is, but there's a waiting list. Much more urgent cases apparently."

Teaps walked over to his desk, switched off the lamp and collected the textbook for Wilson.

"Here you go. Like I said, the Sassoon question is tough, but the other two war poets, well, call me if you need extra ammunition."

Wilson was too pre-occupied to acknowledge the play on words, he needed to buy more time.

"Can I use the loo Teaps? Dying for a pee. Bit difficult to stop once I'm on the scooter."

"Sure. It's not the Savoy, but everything is in working order, just about. It's down there, past Dad's room, at the end."

He nodded towards a passageway that Wilson hadn't noticed.

"Two ticks, as they say."

"Would offer you a brew, but I think the milk's off."

"Nah, I'm good. A quick leak and I'm away."

Wilson took a few steps down the narrow corridor and

saw the door to the bathroom at the end. Which meant the flimsy door to his left, covered with wood-effect, sticky-backed plastic, led to the bedroom of Teaps's dad. It swung open at the slightest touch.

Wilson put his head around the door and peeked inside. The room was neat and tidy. The bed had been made and although the bedspread looked a little threadbare, it was clean with five brightly patterned cushions arranged on top. The wall covering still retained vibrant colours and the sheepskin rugs created a warm and homely feel. A framed print of Teaps as a baby in the arms of his mother stood on a dressing table surrounded by a collection of loose photographs

Wilson made straight for the photos. The images were the same as those he'd seen in The Market Square: Teaps being bottle-fed, Teaps in his highchair. But there was a different one, a new one, a close up of Teaps's mum and dad on their wedding day. The image was sharp and clear with Vanessa's smiling face captured in high definition. Wilson slipped the photo inside his shirt, taking care not to crease it, then shifted the pictures around to fill the empty space. He pulled the door to and walked back.

"I needed that. Wouldn't have made it home without an emergency stop. So, best be off. Mum's cooking Sunday lunch and I have to be back for . . . " Wilson checked the time. "Bloody hell, quarter past twelve! I'm late. Dad's waiting for his drill bits."

"Thought you said he needed weedkiller?"

"Yeah, that as well. Gotta go; he's waiting."

Wilson headed for the door.

"I'll give you the book back tomorrow."

Teaps followed.

"There's no panic. Like I said, call me if you get stuck. Shame you can't stay longer, I could have given you the full tour, including Dad's bedroom. He keeps it just like it was in the old house, for when Mum comes back."

As Teaps opened the door to the stairwell, Michael Clarke, Teaps's dad, lurched in, took two unsteady steps and stumbled to the floor. The stench of alcohol arrived a second later, followed by the stocky, doorway-filling figure of Warren Blamire, their notorious thug landlord. Eddie Spinner followed him into the flat.

"Hey, Wilson, qué pasa?" Spinner, as always, looked uncertain and sheepish.

"Shit" said Teaps.

The four upright bodies virtually filled the flat. Michael was curled in a ball at their feet, like a vagrant, in stained trousers and ripped shirt.

"Don't worry son," he slurred. "Everything will be okay. Just like the golden days." Teaps went to help his father to his feet but Blamire kept him pinned him down with his foot.

"See this excuse for a man Spinner? He's a waste of space. All because of the demon drink. Can't be trusted."

Teaps sprang up and went to shove Blamire away.

"Get your foot off him, you lowlife."

Blamire was expecting the move and grabbed Teaps by his hair, spun him round and clamped a hefty, tattooed forearm around his neck.

Although Wilson hadn't spent that many nights taking martial arts classes in L'École, he was fairly certain Blamire wouldn't be much of a problem, even in such a cramped space. But he was aware of the stolen property tucked inside his shirt and if that got damaged or fell out during a fight, how would he explain *that* to Teaps?

No, best not. That would only make things worse.

"Listen girlie" said Blamire, his ugly mouth inches from Teaps's ear, "me and Spinner, we're like the third emergency service. A Sunday service. Helping those who've lost their way. So I'm telling you, if I see that, that . . . He looked down on Michael with disgust and contempt. "If I see that numpty spending my rent money in The Unicorn again, it won't just be my size twelves making the point."

Then Blamire pushed Teaps away.

"Now, I don't know who this dopy piece of piss is" he said, pointing to Wilson, "but you're lucky he's here, cos I don't want no outside grief. If I don't have my five grand in the next couple of weeks, things will turn a bit sour for you and that muppet you call a dad. Two weeks, five grand. Come on Spinner."

Blamire clattered down the narrow stairwell making as much noise as he could to emphasise the threat. Spinner took off without looking back at Wilson or Teaps.

"Come on Dad, let's get you to bed."

"She's still alive you know" mumbled Michael, as Teaps helped him to his feet.

Wilson felt utterly helpless. His best friend was in a horrendous fix and all he could do was stand there and watch the misery unfold.

"Can't you get any money from social services to help? Disability allowance or something?"

"He's not disabled Wilson, he's an alcoholic and clinically depressed. He doesn't want to be helped. Look, you'd better go" he said, gesturing to the door. "I'll be fine. Just another day in paradise, eh."

"You sure?"

"Yeah, he'll sleep it off and I need to go to work."

Wilson turned to leave.

"Hey Wilson, what about that?"

Teaps was nodding at the textbook on the table.

"Oh the book. Forgot all about it. Cheers mate."

Wilson checked the time as he fired up the Vespa. It was 12.30 p.m. Half an hour to go. He checked the wedding photo was secure inside his shirt. The question of how to return it would be left for another day.

Chapter 33

The Sunday lunch

Sunday 29th October 2017

Wilson arrived home on the stroke of 1.00 p.m. and on opening the front door heard a familiar voice coming from the lounge. Daisy was already there, having an animated conversation with his mum! He retrieved the wedding photo from inside his shirt and placed it between the pages of Teaps's textbook then made his entrance.

Daisy was sitting on the sofa. She was wearing blue jeans and a white jumper and her hair was in the same style as the previous night. She looked amazing.

"Hey, Daisy, wow, you're already here, in the lounge, talking to Mum, and early, that's great. Sorry I'm late, had to go to B&Q for some weedkiller, err, no, sorry I meant this. I had to borrow it from Teaps."

Wilson held the book in the air as though it were a sacred text.

Daisy cocked her head to one side with an uncertain smile on her lips – as though unsure of how to respond to the antics of a naughty but amusing child.

"Yeah, I've met your mum, she's told me all about your bad habits, so I'm leaving now."

Daisy pretended to get up to go. Wilson's mum started laughing.

"Ooh Daisy, stop with that. He'll have an uncontrollable

tantrum and we'll have to call a doctor."

"Okay, very amusing. Sorry I wasn't here when you arrived, and sorry Mum, for not doing the introducing. Had to go and see Teaps. Needed to borrow this book on the war poets."

Daisy's look of incredulity returned.

"Three pieces of prose analysis, on Sassoon and er, Vidal. Needs to be done by tonight."

"Are you alright love?" Gloria was somewhat bemused.

"Yeah, 'course. Why wouldn't I be?"

"I don't know son. You seem to be acting a bit odd this morning. Like you're up to something. Anyway, I'll leave you to it, I need to check on the lamb. Dad called to say he'll be home in ten minutes so I'll have dinner on the table for one thirty if that's okay."

"Sounds and smells perfect, Mrs Arm . . . "

"Please, call me Gloria," she said, patting Daisy on the shoulder.

As she left the lounge she badgered Wilson. "Ask Daisy if she'd like a drink. She is our guest, remember."

Wilson closed the lounge door, sat next to Daisy and with his voice on minimum volume, excitedly started to bring her up to date with the events of the last twelve hours.

"You won't believe what I found out last night Daisy, from Big Mac and Short Cake. I was in The Gateway again and they told me all about the time traces and déjà vu and how straddling involved different energy fields. They said that only people with a pass could visit The Market Square and that we're up to mischief. The Powers That Be know this and I'm sure Big Mac and Short Cake are behind the hospital window and . . . "

At that point, Daisy stemmed the flow of words by placing two fingers on Wilson's lips.

"Slow down, you lost me after the first sentence. Who are Big Mac and Short Cake again?"

"It's complicated, and I'm trying to tell you all of this before Dad gets back. We can't talk about this at the dinner table. I had to tell you, share it with you. It's incredible. It's starting to make sense; I think I get it. I'm joining up the dots. And then there's this."

Wilson leafed through the textbook, retrieved the photo and gave it to Daisy.

"I tried to bring her in last night."

"Who?" Daisy still wasn't following.

"Last night in The Market Square, I tried to bring in Vanessa, to find out what happened to her, to use The Market Square to do something good, just like you said. But I struggled to build a clear image and I couldn't bring her in. So this morning I took this wedding photo from Teaps's dad's bedroom. Look, a sharp picture."

"Wilson, stop, calm down. I'm not following you."

A car pulled into the driveway.

"Damn, Dad's here. We can't talk now. What time do you have to leave?"

"My brother said he'd collect me at four. I have to text him. He's at the Trafford Centre."

"Okay, soon as lunch is over I'll make some excuse to go for a walk and once we're out of the house we can talk properly. I've got an idea, like an experiment and if it comes off, we'll be using The Market Square to do something really good. I need you to help though, because if I do it, but don't remember all the bauble images then . . . "

"Stop Wilson, stop. Okay, 'course I'll help you. Let's try to do something good. Explain everything to me again, later."

Alex had caught his first salmon of the season that morning, a twelve-pound cock fish and as a result, was in a buoyant mood. If there was a veil of awkwardness hanging over the conversation between three of the diners, it didn't show.

The first course was accompanied by Alex's painfully detailed account of 'the one that didn't get away'. It began with how he'd been fishing in Goose Pool on the River Ribble with the river at seven inches, ideal conditions, when a big salmon had jumped towards the far bank. How he'd used a 'double Spey' to cast a fly – a fly he'd tied himself called The Usual Suspect – right on the nose of the salmon. Then an almighty struggle followed until he finally netted the leviathan, only to return it to fight another day.

Alex *then* explained, in step by step detail, the techniques involved in tying the Usual Suspect and the intricacies of the Spey cast, which to Daisy's untrained eye, looked similar to fighting with a lightsaber. Alex was just about to launch into a description of his favourite salmon pool when Gloria said, "Alex, I think that's enough fishing talk for today. I'm sure there are a couple of other subjects under the sun we can discuss. Though probably not with the same level of mind-numbing detail."

Daisy felt sorry to see Alex's enthusiasm curbed so abruptly.

"Well, maybe one day Wilson and I can go with you. I'd like to try it. An afternoon by a river, surrounded by nature – sounds really nice. How many salmon do you normally catch?"

"Two or three, if I'm lucky. I might fish twenty, maybe twenty-five times each season, for about five or six hours each trip."

Daisy did the maths.

"So that's about . . . maybe sixty salmon each year. Sounds great. I'd definitely like to have a go with the old Spey casting." She simulated Alex's casting technique by waving her arms around like Darth Vader.

Alex was shaking his head.

"No Daisy, that's not two or three salmon every time I go fishing, that's two or three salmon each season. Some years I don't catch anything at all."

"But you still go twenty times each year, for five hours each time, and all that travelling and petrol and the Spey casting and then catch . . . nothing?"

Daisy found the idea that someone could go fishing for a year and not catch a fish absolutely hilarious, and though it was probably rude, she couldn't help but break into a fit of the giggles. It was so infectious that Wilson, his mum and then his dad came down with it moments later. Daisy tried to make a joke along the lines of the usual suspect always being the wrong suspect, but couldn't get the words out for laughter.

So I guess you'd call the lunch a success. There was plenty of small talk about Daisy's family. What her mum and dad and brother did, her college subjects, was she going to university, who were her best friends, any pets? All the obligatory subject matter that needs to be covered when parents 'A' are first introduced to girlfriend 'B'. So all in all, it went off smoothly and the elephant in the room by the name of 'The Market Square' was kept well hidden behind the aforementioned veil.

It did slip once though, when Alex asked Daisy where she and Wilson had first met. But Alex recovered pretty quickly and repeated the question, so that, "and where did you first meet?" became "and where did you first eat?" Which Gloria thought was somewhat bizarre. She let it pass though, as Daisy quickly launched into an amusing story about Fabio's restaurant and a packet of wine gums. Gloria was hoping that she would get to see more of Daisy.

"How are you getting home love?" Gloria was loading pots into the dishwasher.

"Oh, my brother said he would pick me up in an hour" she said, checking her watch. "He's out shopping with his kids."

"Oh, that's nice."

That was the cue Wilson had been waiting for.

"Think we'll go for a walk Mum, before Daisy has to go. I'm totally stuffed, need to walk off that second helping." He gave his stomach a series of theatrical pats. "Fancy going down to the park Daisy? I'll show you the ducks."

"What a lovely idea Wilson" said Gloria. "I'll put some stale bread in a bag for you."

Wilson rolled his eyes.

He and Daisy quickly donned coats and scarves, took the bread and headed off.

"Be back in about half an hour" Wilson yelled, before closing the front door and setting off for the park.

"Well, that seemed to go alright, all things considered. Thanks for coming Daisy and meeting my folks. Gives everything a feeling of normality, like feeding ducks."

He raised the bag of crusts and they both laughed.

"But things aren't normal, in fact, far from it. Come on, we haven't got much time and we need to talk."

Wilson dropped the bread in a neighbour's wheelie bin and when they were about a hundred yards from home, they sat in a draughty bus shelter and Wilson began.

"Like I said earlier Daisy, it's incredible, really incredible."

"Okay, well look, we don't have much time, so why don't you start by telling me what's involved in the plan to do something good?"

"Daisy, I went to The Market Square again last night. I saw Teaps and his mum. Before that, The Market Square was a different place. I think I told you there's this huge building, The Gateway, with a Hall of Extinguished Spirits filled with the spirits of dead people, which have been changed into gold bangles, like jewellery bangles, with their names on and the date they..."

"Wilson, you're losing me again. I . . . "

"Sorry, what I think is that The Market Square is like an access point to the energy in people's dreams. Dreams don't just evaporate; the energy of the dream survives. In The Market Square we can log in to all this energy, all the dreams of everybody. The trace of this dream energy, like time itself, the living past, is always out there."

Daisy shifted position and Wilson sensed she was getting frustrated with his foggy theorising. She checked her watch.

Wilson took one of her hands in both of his.

"Look, our Life Path numbers – the special number eleven that you and I have, and my dad – and Stockport Infirmary and The Gateway and The Market Square – they're all connected. I don't know how exactly, but they're all connected. Two nights ago, when you showed me how to bring Teaps into my dream, well, I did it again last night."

241

"Wilson, my brother's going to be here soon."

"I know. I'm nearly at the point; just bear with me. That thing we did with Teaps, when I put my hand on his shoulder, touched him and then we saw those images of his life – they were his time trace, the energy of his past. Like dream energy, always out there. But it's not dream energy, even though we experience it in a dream. It's another type of energy."

Wilson paused.

"When I touched him, that was straddling. I had one foot in a dream energy field and the other in a different energy field of Teaps's past experiences, his time traces. I could sense them both. That's why I was able to see his mum, because as those baubles came towards me, we were viewing all the events of his past life. It seems that everything he's ever done – everything that everyone has ever done – is recorded and stored on some super memory chip of time. And you and I, in The Market Square, can access these memories. Do you follow what I'm saying?"

"I think so. But what happened last night, when you brought Teaps to The Market Square?"

"I focused and focused and eventually I could see loads of stuff with his mum on the baubles – the christening, Teaps being bottlefed. I held onto the image of Vanessa in my head and then I tried to bring her to The Market Square. But my memory of how she appeared on the baubles wasn't sharp. I tried and tried but couldn't pull her in."

"But I thought you said that Vanessa . . . that the police said she could be dead, never found."

"Yes, but she doesn't have a bangle. Big Mac told me that. He said I had to look in The Market Square. So I kind of borrowed this from Teaps."

Wilson once again presented the wedding photo.

"I want to go back to The Market Square again tonight and try one more time using this better image. And I want you to help me. It's an experiment. To test my hypothesis about the energy fields. Look, you said you wanted to try to use The Market Square to do some good. And I think finding out what happened to Vanessa is something we should try to do. A good thing. Tonight."

Daisy studied the smiling bride and groom.

"Wilson, I . . . I . . . yes, okay. I don't understand half of what you're telling me. But hey, since it's only a dream we're talking about, what harm can it do? So, yeah, let's try. I need to go. My brother will be here."

Daisy stood up and was about to head back when Wilson put his hands on her shoulders.

"Daisy, you have to want to go, to want to meet me by the Clock Tower. And if we bring Vanessa in and we see the trace of her past, take in as much as you can. Try to remember all that you see, what you experience – memorise everything as it flashes by. There could be clues, information we can use. If my theory, my experiment works and Vanessa is alive, maybe we can find out where she is."

"So that's what straddling means?"

"Yeah, that's Olympic-standard straddling."

Chapter 34

The Rolling Stones concert

Monday 30th October 2017

Wilson arrived in The Market Square to find himself at a pop concert – something like a scaled down version of the Glastonbury Festival.

The olde worlde buildings and cobbles had been replaced by a new worlde of marquees, tents and food vendors. The jangle of a lead guitar and the thump of drums came from musicians on an enormous raised stage that filled the top end of the square. Wilson was too far away to identify the band. But then he recognised the melody and the words, 'If you start me up, if you start me up I'll never stop!'

How the hell am I going to find Daisy in this mayhem?

Wilson's route to the Clock Tower looked impenetrable; blocked by a human wall of fans. Plastic glasses half-filled with beer occasionally flew into the air followed by raucous cheers. Raised hands held out mobiles to capture selfies. Girls balanced on boys shoulders, sang and clapped and waved their arms in time with the music.

He could see a clock face and the pinnacle of the tower about thirty metres to his right and two lads clinging precariously to their bird's eye view.

She'll be near the bench seats Wilson concluded, before forcing his way into the densely packed crowd.

After a few minutes of argy-bargy he reached a patch

of space near the flower beds and the war memorial. Daisy waved and smiled as he approached.

"Have you seen who's playing?" She nodded her head in the direction of the music.

"Yeah, I know, great isn't it. The Rolling Stones, awesome."

"Want to go on stage and join the band? I'm pretty sure we'll be allowed."

Wilson realised that what was about to happen was beyond even *his* wildest dreams. Beyond anyone's wildest dreams.

"But listen Daisy, seriously, only two songs. We're here to find Vanessa, remember?"

Ten minutes later, Wilson Armitage on bass guitar and Daisy Meadowcroft on jazz flute were centre stage, the new members of The Rolling Stones and loving every minute.

Nobody can ever take this memory from me, even if it is only part of a dream, thought Wilson, looking down on The Market Square filled to capacity with cheering, singing, waving people. As the sun dipped behind L'École, the lighters came out.

Jumpin' Jack Flash, it's a gas, gas, gas.

Wilson turned to Daisy and mouthed a simple instruction: "Come on. We need to go, now!"

They slowly retreated from the limelight with a series of appreciative bows and handed the bass guitar and the flute back to a stage hand. Then they scrambled down a set of metal steps, through a screen of thick black curtains and along an empty corridor.

A door with the words, 'Rock Stars Only' painted in coloured glitter offered itself as the only option so Wilson forced the door and they stepped inside. Four electric guitars were resting against a wall. A clothes rail was filled with leather jackets, colourful silk shirts, drainpipe satin pants, scarves, a feather boa and a black suede Fedora hat. Two bottles of Jack Daniels, a half-empty bottle of Moët Champagne, glass tumblers, two packs of Marlboro Lights and a half-eaten kebab littered the table which stood beneath a dressing mirror bordered with white light bulbs.

"Daisy, I don't know how much time we've got, but we need to do it soon. We have to bring in Teaps's mum."

From the stage above, the muffled thud of drum and bass continued. Someone ran down the corridor shouting "Security."

"So I guess this will have to do."

"What? In here?"

"Yeah, here, now. Or we'll run out of dream time. Plus, we'd never find Vanessa out there anyway."

Wilson sat on the edge of the table, closed his eyes, pictured the wedding photo and zoomed in on the face of Vanessa Clarke. The beaming smile of a bride, the pale complexion, the blonde hair in ringlets. He focused, fine tuned, concentrated and concentrated some more, and then opened his eyes.

Nothing.

"Damn. She won't come."

Wilson tried again, for a full two minutes.

Still the same negative result.

"Why's it not happening? We did it with Teaps and Hoover."

Wilson turned forlornly to Daisy for an answer.

"I don't know Wilson. Maybe it's because you never met her. Or you can only bring in your friends. Or we need to be out in The Market Square, or maybe she's . . . "

"No, she's not dead. I know it; she's not, there's no bangle." Wilson refused to accept Daisy's line of thought. "You have a go at bringing her in. Remember the wedding photo; happy, smiling face, blonde hair. Try Daisy. Maybe you're better than me. A woman to woman thing."

Daisy was about to say something disparaging about Wilson's suggestion, but thought better of it and closed her eyes instead.

There was a knock at the door.

Wilson opened it a fraction and peered through the crack. A man with a clipboard was talking into a microphone projecting down from an earpiece.

"Two minutes, final call."

"Okay, err, thanks. We're ready," said Wilson. He closed the door and turned back to Daisy.

Vanessa Clarke was sitting in the chair, dressed in a long flowing bridal gown with her blonde hair in ringlets, gazing wistfully at her reflection in the mirror.

"Daisy, you genius! You did it!" Wilson was both elated and amazed.

"Is that her? I mean, really her?" Daisy was also questioning her stunning achievement.

Vanessa was reaching for the Champagne bottle and a glass.

"Yeah, absolutely. She looks just like her photo."

Wilson slowly and gently placed his hand on Vanessa's shoulder.

"Yes, I'll be ready in a minute, love," she said, looking up at Wilson.

But there was no power surge. No electrical impulse ran

along his arm.

Wilson raised his hand and again placed it back on Vanessa's shoulder. But still nothing. No baubles and no visions of the past.

He turned to Daisy in frustration. "It's not working. Her traces won't come."

Daisy took a step forward and pushed Wilson to one side.

"Move, let me try. Maybe I have to do it because I brought her here. Maybe it's a woman to woman thing."

Daisy rested her hand on the shoulder of a complete stranger, sitting in a white satin wedding dress, sipping Champagne, in a dream.

Then the music stopped and a transparent curtain of yellow cellophane was drawn across the room. A small, red bauble emerged, followed by a green bauble and in quick succession, white, silver and blue baubles flared like oil drops on water. To the eyes-wide-open astonishment of Daisy and Wilson, floating towards them, reflected in traces of the past, were the events that led to the disappearance of Vanessa Clarke. And all was revealed.

Chapter 35

Mystery solved

Vanessa Clarke was in a state of euphoria as she left The May Fair Hotel and headed north towards Euston station. The business pitch had been hugely successful and the new IBM contract meant promotion to the Premier League of executive recruitment. As she walked through Berkeley Square, with its swanky offices, famous restaurants and luxury car showrooms, Vanessa entertained the notion that one day, V&G Clarke and Partners might also be engraved on a polished brass plaque at the entrance to one of those buildings.

Whether it was the bubbly, or a momentary surge of devil-may-care, it's impossible to say: but as she passed the shop frontage of Nicky Clarke, hairdresser to the rich and famous, she decided that the mumsy hairstyle reflected in the window needed a business class upgrade, in keeping with her new status.

Vanessa was lucky; the salon had just received a cancellation and was told if she came back in fifteen minutes, a cut and colour with the chief stylist, 'wouldn't be a problem'. Vanessa didn't bother to ask the price on the principle that if you had to ask, you probably couldn't afford it. However, she knew that even a Nicky Clarke understudy would be expensive and serious cash would be required.

Vanessa Clarke avoided using a credit card whenever possible, paying with money in the hand was reminiscent of a childhood in Naples and the old-fashioned ways of her father. "Only hard-earned cash in your pocket is virtuous and honourable" he would insist, like it was some Mafia coda. En route to the nearest cashpoint, Vanessa's reflection called out again, this time from the window of an upmarket, clothes shop.

Isn't that old Marks and Spencer raincoat a bit drab? Wouldn't you prefer to be wearing this lovely new camel coat instead? Classically cut, calf length, lambswool and cashmere mix.

Her M&S raincoat wasn't *that* old and it certainly wasn't drab, but Vanessa was sold on the camel coat. She withdrew £1,800 in cash from her business account. This one's on the company she decided and ten minutes later walked back to the hairdressing appointment wearing her new, luxury acquisition. At the same time, the old raincoat, now gift-wrapped in a fancy box, became the property of a homeless woman sleeping under cardboard in a backstreet doorway.

As Vanessa sat waiting for the Natural Light Ash Brown colour to take effect, she reached for her phone and was about to text Michael to say she was taking the later train when she decided against it. The business win and makeover would be a big surprise.

So the woman who walked out of the salon did not look remotely like the woman who first walked in. Vanessa's long blonde hair had been transformed to ash brown, in a classic short bob with a tousled, blow-dried finish, 'to give it a contemporary new take', the stylist had said. With the IBM contract, new hair and a cashmere coat, Vanessa Clarke felt fantastic. It was one of the best days of her life and as she headed for the train station she didn't have a care in the world, other than arriving home to her son and husband later than originally planned.

As she approached the junction where Davies Street meets Mount Street, Vanessa felt something go pop, deep inside her head and stumbled before quickly regaining her balance. She felt nauseous and confused and stood for a few minutes, supported by a lamp post, waiting for the sensation to pass.

Vanessa Clarke had just suffered an ischaemic stroke triggered by a combination of three glasses of Champagne, seven hours' sleep over the previous two days, an inherited condition that causes the narrowing of certain blood vessels in the brain and most significantly, a tiny clot of blood. The blood clot had lodged itself deep in her hippocampus and for two minutes had restricted the flow of oxygenated blood to a cluster of cells involved in speech and memory. The area of tissue damage was tiny, but also irreparable and catastrophic, like a permanent crack across the M6 motorway.

In layman's terms, the hard drive, the storage part of her brain, was still good, but her mental operating system couldn't access it. Which meant Vanessa Clarke was no longer able to remember anything about herself or her past. The memories were still there, but she was unable to retrieve them, or, more importantly, tell anyone who she was. The victim of a random act of violence on a busy street in London. She had been mentally mugged.

The intensely private residents of Mayfair object to overt signs of police surveillance in their gilded borough; so a paucity of functioning cameras meant the blonde figure of Vanessa Clarke, monitored from The May Fair Hotel to Hay Hill, was lost as she entered the environs of Berkeley Square.

Three days after Vanessa was officially declared missing it was discovered that scaffolding, hurriedly erected on the morning of her disappearance, had blocked the field of view of the only camera observing the street with the cashpoint. The camel coat shop was closed when the police conducted door-to-door enquiries and the girl on reception in Nicky Clarke's (who hadn't been working on the day of Vanessa's disappearance) stated confidently that she had "checked the appointments book twice and they had no customer by the name of Vanessa Clarke." The footage on every police camera along the route from Berkeley Square to Euston was pored over, painstakingly, for blonde hair and a blue mac, but to no avail. Vanessa Clarke had simply disappeared.

Of course, the camera at Hay Hill, which captured the last known image of Vanessa, was the focus of most attention. But with over thirty thousand people and four thousand vehicles passing each day, the police constable given the task of studying the tapes could be forgiven for not noticing the smart-looking businesswoman with short brown hair, walking back toward The May Fair Hotel – in the *opposite* direction of Euston station.

In a state of extreme confusion, Vanessa Clarke wandered back up to Stratton Street, where she momentarily stopped outside the entrance to The May Fair Hotel. She then continued on to Piccadilly, through Green Park and down to Victoria coach station, where she boarded an overnight Country Express coach to Inverness.

She handed the driver a wad of notes as she mumbled the word 'Stockland'.

Her eyes were glazed and the driver detected alcohol on her breath. He smiled as he gave her the one-way ticket and change for a twenty-pound note and slipped the rest of the money in his back pocket. Vanessa made her way unsteadily to the back of the coach where she slumped in a seat and fell asleep, totally hidden from view.

Eleven hours later, as the coach made its way through the early morning traffic in Inverness, Vanessa was still sleeping. The coach turned into the bus station, reversed into the allotted parking bay and twenty-two weary passengers disembarked. As the last of the departing passengers stepped down from the coach, a shifty-looking lad, who had been sitting three rows in front of Vanessa, took a few steps back and silently lifted the attaché case belonging to the well dressed lady, still sleeping in the corner at the back.

She's definitely on something, he'd been thinking for the previous two hours, *and it takes one to know one!*

So this scoundrel – who specialised in transporting, twice weekly, two kilos of cocaine from Dover to Scotland – left Inverness bus station, with a case holding over four hundred pounds in cash and all the documents that could be used to identify the presumably pissed-up, drugged-up woman at the back of the coach. The two envelopes, one containing a new credit card and the other, a slip showing the PIN number, were an unexpected bonus.

The credit card was used a few days later in Dover to make a maximum cash withdrawal of £2,000 and then passed to the courier's contacts for use on a return journey to Paris. The attaché case containing a mobile phone, driving licence and a signed IBM contract, was weighted with a brick and somewhere between Dover and Calais, found its way to the bed of the English Channel.

The driver winked at the courier as he departed the coach with the case and after a coffee from his flask and a cigarette he helped Vanessa from the coach.

"Go and get a cup of tea love" he said. "It'll make you feel better."

"Grazie," she mumbled.

The driver handed his coach keys in at the station office then scarpered off to the nearest pub with a wad of stolen beer money burning a hole in his grubby pocket.

Confused, disorientated, unable to remember who she was, not knowing where she was, Vanessa walked slowly from the station down Margaret Street towards the river until she came to a small park overlooking the Ness Bridge, where she sat on a bench seat and waited.

She had been sitting in the rain for five hours when a lady walking a dog brought to a policeman's attention the poor soul sitting in the park 'totally drenched' and 'not quite all there'.

"Come on love, let's get you checked out and dried off," said an ambulance man, as he helped Vanessa into a wheelchair.

"Grazie" she mumbled.

In the ensuing investigation, nobody made the connection between the blonde business woman missing in London; who'd absconded to France and was suspected of fraud, with the well-dressed brunette; found bewildered in Inverness, who'd lost her mental faculties and could only mutter a few words in Italian.

The people running social services for that part of Scotland secretly believed she'd been left on their doorstep by a relative who couldn't cope. Or she'd been brought over from one of the islands, where dementia services were limited, by a family who would rather not see her, than see her not cared for. Either way, the end result was the same. Whoever the mystery lady was, she needed twenty-four-hour care and the health authority for Inverness had a duty to provide it.

Of course, the two people who could have intervened, the drug courier and the coach driver, both had a vested interest in keeping schtum – especially the coach driver, who was told by his accomplice, "jist keep yer trap shut, or yeee'll be havin' a wee accident!"

So for almost seventeen years, Vanessa Clarke had been a virtually mute resident of the South Kessock Care Home. She had a lovely room looking out over the Beauly Firth, but she had no idea of where she was, no idea of who she was and neither did anyone else. That is, until the night Daisy Meadowcroft pulled her into The Market Square.

Chapter 36

So, what now?

Monday 30th October 2017

"Daisy, I can't just walk up and say, 'Hey Teaps, my girlfriend discovered what happened to your mum. She's alive and she's been in a care home in the north of Scotland for seventeen years' can I?"

There had been a flurry of texts between Wilson and Daisy all that morning and after Daisy was threatened with having her phone confiscated during a pottery class, they agreed to speak at lunchtime.

"I know that Wilson. We can't be seen to be involved in this. Teaps has to find out for himself. But first, we need to be certain that the woman we saw in The Market Square is in a care home that actually exists in that part of Scotland and she really is Vanessa."

"Daisy, there is a South Kessock Care Home. It was the first thing I checked this morning. It's owned by a big company and overlooks the sea. The lady will be there and she's Teaps's mum. We both know that."

"But we have to confirm it. I mean, we can't just send a random anonymous message saying who she is and where her family are. Or can we?"

Daisy paused and then corrected herself.

"Maybe Wilson, maybe that's exactly what we do. Just reveal her location anonymously. It couldn't be tracked back to us."

"I know, I was thinking that. But if I was Teaps, it would tear me up to discover that perhaps someone had known all these years and they'd never said anything. I'd go crazy trying to work out who it was. So I don't think that's how we do it.

What if we help someone, perhaps a doctor or a nurse, someone working at the home, to discover Vanessa for themselves. We just have to point them in the right direction. Crop the face from the wedding photo, and then leave it ... "

"But Wilson, there would have to be an explanation of where the photo came from. Anything that leaves a trail can be followed, and as you said, Teaps would go crazy if the trail led nowhere and he was left in the dark. He has no mum for virtually all of his life, then someone leads him to her and he doesn't know who, or why, or why they waited all this time. No, that's not the ... wait, wait, I have an idea. What if Vanessa leaves the trail herself? What if she does something that suddenly reveals a vital clue?"

"Like what?"

"Like her name, scrawled on a piece of paper beside her bed?"

Wilson fell silent.

"Then, maybe, when one of the nurses or a cleaner goes into her room, they see the name, and it's like she's written it, subconsciously.

"They'd take it to a supervisor or a manager, and if we're lucky, they'd have the nous to do an online search. And once they found out that someone by that name went missing all those years ago ... "

"Daisy, you're a genius. That's exactly the way to do it. It'll be like she's trying to send a message, to tell them who she is. A cry for help."

"Exactly. Nobody would ignore her name if it was written five times on a piece of paper. Or even better, if she just wrote, 'I am Vanessa Clarke'. Or just, 'Me, Vanessa Clarke'."

"Yeah, that would definitely work, and nothing suspicious about it. All we need to do is find a way to get to Inverness, get into the home, leave the note and then get back to Stockport, without anybody knowing about it."

"Mmm, that's not going to be so easy." Daisy's enthusiasm for the idea was waning slightly. Wilson however, wasn't daunted by the challenge.

"Daisy, I think only one of us can go. I know you found her and maybe you want to see it through, but he's my mate and knowing his mum's there . . . "

"Wilson, are you crazy? This isn't a bloody movie. There's no way I can go to the north of Scotland, I get lost walking in the garden. You need to go alone, as soon as possible – like tomorrow. And if you go by yourself, we reduce the, 'someone might find out what we're up to' factor by fifty per cent."

"Yeah, you're right. I have to do this by myself. Tomorrow. Daisy speak later – I've got a trip to organise."

Wilson checked his college timetable for the next day and began planning travel schedules and alibis.

No classes after 3 p.m. That's good.

Now, where can I say I'm going to be all day?

A university visit?

No, they'd want to know which uni, which course. Not credible.

Hospital appointment? Curious lump on my leg?

No. Too personal, too lumpy!

Broken Vespa?

No. Wouldn't cause me to be away all day.
Jury service?
Giving blood?
Charity work?
Prince's Trust?
Prince's Trust. That might do it!

Wilson talked through a potential scenario.

"Sir, I won't be in tomorrow morning – until sometime after lunch, at the earliest. I have to go to the Prince's Trust Open Day in Manchester Town Hall with my parents."

No, no. Too forceful.

"Sir, is it okay if I go by myself to the Prince's ... "

But what if he says no? Don't give him the chance to say no.

"Sorry to trouble you sir, but my mum has asked me to ask you if I can help her tomorrow morning. She needs help with an exhibition stand for Oxfam, at the Prince's Trust at Manchester Town Hall. The guy who was going to help hurt his back and she just called to ask if I could ask you for permission. She'd be really grateful. It's for a worthy cause, plus I'd find out about all the beneficial work the Trust does around the world. It wouldn't be four hours wasted."

Bang on.

"Wilson, that is a very public-spirited gesture and you're a credit to your parents" said Mr Finch, his English tutor an hour later. "I'll leave notes at reception for tomorrow morning's double English. What else will you be missing?"

"Err, just one biology class and maths, sir."

"Well, let Mr Edwards and your maths tutor know and tell them I've said it's okay on this one occasion. Highly commendable Wilson. You've climbed a rung on the ladder of my expectations and you'll be pleased to know, you're now on rung one."

"Ha ha ha, thank you sir. Excellent joke."

Old buffoon.

But that was the college alibi sorted.

Now, how the hell do I get to Inverness and back in a day? How far away is it anyway? I know it's bloody miles.

'Trains to Inverness from Manchester. Search.'

The earliest train I can catch is the 6.14 a.m. from Piccadilly. Gets me to Inverness for 13.29 p.m. So would have to be up at 5.00 a.m. and sneak out of the house. Gulp.

I'd have to invent some reason for being up so early.

Okay, worry about that in a minute.

Two changes, Edinburgh and Perth.

And it's a hundred and forty-one quid.

What about the return?

The 15.51 p.m. from Inverness gets me back at 23.28 p.m. Half eleven in Manchester. Back home for nearly half twelve in the morning.

One change.

Another hundred and forty-one quid!

That means I've got two hours and twenty-two minutes in Inverness, to get to the home, do what I need to do, and then get back to the station.

Wilson studied a Google map for the north of Inverness.

'Inverness to South Kessock. Search.'

Eight minutes by car, one point four miles. So I've got two hours and twenty-eight minutes. Will be cutting it fine, but doable.

Now, how do I persuade them to let me into the South Kessock Care Home?

Wilson spent twenty minutes researching the home and its range of services. South Kessock was renowned for the quality of its residential care for those suffering with dementia. As Wilson understood it, you could ring a care home, tell them a relative was at an advanced stage with the illness, that you were looking for a bed in the area and often they'd let you visit to see the facilities.

Wilson dialled the number.

"South Kessock. How may I help you?"

"Hi, it's, err, yes. Sorry to trouble you, I'm ringing about my father. He's suffering from dementia and my mum is struggling to cope and my sister, Daisy and I are, err, we think we need to start looking for a home for him. Dad's doctor told us that South Keswick, I mean Kessock, was, is, a very good home and I wanted to know if I could come and visit tomorrow, at two o'clock in the afternoon?"

"What stage of dementia has your father reached?"

"Oh, he's at an advanced stage. Forgets things all the time. Walks around mumbling about energy fields and a place called The Market Square."

"Well, I'm so sorry to hear that."

"Yes, he's certainly on the downward path."

"Well, we'd be delighted to show you round. Whom shall I say will be calling in then?"

"Just myself. Mum's too upset to contemplate all of this. So there'll only be me."

"Yes, but what name shall I say?"

"Oh, err, I'm Frank. My name's Frank. Mr Frank Spencer."

"Okay Mr Spencer, we'll look forward to seeing you tomorrow afternoon then. Thanks for calling. Goodbye."

"Goodbye."

And that was it, Wilson was in. Now all he had to do was come up with some reason for being out of the house at 5.20 a.m. and back around 12.30 a.m. the following day. He paid for the day return ticket with his debit card and went off to a biology lesson.

He bumped into Teaps in the corridor en-route. He'd been in a fight. There was crusted blood on his skinned knuckles, he had a fat lip and the purple-blue flush of a fresh bruise was swelling on his cheekbone.

"Teaps, what's gone on?"

"You'd better ask Spinner, the slimy little bastard. All the time I thought he was a mate, well, he was spying on me. Watching to see if I was spending money, buying clothes and stuff. Then telling Blamire I was wasting cash when I should be paying our debts. Well, he won't be doing that for a while."

"Why, what's happened, where is he?"

"He's in an ambulance. I just put him in an ambulance."

Then Teaps wiped his eyes with the sleeve of his jacket and tears started to flow. He put his head on Wilson's shoulder and all his frustrations came flooding out, right in the middle of a college corridor.

A girlfriend came over and tried to console him. Students walked past, concerned, but reluctant to get involved for fear of being caught in collateral damage. News of the fight had spread quickly.

After a minute, Teaps stopped crying, composed himself, wiped his eyes and blew his nose on his torn and blood speckled t-shirt.

"I've had enough Wilson. I'm at the end of my tether."

Tears were brimming over the rims of his eyelids.

"Dad was rushed into A&E. He was peeing blood and he'd

collapsed in the flat. I was there on the ward all night. They say he'll live, but only if he stops drinking. But I don't think he can. I can't stop him – I've tried. And when we got home earlier, that little bastard was there in the street spying and laughing at me. So I just lost it. Think I broke his jaw and his arm. I'm going home to check on Dad before the police come. Text you later. See ya, Wilson."

And before Wilson had time to say anything, to suggest Teaps come and live with him, bring his dad, even for just a few nights; anything to help his best mate, who was clearly losing it – he'd walked out of the revolving door of the college and away.

Wilson couldn't concentrate in the biology lesson – and certainly not on dissecting a rat. "Looks like the work of Jack the Ripper," said the class technician as he put the mutilated corpse of Wilson's Rattus norvegicus back in the freezer later that afternoon. Not surprising really. Wilson had carved out a plan that in principle, would allow him to travel to Inverness and back, all in one day, without alerting too much suspicion, and after hearing of Teaps's problems, his scalpel was blunt.

When Wilson arrived home, there was a note waiting for him on the hall table. A divine intervention of sorts.

'Wilson,

Have gone to see your Auntie Rita. She's slipped a disc again, so have to help and stay the night. Dad's in London – back tomorrow. Fish pie in the fridge. Call me if you need me.

Love, Mum X

P.S. Lock the front door when you go to bed!!'

"Half a miracle, anyway," He muttered to himself, scrunching up the note

I'll worry about an explanation for the late return on the trip back.

Wilson called Daisy and brought her up to speed with Teaps's fight, the Prince's Trust excuse, and his good fortune at being able to slip away the next morning under the radar.

"Wilson, I hope that lady in the home really is his mum. But what do you think will happen when she's identified? What if she wants to stay there? What if we make the whole situation worse?"

"I know. I was thinking about that. It's like we're using a dream to change what happens in the future, like a butterfly beating its wings and causing a snowstorm in the Amazon rainforest."

"No Wilson, that's rubbish. It's like playing God. We're in charge of that lady's destiny, manipulating her future because we think it will be good for her and I don't know if we should."

Wilson didn't know what to say.

"But then equally Wilson, if I was Teaps, I'd want someone to find my mum and I wouldn't care what happens after that."

Daisy's voice trembled. "It makes me cry just thinking about it."

She paused for a sniffle.

"Please make sure you text me from the train, especially on the way back."

"I will."

"And don't go to The Market Square tonight. You need some sleep."

Wilson had to laugh.

"Daisy, what do you think we're doing when we're in The

264

Market Square? We are asleep."

"You know what I mean, just try and have a normal dream. Oh, and I forgot to tell you, they're bringing my grandma up from Bournemouth tomorrow and taking her to Stockport Infirmary. She's not got long to live and wants to be close to family. I'm going to see her, so if I don't text back immediately, I'm not ignoring you."

"Okay, I think I'll survive."

"Goodnight and good luck."

"Oh Daisy, wait. Which ward will she be in?"

"3B, I think. Why?"

"Nothing. Tell you another time."

"Okay, goodnight."

"'Night."

Wilson ate the fish pie and watched an hour of TV. He was double-checking train times when his phone registered a text from a number he didn't recognise.

'Wilson, buzz me back if you can.'

Wilson pressed redial. Teaps answered after two rings.

"Hey Wilson, it's me. I'm using my dad's phone. You won't believe this."

"Are you okay? What's happened?"

"Spinner's not pressing charges. The police came round and told me I was lucky, cos I could have been done for assault. Spinner told them he provoked me and got what he deserved. Pretty sure Blamire's behind it. Probably didn't want his little dog spending too much time with the coppers, given the extra-curricular activities."

"Jesus, that's a relief. You must have done some damage."

"Yeah, a fractured arm and jaw and a broken nose. He

"won't be in college for a week. And I smashed my phone."

"Christ, remind me not to get on your angry side. You're like the Incredible Hulk."

"Wilson, I've never hit anyone in my life. I'm a writer, not a fighter."

"Could have fooled me."

"Nah, it was just the spying stuff, but mostly my dad. He's losing it and taking me with him, today was a low point and I just snapped. Now he's in bed, with his arm around a bottle of JD, the surrogate wife. The drinking's not likely to stop and I'll lose him soon. Maybe it's for the best; then they'll be together. Think that's what he wants."

"Teaps, don't speak like that. We need to get you some support. There must be help groups who can get involved. You can't live with this pressure and the money problems and college; you'll have a breakdown."

"Yeah, you're right. Anyway, just wanted to let you know I'm not in a cell for the night, so I'll see you tomorrow."

"Oh wait, I forgot. I won't be in tomorrow – well, not in the morning. I'm helping mum with a charity thing for the Prince's Trust."

"Okay mate, no worries. Say hi from me."

"Will do Rocky."

"Very funny. See ya."

Wilson was in bed for 10 p.m. He read the first three chapters of *To Kill a Mockingbird* and spent some of the night dreaming of Jem and Atticus Finch in Alabama – and not The Market Square.

At 6.14 a.m., as Wilson slipped into seat 23B with a bacon baguette and hot coffee, a shrill whistle trilled along the platform and the Virgin West Coast train slowly pulled out of Piccadilly station, heading north, to Scotland

Chapter 37

North

Tuesday 31st October 2017

Wilson slept for the first hour of the journey but woke as the train skirted Morecambe Bay and the fecund hills of the South Lakes came into view. Wilson was no country boy; he hardly knew a starling from a grayling, but was captured by the natural beauty of the scenery; the comely, undulating contours of fell and field; the silver boil of a rushing stream glimpsed through a canopy of autumn russet and ochre; the grazing sheep dotted on high pasture resembling woolly white pills on green blankets; the purple heather, newly ploughed soil and the endless trails of dry-stone walls. It was a new world to Wilson and he was touched by the pastoral purity of the vision.

A few miles short of the Scottish border, the train charged over a bridge spanning a wide river in which a man stood alone, fly fishing. He was at one with his surroundings, self-absorbed in peace and tranquillity, questioning the ever changing light and the appropriateness of The Usual Suspect at that moment, in that river, at that height. There was something ethereal about the pastime that appeared to include elements both spiritual and sublime and Wilson finally understood why the catch and return of a salmon, the notch in the cork of a double handed rod, was not the point. The real pleasure, was in just being there. Waist-deep in a river with a memory trace as old as time itself. He realised what he'd been missing and vowed not to refuse the next invite from his dad.

An hour or so later, he sent a text to Daisy to say all was running smoothly and he was on a platform at Edinburgh station waiting for the train to Perth. Then a text to his mum to say he'd survived the night 'home alone', the burglars were all in custody and he'd be back late because he was going to see a band with Hoover.

After the Perth train, he caught the connection to Inverness and at 13.29 p.m., bang on schedule, he walked out of the station and climbed into a waiting taxi.

"The South Kessock Care Home please." Wilson tried to make the request sound as routine as asking for the nearest KFC.

"Aye, that'll be the one up on Kessock Road then."

"Yeah, near the bridge, overlooking the sea."

"So what brings you to South Kessock laddie?"

Wilson was feeling nervous and apprehensive and didn't really want to get into a conversation. Until the stark reality of his situation and lack of planning suddenly struck home.

He was about to try and pull off the acting performance of his life; in the role of an anxious son, in a dementia care home in the north of Scotland and needed a script and to practise his lines, quickly!

"Yeah, my dad's not so good. He's got advanced dementia so Mum's asked me to check out a couple of care homes because she really can't cope anymore."

"You're not from round here, are you son?"

That's a point. The home probably wouldn't be interested in talking to someone whose dad lives in Stockport and not in Scotland.

"No, but both my dad and my mum are from Inverness. They were born here and they're thinking of moving back. Mum's got family here, my Auntie Rita, and they all want to be back together for my dad's . . . well, you know, as he declines."

"Aye, that's dementia. We're all living too long. Used to call it old age; now we've got fancy medical terms for everything. How old's yer dad?"

"He's forty-eight."

"Och, that's no age for a man to be taken in."

"Err, I mean, he was forty-eight when he was first diagnosed. He's seventy-two now."

"And he's got a son who's a mere slip of a lad like you? Achhhh, it's all part of the plan of the Almighty up there."

The taxi driver stroked the chain of rosary beads dangling from his rear-view mirror and mumbled a few words in a broad Scottish accent; something along the lines of, "there but for the grace of God go I."

Wilson wasn't really listening, he was too busy rehearsing his story, part of which now required the memorising of a few street names on the fringes of Inverness and some clarity on the age of his father

The taxi pulled to a halt outside a sprawling, two storey, red-brick building bordered by manicured flower beds. Wilson paid the fare, paused for a moment to admire the stunning sea view, filled his lungs with fresh, salty air then pressed the visitors' bell.

A lady emerged from a side office and opened the door.

"Hi, I'm Wilson. Err, Frank Spencer Wilson. I spoke with someone yesterday, about my dad and a viewing. He's got dementia."

"Oh yes, Rosie said you'd be calling in. Perfect timing; they're on lunch. Take a pew and I'll call Celia, the duty manager."

Wilson took a seat in the reception area. Music was playing in the background and a plate of iced buns had been placed incongruously on a small side table. The place smelled of boiled cabbage and bleach.

"Hi, I'm Celia Green, duty manager for today."

Wilson stood up to shake hands with an officious-looking lady wearing a black suit and carrying a clipboard.

"Fill this in and I'll take you for a swish round."

She pushed the clipboard and a pen into Wilson's hands, "I'll be back in five," then she pressed four buttons on a keypad and departed through a door.

Wilson sat down and flicked through the questionnaire. Name, date of birth, address, name of doctor, surgery address, NI number, current medication – and a lot of additional questions he really should have anticipated. The time was exactly 13.56 p.m.

Just under two hours. Should be enough.

He fudged answers to some of the questions, left one section completely blank and sat waiting for the duty manager to return. It was 14.11 p.m. The duty manager reappeared five minutes later and reviewed Wilson's paperwork. Her initial look of scepticism was turning to a frown by the last page. Wilson was prepared for the light interrogation that followed.

"So, Mr . . . Frank . . . Spencer. Rosie told me you're here about your father. He must be very young to have dementia. You can't be more than eighteen?"

"Yes, that's true. But he's not my real dad, he's my stepdad. My mum's real though."

"Well, thank goodness for that."

Wilson jaw tightened as he sensed Celia Green not only wanted to get this over and done with asap, but she was also clearly suspicious of his story and certainly the false name.

"I mean, my dad died and then my mum married an older man, called Alex. Anyway, now he's got dementia and Mum's struggling to cope and needs my help. There's only me and my sister Daisy, but Daisy's away at school, training to be a doctor, so they've sent me to check the place out."

The duty manager raised an eyebrow.

"Where does your father live?"

"Ah, that's the thing you see. He lives in England, in Stockport, with my mum, but he was actually born in Inverness. Mum also. Her sister lives in Inshes, on Culloden Road. Near Inshes Wood. And they want to move up here for family reasons. And so I'm here, you know, to see if Dad would like it."

"We have no funded places I'm afraid."

"That's no problem. Mum's first husband, my first dad, er, real dad, was a football player for Stoke City and so, anyway, she's got money. And err, we think this may be the perfect place. If I could just, you know, have a quick look round. Check out the standards. Then Mum and Daisy can come another time."

Celia Green skimmed through Wilson's completed form for a second time, then lifted her eyes and tilted her head. She was evaluating the questionable personage that went by the highly implausible name of Frank Spencer. Wilson ran through the likely ramifications of her deliberations taking a turn for the worst. These involved a local policeman ringing a startled Gloria Armitage for confirmation that her son was not in college, but visiting a care home in Inverness because his stepfather had dementia. And an urgent phone call being put through to Alex, deep in the House of Commons, from a wife seeking clarification on her husband's mental well-being.

Fortunately, the duty manager decided against dialling 999.

"Okay, Mr . . . Spencer. Follow me."

They passed through the security door and entered a long corridor with small bedrooms staggered on the right and left. On the wall outside each bedroom was a picture frame and beneath the frame, a small aluminium name-holder. Each frame held a montage of family photos depicting happier times from an earlier life.

The duty manager was striding off in front, pointing to this and pointing to that, rota this and prescription that.

Some of the rooms were occupied, but the people in the rooms didn't bear any resemblance to the people in the picture frames. The people in the photos were young and full of life, wearing flared pants and tank tops, drinking beer and dancing at parties. The people in the rooms were grey and shrunken. They were lying in bed in colourless, washed-out nightclothes, propped up with pillows, stroking strands of greasy hair, hypnotised by the movement on silent TV screens. Horribly alive in their other world.

"And this Mr Spencer, is the dining room" said the duty manager, pointing out the obvious in a cursory manner. Vanessa would be about fifty, fifty-five at the most, remarkably young compared to the other residents. After weighing-up each diner, Wilson concluded that nobody even vaguely resembled Teaps's mum.

"Looks very nice – friendly, clean, organised. I think my

dad, my stepdad, would like it. Just out of interest, what's the average age of a resident here?"

"Well, dementia is one of those illnesses that can strike at any time but I'd say the average is roughly eighty and we'll have a resident for about twenty months, maybe two years."

Celia gave Wilson a look that said she was bored and the tour was over.

"Mr Spencer, I really must get back to the office. If you want to bring your mum and sister, call again. We can have a more detailed chat when you're all together."

The duty manager was heading back down the corridor.

"Yes, I'll do exactly that. I'll be back. Looks great," said Wilson, ambling along behind her.

He stopped to check his watch. It was 14.35. *Just over an hour left.* He still had time, but the duty manager obviously didn't. He had to find a reason to stay longer, an excuse to do more looking.

"Who's been here the longest? You know, exceeding all expectations, outliving everybody? I'd like my stepdad to be like that."

"Well, in that case Mr Spencer – and it's strange you should ask – we have our very own mystery woman. An Italian princess, waiting for her handsome prince to come to the rescue."

"Gosh, who's that?" Wilson asked, trying to sound only mildly interested, though his heart rate was beginning to climb.

"Funnily enough, she's right here. We call her Alice."

The duty manager took two steps back and pointed into one of the bedrooms they'd walked past earlier. The picture frame was empty but the word Alice was just about legible on a strip of card inside the name plate.

"Quite the little enigma is our Alice."

Wilson peered tentatively into the room. It was clean and tidy with no TV. Just inside the door, sitting in a tatty, high-backed armchair was a lady who, on first impression, appeared to be *much* younger than the other residents. She was wearing a tweed skirt that had lost most of its colour and her clean, white blouse was fraying at the cuffs.

"Hello," she said, looking up at Wilson in the doorway.

The hair was now more of a creamy grey than a honey blonde, nevertheless it retained a silky sheen. Fine age lines creased the skin around her lips but her green eyes were shining like light beams bouncing off a rippling sea. Vanessa Clarke was definitely still alive!

"Alice is a bit of a strange one. No family, no friends. She was abandoned in a park here in Inverness. It was all well before my time. Apparently, her family, who lived on the Isle of Lewis or Harris, can't remember now, couldn't cope and just dumped her. And she's been here ever since, for seventeen years. We don't think she's got dementia like your father. We did at first, but she's not deteriorated since the day she arrived. Completely lost her memory though. She can say 'hello' and a few words in Italian, but that's it. There used to be a big Italian community on the Outer Hebrides, just after the war, so we think that's where she's from."

Teaps's mum was smiling, looking up at Wilson.

"She's not incontinent, can feed herself, needs no medication and she's no trouble. There's nowhere else to put her in the area, so she's become a bit of a fixture here."

Wilson knelt down and touched the hand of the long-lost, forever-loved and never-once-forgotten mum of his

275

best friend – found at last. He looked into Vanessa's eyes and smiled. It really was her.

Wilson stood up and coughed to check his vocal chords hadn't gone all mushy.

"Right, well, thanks for showing me round."

He put his hand on the pen and paper in his pocket.

"Just need to use the loo if that's okay. Long journey back. Think I saw a toilet sign back there."

"Yes, but that's a residents' toilet. The nice visitors' toilet is this . . . "

But Wilson was off, heading back toward the dining room and the duty manager was not going to stop him.

"Okay Mr Spencer, use that one if you must. I'll be in reception, just press the buzzer."

Wilson ducked into the loo. There was no lock on the door. He fished out the pen and sheet of paper in his jacket pocket and using his left hand scrawled a spidery, 'My name is Vanessa Clarke'. He tore the paper until it was about the size of a cigarette packet and put the pen and scraps back in his pocket. Then he flushed the toilet and stepped back out.

He walked down the empty corridor towards reception and checked over his shoulder. The coast was clear. He ducked into Vanessa's room.

"Hello," she said, as Wilson dropped to one knee and clasped her hand.

"Look, I don't know if you can understand me, or if you can hear what I'm saying, but you're not called Alice. You're called Vanessa, Vanessa Clarke. You have a husband, Michael and a son called Graham. And they love you and miss you and we're going to get you out of here."

Vanessa looked through Wilson as though some distant

familiarity with his words had triggered a memory, a recollection, that was now calling her attention.

"Graham." The two syllables were released as barely a whisper.

"Yes. He's coming to get you. We all are. All the cavalry."

Wilson pulled the scrap of paper and pen from his pocket and placed them both in Vanessa's lap.

In the lap of the gods!

He kissed her on the forehead, squeezed her hand and then strode briskly down the corridor, through reception and out into warm, afternoon sunlight and a fresh, liberating breeze flavoured with seaweed and strong enough to taste.

Waiting for the taxi, Wilson reflected on the building in which Vanessa Clarke had been held captive for seventeen lost years. He thought of Teaps and his dad and all they had missed as a family apart and his emotions gained the upper hand. "Jesus" he exclaimed, trying to stop a lump rising to his throat, "it's like watching *It's a Wonderful Life* on Christmas Day."

An hour later, Wilson was on the train heading south with mission hopefully accomplished. There was just one station change on the journey back, but he hoped a more seismic change was also in motion.

Chapter 38

South

Tuesday 31st October 2017

'DAISY. WE FOUND VANESSA. ONE HUNDRED PER CENT. WE DID IT!'

Wilson didn't want to tempt fate, so he waited until the train had left the station before he sent the text message.

Twenty minutes later he was still waiting for a reply.

He checked the BBC website for any breaking news. There was no startling headline. Wilson was fidgety and experiencing something of an anti-climax after his heroics, like a soldier high on adrenalin after a successful mission. With Daisy's help, he'd pieced together the mystery of Vanessa's disappearance, used dream power to track her to a care home in Scotland and then travelled to Inverness to leave a secret message. But now, as he was stealthily making his way back home, totally incognito, the blue touchpaper seemed to have gone out. Not surprising really, given that he was still only sixty miles south of Inverness. After a further half an hour, the hypnotic, clickety-clack of the moving train began to placate Wilson's understandable impatience and he dozed off.

The ping of a message an hour later woke him with a start. He read the lines from Daisy and replied.

'Yep, mission accomplished. Can't speak on the phone — train packed. On my way back. Inverness is a long way! But enjoying the views. You okay?'

A minute later she texted back:

'All good. Just off to see Grandma at SHH. Well done. Fingers crossed. luv D'

'Text later. W x'

Wilson was pleased to see the word 'luv' in Daisy's message and so signed off his reply with the more expressive and heartfelt 'x' rather than a thumbs-up emoji. A small, yet significant step forward in the evolution of their relationship.

Wilson checked the time. Another six hours to go and a platform change at Edinburgh. His mind started to wander.

No messages from Mum. That's good. No suspicions. Looks like I might just get away with it. With luck I'll be back for quarter past twelve; a reasonable time to get back from a night out with your mates, having watched a local band and actually, the hour's not the issue. I'm eighteen; my folks won't be bothered if I'm home at quarter past three. It's the lie that's the point. You tell lies, you get found out and no one can ever find out about this little trip. When Vanessa Clarke is discovered it could be huge local news, maybe national news and there's no way anyone can connect it with us.

Wilson slouched down in his seat, pulled up his jacket collar and urged the train to continue eating up the miles. The final leg of the journey was completed under the cover of night. Station after station flew by with a sudden phhuuuudddummm and a blur of lights. Wilson had completed a stack of college coursework during the seven hours travelling up to Inverness, but now, with nothing further to read and no countryside to contemplate, he was left gazing at himself in the carriage window. He studied the reflection of the old lady opposite as she nibbled at a homemade cheese sandwich and the grandson, as he played Candy Crush on his phone. The refreshments trolley came and went. Passengers wobbled and lurched in the direction of the loo. Then they wobbled and lurched back again. Unstructured thoughts floated through Wilson's mind. Thoughts about energy and the time trace of a fast-moving train. Would it create more Polaroids? Polaroids closer together? Or thinner Polaroids? As he peered out of the train window, past his own reflected image and into darkness, Wilson's consciousness, his perception of that very moment, slipped anchor and found a new mooring in a different channel of cognition, as if he'd been self-hypnotised. It was a slight but very palpable shift; as though he'd gone through a door never opened before and was now thinking with, or from, a new part of his brain. Could it be that in this 'side room' the location of the data server, the router for a WiFi of dreams could be found? Wilson was about to explore the topography of this new mind scape when quite bizarrely, the image of a river, but a river flowing backwards and away from the sea, commandeered his thoughts. Wilson's psyche no longer seemed to reside within his own body. It had taken wing and was flying above this river, a river flowing in reverse. One Wilson was tracking the current back upstream, over fast, broken water and pools with mirror finish glides, like a duck flying home to roost; while the other Wilson was staring through the window of a train in an altered mental state.

When the river foked into two tributaries, Wilson the aviator chose the path of the smaller and followed its winding journey up a steep valley overgrown with trees. At the head of the valley, as the canopy of green thinned out and the last tree standing surrendered to moorland, the river was already reducing to the size of a narrow stream. Flowing backwards in time; past rocky crags on a moorland fell of heather and bilberry bush, shedding rivulets and runnels along the way; the stream diminished to the merest trickle as it ran between moss covered pebbles to its source as a gurgling spring.

The dimly lit carriage hurtled through the wet night. As the train roared into a tunnel, the sudden thump of displaced air brought Wilson back from his out-of-body experience. The old lady had fallen asleep. The grandson was still playing Candy Crush. The lights in the carriage sparkled on streaks of rain running down the window. Wilson followed the translucent, meniscal path of a single drop as it meandered then rushed, down the glass. For the raindrop, this single, living cell of liquid, this embryo of a river, the journey to the sea was already in motion.

Wilson blinked, in order to end the introspection, but the psychoanalysis was far from over as a new way of seeing things was spelled out in the tiles of a Scrabble game played on a window of tinted glass.

The letters for 'energy field' formed a vertical line. Fifteen tiles spelling 'the market square' then dropped into position with the second 'e' in 'energy' also forming the 'e' in 'market'. More letters fell into place, inter-linking like a self-completing crossword. 'Dream', 'eleven', 'time', 'numerology'; words from the lexicon of The Market Square all found a niche on the board and in so doing, spelled out the epiphany Wilson had been seeking.

The explanation had been there all along - he just hadn't been looking for it from the perspective of the side room.

An explanation for how the dot of meeting a girl in a dream could be joined to the dot of meeting her in real life. On the scrabble board of Wilson's mind, the letters spelling 'The Gateway' finally completed the puzzle and it was those ten letters, eleven with the blank space, that added up to the answer.

Chapter 39

Home

Wednesday 1st November 2017

It was quarter past twelve in the morning when Wilson eased the Vespa into the garage and pulled down the door. A light was shining from the lounge and through the window Wilson could see his father, illuminated by a table lamp, reading a book on the sofa.

"Hey Dad. Everything okay? Can't believe the time, the night just flew by."

The breezy greeting from the hallway rang hollow as he closed the front door; even Wilson could hear the trace of guilt in his voice.

"Yeah, just catching up with some papers and research reports."

Wilson entered the lounge as his father looked up from his book.

"Mum's in bed. Your Auntie Rita's tired her out. How was the concert?"

The trepidation was downgraded to apprehension.

"Oh it was great! One of Hoover's mates plays in the band and we went backstage afterwards. That's why I'm late. Anyway, pretty tired myself, so I'll be off to bed. 'Night Dad."

Wilson was three steps in to making good his escape.

"So what's all this about missing socks then? And a

website that Hoover and his brother have been working on all night?"

Wilson stopped in his tracks.

"Oh that? It's just a crazy idea of Hoover's. You know what he's like. He believes there's some kind of missing sock conspiracy and by building a website with pictures of odd socks – you know, people's missing socks – he can repatriate them."

"Yeah, it's a great idea. Won't work of course. But I like it! I told Hoover I'd upload some photos of my own. I thought Gloria was hiding my socks on purpose to wind me up. I didn't realise it was actually a global phenomenon."

Alex closed his book.

"But son, that's not what I meant. My question wasn't about the website. It was about something far more bizarre than a website for missing socks. It was a question of how Hoover and his brother could be working together, tonight, at Hoover's home, when he was also with you at a concert? Now, a website that can explain things like that – that'd be huge, don't you think?"

Wilson slumped in an armchair. He was angry and tired and didn't want a stupid mind game with his dad, who was gloating because he'd managed to trip him up.

"What did you do Dad? How did you find out?"

"Ah Wilson, you know . . . "

"Dad, shut up. What did you do?"

"Sorry! What did you say Wilson?"

"*I said*, what did you do? Tonight! To find out? I'm not playing games Dad and right now I haven't got the patience for your Sherlock Holmes routine.

"Something important has happened that no one can ever

know about, even you. What did you do?"

Alex paused for a second, sensing from the tone of Wilson's voice, and the look on his face, now was not the moment to be acting like a sitcom dad.

"Nothing son. You're safe. Look. All night your mum's been worried about you. She said she sensed something was happening; that you weren't at the concert. To be honest, I felt exactly the same. So I said I'd call Hoover's dad and without blatantly noseying, ask him if Hoover was with you at a concert."

"Dad. Jesus, you . . . "

"Wait Wilson, wait. I know Hoover's dad. I used to go coarse fishing with him. So I called him up about two hours ago on the pretext of asking him about catching carp in salmon rivers. I'm sure he thought I'd lost the plot. Anyway, I was about to mention the concert when Hoover came to the phone and told me about his sock project. I didn't drop you in it and I told your mum you were in town with him . So you're in the clear and no one knows what you've been up to today – including me!"

"I can't tell you."

"Why not? I told you I'm here to help. Remember our conversation in the canteen?"

"Dad, what does The Market Square look like?"

Alex started wringing his hands. He was about to speak, but stopped. Then he said in a clear and certain voice. "The Market Square can be anything son. Just like a dream."

"I know Dad. But what does it look like? You know what I'm asking. What does it look like?"

Alex paused again and shook his head. He was buying time as his eyes followed the pattern in the carpet.

285

"Why Wilson, why are you asking me that?"

"Because I want to know."

Alex held his breath for a moment that seemed to fill a minute.

"The Market Square has a Clock Tower."

Wilson flipped – tiredness, stale adrenalin, his wired, mental state, they all got the better of him.

"Bloody hell Dad! So you've really been there! You've known about that place for years and never thought to give me help or support? Have you any idea how it messes up your head. You think you can grow out of that as a passing phase? Seriously? I so wanted to bloody well grow out of it. I thought I was becoming a bloody schizophrenic – until I met Daisy."

"Wilson, language! And volume, your mum's in bed."

"I really don't care Dad! And you should have said something a long time ago."

Wilson paused and then addressed his father without any trace of guilt whatsoever.

"You're a coward Dad! You chose a career outside your daft swimming pool metaphor, because you were too scared to dive in and get wet and . . . "

"Wilson, yes, okay, you're right, I can see that, but for good reason. When I met your mum and the twins came along, I decided to stop going to The Market Square because deep down, I felt there was a possibility it could actually be dangerous. I had a family and a wife. I didn't want it to jeopardise my personal life, my children or my home. Then you came along, a master number and I knew there was a chance you'd discover The Market Square. I just hoped you wouldn't find it, or you'd blank it out after a while and stop. But I guess a part of me also wanted you to go there – to explore, to learn, to find out more about the energy."

"Stop for a second." Wilson leant back on the sofa and took a deep breath. "That is so messed-up."

He raked his fingers through his hair as he sought to compose himself for what was about to follow. Wilson leant forward and as his eyes locked onto his fathers, he declared in a calm and even voice.

"I'm going to stop swearing now Dad, because in about ten seconds, I guarantee, it'll be your turn.

"You know how you just said you wanted me to explore, to find out more about the power of The Market Square? Well I did. I conducted a little experiment, which is why I was late home. But the good thing is, the experiment was a big success.

"Daisy and I did a bit of detective work and we discovered something quite incredible. So I went all the way up to Scotland today, to visit a care home, in a very nice place called South Kessock. It's near Inverness, and it's where I found a lady by the name of Alice. She'd been there for seventeen years without a single visitor. But she's not really called Alice, because, believe it or not, she's actually called Vanessa. Vanessa Clarke. In other words, Teaps's mum!"

There was complete and utter silence as the full meaning of Wilson's confession registered. Alex's response was understandable, all things considered.

"Son, have you been taking drugs?"

"No Dad. It really was, I mean, is, Teaps's mum. Something happened to her when she was in London, I think it might have been a stroke. She lost her memory and travelled all the way to Inverness, where her bag was stolen, and then nobody could identify her because she'd changed her hair and could only mumble a few words in Italian."

"But I thought she was dead or she'd absconded to France . . ."

"I know Dad, but that's not true. She was in a care home in Scotland all along, for all those years And that's where I've been today. To find Teaps's mum. Who is so definitely alive!"

Wilson was right, Alex did swear a couple of times at the end of that last sentence.

Chapter 40

Talking into the night

Wednesday 1st November 2017

Alex made two mugs of coffee and returned to the lounge for round two of revelations.

"Bear with me Dad, this story's going to jump about a bit and I'm still not sure I've got everything clear in my own head."

Wilson continued.

"You know I can speak different languages right, French for example. And if there was a helicopter parked outside I'd be able to fly you up to visit Vanessa."

Alex smiled at the notion.

"So Dad, The Market Square is where you access all this information, but it's also a chicane, where other forms of energy converge. Now, put those facts to one side and consider Morphic Fields. Morphic Fields are thought to be based on a memory of actions that animals access like a WiFi of nature."

Alex nodded.

"So a baby spider logs in to the 'WiFi of nature' to access the instructions to build a web left by billions of other spiders. Those instructions must be a form of energy, because they don't get destroyed. They're always out there. Like my internet WiFi, which is also energy?"

"It's a microwave actually, son. But yes, it's made of photons, which are essentially small bundles of energy."

"Okay Dad, so if our internet WiFi is an energy field, let's assume the WiFi of nature is also a type of energy field."

"Yes, I'll go with that. If it exists, of course, but . . . "

"Dad. Dad, just give me two minutes and I'm done. A few weeks ago you told me about energy fields that were waiting to be discovered. Well I think a Morphic Field and a dream energy field could be two of those. And when we dream, all that dream energy somehow flows into The Market Square. My laptop takes the energy in a WiFi signal and builds a web page. In The Market Square, I take the energy from dreams to learn to play the guitar. From all the people who have ever played a guitar in their dreams, or from the dreams of people who can play the guitar, I can't say. But what I do know is that they leave a trace. I can access the data, this knowledge, I can feel it, that's our special gift – mine and Daisy's and yours I guess. But there's even more to it. It can take six months to get your head round a new language, but I can reach the same level after just six nights in The Market Square. And this is the thing, this came to me on the train today. Learning a language involves time. And time, this very moment, me and you drinking coffee, leaves a trace, a little package of energy on a Polaroid snapshot of right now. And a million, billion nows altogether, make the past. And all those traces, everyone's trace, the energy of time also runs through The Market Square."

Wilson paused for breath as he prepared to make the final point.

"Are you still with me?"

"I'm with you so far son. Go on."

"In The Market Square, all those Polaroids can be pushed even closer together, like compressed data, like the zip files on my laptop. So you can experience, or absorb, more of the past in a much shorter time. In The Market Square, you can access the energy of past dreams to find piano lessons. And if you combine that with a time energy field, you can zip-up weeks of tuition and store it in a file that I can download in minutes. That's what we did, to find Vanessa."

Wilson knew his father was keeping pace. He was nodding to acknowledge a degree of understanding and the recognition of a truth both unfathomable yet real in the words he was hearing.

"Daisy logged in to the WiFi of dreams, the energy field, to pull Vanessa into The Market Square; a foot in one camp so to speak. Then once Vanessa was there, she accessed the time energy field, straddled the two and brought up all the traces of her life. When we opened the zip file, we did a search going back seventeen years and saw everything that happened on the day she disappeared."

It took a moment for Alex to reply.

"Wilson. That, that is just the most incredible thing I've ever heard – anyone has ever heard. If what you're saying is true . . . I don't have the words. It's incredible. We believe in the space-time particle and we're getting close with the Higgs Boson, but this could be the most significant scientific postulation of all time. Every physics book, every nature book, all the major religious texts, the Bible, the Koran, would all have to be rewritten!"

"Funny you should say that Dad. You see, rescuing Vanessa was easy, we used dream energy to find her and then time energy to look through her trace, then a trip to Inverness. But something makes it more complicated, mind-blowing, as you'd say, because I think there's another type of energy."

"I'm mind-blown enough son."

"Dad, here's a question: how did I know Vanessa wasn't dead?"

"You mean, how did you know she was still alive?"

"Yeah, how did I know she was still alive?"

"A lucky guess, a hunch."

"No Dad, it wasn't a guess. How did I know Vanessa Clarke was still alive even before Daisy and I brought her to The Market Square?"

Alex was struggling to follow the logic.

"I've no idea son."

"Someone told me, that's how. I don't know who these characters are, but they told me about another type of energy. The energy of the human spirit. And they told me in a dream, in a place called The Gateway, that Vanessa's spirit had not been extinguished because there was no gold bangle and I'd find her in The Market Square. Big Mac, one of these characters who works for The Powers That Be, told me that Teaps's mum was still alive. And while we're on the subject I think The Market Square is connected in some way with Ward 3B of Stockport Infirmary and I know exactly how déjà vu comes about, because Short Cake, who also works for The Powers That Be told me."

Alex Armitage said absolutely nothing, then rose to his feet and went directly to bed. Unsteady on his feet, both hands held the bannister as he climbed the stairs. One of the effects of breathing in smoke and having your mind-blown.

Chapter 41

Any news?

Wednesday 1st November 2017

The first thing Wilson did when he woke the next morning was check BBC North West on his phone. There was no story about Vanessa Clarke. He checked BBC Scotland. The same.

A text message arrived from Daisy.

'Hi W. Sorry I went silent on you last night. Major issues with Grandma, but she's in SHH, comfortable. Going to see her again later. Any news? D x'

'No, nothing yet. Thinking maybe a dozy cleaner binned the paper. Please God, no. Don't think they'll let Frank Spencer back in that place. Call you later. W x'

'Frank Spencer?'

'From some old comedy programme Dad watches. His name just popped into my head. I'll explain later.'

Teaps and Hoover were eating cheese toasties as Wilson crossed the college canteen to join them. All appeared to be normal.

"How's it going, boys?" Wilson asked, his eyes searching Teaps's face for a sign of elation.

"Fair to middling," said Hoover, through a mouthful of hot cheese, "we've got six hundred socks now."

That really wasn't the elation Wilson had been hoping for.

"Any matches?"

"No. We had a false alarm from Ecuador though. Same colour, same pattern, but wrong size. The guy in Cardiff was an eight and the guy in Ecuador was a twelve. Not even close."

"How are you Teaps? All okay?"

"For now, yeah. Dad was alright when I left him, nursing a hangover, but let's see what this afternoon brings. And I've got no phone at the moment; Spinner's nose broke it."

"How was the Prince's Trust thing?" Hoover asked.

"What Prince's Trust thing?"

"Yesterday? Town Hall, your mum, charity, day away from college?"

"What? Oh that. Err, yeah, I met the Prince."

"Riiiiiightttt, yeah, as if" said Hoover.

"No way" said Teaps.

"Way" said Wilson.

"Bollocks" said Hoover.

A bell rang to signal the next period of classes and herds of students, saddled with bags and backpacks, filed out of the canteen and trailed across the recreation square.

"Like wildebeest crossing the Serengeti" said Hoover, who was heading to the same part of the college as Wilson.

Teaps's IT room was in a different building and Wilson watched him walk away, joking and chatting up one of his ex-girlfriends. Perhaps the dozy cleaner *had* binned the slip of paper after all.

Nobody told Wilson that half an hour into his Computing class, Teaps was passed a note asking him to report urgently to the Principal's office; but when Wilson arrived home later that afternoon, he found out. The seismic change had arrived. Magnitude 11 on the Richter Scale.

Gloria came rushing into the hallway as Wilson was

halfway out of his jacket, grabbed his arm and dragged him into the lounge. The TV was on.

"Isn't it just the most incredible thing Wilson, the most incredible, unbelievable thing."

His mum was weeping into a damp lace hanky.

Wilson removed the other half of his jacket and threw it on the sofa.

"It's a miracle Wilson, that's the only word to describe it. A miracle for that blessed boy and his poor father."

Wilson's mum was sobbing uncontrollably.

The image on the TV was of a reporter standing outside a red-brick building, the tail fin of a police helicopter was jutting into the shot. Directly behind the reporter stood a sign that read: 'The South Kessock Care Home'.

Wilson sat down on the sofa. His mum joined him, still sobbing, and put her hand on his knee. They listened to the reporter.

"I'm standing here in South Kessock, a quiet, peaceful suburb just a few minutes from the centre of Inverness in the north of Scotland. You can forget biblical stories of turning water into wine, because yesterday, in the building behind me, a real miracle occurred, witnessed by the staff of the South Kessock Care Home."

The camera then cut to a photo of Vanessa from around the time of her wedding. The reporter continued as a voiceover.

"One morning, seventeen years ago, Vanessa Clarke, a successful businesswoman, left the family home in Stockport to attend a business meeting in London and seemingly walked out of the lives of her husband and one-year-old son forever..."

Wilson's mum didn't know whether to be happy or sad, to laugh or cry, and in the space of a minute had sampled all four.

"... around the same time, this lady, known only as Alice."

The screen switched to a grainy picture of care home residents enjoying Christmas dinner. The face of a smiling Alice was circled in red.

"... was found sitting in a park in Inverness, cold, alone, with no knowledge of who she was or where she was. That is, until late yesterday afternoon when a nurse made an incredible discovery."

Cut to the interview recorded earlier with the nurse.

"Well, I was taking Alice her afternoon cup of tea. She always has it in her room. She's such a lovely lady; never any trouble. So, I placed the cup on her bedside table and I was just about to leave when she pulled at my skirt and I turned around, and ... "

The nurse hesitated for a moment and wiped a tear from her eye.

"Yes ... and she pulled my skirt ever so gently."

She paused again but needed the back of both hands to wipe away the tears this time. Wilson's mum was listening intently and copying her actions.

"And then I looked down, and she was, like, looking up at me and, you know, she was crying ..."

The nurse was really struggling to contain her emotions.

"And then she slowly handed me a scrap of paper and on the paper she'd written, 'My name is Vanessa Clarke'. So I ran and grabbed the duty supervisor and then ... and then ... Sorry, I have to stop, it was a miracle."

Now Wilson couldn't stop *his* eyes watering.

The screen switched back to the reporter who was now standing with two men. One wore a suit and the other was a policeman.

"I'm joined here now by Vincent Machonachie, company operations director for the South Kessock Care Home and Sergeant Derek Jordan, the officer with the North Caledonia Constabulary who took the call yesterday afternoon.

"Gentlemen, thank you for joining me on this truly amazing day. We've just heard from the nurse who found the note, so Vincent, can you tell us what happened next?"

"Well, it started with a call from Celia Green sometime around 5 p.m. yesterday afternoon. Celia told me there'd been an incident and they weren't sure how to deal with it. She wouldn't say anything over the phone, so of course I came down immediately. At first I thought it was all a prank. But when Celia took me to her office and showed me the story on the internet about Vanessa Clarke, and a photo, we realised *that* person was also *our* Alice. The facial similarity, even with the passage of time, was striking – plus, how else would Alice know about Vanessa Clarke? We didn't even know she could write."

"So what happened then?"

"I called the police and spoke to Sergeant Jordan."

"Sergeant Jordan, good afternoon. Talk us through what happened next."

"Well to be honest, when I got the call, the message was like gobbledygook. I thought Vincent had been on the whisky. So I rushed down here and they told me about the discovery. Then I got on to Scotland Yard, who sent us the incident and missing person files, and for the next few hours we tried to make sense of everything, and we're still doing that."

"I understand that Vanessa's husband Michael and son Graham are here right now?"

"Aye. We had trouble tracking them down, but earlier

today, a police helicopter picked them up and brought them straight here."

"What did they say? Who broke the news to them?"

"It was funny actually. My colleagues in Greater Manchester told me the lad thought they'd called to arrest him. Anyhow, they told Graham and his father there'd been a sudden development in the search for Vanessa and asked for help with enquiries. We have to be careful though. While it seems likely that Alice and Vanessa are one and the same person, we won't be a hundred per cent sure until we get the DNA test results back."

A second policeman then came into view and whispered something in Sergeant Jordan's ear. Sergeant Jordan smiled and cleared his throat.

"Err, I've just been told by my colleague that Alice's DNA was a one hundred per cent match with the boy's. So we can now say with certainty that Alice is Vanessa Clarke."

Cheering could be heard in the background. The camera scanned the perimeter of the care home. There was a battalion of photographers, TV cameras, mobile broadcasting units and a sizeable group of locals of all ages waving at the cameras.

"Bloody hell," said Wilson. "I never thought all this would happen."

"Me neither. Though I did pray for it, I really did," said Gloria, not fully appreciating Wilson's point.

The reporter had his finger on his earpiece.

"I'm being told that the father and son – that is, Michael and Graham – are coming out in a second to give a brief interview in advance of a full statement later."

The broadcast editor switched to a camera focused on the front entrance of the care home. The door was pushed open by a policeman as Teaps, his dad and Celia Green emerged to face TV cameras and journalists shouting questions.

Wilson could see from the puffy eyes that Teaps had been crying.

"I'd just like to read this prepared statement, if I may," said Celia.

"The staff and management of South Kessock Care Home and myself, would personally like to say . . . "

A reporter put his microphone in front of Teaps, who had his arm round his dad's shoulders and a camera instantly zoomed in. Celia Green was jostled to one side.

"Mr Clarke, tell us about the emotions you're feeling right now. Can you put them into words?"

Michael was standing tall and straight with his shoulders back and at first Wilson didn't recognise the person he'd seen cowering at the feet of Blamire.

"All I can say is that my son and I never doubted that Vanessa would come back. She loved Graham with all her heart and would never have left him. I told everyone that at the time and I knew we'd find her one day. We never, ever, gave up hope."

"Is there a chance we'll get to see her?"

"No, I don't think you'll ever see her. When Graham and I take her home, we won't be letting her out of our sight again. She's back for good this time."

Then Michael had to stop because he was too emotional to speak so the reporter turned to his son.

"Graham, how does it feel to have your mum back?"

"It's just incredible. I was only a baby when she disappeared so I don't really remember her. But of course, I missed not having a mum, like my friends. And I always felt she was still alive, just like my dad said. He never once stopped willing her to come back to us, praying for it. The pain almost ruined his life, but I think we'll be just great now and that's the main thing."

Then Teaps hugged his dad and someone ushered them back inside the home and the door closed.

"So there we have it, a modern-day miracle. A missing mum back in the arms of her loving family after being lost for seventeen years. Questions will be asked as to why the tragic stories of the two missing women, Alice and Vanessa, were never pieced together, and no doubt there will be a full inquiry. But for now, as night draws in on the beautiful Beauly Firth, this is Felix Armstrong for BBC Scotland saying a miraculous good evening from the South Kessock Care Home."

"In other news now . . ."

Wilson switched the TV off. He sensed a moment for quiet reflection and the curative powers of a cup of tea were needed. Gloria was still staring at the blank TV screen dabbing her eyes.

"You were back late last night love. Your dad and I had a funny feeling about you, like something was wrong."

"Nah, the gig just went on a bit. And then I got chatting to Dad for an hour or so."

"I know. I don't think he slept well last night. Then he was up and off for the early train. He'll be shattered. Do you think he's heard about Graham?"

"Oh I'm pretty sure he will have Mum. Certain in fact. I'll go and make you a cuppa. I think you might be suffering from shock. I know I am."

"Think of it Wilson. That poor woman, trapped in that place for seventeen years, almost like a hostage. Why didn't she say something, tell someone?"

"I don't know Mum. I've no idea."

"It's a scandal. She never got to see her baby grow up."

As Wilson waited for the kettle to boil, four hundred miles away, more steam was rising. Having been snubbed on national TV, Celia Green was thinking through the previous day's events. She was putting one and one together and it was adding up to an eleven by the name of Frank Spencer. It was too much of a coincidence that a resident, who had never communicated in any way and with no visitors for seventeen years, would suddenly write a help note on the same day she'd been the focus of attention for a suspicious young lad.

Celia picked up the phone and dialled Sergeant Jordan.

Chapter 42

The hiccups

Thursday 2nd November 2017

That night, and into the morning, Wilson and Daisy celebrated the incredible, miraculous result of their detective work.

The Market Square was wearing dancing shoes and resplendent in the guise of the magnificent ballroom at the top of Blackpool Tower. Cobbles had been replaced with a sprung floor of mahogany, oak and walnut. A domed ceiling, decorated with finely detailed frescoes and faux-neoclassical plaster relief, arched over the entire square. The candle light from three, magnificent crystal chandeliers sparkled and bounced off a slowly turning mirrorball like facets on a diamond. The shops and cottages on the perimeter of The Market Square had all been remodelled to feature at least one theatre-style box jutting out over the ballroom floor at circle level like a private balcony. Each box held an audience of five or six people all attired in splendid Edwardian costume. Music, which rolled and cascaded around the entire Market Square like the soundtrack to a carousel ride, came from the ornately decorated Wurlitzer pipe organ blocking a view of the Clock Tower.

"*Strictly's* in town," said Daisy as Wilson arrived to join her.

The floor was a twirling, whirling, quadrangle of vibrant colour and interlacing choreography. For the ladies, the dress code included ball gowns in every shade of satin and silk with feathered hats and opera gloves. For men, black tie and tails, handlebar moustaches and hair slicked back with pomade was de rigueur. A rotund, pompous-looking chap with a flushed, red face and bushy whiskers strode over and with a polite bow, enquired as to "the possibility of mademoiselle honouring me with the pleasure of the next waltz."

Daisy took the man's pudgy, pink hand and curtseyed, which Wilson thought was completely over-the-top. She was wearing a voluminous pink hoop skirt, long white gloves, black Doc Martens and her hair was in finely coiled ringlets. Daisy pulled her tongue out and winked at Wilson as she twirled across the floor.

Somebody tapped Wilson on the shoulder and he turned, only to be confronted by a lady standing at least a foot taller than himself. Her gown was made from blue silk with a white lace trim around the edges. The protruding bustle created the impression of a small child hiding beneath her underskirts. She had the waist of an egg timer and the bodice of her dress, pulled-in tight like a corset, was tailored with all kinds of fancy trimming and embroidery. A monocle was wedged in one eye and her hair had been braided and then pinned to form an elaborate stack, from which some of the braids were tumbling free. She reminded Wilson of a praying mantis or, more accurately, a gorgon.

"You really can't just stand there ogling" said the Medusa with a haughty, plummy accent, "it's not polite."

She took Wilson's arm and with surprising force, dragged him onto the dance floor. The button-fronted breeches Wilson was wearing were far too tight and gave him a wedgie. The frock coat was too big and the cravat pinched his neck.

Nevertheless, over the course of the next hour, under the expert tutelage of Medusa, Wilson managed to master the timing and footwork for the waltz, the samba, the paso doble and the tango.

"She was good fun, in a matronly sort of way" he said to Daisy as they sat drinking Champagne in a private box for two. They were looking down upon the graceful choreography of what Daisy identified as 'the foxtrot'.

"I feel like the Queen," she said, as bubbles tickled and fizzed somewhere inside her nose. She raised her Champagne flute and they toasted the liberation of Vanessa Clarke.

"Do you think we'll have hangovers tomorrow?"

Wilson started laughing.

"You know what Daisy? I never considered that. It's a great thought though. However much we celebrate, we'll still be completely sober when we wake up in the morning. What an excellent place this Market Square is."

"Another bottle then my dear?" Wilson asked playfully and adjusted his cravat.

"For sure . . . err, I mean yes, my dear Lord Armitage, that would be truly delightful" said Daisy, giggling and hiccuping as Wilson departed to find the waiter in charge of their Royal Box.

"But not a bottle Wilson" she called after him, "get one of those big magnum thingies and make sure it's the most expensive. In fact, get two!"

Chapter 43

Smile, you're on Sky News

Thursday 2nd November 2017

Wilson woke early to the ping of a message from Daisy.

'Wilson, have you seen it? The news? Teaps is everywhere. The front page of the papers, on breakfast TV, he's all over social media. He's gone viral!!'

Wilson sat up in bed, clicked a 'news' app on his phone and waited.

The first chunk of data delivered a photo of Teaps and his dad. They were smiling with their arms around each other's shoulders outside the South Kessock Care Home.

Then came the headline: 'Husband and Son Reunited with Missing Mum After 17 Years'.

Wilson knew the story of course, but the online report carried much more detail than the TV broadcast the previous evening. There were links to the old coverage about Vanessa going missing in London and the subsequent police search. One report from a local paper in Inverness talked about a woman who had 'probably been abandoned by one of the crofting families on the Outer Hebrides'. A policeman from Inverness had been interviewed that morning and was quoted as saying, 'we made enquiries at the time, but in the absence of any evidence or other possible line of enquiry, the investigation was eventually dropped'.

When asked if it was true, as suggested by a source

inside the local police, 'that the case was given a low priority because the woman had impaired mental faculties', he said there would be a full internal investigation. The statement was accompanied by a photo and from his facial expression, it appeared that Assistant Chief Constable Simon Montague was not chuffed to find himself in the spotlight for all the wrong reasons. There was no mention of the current whereabouts of Teaps and his parents, but Wilson was certain they wouldn't be back in their dingy flat opposite the pub. He checked a few other media sites, Twitter was all of a flutter with the news.

As Wilson ate breakfast, his mum was in the lounge watching *Good Morning* on TV. The presenters were interviewing a vicar from Romiley, who was outlining the care and time for healing that Mrs Clarke and her family would need over the coming months and years.

Gloria was still sobbing and simply said, "goodbye son" as he left for college.

Wilson had a sense of foreboding about the day ahead; the discovery of Vanessa had been meticulously planned, but the aftermath was completely out of his control. There was a major plus point to be thankful for though, because even after downing two magnums of Moët with Daisy in The Market Square, he'd woken with a perfectly clear head.

Twenty minutes later, Wilson eased on the brake of the Vespa and indicated to turn left into the college car park. A security guard in a hi-vis orange jacket barred his entry through the gates and informed Wilson that the car park was closed for the day and he would have to find a space further down the road. Wilson drove past the college grounds and glanced through the railings. The aftermath had arrived. The car park was rammed full with outside broadcast vans, reporters and cameramen. After about three hundred yards, he managed to find a gap for the Vespa, then he walked back to the gates, showed his student pass to the hi-vis man and entered the college grounds.

Sky News, BBC, ITV, Channel 4 and French and German TV broadcast vans, with logos on the sides and aerials on the roof, filled every bay in the car park. A Japanese TV vehicle was parked with two wheels on the steps leading to the college's main entrance, in front of which, Mr Proctor, Teaps's personal tutor, and Miss Patel, an English teacher, were being interviewed.

Wilson skirted around the back of the melee and made for the common room, but he was confronted by another pack of eager reporters grilling anyone and everyone, on the subject of Graham Clarke.

"Did he ever mention his mum or talk about her?"

"How did he get the nickname Teaps?"

"Woz 'ee ever down or, 'ow you say, melancholeee?"

"Who are his best friends here at the college?"

Wilson retreated deeper into the hood of his parka on hearing the last question and searched for a different route to the sanctuary of the common room. His phone vibrated on silent and he tapped the screen. It was the unknown number from the other night.

Teaps's dad. It's Teaps!

Wilson turned from the scrum and headed for the empty tennis courts on the periphery of the college grounds and well out of earshot. He answered the phone on the move.

"Hi, it's me, Wilson."

"I know Wilson. I've just called you."

"Mate, it's incredible! Just unbelievable! How are you?

307

Your mum, your dad? The cameras are all over the college. You're on TV. You're on TV. You're famous man. My mum's not stopped crying since she heard."

"I know. It's a miracle."

From the hushed tone of his voice, Wilson suspected that Teaps was trying to speak without being overheard.

"I haven't slept since I . . . Awww, man, I still can't get over it. I was calling to let you know everything's okay."

"Thanks pal. Wasn't worried, obviously. But I was waiting to hear from you. So how is your mum? And your dad? What did you think when you saw her in that room? Will she get her memory back? Does she remember you? Where are you now?"

"I can't really speak. We're at a private hospital, like a rehabilitation place, somewhere near Chester. Dad's become a changed man, virtually overnight, he really has. Don't tell anyone where we are though, even Hoover – especially Hoover. The world has gone crazy mate. An agent from Ok magazine wants an exclusive on the story and we've to keep everything secret. But the main thing is, my mum's here. She's back after all these years. I can't believe it. Look, I gotta go. I'll text you later when I've got more time."

The call over, Wilson and Teaps picked up where they'd left off.

For Teaps, that was sitting in a private room with his dad, watching his mum sleeping. As he did so, it struck him as odd that Wilson knew his mum had been in a room, and that she had memory loss. How did *he* know? A doctor had only just told them about that!

"We can see from the scans that some years ago Mrs Clarke suffered a small but severe stroke that damaged cerebral connections to her memory. Probably around the

308

time she went missing in London. We don't believe her memory has been wiped clean as such, because the damage was limited to the neural networks that govern retrieval, rather than memory storage itself. With cognitive therapy at the time, those connections might have been restored, but in my professional opinion that's not likely to be possible after all these years."

Wilson meanwhile, had headed back to the common room where he was cornered by a reporter after being pointed out by a girlfriend of Teaps.

"Jan Smith, Sky News. I understand you're Graham Clarke's best friend. What do you think of the news?"

A microphone was thrust in front of Wilson's face and the intrusive lens of a camera followed.

"It's, err, it's just sensational. The best news ever."

"Did Graham ever think he would see his mother again?"

"Err, I dunno really. We spoke about her sometimes. I know his dad never stopped believing that she'd come back. He knew she hadn't run away or anything like that."

"Where is Graham now?"

"I don't know. He couldn't tell me."

"He couldn't tell you? So you've spoken to him then?"

"Yeah, really briefly, but he, err . . . I don't know where he is."

"Is it true that Ok magazine have offered a million pounds for an exclusive?"

"I can't say. I'm just so happy his mum's back. I gotta go. Thanks."

Wilson pushed the microphone and camera away and forced his way through the doors of the common room – where he then caught sight of himself pushing the microphone and camera away. He was following his own footsteps via a TV mounted on the wall.

"It's like déjà vu" shouted Hoover, waving him over.

Hoover was sitting with six or seven others watching the story unfold on TV. Spinner was with them; his arm was cradled in a sling and one side of his face was a swatch book of purple and yellow bruising.

"Thought you were in hospital Spinner?"

"Discharged myself didn't I, when I heard about the commotion and the good news."

"You're the news mate, and it's all bad news" said Wilson.

Hoover's arm reached out like that of an orangutan to keep Spinner in his seat.

"Leave it out pal" he said glaring with intent. "In fact, don't know why you're here with us anyway. Go and sit over there, in the naughty boys' corner. Go on, clear off."

Spinner got up and trudged away.

"What a low life" said Hoover.

Wilson sat on the vacated chair and watched the images on TV. He couldn't hear the voice-over for all the din in the common room. The screen was showing a photo of a happy Mr and Mrs Clarke on their wedding day, but the caption underneath was referring to an internal investigation within the North Caledonia Constabulary.

"I'd have said there was more chance of one of your socks turning up than this happening" said Wilson.

"Wilson, do you want to go and join Spinner over there in the naughty boys' corner . . . oh, what the hell does he want now?"

Spinner had hobbled back over to thrust a mobile phone into Wilson's hand.

"It's Blamire. He wants a word."

Wilson put a finger in one ear and pressed the phone to the other.

"Hello?"

"Hey, Winston, how are you my friend? It's me, Blamire? The good-lookin' fella, the landlord for your friend Teaps and his muppet of a dad. We had a discussion in the flat the other morning."

"I know who you are."

"Well, I was just thinking, about all of this bein' a bit of a turn-up for the books. You see, there I was at home last night, readin' the kids a bedtime story, when me missus shouts me to come and see what's happening on TV. Can you believe it, there was the muppet and son, complete with a mum. All happy families again."

"Listen Blamire, can you get to the point?"

"So when I heard this morning, that some gossip mag' me wife reads is gonna fork out a million quid for the exclusive story, it got me thinking! So I alerted my pet hyena and told him to get out of his sick-bed and back to school, cos he could learn how to make a bit of bunce."

Wilson turned to Spinner.

"And then, a couple of minutes ago, when you let slip about your chat with our Mr Teaps, I thought maybe you could pass him a personal message about interest on the interest. Like my little phrase Winston? Interest, as in, on top of the five grand he owes me, and interest, as in, he'll be a rich lad in the next couple of weeks from all the stories in the papers. So tell him the interest on the interest now makes what he owes me eight grand, and he's got two weeks – or his mum might go missing for another seventeen years. I'll be in touch."

311

Wilson stood up with a purpose and headed over to Spinner to hand the phone back. As Spinner took it, Wilson grabbed his thumb and bent the knuckle down into the palm. Spinner winced in pain but didn't scream out. Wilson wasn't applying that much pressure, just enough to let Spinner know he was being serious and to shut up and listen.

"Spinner, whatever Teaps did to you the other day, you deserved, because you're a slimy little rat."

Wilson exerted a bit more pressure and Spinner felt it.

"If I ever see you in this common room again, you won't be getting out of hospital quite so quickly the next time. You'll have a permanent bed somewhere, a bit like Teaps's mum — you know, Teaps, your friend? Tell Blamire not to use his little dog to deliver his messages anymore, get him to call me himself. You've got my number pusher-man."

Wilson gave the thumb a final squeeze.

As Spinner squealed and everyone in the common room turned to the source of the distress, Wilson was heading back to Hoover.

"What was that all about?"

"Nothing. Just giving Spinner a message to pass on to someone."

A different directive then came over the college tannoy system.

"As a result of the current media interest in the college and the major disturbance to our schedules, there will be no further classes. The business of education will resume as normal tomorrow."

For the next hour, Wilson and company sat around drinking coffee, watching the news, laughing at Wilson's crap TV interview technique and generally speculating on what the future held for Teaps. They didn't see Spinner slouch off, but Blamire got the message. Wilson's phone beeped with a text.

'Winston. Tough guy. Will be in touch. Still eight grand. Don't care where it comes from. Blamire.'

Then his phone beeped again. Wilson was sufficiently wound up to fight fire with even more fire, but the text message was from Daisy.

'W, going to Stockport this afternoon to see Grandma. Want to come and meet her? Don't worry, will only be me. No parents etc. D'

Wilson had a free afternoon and he was definitely interested in meeting Daisy's grandma, she knew about The Market Square. Plus, there was another reason he wanted to go to Ward 3B.

'Yeah, for sure. What time?'

'Three thirty at the main reception.'

'Okay.'

Then Wilson had second thoughts.

'No, meet at the entrance to the main car park, in front of the new bit of the hospital. By the information signs.'

'Err. Okay. D X'

Chapter 44

Ward 3B

Wilson arrived at the hospital car park ten minutes early and whiled away time reading the information boards. One sign was for the purpose of navigating the hospital grounds and directed visitors to Reception, X-ray, Outpatients and so on. The other carried details of the NHS Foundation Trust and the history of the site.

The hospital consisted of an expansive, state of the art, new build structure, fabricated with panels in calming pastel shades and a dilapidated red-brick building, from the Victorian era, that had to be retained because of its Grade I listing. The facade of the old section fronted the A6 and was dominated by a huge, mullioned window set between two ornately carved sandstone columns. It was a window Wilson knew only too well!

The new building housed the core of the hospital's services. The old building, propped up with scaffolding in keeping with its elderly status, provided palliative care for the terminally ill. Daisy's grandma had a bed in Ward 3B, a ward Wilson suspected was home to certain energy fields and the likely source of his déjà vu headaches.

Daisy arrived with a wave and a smile that carried both affection and diffidence.

"Thanks for coming Wilson."

"No, I wanted to come, I wanted to meet your grandma."

"Well she's not really with us anymore. They've stopped feeding her and it seems cruel, but there's no quality of life. I wanted you to meet Gran, before she leaves us. She's called Gwendolyn. Mum's not here, she's gone home to shower and change."

They walked to the building hand in hand.

"Have you seen Teaps?"

"No, but I spoke to him briefly. He's with his mum at a private hospital near Chester. He didn't say where exactly, but I've never heard him sound so happy or so upbeat."

"The story's never been off the news. Even Mum was going on about it. I didn't tell her Teaps was your best friend."

"To be honest, I just want it to blow over now. Not for Teaps or his dad, I meant it's strange; although we've done this incredibly good thing, made a miracle happen like they say on TV, it actually freaks me out."

Wilson stopped and turned to Daisy.

"Do you think we've been playing God? We made something happen that maybe, wasn't supposed to. We held Vanessa's future in our hands and decided what happens next. All the repercussions that follow, like college closing for the day, are a result of our actions."

"Yeah Wilson, I've been thinking that as well. But then I thought it could also be God who showed us The Market Square in the first place, and how to look back in time to find Vanessa. Maybe this was always meant to happen and we had no say in it.

"I don't know much about philosophical stuff, you know, free will and fate and all that, but I know I'd do it again. And if I was in the same situation as Teaps, I'd want someone to do the same for me, to find my missing mum. I wouldn't worry about playing God, I'd just want Mum back."

"Yeah, I know Daisy, it's great that we rescued her, but what if we cause a chain of new events that are so bad, it turns out she was better off, everyone was better off, when she was in South Kessock. Does that make sense?"

"Wilson, I get your concerns, I really do, but right now we're here to see Grandma, so can we talk about this later."

Daisy wrapped both arms round one of Wilson's as they carried on to the hospital entrance.

"Wilson you're a good person. That's all you need to know."

They crossed the reception area and entered a long, wide, corridor. Smaller corridors led off at intervals, to Maternity Ward 2, Coronary 1 and Neonatal 2. Wilson and Daisy continued walking until they eventually reached the structural scar where the concert block and steelwork of the new hospital was grafted to the red-brick of the old one. They made a ninety-degree turn beneath a sign pointing to Ward 3B and Wilson immediately felt the growing pressure of a vice clamping down on his temples. As he took the next few steps, a déjà vu sensation on a repeat play loop arrived. Waves of pain crashed one after the other with increasing fury and the pounding in his head felt like something trying to punch a way out of his skull. After taking another three steps, Wilson's legs gave way and he collapsed on the floor throwing up the foul soup of a half-digested breakfast in the process.

"You've probably picked up the stomach bug that was sweeping the town last week. Your temperature and blood pressure are good. Lots of water and you'll be fine" said a doctor, having checked Wilson over. Wilson and Daisy were no longer in sight of Ward 3B. They were sitting in an empty waiting room just off the main corridor.

"Daisy" said Wilson, wiping his mouth with a tissue and looking green around the gills, "I have to tell you something."

"That wasn't a stomach bug was it?"

"No it wasn't. It was caused by this place."

Wilson paused to get his thoughts in order and took a sip of water from a plastic cup.

"Daisy, I don't think it's a random coincidence that you and I were born here, my dad, and possibly your grandma too. I also don't think it's by chance our birth dates align, we're all a number eleven and we all visit The Market Square. My dad described the Clock Tower; he's definitely been there."

Wilson started to laugh at how ridiculous he was sounding.

"For years I've been coming past this hospital and even as a little kid, in the back seat of Dad's car, I'd always get a fleeting sensation of déjà vu. An impression I'd been here before. Recently, these feelings have become more painful, like the most powerful déjà vu mixed with a migraine but ten times stronger. That's what happened just then, when we turned the corner to Ward 3B and I think I know why."

"Go on" said Daisy, anxious to hear Wilson out before they were disturbed.

"The explanation came to me on the train the other night, in a sort of visual analogy. Years ago, when I was at junior school, we went to Saddleworth Moor with a teacher. It was raining and were all wearing these yellow cagoules." Wilson smiled and shook his head at the memory. "Anyway, the teacher showed us how to make these little paper boats and we followed them down this trickle of water running between pebbles. The boats soon became waterlogged and turned to pulp, but we carried on following the trickle as it merged with other trickles and soon became a small stream. The stream merged into other streams and within a mile or so it had grown into a small beck and eventually we came to a road, where all this gushing water was directed into a concrete tunnel and released on the other side to prevent a driving hazard.

"I think that when we dream, all the dream energy merges and flows together, like a beck. Every moment in time, every trace we leave behind, also combine to make another beck. And in some places, they meet. So there's this gushing flow of energy that needs to be channelled through a pipe, to avoid flooding. I think that tunnel is in the corridor outside 3B.

"I also believe, to end the analogy, that we can put a foot in a beck of dream energy and feel people's dreams flow by. At the same time, we can put the other foot in a beck of time energy and straddle both. We combine dreams with the time traces of people's lives, their past and that's how we found Vanessa. Somehow, in that corridor, the two becks merge together and the energy flow is so strong and deep it makes me feel ill. I don't know why it didn't affect you in the same way though."

Wilson threw his head back and emptied the plastic cup.

"Wow" said Daisy, feeling the need to at least say something.

"You need to be my wading stick."

"Your wading stick, what the hell is that?"

"Dad uses one to steady himself against the current when he's fishing in a river. You didn't feel anything when we turned the corridor to 3B, so I want to try walking down there holding on to you. Like a wading stick."

"You certainly know how to flatter a girl Wilson."

They gathered their belongings, left the waiting room and headed back down the corridor and stopped at the 3B sign and the ninety-degree turn.

Daisy held Wilson's arm.

"Ready?"

"Ready" said Wilson.

They turned the corner and directly ahead, thirty metres away, was the swing door entrance to the ward. This time, with his arms entwined with Daisy's, there was no excruciating headache, no super strength déjà vu, no nausea. Wilson could sense prickly spikes of energy in the air, like the static you can almost touch as a thunderstorm builds, but it was no longer debilitating.

"Let go, just for a second."

Daisy slowly extracted herself and set Wilson free. He winced with pain immediately and Daisy rushed forwards to grab his arm.

"Thanks" he whispered. "Keep going."

They continued at a snail's pace, arm in arm, drawing ever closer to the frosted glass and wood-panelled swing doors of Ward 3B. Wilson closed his eyes and slowly moved his head from side to side and then up and down as though playing a game involving a blindfold.

"Why have you closed your eyes?" whispered Daisy.

"Because now I can see everything" he said.

Wilson stretched out an arm as if reaching for an invisible object on a shelf that only he could see. Daisy looked over her shoulder to make sure nobody was following them, men in white coats possibly? They resembled an elderly couple shuffling towards a geriatric ward.

When she turned her attention back to Wilson, he had

a white plastic rocket in his hand, like a small boy's model construction from an Airfix kit. Without looking down at the object, Wilson scratched at a transfer on the body of the toy with his finger nail; it was an American stars and stripes flag that had been positioned on the rocket upside down. Wilson smiled at a distant memory, his eyes still firmly closed. Then, as though drawn to a new toy on the imaginary shelf, he let the rocket slip through his fingers and fall to the floor. It zoomed away past Daisy's leg. When she turned, open mouthed, to monitor its progress, the model was nowhere to be seen. Now Wilson had a small doll in his hand. He was playing with the stringy little toy, all arms and legs and platform shoes. He let the doll drop to the floor and again it flew past Daisy's leg. But this time she managed to follow the journey as the doll disappeared into thin air — as though an invisible current, a transparent river of energy, had carried it away downstream and a strong undertow had pulled the helpless toy beneath the surface.

Wilson opened his eyes.

"Take me back Daisy" he whispered hoarsely. "I'm very tired. Need to go back, now, quickly."

She kept her arms firmly wrapped around his as they turned and trudged back up the corridor, around the ninety-degree turn and out of sight of Ward 3B. Daisy slowly released her grip on Wilson's arm. He collapsed to the floor, as though someone had stolen his bones. A few minutes later a doctor and two nurses from A&E came flying down the corridor quickly followed by a porter pushing a trolley bed.

Chapter 45

They never thought of that

Friday 3rd November 2017

"So, Sergeant Jordan, like I say, it's all too much of a coincidence. Alice is here for seventeen years without a single visitor, then this nervous young lad turns up with some cock and bull story about finding a home for a stepdad who lives in Stockport. While he's here, he shows a lot of interest in Alice and then two hours later, she miraculously writes a message to say she's really called Vanessa Clarke, who also happens to come from Stockport."

Sergeant Derek Jordan was taking notes, not convinced that the heartwarming elation of the last few days could ever warrant a police investigation. However, having been snubbed live on TV, the duty manager had grabbed a bone and she wasn't letting go.

"So I'm not buying it! Something strange was going on with that lad and in my opinion he knew about Alice being here and knew where she was from and what happened to her."

"But Celia, I thought you said the boy looked about sixteen. That means Alice, sorry, I mean Vanessa, was already in South Kessock before he was born. Not sure how he could have influenced much back then, given that he was just a glint in his dad's eye."

Celia Green was not amused.

"Look, I don't know what he was up to. All I'm saying is

that, that lad, Frank Spencer, or whatever he's really called, was involved in this and it's your job to find out how."

The sergeant closed his notebook, clipped his pen in his shirt pocket and stood up.

"Well Celia, in the absence of an obvious crime I'm not really sure how to go about this, even if the boy was involved, strikes me he's done the family a big favour in bringing them all back together again. Think he deserves a medal, not a police enquiry."

"But what if he'd known she was here, for a long time? Or he was part of a trafficking gang – maybe his dad was involved years ago and they left her here, alone, knowing the family were looking for her, thinking she was dead? Maybe he could have acted earlier? That would be wrong wouldn't it, a crime possibly? Obstruction of something?"

"Yeah, okay. Look, maybe you've got a point, let me think about it. I can see there's a strange coincidence. Let me have a word with the chief, get his take on it. It does all seem a bit odd, the chain of events. So thanks for bringing it to my attention Celia, I'll take it further, I promise."

Sergeant Jordan was heading out of the building when he had an afterthought.

"Celia, are there any cameras in the home, maybe on the car park, something that might have caught his image?"

"No, I thought of that. But we don't have any."

"Shame, would help if we had an image of young Frank."

With that the sergeant said goodbye, left the building and climbed into the police car parked directly in front of the South Kessock Care Home.

"Frank Spencer eh," he said, smiling at the thought, "the lad's certainly got a sense of humour."

322

When Sergeant Jordan arrived back at police HQ, he popped up to see the Assistant Chief Constable's secretary and asked for a quick ten minutes with the boss.

"Leave it with me, she said, I'll see if I can find you a slot. He's still full on with the media after the Alice discovery, you know, given his role in the case at the time."

"Yeah, I've seen he's getting a fair bit of stick, but it's actually the Alice thing I want to talk to him about."

Half an hour later Sergeant Jordan's conversation with Assistant Chief Constable Montague was coming to an end.

"I'm not sensing a major misdemeanour here Derek, but as you say, it would be nice to know the full story. It does seem massively coincidental. Don't think we need to go about it mob handed though. Where are Vanessa's family from again?"

"Stockport, sir."

"And the lad didn't have a Scottish accent and too young to be driving you say?"

"Aye, that's what Celia Green at South Kessock told me."

"Well sergeant, he's not likely to have ridden his push bike all this way. So driven by someone? There's a good possibility, but it'd take a lot of man hours to check that out so let's start with a train. Probably from Manchester. Make it discrete Derek. Not sure what we're dealing with here and that family have suffered enough at the hands of the North Caledonia Constabulary, let's not compound their distress. Keep it under the radar, in fact, just between you and me on the off chance this thing has legs. Get a description and start with the train station, trains to Manchester, just platform footage. You said the receptionist at the care home thought he'd arrived in a taxi? Well try and track down the driver. If you get a match on anything, get back to me."

"Yes sir, I'm on it. I'll check the phone records at the home also, the receptionist said the boy called the day before to make an appointment, perhaps he was careless with a mobile number?"

Later that evening Sergeant Jordan was studying two black and white images. One showed a young man in a parka sitting on a south bound platform at Inverness train station. The other showed the same young man leaving Piccadilly station on a Vespa scooter. The registration plate of the Vespa was clearly visible. It belonged to Wilson Armitage of Midland Drive, Bramhall, Cheshire.

Chapter 46

Ward 7

Friday 3rd November 2017

When Wilson woke he was still in the hospital, but in the new building, in a bed in intensive care on Ward 7. He had a drip in his arm and a monitor bleeped metronomically as it took readings on his vital signs. Wilson peered groggily around the room. He recognised Daisy sitting to his right and the blurry forms of his parents at the foot of the bed and didn't have the strength to keep his eyes open long enough to fully focus.

The following day, when able to sit up in bed and with enough energy to stay awake for more than five minutes, a consultant doctor gave his verdict.

"Quite extraordinary. You're a very lucky young man.

Wilson's eyelids felt as heavy as manhole covers.

"You've had a catastrophic neutralisation of plasma electrolytes. Basically, the positive and negative ions were neutralised and every system in your body shut down. Similar to having a flat battery. If we hadn't got you on a drip as quickly as we did, I shudder to think what the outcome would have been. The old ticker doesn't run so well on a flat battery. The only other time I saw something remotely like this was in a farmer who was hit by lightning, and he didn't make it, poor chap. No idea what you've been up to Wilson. Burning the candle at both ends, no doubt; what we call a toxic lifestyle, eh? But I wouldn't do it again if I were you.

"Anyway, all the tests indicate you're getting back to normal. We'll keep you in for a few more days of observation, keep you plugged in to our machines, make sure you're fully charged and then all being well, you can go home. Cheerio."

Wilson went back to sleep.

Chapter 47

Home time

Tuesday 7th November 2017

Four days later, Wilson was given the all-clear and permission to go home. Daisy arrived at the hospital with a bowl of fruit partially covered with cling film and the latest copy of *Scootering* magazine.

"Some of the pages are stuck together," said Wilson, as he tried to thumb through the magazine. And half the grapes have been eaten!"

"Well, I've no idea how that could have happened while I was on the bus, on my way here, feeling hungry and with nothing to read. Anyway Wilson, stop complaining. The doctor said you're not at death's door anymore. I'm going to see Gran in half an hour and it's so handy having you both here. Like killing two birds with one stone. Which is a totally inappropriate thing to say!"

Wilson laughed weakly, coughed and told Daisy he wasn't sure if he had the strength to cope with her fully charged battery.

He couldn't remember much about the last few days, just vague recollections of blurry comings and goings. His parents being at the bedside with Kate and Megan; conversations in which his mother sounded anxious and upset; an impression of Daisy and Hoover being there.

"It's all the excitement of his best friend finding his mum.

It must have been too much for him, a bit of a shock I expect" he remembered her saying.

Daisy helped Wilson higher up the bed and adjusted the pillows. They made light conversation for a few more minutes until it seemed timely for Daisy to broach the subject.

"You had your eyes closed all the time, but what could you see?"

Wilson sank back into his pillow and for a moment stared blankly into space, looking for words to explain an experience that was quite simply, inexplicable.

"Daisy, it was just the most incredible feeling. As though I was standing in a wind tunnel facing this strong breeze, but it wasn't a wind that was blowing, you know, like air rushing by; it was a billion impressions of life, my life, your life, everyone's life, the world was flowing past at a million miles an hour. It's impossible to put into words, because I didn't see anything visual to describe. I was feeling pictures rather than seeing them. It was as if my brain could create an image from the signals, the data it was receiving, but without my eyes needing to be involved. This torrent of energy, the particles of moments from the past, were rushing down the corridor and I was standing in the middle of it all. I could feel them brushing past my hair, passing through my body. Like when you put your tongue on the end of a battery and you get that burning buzz. That sensation was inside me. There was this feeling of energy all around, zooming through me. I could capture it, sense it, when I closed my eyes. It almost fried me though, there was too much, it was too strong and too powerful."

Wilson turned to Daisy and reached for her hand. The little colour that *was* in his cheeks had been blanched by the effort of recollection.

"You weren't my wading stick Daisy. That analogy was wrong. You were my lightning rod, cos I think through you, some of the energy was kind of earthed and you diminished the power of the flow."

"Okay, stop Wilson. That's enough for now. We can return to this when you're feeling stronger. Here, before I eat them all."

She popped a grape into his mouth.

"But one last question. Do you remember the toy rocket and the little doll?"

"What?"

"The ones you plucked from thin air, like a magician."

Wilson chuckled at the suggestion.

"Yeah, vaguely, now you come to mention it."

"And when you let go of them, they just flew away and disappeared again. It was a great trick."

"I don't fully remember Daisy. But whatever I did, it discharged my battery pretty quickly."

"Well, making a plastic model suddenly appear out of nothing and then making it disappear again, I can understand how that would be a bit draining. Anyway Dynamo called again. He wants to meet up and pick your brains about conjuring an elephant out of thin air."

"Oh yeah, are the flowers from him?" Wilson asked, nodding at a sorry looking bunch of daffodils in a vase on the window sill.

"No, they were delivered a few days ago. We don't know who sent them, but they came with a message, it's here."

Daisy retrieved a small card from the bedside cupboard.

"It says, 'From me and the missus and the boys, hope you get your strength back soon, Blamire.' And he spelt strength with no 'g'."

"I know who that is Daisy and you can chuck those fly-traps in the bin."

There was a soft knock followed by Wilson's dad popping his head around the door.

"Taxi service?"

Wilson was way off his personal best when it came to getting dressed and the final hurdle of pulling a sweater over his head left him panting for breath. His dad pushed him to the car in a wheelchair.

"Don't go on the A6 Dad," Wilson said, as they pulled out of the car park, "can you go the back way please?"

They had been driving in silence for ten minutes when Alex broached the inevitable by asking, "want to talk about it son?" There was no pressure or a feeling of necessity in his voice.

"Not right now Dad. But I know what happened."

"Me too. Catastrophic neutralisation of plasma electrolytes caused either by lightning or inhaling too much smoke. Didn't I tell you about the dangers of smoking?"

"Yes, you did Dad, you certainly did."

Wilson started to laugh and cough at the same time.

"It all goes through there Dad. All of it. Through Ward 3B. You should put an energy detecting machine in there."

"I will Wilson. The MPs on that committee would love that. Especially when I explain the theory behind it."

They sat in silence for a while, enjoying the reassuring normality of a car journey in heavy traffic. The queue at the lights outside Davenport train station had backed up all the way to the A6. If the cause was an accident, Wilson crossed his fingers for an ambulance to already be in attendance.

"Listen son, I'm just glad you're okay. Plus, I'm still trying to get my head round what you did for Teaps. This is what happens if you smoke; you nearly kill yourself, but on the plus side, you can find missing people. Just don't do it again son, please, for your mum's sake."

Chapter 48

Birthday girl

Wednesday 8th November 2017

After twelve hours of revitalising, dreamless sleep, Wilson felt a resurgence of vigour when he woke the next morning; as though the dead weight of his limbs had been inflated with air and a dimmer switch had turned up the light in his eyes. Gloria served breakfast in bed.

"Just so happy to have you home love. Two miracles in the space of a week."

When she finally stopped fussing, tidying his room and chattering to herself, Wilson managed to get a word in edgeways.

"It's Daisy's birthday today Mum – she's eighteen – and I haven't had a chance to buy her anything."

"Well, are you up to a trip to the Trafford Centre? I can park right outside the entrance to Selfridges."

"Think so. Let me have a shower and we'll go." Wilson suddenly remembered his phone.

"Mum, what happened to my mobile?"

"Oh, it's downstairs on the bureau love. Your dad brought it back from the hospital the night you were admitted. Do you want it?"

"Please."

Gloria scurried downstairs as Wilson went to take a shower.

When he returned, his phone was on the bed. Nine missed calls from Teaps, lots of 'get well' messages on social media and a couple of nasty texts from Blamire.

Teaps had been waiting anxiously for his calls to be returned.

"Wilson, what happened to you man? Called you about a hundred times. How come you were in hospital?"

"Ah, it was something or nothing. Think I was a bit run-down and then I got a stomach bug in the hospital, so they kept me in."

"Wilson, you were in Intensive Care for three nights and your dad told Hoover's dad you had absolutely no energy, no strength left in your body."

"Think that's a bit of an exaggeration Teaps. Anyway, I'm alright now. More to the point, what's happening with you? Bring me up to speed."

"Phew, don't really know where to begin. In the words of Alex James, it's been a bit of a *Blur*. The most important thing though is that Mum's okay. Physically fine. She can speak a little bit, about things that happen during the day, in a jumbled up sort of way, like she'll remember what she had for breakfast, but then not know what breakfast is! But all the old memories have definitely gone. She doesn't really remember me and Dad – seems to sense that we're her family, that I'm her son, but can't explain why or how."

Teaps paused for a moment as the intonation in his voice changed.

"Wilson, I've got to ask you something. Something that struck me as strange."

"What's that?"

"Well, when I spoke to you, on Dad's phone, the morning

after we found Mum, remember? I called you and you said, "What did you think when you saw her in that room? Will she get her memory back?" Wilson, how did you know she was in a room or that she'd lost her memory? Nobody knew that. Not even me and my dad, not until the doctor told us. But you knew she'd lost her memory."

"Well, err . . . I don't really remember what I said in all the excitement. Probably meant 'that home' when I said 'that room' and I'm sure I heard it on the news that she had some impaired mental abilities. I just presumed it was to do with memory. Yeah, and my mum said it. I remember now – she was watching the news on TV and she said your mum's memory must have gone. Think it's cos she spends a lot of time with the elderly people in the shop, she has experience of that type of thing. Anyway, what does it matter? It's not important. Where are you?"

"We're still at this private rehabilitation place near Chester, but everyone knows we're here. It's been in the papers. Cameras and TV trucks have been camped outside all week. But some amazing things have happened. First, the Housing Department at Stockport council have been in touch to say they've put us at the top of the waiting list now that Mum's back and needs special care.

"Plus, a few – quite a few actually – of Dad's old customers have been calling and asking if he's interested in going back to do their gardens for them.

"And there's some really unbelievable news. When Mum went missing, she had some junior partners in her firm, people she'd trained up, and they carried on running the business thinking she'd come back. As Mum was never pronounced dead, the company stayed in her name. The partners told Dad at the time but he was so upset he said he wasn't interested and they could keep the business. The publicity and mystery of her disappearance brought in loads of new clients and now they employ forty people. They've even got an office in London! Mum was allocated chunks of profit every year and it turns out she's pretty wealthy now. There's certainly enough to avoid having to return to Blamire's fleapit. And I've packed in my job at Morrisons!"

Wilson started laughing and Teaps did the same, coming over like an echo on the phone.

"I'm so happy for you mate, I really am. What will you do about college?"

"I'm taking a gap year. Might not even go back. I want to spend all my time with Mum for now. Dad's asked if I'd like to get involved with his landscaping business but to be honest, I think recruitment and the London office is more up my street."

"Okay, well keep in touch, and if you need any help with anything . . . "

"Yeah, will do."

"Say hi to your dad – hey, and your mum! Sounds strange saying that. Teaps's mum, Vanessa, your mum. It's just brilliant."

"Yeah, I know. See you Wilson."

"See ya, man."

The yell from an impatient mother standing in the hallway fishing for car keys in her bag, brought Wilson back to earth. "If you want to go shopping for Daisy's present, we need to go now Wilson."

"Be down in a minute."

He quickly read Blamire's texts, both of which regurgitated the same menacing threat, then deleted them.

An hour later, Wilson was feeling somewhat bewildered and challenged by the world of fashion offered by Miss Selfridge.

"I don't know if she's an eight or a ten or a twelve Mum. Actually, no, I'm sure she's an eleven."

"Wilson, don't be silly, she's an eight, besides, there's no such thing as an eleven!"

"Oh, I'm pretty sure there is Mum."

Since clothes were clearly out of the question, Wilson bought Daisy a fine gold chain necklace with a St Christopher pendant, a pair of black suede gloves, a book entitled A Guide to the Meaning of Dreams and a jumbo bag of Midget Gems. Gloria wasn't sure about the last two presents but was okay with his choice of the jewellery and gloves. She made him drink a bottle of Lucozade and eat two energy bars during the journey home.

Around seven thirty, Daisy and her mum, Frances, called in. Gloria and Frances had been introduced during Wilson's time in Intensive Care. They sat chatting and drinking tea in the kitchen while Daisy opened her presents in the lounge with Wilson.

She loved the necklace, said the gloves fitted, 'like a glove', playfully hit Wilson with the book and then started eating the Midget Gems.

"Sorry we couldn't do anything better, something special to mark your eighteenth Daisy. The doctor said I need early nights and lots of rest, and to be honest, much as I'd like to ignore doctor's orders, I still feel absolutely knackered."

"Wilson, shut up. I'm eighteen years old now, an adult. You can take me to Fabio's next week and I'll interpret all your dreams with my new book."

"Sounds like a plan."

"Speaking of dreams, I don't want to go back to The Market Square again. It doesn't feel right anymore. In some ways it scares me to be honest. When I think that the force of energy in the hospital corridor, and the damage it did to you, could also relate to our dreams in The Market Square, while we're asleep in bed. That can't be a good thing Wilson, I enjoyed the dancing the other night, but it's not real. I want a normal relationship like everyone else and I want to get drunk and feel the hangover the next day. Let's try to stop. We did a good thing there. Let's end on a high. I was really worried when you were in hospital. And I missed you, a lot!"

"Me too. I mean, I didn't miss myself a lot – well, I did actually, but I also . . . "

Daisy thumped Wilson on the shoulder and tried to force a black Midget Gem into his mouth as punishment for being so blasé about her concerns. He retaliated by tipping a handful of Midget Gems down the back of her sweater, which became the signal for Frances to say it was time to go and she would be waiting in the car.

"Seriously Wilson," said Daisy, buttoning up her coat, "no more Market Square and no more Ward 3B and energy tunnels. Look, it gives me goosebumps on my arm just thinking about it."

"Okay, I agree. But it might be that we can only stop after tonight."

"Why, what's happening tonight?"

"I can't be certain, but I think there's a good chance I'll be seeing you later, it being your eighteenth birthday and all."

Chapter 49

The fatal attraction

Wednesday 8th November 2017

Wilson was the first to arrive in the poppy fields. The lilting breeze made the slender green bodies and crimson cup hats sway in harmony like a Mexican wave. The outline of The Gateway rippled in the heat as pearl-tinted clouds drifted across the sky. The clouds seemed to pause while passing across the sun, as though basking in a moment of celestial superiority, before fragmenting and dissolving – the price to be paid for impertinence.

After a while, Wilson felt a warm, soft hand slip into his. There was no need to look; the birthday girl had arrived. The waves of flowers parted like a biblical special effect and in no time at all, Wilson and Daisy stood facing The Gateway.

"Jeeeesssus," said Daisy, craning her neck to take in the monumental scale of the building. "Whose palace is *this*?"

"It's called The Gateway. The place I told you about, remember, where they keep the extinguished spirits."

"You never said it was this big, how do we get inside?"

"You follow me."

As they made their way up the wide stone steps hand in hand, Daisy paused to take in the battle scene carved into the pediment of the portico. She caught up with Wilson in front of two doors, which he explained were completely independent, two separate entrances: one for visitors, the other for residents.

"We're definitely visitors" he said, pushing the door open sufficiently for them both to squeeze through.

Daisy stood transfixed, eyes and mouth agape, taking in the magnificent spectacle; the shafts of milky light pouring through a never ending row of arched windows; the colossal expanse of the cathedral like interior and the towering stacks of gold bangles.

"Tell me again where we are" she said, turning full circle while gazing upwards. Dust particles were swimming in pools of stained glass colour.

"He's already told you. It's called The Gateway."

Startled by the voice, Daisy instinctively turned back to Wilson and blinked in surprise at the two comical looking characters standing either side of him dressed like undertakers. Wilson had his hands in his pockets and was rocking on his feet, grinning.

"This is The Hall of Extinguished Spirits" said Short Cake, sweeping his arm outwards in an imperious manner.

"These are the guys I told you about."

Daisy was still coming to terms with the ineffable magnificence of the hall, the gleaming mountains of gold jewellery and if that wasn't enough, the men in black.

"Yeah, Big Mac and Short Cake look after the place, but the other way round – cos he's not big and the other one's not short – it can be confusing." Wilson pointed out the disparity by way of introduction.

"So what's with all the jewellery then?"

The dumpy figure of Big Mac waddled towards Daisy – his small feet and short legs just about able to keep his top heavy frame upright. He reminded Daisy of a round-bottomed toy, a Mr Roly Poly or a Wobbly Man.

"Each gold bangle Daisy, is the Outer Shell of a human spirit, the extinguished 'will to live' of a dead person." Big Mac held one of the bangles aloft as he continued to explain.

Knowing that the dialogue to follow was for Daisy's benefit, Wilson turned to Short Cake, who swivelled his head ninety degrees, owl like, in response to Wilson's attention.

"We loved your rescue mission in Scotland Wilson, we really did. Even The Powers That Be enjoyed it and they usually hate that magnitude of mischief. Yes, you really put the cat amongst the feathered rats with that little stunt. So ingenious, stealing the wedding photo, writing a secret message, the lovely train journey and the chat with Dad. We loved it. And we saw you on TV! Big Mac even shed a few tears when he heard how concerned you and Daisy were at playing God.

"But Wilson," Short Cake continued, "when I say, Big Mac shed tears, I don't mean he was crying at the emotion of it all. I mean he was splitting his sides laughing." Then he bellowed at the top of his voice. "AND NOT IN A GOOD WAY!" Which once again gave Daisy a start.

"I don't get you" said Wilson.

Big Mac had concluded Daisy's truncated introduction to The Gateway and now turned his attention to Wilson.

"Mr Armitage, you are a very clever chap. Over-indulged possibly, and certainly an above-average eleven, but then you were turbo-charged with extra . . .abilities, shall we say."

"Just for the flippin' hell of it" announced Short Cake, stamping his foot like a spoilt child.

Big Mac ignored him.

"We don't know why they gave you and Daisy the status

of eleven-plus Wilson and I believe they're now of the same opinion, especially after your rocket-conjuring trick. That was another first and took us all by surprise."

"Gateway, this is Short Cake. We have a problem."

"Stop, please stop, just for a minute. Can someone tell me what the hell's going on here, in ENGLISH?" Daisy had heard enough of the nonsensical chatter. She was lost in someone's daft idea of an intriguing, birthday dream, Wilson's most likely, and she was not enjoying it at all.

"Ah" said Big Mac, his face lighting up, "I'm so happy you asked that Miss Meadowcroft. Happy birthday by the way. Many elevens come here for a meet and greet when they come of age. May I be allowed to answer your question at the macro level?"

Oh, be my guest thought Daisy, wishing he'd quickly get to the bloody point.

"Earth is but part of a universe forever expanding outwards. The space into which the universe expands is where The Powers That Be reside, running their giant train set."

"It's just the best toy . . . ever." Big Mac made a point of ignoring the puerile silliness from you know who.

"And so Daisy, they let uncontrollable variables like you and Wilson mess up the schedules with your mischief on purpose, so they can place bets on all the possible outcomes. You two are very hard to predict and so difficult to wager. The Powers That Be like you Wilson, they really do."

"But stop meddling with stuff that don't concern you!"

Daisy was now certain Short Cake had mental problems and was so irritated by the conversation she decided to go and explore.

"I'm just going to see if there's a sale on in Tiffany's" she said, nodding at the steep valley running between the hills of bangles.

Big Mac returned to the point he was making.

"What I'm trying to say Wilson, is that you're only supposed to be in The Market Square to bring a light dusting of snow – not to rescue missing people and cause blizzards. They gave you too much power Wilson. You make the gambling difficult, harder to calculate the odds – the ripples from some of your actions have the bookies beaten. Not to mention all the damage limitation required and the knock on effects of snow falling on the Amazon. Remember?"

Big Mac raised an eyebrow questioningly.

"Okay, okay, I get the message" said Wilson, "and we're sorry, but we were only trying to help, to do something good. Daisy even reckons it could have been God that made us do it in the first place. That would count in our favour, wouldn't it, with The Powers That Be?"

Wilson knew Daisy would soon return and insist on leaving The Gateway so he jumped to the question that had been on his mind since the point was raised on sports day.

"There's one thing I don't understand; who decides what The Market Square looks like when we arrive?"

"Ahhh, good question Wilson. Well, to use the terminology of the day, it just happens to be what's trending. The consensus of dream energy mixed with tomfoolery from The Powers That Be – rigged dice, five aces, that sort of thing. But the Blackpool Tower ballroom was all their idea. They thought you might want to celebrate."

"So will they stop us visiting The Market Square soon, you know, because of our mischief?"

"They're certainly working on it, but yours is more of a

VIP pass and more difficult to nullify. So until the matter is resolved, I suggest, no, I absolutely recommend, you refrain from further disruptive activity."

Big Mac had chosen his words carefully and it seemed to Wilson that he had finally got to the point. He and Daisy were being told in no uncertain terms to stay away from The Market Square, or at the very least, to avoid making mischief.

But how is it possible, in practical terms to cease visiting The Market Square? How can Daisy and I choose not to go when we don't want to be here now? Assuming The Gateway and The Market Square are connected that is.

Wilson put the questions to Big Mac.

Daisy was about twenty metres away, standing at the foot of the inventory for 2006. The bangles resembled golden scree on a sloping hillside. She selected three bangles and slipped them onto her wrist. *Nice and heavy, definitely real gold* she thought, letting them shake and jangle on her arm. She turned to walk back to Wilson. Big Mac was still droning on. Short Cake was rising and falling on the balls of his feet with a gormless expression on his face.

Whether it was a lack of sustenance in his body or because the 'end by' date of the dream had arrived, it's hard to say, but at that moment Wilson began to yawn, he then dissolved into a translucent shadow of his former self and departed The Gateway.

Daisy was scratching at what appeared to be a hallmark or an inscription on one of the bangles hanging from her wrist, when she also started to yawn and moments later, returned to the 'no longer dreaming' phase of sleep.

At 5.45 a.m. the next morning, Wilson was stirred from

slumber by a text from Daisy.

'Wilson, I'm lying in bed and I've got three ******* gold bangles on my ******* wrist!'

Wilson read the text with one eye open, half asleep, and was so convinced the message was just a straggling remnant of the previous night's dream, he went straight back to being fully asleep.

Chapter 50

A spanner in the works

Thursday 9th November 2017

When he read the text message for a second time, Wilson replied with one of his own.

'Morning, I've just read that message from earlier – I'm right in thinking you only *dreamt* you had three bangles on your wrist?'

'No. I really have. They were still on my wrist when I woke this morning. The same bangles I was trying on in that Gateway place last night.'

Wilson called as fast as his fingers could move over the phone.

"Daisy you realise this can only mean one of two things. We're going to be rich beyond our wildest dreams by selling mountains of gold jewellery that doesn't belong to us, or we're in a lot of trouble. But let me tell you for certain; we'll never be allowed to sell gold bangles that represent a person's extinguished spirit. Especially when they've got the name of the owner written on them and that person is DEAD!"

Wilson was shouting as he delivered those last few words.

"This is incredible, I wonder how I did it."

He could hear the illegal exports jangling on her wrist.

"I don't think anything bad is going to happen."

"Oh yes it is Daisy, because The Powers That Be are going to say something along the lines of 'we're also called The

Powers That Kick People's Head In For Making Even More Mischief When They've Been Told Not To'. Do you get where I'm coming from?"

"Come on Wilson, they won't miss three. They had millions of them."

"Jesus Daisy, you're not listening to me, of course they will."

"Who will?"

"The people, the spirits, the Residuals who moved on to eternity. The people whose names are on the inside of those bangles! They'll bloody well miss them."

"What names?"

"Daisy, please, the names that are inscribed on the inside of each of those bangles in very small, but very clear writing. Weren't you listening to what Big Mac told you?"

"Yes, but I thought it was some made up story, part of the dream."

Wilson heard her shake one of the bangles free.

"You mean, err, let me see . . . God, it's tiny writing. Er, Andrew Latchford. Nineteen fifty-four until two thousand and six."

"Yes, and the others?"

"Er, hold on a minute . . . Edward Riley, nineteen thirty-two until two thousand and six. And err, Emily Broadstairs. Eighteen forty-five until two thousand and six."

"So Daisy, the name is the name of a person and the numbers are the years they were born and then died. The year they died is the year they entered The Gateway, where we were last night – where I knew we'd end up because it was your eighteenth birthday and for some reason you go there when you're eighteen. The hall is where the will to live, energy that can't be destroyed by death, the outer Shell, is turned into three ounces of gold, leaving the final chunk of energy, the soul, to go through the door to eternity and live with The Powers That Be. Didn't Big Mac tell you all this last night?"

Wilson was becoming increasingly frustrated.

"Yes, but he didn't say each bangle was personalised. So let me see, Andrew Latchford was fifty-two when he died. And Emily was, err, sixty-one. No, one hundred and sixty-one. Wilson, nobody lives to be a hundred and sixty-one."

"Correct Daisy, they don't. But in her case, she was probably only seventeen when she died, from TB or an accident in a mill – certainly before she wanted to."

Wilson was dismayed with Daisy's inability to grasp the gravity of her transgression, the dire situation she, *they*, were in.

"Listen, if you look on the internet, there's every chance you'll find a ghost called Emily Broadstairs who haunted some old building. I know all this because I did the research. I've got the t-shirt for Eric Murphy!"

Wilson exhaled. He'd just woken up and was already exhausted.

"Maybe they won't notice these three are missing?"

"Daisy, THEY WILL! They already know, I'm sure. The question is; what are they going to do about it? And the other question is; how do we get them back? Sharpish!"

"Do you think we're in trouble?"

"Yeah I do. I really do. There's going to be serious repercussions about this."

"But I didn't steal them on purpose. I was only trying them on. They're so nice. I wasn't really listening to you talking to Big Cake so I put them on my wrist. And then I became tired and when I woke up, they were here, on my wrist."

"Daisy, I know you didn't steal them on purpose. I tried to borrow a special spanner from Sampson's one night, when I was doing up the Vespa, but it wasn't in my pocket when I woke up the next morning. That's because The Market Square seems to be mostly about two kinds of energy, dreams and time. But The Gateway is different, it's involved with another type of energy altogether, the energy of the human spirit. And somehow you managed to wander back to bed with part of it, the Outer Shell, dangling from your wrist. Actually Daisy, now I come to think about it, those bangles *are* like spanners, spanners in the works of The Gateway – maybe even spanners in the universe."

"Shit" said Daisy. "Well, when you put it that way, yeah, it does sound serious. What am I gonna do?"

"I've not got a clue Daisy, but above all else, don't lose those bloody bangles."

The red army

Thursday 9th November 2017

A few minutes after he'd finished the call to Daisy, Wilson's mum delivered milky tea with extra sugar, a sausage sandwich and two bottles of Lucozade. She checked his temperature and told him she was nipping out to the shops but would be back in an hour. Wilson made an attempt at the sandwich but with no appetite, each mouthful had to be washed down with a gulp of tea. He was trying to digest the implications and ramifications of their predicament, the consequences of bridging the gap between a dream and real life by stealing other-worldly artefacts. When his phone rang, Blamire was on the other end.

"Hello?"

"Hello Winston?"

"It's Wilson, you idiot."

"Hello Wilton."

"What do you want Blamire?"

"I was just ringing to check on my investment."

"Blamire, overcharging someone for a poxy flat that should be condemned and then ripping them off at some extortionate interest rate isn't an investment, it's extortion – an extortion racket by a slum landlord. You've done this before, haven't you? Probably to the people who were in that flea pit before Teaps. You know, I think the police would be interested in your little scam."

"Yeah, I'm sure they would, but going to the boys in blue wouldn't be a smart move would it Winston, cos now I've got another option? You see, I've been talking to a couple of handy lads from Salford, from a well-known firm. I brought them up to speed with my predicament and they made me a business proposition. They expressed an interest on my interest on the interest. Seventy-five pence in the pound. Which means I get six grand today and they become the new debt collectors.

"So I need eight grand by the day after tomorrow, or the reds will come marching in. Those boys really don't give a shit about whether you tell the police or not. They'll definitely be well up for kidnapping Teaps's mum if they don't get paid. She's loaded apparently. Two days Winston. You've got my number."

Then the line went dead.

Wilson threw the phone across the bedroom. It bounced off the carpet and hit the skirting board but fortunately didn't sustain any damage. Which was just as well, because two hours later it rang again.

"Wilson, it's me. I have to tell you something."

Daisy's voice was flat and lifeless, as though she'd taken a strong sedative.

"I'm in the nurse's room at college. I think I've got a broken finger. Someone slammed my locker door on my hand. But there was nobody there. I'd forgotten my book and there was only me by the lockers. The door really whacked my finger, like a hurricane or a tornado had blown it shut. It was so quick and powerful. And I'm sure someone's been following me ever since I left the house this morning."

"Have you seen anyone?"

"No, but I sense someone's watching me; and don't have a fit, but I think they might have tried to push me under a bus at the station."

Wilson sat bolt upright.

"What? You're saying you think someone tried to kill you?"

"No. Yes. I don't know.. I just felt this shove and my feet tripped on the kerb and I was about to go under the wheels when this man standing by my side grabbed me and pulled me back. And we couldn't tell who'd pushed me. So people thought I was trying to jump or I'd lost my balance. Wilson I'm scared. Really scared. I don't know what to do."

Daisy started crying, a doleful, 'how could I have been so stupid to get myself into this mess', sort of cry.

Wilson knew Daisy's fear was well-founded, the threat was very real. You can't steal priceless jewellery and not expect the owners to come looking for it – especially when the owners know who the thief is and where she lives.

"Daisy, Daisy, listen to me. Where are the bangles?"

"They're in my bedroom at home. I wrapped them in paper and hid them at the back of the drawer in my bedside table."

"Okay, well they're safe there. Daisy, try to pull yourself together. Be strong. Look, I don't know what's going on exactly, but I'm sure what's happening now is all connected to you taking the bangles from The Gateway. But they're also playing with me, with us, teaching us a lesson because we found Vanessa. They're demonstrating how actions, playing God, can have dire consequences, like Blamire blackmailing Teaps."

"What?"

"Nothing, nothing, another problem. Daisy, stay close to

people all the time. Be with someone as you move from class to class; don't be alone. Call me when you get home later. Be careful okay? I'm going to work out how to sort this."

"I want to call the police."

"You can't do that. Daisy that's ridiculous! What story are you going to give about the bangles? If the forces of the universe are after you, how do you think the police can possibly help. We've got to get those bangles back quickly and hope that's all we need to do."

Wilson then paused for a second as bald awareness of the unfolding drama implanted a thought not based on any rationale or logic.

"Daisy, I don't know why I'm thinking this, but I feel you might be safe with your grandma in Ward 3B."

"With my grandma? She's dying Wilson. She can't move, can't speak, and you think she can protect me from an invisible man pushing me under a bus better than the police? Why would you think that?"

"I don't know, I just do. They want the bangles back above all else, but they know you didn't take them on purpose. They'll have seen your trace. It was just bad timing. They're trying to frighten us and they're doing a good job, but I think we have time. They'll give us time to put it right."

"But what if we can't?"

"We will. I'll think of something. Listen, call me later. Okay?"

"Okay. I will, I promise."

"And don't worry, I'll sort it."

The call ended with Daisy trying to rally her self-composure and curtail the sobbing. Wilson tried to stay calm and think logically but the parameters of the problem made any conventional approach to solution seeking impossible. What he had to do was think illogically, instinctively. Like the idea that Daisy would be safe in Ward 3B. There was no reason for that, but it felt right. And what if Daisy had been allowed to leave The Gateway with the bangles on purpose, for some ulterior motive? A torn pocket was one thing, but the embodiment of human spirits being extracted from a dream, well, that was unthinkable. Wilson knew one thing for certain however, he was sure The Powers That Be would give them more time to solve the problem. After all, they were betting on it!

Wilson lay in bed for the rest of the afternoon, charging his batteries and boosting his energy levels with bananas, high-protein bars and cocktails of vitamins and mineral supplements.

He would sleep fitfully, then after twenty minutes of tossing and turning, wake up with his mind darting in each and every direction in search of a sign post that would point to a solution. This routine continued until his phone rang.

It was Daisy and from the detached delivery of her words, it sounded to Wilson like she was in shock, in another world, a distant place.

"It's me. I'm home. Dad's here. He had to come back from work early. Something really bad has happened and . . . " Her voice fell away, as though she'd witnessed something too terrible for words. Wilson could hear voices in the background.

"Daisy, find somewhere quiet where we can speak."

"I can't now Wilson. I don't know what to say to you."

"Daisy, we have to . . . "

But she'd closed her phone.

He rang back constantly for the next hour and sent

umpteen messages. Gloria served sausage and mash for tea, followed by a bowl of rice pudding with a blob of jam in the middle, Wilson's favourite. There was a look of concern on her face as she gave him the tray of food and asked if he was feeling okay.

"You look tired son, and all washed out again."

Wilson had been planning to go and see Daisy on the Vespa, but he knew his mum would be devastated if he tried. Besides, he wasn't sure he had the strength to steer the scooter.

Daisy called him back around ten thirty.

"Daisy, about time! I've been calling you all night. What happened?"

"The house was burgled this afternoon, while we were all out. Everything was upside down and strewn across the floor."

"Burgled? Is there much damage? Was anything taken?"

"There were no signs of a break-in Wilson. No smashed windows or broken doors. Nothing was taken, just messed up. It was like a demonstration of what a burglary looks like. The policeman blamed it on an animal coming down the chimney. A squirrel. With no damage and no fingerprints, that was the best he could come up with. My room was the worst though. Some of my clothes had been ripped to shreds and then placed back into the cupboards – I mean, lacerated with a knife. Sliced into strips. It wasn't a squirrel."

Daisy's voice was cold and emotionless, as though resigned to accept the terrible judgement and sentence coming her way.

"Whoever it was, they found the bangles. The paper I'd wrapped them in was all torn up on the floor, but the bangles had been thrown back in the drawer. It was like a message to say they knew the bangles were there. Wilson, I have to tell my dad."

"Daisy, don't. I'll find a way to stop all this."

"I don't know Wilson. I'm scared and worried, Mum's crying – what's gonna happen next?"

"Nothing. They're just sending us messages. Playing with us. I'm sure they'll give us more time to give the bangles back."

"How much time though?"

"I don't know. A bit."

"Wilson, I'll probably be at the hospital all day tomorrow. They think Gran will pass away. Mum can't cope. I have to go."

"Alright, sorry for your gran and your mum. I'll call you tomorrow."

"Bye."

"Oh, one thing; keep those bangles with you at all times. If they go missing that'll be an even bigger problem."

"Okay."

Wilson closed his eyes, his mind frantically seeking a way to make the impossible happen, to return three tangible, metal objects to their rightful owners in a dream. A solution. An illogical solution. Any solution.

Over the course of two hours he revisited every dream with Daisy, from that first meeting in Sampson's to their last visit to The Gateway. He was looking for the needle in a haystack that would enable him to stitch a remedy together, but he was clutching at straws.

Wilson reached the conclusion that he needed to go and search The Market Square, that night, alone. Perhaps someone was betting on it?

Chapter 52

The fragment

Friday 10th November 2017

As Wilson strode into The Market Square the sense of drama was tangible in the atmosphere. Dense clouds, the colour of pewter and gunmetal, were banked in layers across an angry sky and intense flashes of sheet lightning erupted with unpredictable regularity. Deep rumbles of thunder trundled along moments later like giant footsteps hurrying to catch up.

A storm. That's a first.

Wilson knew the dramatic lighting and special effects were being orchestrated just for him. A soundtrack and setting to accentuate the dark mood of the moment, courtesy of The Custodians of The Gateway.

He began his search at L'École but the entrance gates were padlocked and the louvre shutters folded and secured over the windows. The tulips in the window boxes were drooping and colourless, a section of loose guttering was hanging at a dangerous angle and paint was peeling from the walls like patches of flaking skin.

Wilson walked along the flagged pavement with the Clock Tower to his left. The butcher's shop was closed and just like L'École, the building showed signs of neglect. The broad, bay window, normally filled with fat sausages and bloody steaks, was empty. There were no pheasant or grouse hanging to age. Display trays were covered with a film of grey dust in which flies and wasps lay mummified.

Wilson was reminded of one of his dad's jokes:

A man walks into a butcher's shop and asks for a pound of dead wasps.

"I'm sorry sir," says the butcher, "we don't sell dead wasps."

"Yes you do," says the man, "you've got loads in the window."

The cheese shop and the greengrocer were similarly afflicted – empty, dilapidated and abandoned. The once vividly colourful Market Square was now sepia-tinted and derelict, as though blighted by a wizard's sorcery. No inhabitants, no lights in buildings, just an eerie, flickering glow from street lamps running on economy setting. The rate of lightning flash was increasing and thunderous rumbles were growing louder. The giants were marching with purpose. Wilson made his way across the cobbles and headed for Sampson's workshop.

There's a possibility he'd know how to return the bangles. After all, he's a resident here.

But Sampson's workshop was also closed. The hanging sign above the door had crashed to the ground and splintered wood littered the pavement. Wilson brushed the dust from a window with the sleeve of his hoodie and peered in. The workshop wasn't just closed, it was completely empty. The bikes, the scooters, the tools, the wooden workbench – all gone. Wilson turned away.

The Powers That Be are really pulling out the stops with this stunt. An illusion of decay – all for my benefit.

As if to punctuate his thoughts, a slate roof tile crashed to the ground and shattered at his feet, Wilson stepped off the pavement, out of reach of further danger and headed back to the Clock Tower to consider his next move. The egg hunt was going nowhere and Wilson's basket was still empty.

The sandstone mouldings around the clock face had started to crumble. Large chunks of stone, with a partly sculpted side or a bevelled edge, lay strewn on the ground. The polished sheen of Mr Abingdon's bronze statue – or was it Mr Ludlow? – was now tarnished with a dull black patina like a skin disease and his left arm was missing. The wooden slats of the bench seats were afflicted with wet rot and fungi. An armrest was missing. Wilson sat down.

They're watching me, I know they are. Betting on me finding a solution. Or not finding it. They're gambling on what happens next. That's why I'm here, to up the stakes in their stupid game. Turbocharged Wilson, the loaded dice. It's like I'm in some kind of problem solving computer game or TV show. The Crystal Maze. The Midnight Castle.

Wilson continued to expand on those thoughts, working through each step.

So, if they're betting on me, that means I'm either going to win, or I'm going to lose. So only two things can happen next. I discover how to return the bangles, or I don't. And if a chance exists to win, then the answer must be here, in The Market Square, otherwise there's no bet!

Wilson surveyed his surroundings; from L'École up to the far right corner; then past the old coaching house to the corner opposite; then back down past Sampson's to the ominous looking building directly to his left; The Bank.

What exactly is it I'm looking for? Give me a clue, point me in the right direction.

Seemingly on cue, an emphatic burst of sheet lightning seared across the heavens above Wilson's head and for a fleeting moment, illuminated a long-forgotten scene in a dream; only a fraction of a second of insight, but it was enough. Wilson closed his eyes and went instantly in pursuit, opening, scanning and closing every dream memory along the way. Tasking the most powerful part of his brain, his side room, to find the connection. As heavy rumbles of thunder reverberated around The Market Square, Wilson journeyed all the way back to being five years old, to the night of his first arrival in The Market Square, to the night he discovered L'École. There, dimly lit by a single bulb, deep in the darkest recess of his memory, he saw the tell-tale fragment of a dream that could never be extinguished. A trace of polaroid snapshot from a moment long forgotten in time. When the light faded, the gas lamps glowed and the rocket and giraffe exited stage left. When the air turned cold and a doorbell rang as a candle flickered to life. The muffled conversation and two pairs of eyes observing him, then movement from two silhouettes, one round, one tall and thin – looking down from a room above a hanging sign.

I don't want to become the boy that is eaten by the wolf.

Wilson sprinted from the bench seat, across The Market Square and up the four stone steps that led to the entrance of The Bank building. The door was covered with dust and cobwebs but the round brass handle reluctantly turned and when combined with the push of a shoulder, the door slowly creaked open. It was pitch black inside, Wilson reached for his phone and swiped the torchlight.

He was standing at the foot of a staircase on a brightly coloured mosaic floor in which a familiar battle scene had been recreated in a patchwork of tiny stone tiles. Wilson recognised it as the one above the entrance to The Gateway.

He illuminated the route forward. Each stone step was worn smooth in the centre like a shallow platter. A hardwood bannister spiralled upwards supported by white-painted spindles. As he climbed to the first floor, Wilson tried to keep his bearings in relation to the room above the sign.

This is it, he thought, standing in front of an antique oak door with a lion's-head knocker in polished brass. There was no nameplate or numbering. Wilson twisted the fluted glass door handle and pushed. The door didn't open. He applied his shoulder again, but it still didn't budge. He raised the lion's jaw knocker and let it fall. An authentic roar echoed down and back up the staircase – followed by silence. Wilson almost smiled, he knew the animalistic sound effect had been added for his entertainment. He tried the knocker a second time and again, there was no reply.

Wilson smashed his clenched fist against the solid wood.

"Look, I know you two are in there, so open this bloody door."

More silence.

Wilson kicked the door repeatedly. "Let me in, I need your help, urgently."

More silence.

Then a voice.

"What's the magic password?"

"Err, let me think. Oh yeah, I know it: open this door before I break it down and smash your face in."

"Yes that's it, well done."

The door swung back on its hinges and Wilson entered a spacious room with a high ceiling, the corners of which were lost in shadow. Big Mac and Short Cake were sitting in black leather chairs behind executive style desks on which shining table lamps were poised at the same angle.

"So this is where you jokers hang out, is it?"

"Our office in town" said Short Cake, reclining back in his chair and grinning, with his hands behind his head.

"Listen guys, I'm feeling a bit stressed and tired at the moment, in fact, I could go any minute. I'm also totally hacked off. You know as well as I do that Daisy didn't steal those bangles on purpose. It was just bad timing. Or you planted them on her as part of one of your games, a challenge."

"Oh, we know she didn't do it on purpose" said Short Cake.

"So how . . . " Wilson had stifle a yawn " . . . how do we get them back? Back in the correct year pile."

"Oh, it's very easy. Someone has to bring them back" said Big Mac, spinning his fountain pen on the surface of his desk like the arrow on a Wheel of Fortune.

"We don't care who. It can be you or Daisy" said Short Cake.

"Any*body* in fact" said Big Mac.

"Good. So where do we bring them?"

"Back to The Gateway of course."

"To The Hall of Extinguished Spirits."

"Through the residents' entrance" said Big Mac.

Wilson's leapt to the practicalities of the requirement and immediately hit a brick wall. It left him stunned.

"Hold on a minute. I thought only dead people could get into the hall through the residents' entrance, the one on the right."

"Spot on" said Short Cake.

"So either Daisy or I have to be *dead* to bring the bangles back into the hall, is that what you're saying?"

Wilson had to swallow down the lump of something that

361

had risen to the back of his throat.

"Spot on again" said Short Cake.

"I agree Wilson, it does seem harsh," Big Mac continued, "but the problem is, we don't have a door that's signed 'The Gateway: for the bearers of accidentally stolen human spirit bangles'. Obtaining planning permission for that would take ages. Far longer than *you've* got, I'm afraid."

Wilson paused for a moment, captured by the irony of knowing that he would not be in a position to say the next morning, "thank goodness, that was all just a dream." Daylight was not going to bring an end to this nightmare.

"You're having me on, right. You're just joking?"

"Not at all. To bring the bangles back they must come through the Residents Only door. With, or more accurately, on, a dead person."

"Choo-choo," said Short Cake, pulling down on the cord of an imaginary steam train whistle.

Wilson had to restrain himself from throwing a punch.

"Listen, I know The Powers That Be are mad with me because I played God and derailed their train set or whatever. And I said I'm sorry. But Daisy and I were only trying to do good."

"Just like The Powers That Be then" said Big Mac.

"That's bollocks, there are people starving in Africa, tsunamis, civil wars, terrorism, diseases and cancers. All The Powers That Be seem to do is play cruel gambling games while the rest of the world suffers."

"Wilson, dear Wilson, let me tell you something, let me explain," said Big Mac, rising to his feet. Once upright, he stood no taller.

"Millions and hundreds of years ago there was a special

place created by The Powers That Be for human people. It was what you might call a paradise, with no disease, no crime, no tsunamis. But humanity soon became bored with everything being perfect every day and so animal instincts surfaced to create wars and terrorism and serial killers. So The Powers That Be designed a better paradise. One that wouldn't always lead to *Lord of the Flies* scenarios. A paradise-lite, if you like. The point is, the accidental car shunt, the odd tsunami is okay. They add the necessary spice to human life."

"And you should be thankful" said Short Cake "for all the civil wars, plagues and terrorist attacks The Powers That Be manage to prevent."

Wilson was taken aback and momentarily lost for words.

"So what you're basically saying is that things would be far worse without The Powers That Be. That they try to minimise the bad things that can happen?"

"Yes. You humans don't like it all controlled and you kill each other if it's not. So they try to maintain the optimal balance of cause and effect, by allowing your *mischief*, as I've told you on numerous occasions. Gambling on outcomes is their *guilty pleasure*."

"And there's quite a few bobs on you Wilson, quite a few bobs," said Short Cake, gleefully, "one of The Powers That Be has made an extraordinary bet that the ripples from Wilson to the rescue will cause at least three thousand unscheduled deaths. They'll be busy trying to keep that down to a manageable level if it all comes to pass."

Wilson's stomach churned at the thought.

"And the one behind the burglary at Daisy's, the nasty one, who snapped her finger – well, he really wants to win."

"One more very important thing Wilson, about the

bangles" said Big Mac.

Wilson was listening intently. In fact he was hanging on to every word. But he was growing tired, irresistibly tired and began to panic at thoughts of suddenly vacating the dream.

"No, not now. Wait, give me a minute, just another minute," he pleaded to Big Mac and Short Cake, "don't let me go without knowing, tell me quickly, please."

Short Cake smiled and simply shrugged. His fingertips tapping out a sequence of notes on the black, lacquered surface of his desk.

"Come on, what is it, what's the one more important thing?"

Wilson lurched forward and grabbed the armrest on Big Mac's chair, trying to anchor himself to the moment, to stay inside the dream.

"Please, tell me, what's the important thing, how do I save Daisy?" He was desperate for a few more precious seconds of conversation but it was too late. He'd run out of time and the dream had reached its expiry date. Wilson began to fade away and in a moment of extremely bad timing he vacated the premises, never to hear Big Mac's last words.

Big Mac turned to Short Cake.

"Well. How rude was that? You don't just leave without hearing the 'one more thing'."

"Indeed" said Short Cake "particularly when the 'one more thing' relates to the crucial imperative of returning the bangles by tomorrow night if Daisy is to avoid a fatal and inexplicable accident – thereby delivering the bangles by default, *ipso facto*, as they say."

"Correct" said Big Mac with a callous chuckle.

Chapter 53

A scratch I can't itch

Friday 10th November 2017

No combination of words could ever convey the magnitude of the emotional maelstrom raging in Wilson's head when he woke the next morning. He felt like someone who'd driven to the pub with his mates, free as a bird, only to wake up in a police cell the next morning facing life imprisonment for killing a family of five through drink driving. With no possible way to rewind the clock, he was condemned from that moment to a life of torment.

Gloria called him down for a bowl of soup at lunchtime and he joined her, despondent and forlorn, still in his pyjamas. He considered confessing everything, a plea for help; but his innocent mum didn't deserve to be involved in his self-inflicted catastrophe.

Teaps was still making news on TV. The latest angle focused on Vanessa's mother and how she'd died from sorrow barely a year after her daughter had gone missing.

"She'll be watching from heaven with a smile on her face" said Gloria, absorbed in the unfolding story.

Struck by something in his mother's words, Wilson stopped sipping soup, closed his eyes and returned back to last night's dream.

What exactly was it that Big Mac had said?

"Oh, it's very easy. Someone has to bring them back."

"We don't care who. You or Daisy."

"Anybody in fact. To bring the bangles back, they must come through the Residents Only door. With, or more accurately on, a dead person."

So anybody can take the bangles back, they don't care who it is — it can be anyone who's just died, or someone who's about to die.

Wilson shot upstairs to get dressed. He called Daisy and started speaking the moment she answered.

"Daisy, Daisy, I've worked it out, I know how to get the bangles back, I know how to do it" he said, trying to pull his socks on at the same time.

For a second there was no reply. Wilson thought the connection had been lost.

"Daisy? Are you there?"

"Yes, I'm here, Wilson."

Daisy's voice was that of someone in a trance.

"Daisy, what's wrong? Don't worry. I have a plan. I know how to get the bangles back — it's all going to be okay."

There was another pause.

"Wilson it's too late. It's gone too far."

"Daisy don't be silly. What do you mean, gone too far?"

"I was attacked in my bedroom last night. I think they're going to kill me."

Wilson's stress level was already in the red, but now the needle was off the gauge.

"What! What do you mean you were attacked in your bedroom? What the . . . Jesus . . . Are you okay?"

"Yeah. My back's a bit of a mess. I really can't speak now."

"Why? Where are you?"

"I'm in hospital, but not for me, I'm in Ward 3B. A priest

is here for Grandma. She's going Wilson, she's only has a few hours left. She's not moved or opened her eyes."

"Have you got the bangles?"

"Yes. But . . . "

"I'm on my way. Talk to her, do anything, you have to keep her alive until I get there."

Wilson dashed downstairs.

His phone beeped with a text from Blamire.

'The red army is moving out in two hours!'

Wilson checked his watch then quickly texted back.

'Got something loads better than cash. Meet me in the car park at the entrance to Stockport Infirmary in twenty minutes.'

He grabbed his jacket and was on the Vespa, accelerating down the driveway before his mum could object. At the first set of red lights he sent Daisy a text.

'Meet me in the car park, usual place, in ten minutes. Bring the bangles!!!'

The muscles in Wilson's arms and shoulders began to ache as he weaved through traffic, his body functioning on a diminishing power output. He turned onto Bramhall Moor Lane and then pulled into the car park of the hospital. Daisy wasn't waiting but Blamire was and he sprang out of a black Mercedes with tinted windows the second Wilson pulled the scooter to a halt. Blamire was accompanied by a stocky, shaven-headed bloke and the phrase 'knuckles trailing on the ground' could never have been more applicable. Wilson removed his helmet and looked anxiously at the hospital building.

Daisy, come on, come out of the doors now, please.

"What you got for me then?"

Blamire thrust his stocky barrel chest out and his pit-bull mate did the same.

"It's not money, right, not the eight grand" said Wilson, taking a step backwards.

"Are you wastin' our bleedin' time? Cos if you are, we'll be takin' it out on your face. Broad daylight or not."

"No, wait, give me a second. Look, you have a pawn shop, or a buy-and-sell-gold or whatever it is, on Mersey Square, right?"

"Yeah, what of it?"

"Well I've got some gold, solid gold, the best gold you'll ever see."

"Where is it then?"

"It's coming. My girlfriend's got it. The gold used to be her grandma's. She's in the hospital. I just texted to say I've arrived and she'll be here any second. Check my phone if you don't believe me. It's the best gold, fifty carat. Worth loads more than eight grand."

"I don't friggin' believe this. You call me down here promising the dough and then you tell me it's fifty-carat gold."

Blamire took a step forward.

"Fifty-carat gold don't exist, you numpty."

Blamire then stepped back.

"Give him a slap Andy. Remind him who he's dealing with."

Wilson was focusing on the hospital entrance. What if Daisy hadn't got the message to meet him in the car park? What if her grandma had died and it was all too late?

Blamire's bruiser stepped forward and swung a gym-muscle forearm and a tattooed fist at Wilson's head. But Andy was too slow and too out of condition. His fist slammed into

Wilson's crash helmet, which Wilson then smashed back into Andy's jaw, just as he brought his foot down at an angle onto the side of Andy's knee joint, snapping ligaments and tendons. Andy screeched in pain and crumpled to the floor. Wilson stepped back, on his toes, waiting for Blamire to make his move.

"What the…!" Blamire's face was fuming with psychopathic rage. "I'm gonna rip your fff…"

"Wilson! Wilson!"

It was Daisy. She came waving and running across the car park. Breathlessly, she handed him a paper bag. Her broken finger was bandaged and locked straight in a splint.

"Wilson, she's almost gone. I've got to go."

As Daisy turned to hurry back, her sweater lifted an inch or so and Wilson caught a glimpse of thick, red scratches, like claw marks, running across the base of her back.

"So what's your fairy godmother brought ya?"

Wilson handed the package to Blamire, who opened it, lifted out one of the bangles, felt the weight, scratched at the surface with a tooth and whistled.

"Tasty bit of colour. Where did you get these then?"

"Like I said, an old family heirloom."

"Nice Winston, very nice."

A second car then pulled alongside and a tinted window came down. Blamire handed the package to the driver with the instructions: "Get these in the safe in my office, now."

The driver nodded, took the package and drove off.

"You were right Winston, that is premium quality merchandise. Vintage, twenty-four-carat gold. Worth about three grand each in the shop. I'll use some of that to get Andy patched up. Don't suppose you know if there's a hospital round here?"

"We finished Blamire?"

"Yeah. For now. Give us a bell if you get any more trinkets like that."

Wilson rang Daisy as he sprinted across the car park towards the hospital entrance.

"Daisy, meet me in the corridor at the corner, just before the turn to 3B. Coming now."

Daisy was waiting, tears running in tracks down her cheeks, when he arrived.

"Grandma has left us Wilson. She's gone."

"No, maybe we have a few seconds more. We've gotta try."

"Try what? What do you want to do?"

"Daisy, hold my arm. I need to get closer to 3B."

"No Wilson, you can't go down there. You almost died the last time."

"Daisy, trust me. We don't have any other option."

"No, I can't, I can't do it."

"Well then, I'll have to do it myself."

Wilson turned into the corridor and immediately felt a chisel gouge splinters from inside his skull. He tried to force a second step, but a wall of agony stopped him in his tracks. He tried to push through the excruciating pain, but it was impenetrable. Then a soft hand closed around his own, the pain quickly ebbed away and his beautiful, reassuring, staff-of-life supported him as they slowly walked in the direction of the swing doors.

Wilson closed his eyes and began to turn his head from side to side, up then down, searching for something in the streaming torrent of time traces and energy flowing down the corridor. They stood in front of the swing doors to 3B as

Wilson raised one hand into the air, reaching out to an invisible object, seemingly suspended in mid-air, an arm's length away. Precious moments passed. Daisy could feel Wilson slumping in her arms, his stamina failing, his energy, his electrolytes being obliterated.

"Wilson, please, we have to go back."

With his eyes still closed, Wilson turned to Daisy and offered her his hand. Three gold bangles were nestling in the palm, plucked from thin air, the startling climax to an incredible conjuration. Daisy stared, astonished, unable to comprehend the reality of the illusion.

"Daisy . . ." Wilson could hardly speak; he was wheezing and coughing. "put . . . put them on . . . your grandma's wrist . . .now. Run Daisy, we might not be too late, your life. . . . "

She supported Wilson as he slumped to the floor, grabbed the bangles from his hand and ran to her grandmother.

On the other side of the bed and out of sight of her grieving mother, she slipped the three gold bangles over a still-warm hand and onto the narrow wrist beneath the covers.

Then Daisy turned and sprinted back to Wilson as though *his life* depended on it. And it most certainly did, because Wilson was flat on his back in the middle of the corridor and not moving. His lips were turning blue and his face cadaver grey. Daisy wasn't sure if he was breathing. She dragged his lifeless body back down the corridor, round and out of sight of the swing doors to 3B.

She smashed the glass covering an emergency alarm with her fist and started screaming and screaming for help, from anyone, from everyone, from anywhere.

Chapter 54

Who dunnit?

Friday 10th November 2017

Blamire helped Andy hobble to A&E reception where a nurse told them to take a seat and wait to be called. Andy sat in a wheelchair as more pain was inflicted.

"It's not acceptable pal. A skinny kid like that showing me up. If you work in my team Andy, you've gotta be able to handle yourself. I mean, if word gets out, it's my reputation that takes a batterin' not you. Everyone'll start taking the Mick."

Andy was struggling to reply. Not because the conversation was particularly erudite, but because his jaw was fractured in three places.

An urgent message came over the tannoy system.

"Crash team to Ward 3B. Crash team to 3B."

"I think it's better Andy if you find a new career. Something you can handle. Open a flower shop with yer missus. Get a stall on the market and sell cards."

"Doctor Khan to Ward 3B. Doctor Khan, urgent call for Ward 3B."

"Christ, what's goin' on in 3B? I bet it's that Wilson kid kicking off again. Anyway Andy, don't call me, right, and keep your trap shut. You don't want to be spending time in here again . . . with a crash team in Ward 3B. Know what I mean?"

Andy grunted in reply. He'd got the message.

Blamire hurried back to his premises on Mersey Square, anxious to check his instructions had been followed to the letter. As he entered the pawn shop, the driver of the second car, who was now behind the counter serving a customer, nodded to confirm the jewellery had been locked safely away.

He entered his office, locked the door and opened the safe. It contained a loaded hand gun, eighteen thousand pounds in cash, twelve thousand euros in forged notes and a kilo of cocaine. The gram of dope was purely for personal use. There was also a white paper bag – with nothing in it. Blamire frantically emptied the safe, leaving the tools of his trade scattered on the office floor. Then he went back out to the shop.

"Are you pullin' my pipe, Dickweed? Okay, very funny. Where's the booty, the bangles?"

Dickweed was still serving the customer but looked up the moment his name was mentioned.

"In the safe boss."

The customer said she'd come back later.

The fight didn't last long. That's assuming you can call Dickweed being thrown over a glass counter, through the front door and out into the street, *a fight.*

The police squad car arrived just as Blamire was about to throw Dickweed back into the shop, through the front window, the entrance door no longer being fit for purpose.

The police loved the interior of Blamire's office.

After considerable effort, three burly officers eventually cuffed an altogether different style of bangle onto Blamire's wrists and dragged the spitting, red-faced maniac back to the sanctity of *their* office.

Chapter 55

Knock, knock – who's there?

Friday 10th November 2017

Blamire had hit the nail on the head. Wilson had indeed been causing trouble outside Ward 3B and was now lying horizontal and unresponsive, his eyes wide open, fixed on the strip light directly above his head.

A team of emergency medical professionals, including Doctor Khan, were desperately trying to jump-start a flat-as-a-pancake heart. Only Wilson's legs from below the knee were visible, protruding from the tent of crash team jackets he was hidden under. The soles of his trainers correctly gave the time of the incident as ten minutes to two. Daisy was collapsed in a heap three metres away; a heartbroken marionette whose strings had been snipped. Her cheek was pressed hard against the cold concrete of the corridor wall and floods of tears had created small puddles on the floor. Her bloodied fist was pounding the wall, but the rhythm was slowing in sync with her sobs, and Wilson's heartbeat.

Around the same time, at The Gateway, there was the gentlest of taps on the door of the residents' entrance. Big Mac greeted the new arrival.

"Ah, Gwendolyn, you're finally here, we've been expecting you."

"Do come in" said Big Mac, opening the door fully.

"Looks about a three-ouncer to me" said Short Cake, eyeing up the frail frame and wrinkled countenance of Daisy's grandmother.

Gwendolyn took a step forward and was about to cross the threshold when she stopped, turned her head and looked back over her shoulder. It was as though she'd heard someone mention her name, from the other side of a room, in a cocktail party conversation.

"Actually" she said "I think I'm a fraction over the three. Better go and spend that last tad of energy on something valuable."

Gwendolyn's Outer Shell then carried her Residual back to Stockport Infirmary where it settled into her recently deceased body for just a moment, before returning back to The Gateway.

Big Mac and Short Cake were waiting when she arrived. They knew exactly where she'd been.

"Sorry" she said with a knowing smile "I forgot to bring the bling."

The about to be extinguished spirit of Daisy's grandmother then raised a bony arm and started jangling the bangles.

"Come on in Widow Twankey" said Short Cake. "It's time for you to climb that stairway to heaven."

He began singing the words to the Led Zeppelin song

"There's a lady who knows all that glitters is gold . . . "

Big Mac closed the door.

"I wonder who's won all the money then?"

Chapter 56

Daisy's dream

In all the chaos, Daisy never found the time to tell Wilson how she got the claw marks across her back and the bruising on her upper body, but I thought you might like to know.

Following the burglary, it took Daisy two hours to restore her bedroom to something like its former self and secretly dispose of the shredded clothes. At 11.00 p.m. she took the sedative her mum said would help with sleep and for an hour lay in bed feeling frightened and vulnerable. She cursed The Market Square and her stupidity. Daisy didn't have the faintest idea on the way or the means to return the bangles or where to begin such an impossible thought process. She prayed Wilson was having more success.

Around 3.00 a.m. she woke for no apparent reason, other than the allure of a bead of light shining beneath the bedroom door. After slipping into the red dressing gown and a pair of matching slippers at the foot of her bed – a gown and slippers she'd never seen before – Daisy left the room. The house was silent as she walked across the landing towards a wall switch with the intention of turning off the light.

A tall figure, half-hidden in its own shadow, was standing at the foot of the stairs covered from head to toe by a black, woollen cassock. A voluminous pointed hood enshrouded the figure's head completely and the existence of a face was not apparent, only a dark, oily void. As Daisy stood transfixed by the monk-like figure, an invisible force, completely beyond her control, enticed her down the stairs. Half-falling, half-flying, she landed in a heap at the feet of the figure who stooped down, enveloped her within folds of heavy, coarse fabric and began to tickle her.

"Tomorrow is judgement day" the figure whispered in her ear, before cackling with the cruel laugh of someone or something savagely amused.

When Daisy woke, her body bore the signs of a brutal assault.

Chapter 57

Limboland

Sunday 12th November 2017

After thirty-six hours of intensive care, Wilson's distraught family and friends were finally given the news they'd been dreading. Despite the medical team's best efforts and the extensive resources of the hospital, Wilson was in an irreversible coma. Alex, Gloria, Kate, Megan, Daisy, Teaps and Hoover were all in attendance, grief-stricken and inconsolable.

Putting my ambivalent indifference to one side, or perhaps watchful neglect would be more apt, I have to admit, it was all desperately moving and extremely sad; but not all bad news. Because just after Doctor Khan had delivered his prognosis, Wilson's phone, which was lying on the table beside his bed, let out a sharp ping. Hoover picked up the phone and keyed in Wilson's passcode.

A photo message popped open.

It was a picture of a Japanese boy with a big happy face and an enormously broad smile. He was holding in front of the camera a green sock with a Ralph Lauren logo embroidered onto it.

Dumbfounded, Hoover turned to face Wilson's dad. "We've found Wilson's missing sock" he said.

The following day, an eminent neurologist met with Alex

and Gloria and during a grave and stony-faced discussion, he told them the Intensive Care Unit had done all that could be done for Wilson. The brain scans and the consultations between doctors and specialists had all delivered the same conclusion. Wilson was in a persistent vegetative state, or PVS for short, and always would be. Wilson's brain was the equivalent of a dead battery. The component parts were in perfect working order, but the liquid charge being drip-fed into his arm was having no effect. Put simply, Wilson couldn't be jump-started.

Two porters pushed his bed to a small private ward and passed an arrow pointing to 'The Chapel' on the way.

The ward only had space for three beds. One was taken by Wilson. The second, by a young lad called Tom who'd fallen and cracked his skull while having a laser-gun fight with his brother. In the third bed was Sally Bennett, the victim of a car crash outside Davenport train station. All three were connected to EEG machines and a spot of light was tracing a line across each screen.

On the screen above Sally's bed, the spot was peaking and troughing and bleeping with signs of life.

On the screen above Tom's bed, the spot was more subdued. Above Wilson, the needle of light was flatlining.

Alex, Gloria and Daisy sat around Wilson's bed and even the most poignantly crafted sentence could never begin to convey the depths of their grief, torment and suffering.

Gloria had brought Wilson's alarm clock and lovingly placed an old toy giraffe with a missing ear on his pillow. Wilson appeared to be dreaming, like the little boy she remembered, sound asleep under a Batman duvet and dreaming of who knows what? Firemen, faces in spoons?

Doctor Khan quietly entered the room and checked Wilson's pulse, then he lifted an eyelid and shone a torch on the iris. No response. He put the torch back in his pocket and appraised Wilson for seconds that were filled with disappointment, sympathy and sadness.

"I'm sorry, but I can't change my prognosis Mr and Mrs Armitage. In my professional opinion, your son won't be coming back."

Alex had aged ten years in just a few days. Saggy half-moons of skin drooped beneath his eyes and a corrugation of worry lines ran across his forehead. The guilt was almost too much to bear, and the thought of telling Gloria the full story of the cause of Wilson's life ending tragedy made him feel nauseous and mentally unstable.

"As you know" Doctor Khan continued, "I've instructed the nurses to implement a regime of 'nil by mouth' in three days' time." He checked the date on his watch.

"Let's say from Friday morning then, shall we?

"Of course, you can appeal against my decision and I can put you in touch with the lawyers here at the hospital. Though speaking as a father, and someone who understands the utter heartache and despair you're facing, and having seen the appeals process and the further pain it brings, I would advise you to put your emotions to one side and do the right thing for Wilson, and above all, yourselves."

Gloria was staring into space, not listening, trying to convince herself that this wasn't happening. She started folding the lace hanky in her lap into increasingly smaller-sized rectangles. She was picturing herself in the kitchen cooking Wilson's sausage and mash.

"But how can he go, just like that?" Alex's voice was cracking under the strain.

"He was getting better" pleaded Gloria.

"Mr and Mrs Armitage, the brain is a complicated instrument and we still don't fully understand some of its functionality. Take the case of Sally here. Her brain is not . . . how can I put this? Her brain has always showed some signs of life. Over the last few weeks, cerebral activity has become stronger as her brain has started to repair and reorganise itself. Patients like Sally will, with time, pull through. In actual fact, she was wide awake yesterday for a few hours. This often happens as the brain continues its running repairs. Some do come out of their coma with a degree of disability it's true, but others make a full recovery.

"But as I said, I can't give you false hope, because that won't be the case with Wilson. There are no impulses, not even the tiniest amount of activity to indicate his brain will return to consciousness. I'm sorry."

"Doctor Khan" said Daisy, "could Wilson be alive and just . . . dreaming somewhere? Like resting, recovering in some kind of . . . altered state, just waiting to come back?"

Alex so desperately wanted to clutch at that straw also.

"No Daisy, I'm sorry, that's completely impossible."

Doctor Khan's pager bleeped and after checking the message, he apologised, said goodbye and left the room.

Daisy sat motionless, her mind and body numb, unable to believe, to accept, the horrifically unhappy ending to their fairytale.

Gloria was silently crying, tears free-falling onto her hanky. Slowly she looked up at Daisy, her eyes both crazed and questioning and her lips trembling. She was on the verge of hysterics and a primeval plea for truth erupted from the depths of her soul.

"Daisy" she screamed, "what did you do to my son?"

Alex shepherded his distraught wife from the room and told Daisy they were going home for a few hours. He also said that they would need to have a private conversation at some time in the future.

After they'd left, Daisy moved her chair next to Wilson's bed. Her eyes were bloodshot and her cheeks lined with the varnish tracks of dry tears. She held Wilson's hand and smiled at his lovely face, his crazy, spiky hair and the small, dark mole on his chin. His wax paper skin had a milky sheen and the raised corners of his mouth even suggested a smile. Daisy remembered all the carefree, happy moments. Wilson waltzing with the Medusa in those ridiculous, tight breeches. Singing in Fabio's with Chanelle and the Eager Beavers. The first meeting in Starbucks, then standing in the rain under the umbrella and that amazing, wonderful first kiss beneath the fireworks of Ferris the Catherine Wheel.

Daisy leant forward and kissed Wilson's lips and when she did so, his eyelids suddenly, and most definitely, fluttered – as though displaced by a rapid eye movement beneath the surface.

Daisy's heart missed a beat.

She kissed him a second time and his eyelids pulsed and flickered again, from side to side, then up, then down. Daisy's heart missed a second beat and in that instant, she instinctively knew Wilson was still with her. A message from her heart, from somewhere, from Wilson, was telling her that he was not dead, just dead to the world.

Daisy grabbed her bag and coat, kissed him again and whispered in his ear "Wilson, I know where you are, and I'm coming to get you."

Chapter 58

Calamity Jane

Monday 13th November 2017

Travelling home on the bus, Daisy tried to shackle euphoria. She didn't want to be overly optimistic but her hope against all hopes was that she would find Wilson and somehow bring him back. She had no idea how, but that wasn't the point. She knew Wilson was still alive, trapped in some kind of limbo between coma-land and being properly alive, breathing and laughing and joking and making her fall in love with him. Daisy was fairly certain she needed to start her search in The Market Square, Wilson's eye movements had confirmed that, but her plan had evolved no further. She had to admit it wasn't a great plan, but something inside was saying there was no need to consider any other possibility.

When Daisy arrived home and opened the front door, her mother was standing in the hallway, expecting the worst. Frances was holding on to a bannister for support in case her legs gave way. The moment she saw the look on Daisy's face however, she knew something had happened and it wasn't the tragedy she'd been expecting. Daisy wouldn't admit to anything by way of good news though – on the contrary.

"No Mum, he's still the same. They're planning to stop giving him nutrition and after that, it's just a matter of time."

Frances advanced to give Daisy a hug, fully expecting her to break down in tears, to let it all out, to have a good cry on her shoulder, but she didn't. She simply said, "don't worry Mum. They have top doctors at the hospital and I'm sure one of them will come up with something. Sorry, I'm really tired, I haven't slept too much over these last few days. I'm going to lie on my bed for a while. I'm not hungry, so don't bother with any tea for me. Just need to be alone with my thoughts."

She then entered the lounge, grabbed her laptop, said "hi" to her dad, and two steps at a time raced up to her room.

Daisy's father appeared in the doorway, caught the eye of his wife and shrugged as if to say, 'What the hell's bells is going on with Daisy?'

Frances scratched her head.

That was odd, she thought, *I could have sworn Daisy was singing that Britney Spears song as she closed her bedroom door.*

It was only half past seven but Daisy changed into a fresh pair of pyjamas, brushed her teeth, combed her hair and climbed into bed. She was filled with nervous anticipation, trembling at the prospect of bringing Wilson back, but first there was prep work to do. With the laptop resting against her knees, she pulled the duvet under her chin and asked Google to disclose all it knew about PVS, or persistent vegetative states.

For two hours Daisy read the results of every conceivable search term relating to the word 'coma' including 'coma recovery', 'coma phenomena', 'comas and dreams', 'comas and miracles' and so on. When Daisy finally arrived at the search term 'comas and the human spirit', she knew her work for that part of the evening was done and thankfully, she was tired. It was nine thirty when she switched off the light, closed her eyes and an hour later began the journey to rescue Wilson.

385

"Hi there, little missy."

A cowboy was tipping the brim of a Stetson hat and his grinning face was inches from Daisy's. Most of his stubby, yellow teeth were missing, his hair hadn't been washed in years, he smelt of horse manure and whisky and his clothes were filthy. The handles of a pair of six shot revolvers, nestling in holsters on a belt full of bullets, were in the grip of his filthy, nicotine-stained fingers.

"God," said Daisy, rolling her eyes, "that's all I need, Dodge City." Slowly she turned on the spot, taking everything in, irritated with the unnecessary antics of The Market Square.

The flagged pavement normally framing the perimeter of the square was now a raised boardwalk with lines of hitching posts. Saddled horses stood patiently, tethered at the bridle.

The cobbles of the square were covered by a thick layer of sun baked, red earth. The fascias of the once familiar buildings had all been refashioned with wooden planking in keeping with the night's theme and re-branded with hand lettered signage as the 'Saloon' or a 'Telegram Office', a 'General Store', a 'Jail' and an 'Hotel'. Cowboys, in leather chaps and waistcoats and stack heeled boots with silver spurs jangling and thumbs tucked in belt loops, clomped along the boardwalk. Two American Indians riding bareback trotted past a colourful teepee painted with crude images of a buffalo hunt. Beyond the Clock Tower, (which now resembled something like a totem pole), at the bottom end of the square, a Mississippi paddle steamer was moored on a wide river alongside a long wooden jetty. The river boat was four decks high and the word Casino was emblazoned on the bow.

Daisy walked to a bench seat where an old, piebald mare, with a long fringe of coarse hair covering one eye, was saddled up and reined to the backrest. The horse was chomping on a mouthful of hay.

"Why howdy, ma'am" said the horse.

The huge, protruding incisors and thick lips reminded Daisy of her grandad adjusting his dentures. The image wasn't welcome. She ignored the horse, sat down with her arms folded and began looking around for Wilson. In truth, she was surprised that he wasn't already there, waiting for her by the Clock Tower or on a bench seat, but gazing across The Market Square, she realised why. The Wild West backdrop was a dream playground for Wilson.

He'll be out there acting like some bad-ass outlaw or a sheriff laying down the law – so I'll just have to go and round him up.

Daisy was about to start her search in the far corner of the square, where L'École was now masquerading as a saloon called The Golden Nugget, when the horse whinnied for attention and then spoke.

"Can give you a lift, if you like?"

Daisy shook her head at the sheer ludicrousness of the suggestion but then quickly saw advantage in the offer.

I'll be able to cover more ground and track him down much quicker.

Daisy had never ridden a horse before but soon got the hang of it, thanks to expert advice, straight from the horse's mouth, so to speak.

"What's your name darlin'?"

"Daisy. What's yours?"

"Trigger" said the horse.

"Come on then Trigger, giddy up, let's go and round up good ol' Sheriff Wilson."

After searching for what could have been hours or only a matter of minutes in dream time, Daisy still hadn't found Wilson. He wasn't in the saloon, in jail, or playing poker on the steamboat. He hadn't checked into the hotel and wasn't involved in the gunfight or the brawl in the middle of Main Street. Even the smoke signals from Big Chief Sitting Bull failed to reach him. There was no sign of Wilson anywhere.

Daisy climbed down from Trigger and patted him on the shoulder. "Sorry we couldn't find him" said Trigger, dejectedly.

"Yeah, I know. Thanks for the help anyway."

Trigger walked away disconsolately, his nostrils almost touching the ground and his tail swishing from side to side.

Wilson hadn't arrived at the bench seats during Daisy's absence and she was stumped.

Cramming all that ridiculous information about comas was a complete waste of time. Reading a book about Billy the Kid would have been more useful.

It was at that moment that Daisy began to feel anxious and deeply uncertain about everything. She had been so sure that Wilson would be waiting for her in The Market Square, her plan had never allowed for any other possibility. However, what if Wilson really was in a permanent coma and not lost in The Market Square at all? What if she couldn't find and rescue him? What if they did stop feeding him at the hospital? Daisy was finding it difficult to stop disturbing thoughts hijacking her fragile psyche. She began to weep, with real tears, a first for The Market Square, but then a stern voice from deep within demanded she pull herself together.

Daisy come on, keep going, don't give in. Think like Wilson – what would he do? He certainly wouldn't give up on you, ever!

So Daisy thought just like Wilson and three familiar words soon arrived to restore her self-confidence and give fresh impetus to the quest: Sampson's Motorcycle Workshop.

What an idiot! How could I have been so stupid? Wilson knows it's impossible to find him in this cowboy madness, so he's waiting at the obvious meeting place. And all this time I've been prancing around on a bloody horse.

Daisy stood up, laughed and wiped away her tears as she tried to get a fix on the sign outside Sampson's workshop. It wasn't easy to spot because a cloud of thick red dust was following the head of cattle slowly being driven over The Market Square. The Texas Longhorns mooed and bellowed as they succumbed to the shouts and the crack of a whip herding them along. As the stockmen finally steered the last of the stubborn cows past Daisy and down to the river, she saw the distinctive lettering on a sign above a doorway. She knew that even if Sampson's workshop was labelled as the Dodge City Blacksmith, Wilson would still be there and waiting.

Daisy left the bench seat and sprinted in the direction of Sampson's, but strangely, the more she ran, the further away the workshop seemed to be. She was covering yards of dusty earth, but more ground was slipping back beneath her feet. One step forward became two steps in reverse. Running even harder, meant getting no closer. But she was desperate to reach Wilson. So she ran and ran and ran, faster and harder than any dream could ever follow. Faster than the feeling of panic draining the energy from her aching legs. Finally, with muscles burning and her lungs about to explode, she burst through the dream barrier and crashed through the door of Sampson's workshop, where she fell to her knees, gasping for air.

As her heart rate dropped and her breathing returned to

normal, Daisy looked around and could see there was nobody home!

"Wilson" she yelled at the top her voice. "Wilson, it's me, Daisy, I'm here. Wilson, where are you? This isn't funny anymore Wilson. I'm getting scared."

Mark Sampson emerged from his office. He was wiping his hands on a grubby cloth.

"Can I help you?"

"Mark, thank goodness. It's me, Daisy, Daisy Meadowcroft. I'm here for Wilson – you know, Wilson Armitage. Where is he? He should be here waiting for me."

"Can I help you?" Sampson gave the same blank reply for a second time.

"Yes Mark, you can. I just told you, I'm here for Wilson."

"Can I help you?"

"Mark, stop playing silly games. This is serious. Where's Wilson? Wilson Armitage. Where the hell is Wilson?"

"Can I help you?"

Daisy stopped speaking. Something was clearly wrong and terribly confusing.

"Mark, it's me. Don't do this, please, I beg you. We don't have much time, I could go at any moment and still haven't found Wilson."

"Can I help you?"

Standing on the brink of hysteria in a dream, Daisy frantically ran her fingers through her hair. *Please, please say this madness isn't happening.*

Sampson's facial expression hadn't changed throughout the entire conversation. There was no look of concern, no change of emotion. He was role-playing the robot, dressed in grimy overalls, mechanically cleaning his hands on an oily rag.

"Do you understand me Mark? I'm talking about Wilson — you know, Wilson Armitage, the boy with the Vespa."

At the word 'Vespa', Sampson's entire demeanour changed. He stopped wiping his hands and smiled.

"Ah yes, the 1959 GS 150. A classic. How's he getting on with it?"

Daisy had finally pierced through the false persona. It was all part of an act; a scene of meaningless obfuscation.

"Hallelujah! Listen Mark, Wilson's had a terrible accident and he's in hospital, in a coma. He fluttered his eyelids this afternoon, telling me to come and find him. I searched all over the wild west, but he wasn't out there, so he has to be here, with you. So where is he?"

"Can I help you?"

Daisy froze, she was still talking to an android.

"Would you recommend a Suzuki?"

"No, cheap and unreliable. Wouldn't touch one with a bargepole. If you want a Japanese bike, get a Yamaha. Can't go wrong with a Yamaha."

Sampson turned to a row of bikes that were lined up for sale.

"You see, take this Yamaha 250. The engine runs . . . "

Daisy stopped listening because she suddenly understood what was happening. Sampson wasn't real. He couldn't help. He was just a prop, a talking mannequin. Ask him the time and he'd have no answer. Ask about a bike and he'd give a programmed reply, a pre-recorded message activated by the relevant prompt.

"What day is it Mark?"

"Can I help you?"

Daisy left Sampson's shop agitated and frustrated by

her endeavours not concluding as intended. A new idea was needed, the Plan B that would lead directly to Wilson. She peered across an empty Market Square looking for a pointer, an indicator of what to do, where to search next. The Clock Tower was fading into twilight shadow as Daisy tried in vain to stifle a yawn.

So where do I go now?

Back to bed, came the answer, as she was consigned to leave Wilson, helpless and alone, somewhere in The Market Square.

Chapter 59

Knockout drops

Tuesday 14th November 2017

'The worries of a sleepless night mean nothing to the morning light.'

Daisy couldn't recall where she'd heard the quote, but lying in bed, she knew the sentiment wasn't true. Half her mind was still frantically roaming The Market Square, the other half was at Wilson's bedside, where the grim reaper was about to cut short his life. She dressed quickly and slipped out of the house without saying goodbye to her parents. The note on the bedside table would explain.

An hour later she was in the hospital, one step away from entering Wilson's room, when she paused at the sound of excited chattering and laughter coming from within. Her heartbeat fluttered with joy, Wilson had found his way back all by himself. Daisy cautiously pushed open the door and entered.

Wilson was still lying prone on his bed, in the exact same position as the previous day. So too was Tom. Sally's bed though, was hidden behind a curtain and the thin partition of fabric was struggling to contain the lively conversation on the other side. The car crash girl was awake.

Daisy went for a coffee feeling utterly deflated. When she returned half an hour later, the curtain had been pulled back and Sally was propped up on two pillows, sipping juice from a plastic beaker. Her head was bandaged and her arm was in a sling, but apart from that, she appeared well on the way to recovery. All but one of the earlier visitors had gone, so Daisy assumed that the lady remaining was Sally's mum. She was in fact Kay, Sally's aunt and guardian.

Daisy offered a polite "hello" and took the chair at Wilson's side.

Sally returned the greeting with a timid wave.

Kay simply said, "Morning love. We've got our fingers crossed for him."

Daisy forced a smile, "thanks, I'm glad you're okay," and then she turned back to Wilson.

Something was different, he looked older somehow and there was a sickly smell coming from his bedclothes. Not body odour; more the sweet, mustiness of decaying fruit. The pallor of Wilson's skin had also changed. It had acquired a sallow, grey tinge and his lips were lined with a trace of blue. Daisy's heart sank. She didn't need to look at the EEG monitor to know that during the night the grim reaper had taken a step closer with his scythe.

"Sorry," she said, pulling the curtain back between the two beds.

Daisy wanted privacy, to be completely alone with Wilson.

"It's alright love" said Kay softly, "I know how you feel."

The conversation between Kay and Sally continued but at muted volume.

Daisy adjusted the bedsheets to fully cover Wilson's shoulders.

On the bus that morning, all the way to the hospital in fact, she couldn't wait to kiss him one more time. To prove that her female intuition – no, more than that, her number eleven instincts from the previous day were not just some kind of delusional self-deception.

Wilson's eyelids definitely flickered when I kissed him, without a doubt.

But were they really signalling his dream sleep? Or could the flicker have been a twitch, some kind of involuntary reaction to being kissed? So Daisy kissed Wilson one more time and kept her eyes fixed on his. No response. She repeated the kiss. Still no response. Then she kissed him again, more forcefully, with all the feeling she could impart. But the dream was no longer running in Wilson's head, there was no action for his eyes to follow and the twitch theory was also wrong. When Daisy overheard Sally whisper something to her stepmother about 'mountains of gold bangles', she had to bite on a clenched fist to stop from shrieking.

Daisy tiptoed round Wilson's bed, stood with her ear to the curtain and checked her feet weren't poking out underneath.

"Yeah, it was such a weird dream Auntie Kay. I'll never forget it. This strange white room with people just standing around, all dressed the same. It felt like I was in that white room forever. Then a door opened and I walked into a huge church filled with those golden bangles where two funny men helped me to escape to cowboy-land. Then I woke up and look, all my eczema's nearly gone!"

Daisy held Wilson's hand as she stared into space with eyes like lasers. She was opening, scanning, closing every memory from The Market Square. Searching for a lifeline, a sign that would direct her to the white room in The Gateway. Every dream was mentally dissected into its component parts. Finally, after an hour of examining and probing, at the very end of the road, hidden deep inside the very first night she met Wilson, Daisy found the visual cue, the motif she was seeking – they were in a glass bowl, on a teacher's desk, in a French language lesson, in L'École.

Ten minutes later, Daisy was in the hospital pharmacy.

"Do you sell sleeping tablets?"

"We do, but I can only sell you certain ones without a prescription. Who are they for?"

"They're for me, I'm going to Australia with my dad tomorrow and I hate flying. I need to knock myself out quickly."

The assistant turned to the various medications on the shelves behind her and asked "How old are you?"

"I was eighteen a few days ago." Daisy flashed her college ID card.

"Well, these will do the job. They're adult strength, so you'll only need to take one, about half an hour before you fly."

"What if I take two?"

"The recommended dose is one in any twenty-four-hour period. So two will certainly send you down under."

She paid for the knockout drops and rushed back to Wilson. Daisy swallowed two pills from the blister pack, drew the curtain to fully enclose Wilson's bed and lay down beside him. She didn't have time to wait for night to arrive – Wilson was dying and she needed to fight for his life there and then. Twenty minutes later Daisy was on her way and knew exactly who to pick a fight with.

Chapter 60

The grand finale

Daisy hit the ground running and headed straight for L'École.

She dashed up the flight of steps that led to the main entrance and stopped to get her bearings in the foyer. Through a window to the right she could see a small office in which an elderly lady sat touch-typing at an old fashioned typewriter. The corridor ahead was empty but Daisy could hear the voices of night class teachers running their crash courses. She couldn't recall the exact room in which she first saw Wilson, but remembered the teacher's name. Following a double tap on the office window, the lady hobbled over and with a warm smile slid the window to one side.

"May I help you?"

"Hi, really sorry to trouble you, but I'm looking for Miss Angeline. She was a French teacher, many years ago. Is she still here, I need to speak with her urgently?"

"Yes child, Miss Angeline still teaches in our language department. I'd be delighted to pass on a message for you."

"No, no you can't. Sorry, it's a personal thing, about a former student; there's been a terrible accident and I have to let her know, face to face. I promised. It'll only take a few minutes."

"Well, up you dash then dearie. She's in Classe 6a, first floor, first on the right."

"Oh thank you, thank you so much."

"Well, I do hope your . . . our alumnus is soon on the road to recovery."

"Yeah, I'll tell him" shouted Daisy as she charged up the stairs.

On reaching the top step, familiarity with the first floor came flooding back. The white mosaic floor tiles, the rose pink walls, the smell of fresh flowers and on the right, the door to Classe 6a. Daisy knocked and entered.

The classroom was filled with children seated at wooden desks. The boys wore blazers with a large sun embroidered on the breast pocket, the girls wore stripy pinafore dresses. Daisy felt something glow inside her heart when she saw the little wooden desk in the middle of the front row from which she'd once passed shy smiles to Wilson.

"May I be of some assistance?"

Daisy turned at the sound of the curt voice and instantly recognised Miss Angeline. She was wearing the same, matronly, tweed skirt and jacket, her hair was tied in the same tight bun and she hadn't aged a day. Crucially, the large glass vase filled with flaming-red poppies, was still there, on her table.

Daisy's hunch was going in the right direction.

"Look, I'm really sorry to trouble you Miss Angeline but I need to know where you got those flowers?"

Miss Angeline faced up to Daisy with a puzzled expression, as though she was being addressed in a language she'd never heard before.

"Please, it's a matter of life and death. I have to know, quickly."

"Why, I cut them myself, just this morning, fresh from the meadow."

398

"Fresh from which meadow? Where is it and how do I find it?" Daisy's words tumbled out in an anxious rush.

"You'll find it out there of course."

Miss Angeline pointed to a large sash window to the right of the blackboard. It was set in a wall at the back of the room, in an elevation that couldn't be seen from The Market Square.

Daisy dashed to the window, hardly daring to look, too frightened to contemplate the possibility of being wrong. She needn't have worried though, because expanding outwards and onwards for as far as her eye could see, were thousands of vivid crimson flowers murmurating in a gentle breeze. On the horizon, shimmering in a heat haze, was the colossal structure of The Gateway itself.

Scarcely able to control her joy, she shot back downstairs and in a flurry of words asked the lady in the office for directions to an exit that would lead out to the poppy meadows. The elderly secretary was happy to oblige.

"You go through the front door and take the alleyway on the right" she said.

Daisy stood in the cool, shadowy shelter of the portico, facing two familiar doors.

The brass plaque on the left stated: 'The Gateway. Visitors Only'.

The plaque on the right: 'The Gateway. Residents Only'.

Daisy pushed the door on the left, just as Wilson had done, but for some reason, this time, it wouldn't budge. She shoved a little harder but it still didn't shift. Then she really put her back into it, the door budged an inch and then slammed shut again.

She heard voices whispering on the other side. Someone had a foot wedged against the door and she didn't need a prize for guessing who.

"Hey, I know you two are there, so let me in. I've come for Wilson. I'm serious. I'll smash this door down if I have to."

She heard further mutterings.

She pushed again with all her might. The door edged open a fraction and again slammed shut. Daisy felt groggy, but not from the exertion, the sleeping tablets were fully kicking in. She was struck with the bizarre notion of falling further asleep inside her own dream.

I hope not, please, not right now.

She hit the door with two sharp raps.

"Look, I'm sorry I stole your bangles. It was a mistake – you know I didn't mean to. But Gran gave them back. And now Wilson is seriously ill as a consequence. I think he's stuck somewhere in a white room and I need to rescue him, urgently."

No answer.

"Please guys, please let me in. Wilson hasn't got much longer. He's going to die if I don't find him."

Daisy waited a moment and shoved the door again, to no avail.

Then came the realisation that the miscreants on the other side were aware of this. They knew exactly where Wilson was. They'd kidnapped him and were slowly snuffing out his life, murdering him as punishment for playing God. Daisy's blood began to boil and she put her mouth close to the door.

"Listen, if you two don't want a pair of new bangles with your bloody names written on them, OPEN THIS DOOR, NOW!"

Further mutterings, then at last, a reply in a high pitched voice.

"We're closed today."

Daisy took three steps back and charged at the door, but it still held firm. She slumped to the floor rubbing her shoulder. A feeling of deep despondency immediately descended. Wilson was running out of time and every plan was leading to a dead end. Daisy clambered to her feet, walked back beneath the portico, down the flight of stone steps and turned to survey the building.

There must be another way to get in. Another door possibly, or perhaps...

A penny dropped.

...an open window. Exactly, I'll climb in through an open window – or break one if I have to.

With renewed optimism, she studied the row upon row of elegant Georgian-style windows along the left and right wings of the building, but they all looked shut and more to the point, the lower floor was completely inaccessible, over ten metres above the ground. Also, she couldn't see any signs of the stained glass windows that were visible once inside The Gateway, which struck her as being odd.

So where the hell do I start looking for a ladder.

Daisy pictured the local window cleaner and more specifically, the extension ladder that was always strapped to the roof of his van. She contemplated bringing him to The Market Square but couldn't be certain he'd bring his ladders as well.

So who else can I reach out to for help?

That train of thought rumbled on, and was going nowhere, until a stroke of inspired thinking brought a far more reliable accomplice to mind. Daisy closed her eyes, pictured the sharp image of a familiar face and pulled her personal hero into the drama. When she opened her eyes, Gwen Burton, the six-foot-tall hockey teacher with flaming ginger hair, was standing two feet away, complete with hockey stick.

"Wait there" said Daisy, "we'll need some reinforcements."

A few moments later, Miss Wetherington, the head of PE and a fourteen stone battleaxe, was also standing on the first step, with *her* hockey stick.

"Morning Miss Burton. Morning Miss Wetherington."

"Morning Daisy, and how are you on this beautiful day?" Gwen Burton was swishing her stick in anticipation of a bully-off.

"Well, to be totally honest, I'm not so good. I'm trying to get into this building, through that door, up there on the left, to rescue my boyfriend. But the two guys on the other side, who've kidnapped him, won't let me in."

Miss Wetherington turned to Gwen Burton and her face quickly turned an angry, beetroot red, as her neck and rugby-player shoulders began to hulk up.

"Well, we'll see about that."

As though summoned to quell a disturbance in the sixth-form common room, they raced up the steps, then paused for a second before taking a combined run at the door on the left, almost smashing it off its hinges.

All three marched triumphantly into the hall.

Big Mac was sprawled out in a daze at the foot of the mound of bangles for 2017.

Short Cake was losing his footing as he tried to scramble down the pile from 2016.

"I'm not sure that was completely necessary," said Big Mac, dusting himself off. "You should have said if it was that important."

"Grab 'em both" said Daisy "and follow me."

They marched round the back of the 2015s where Miss Burton and Miss Wetherington shoved their captives into their matching chairs. The teachers sat, one on each desk, menacingly tapping the business ends of their hockey sticks on the polished wood surface.

"Where's Wilson?" Daisy demanded. "Where are you keeping him? Where's your white room?"

Short Cake was scowling and Big Mac was sulking. Neither of them said a word. Miss Burton raised the tip of her hockey stick and turned to Daisy, about to ask permission to use it.

"No, not just yet. Let me think."

Think like Wilson again, act like Wilson.

Daisy read the words on the signs above the three doors behind the desks. Big Mac had mentioned something about them but neither exit appeared to relate to a white room.

Peering across the cavernous space she was bewildered by the challenge.

The white room could be anywhere in here, and it would take me a year to search it all, maybe forever.

Daisy was still considering how and where to start when she heard a scream, as though someone was being inflicted with pain, or tortured! A second yelp was accompanied by a burst of mocking laughter which Daisy was able to trace back to its source; a hole in the wall, roughly twenty metres to the right of the three doors.

Big Mac gasped and then started whimpering as Daisy, with some trepidation, began walking slowly towards the hole. She looked back, Short Cake was shifting uncomfortably in his seat and the skin stretched over his horrified face was chalk white. Big Mac gasped for a second time as Daisy peered into the hole. She couldn't see the bottom, it was an inky black void, but there was certainly something bad happening down there; she heard another scream and a desperate plea, "No, please, show mercy for heaven's sake!" This was followed by an angry booming voice shouting "Oh very funny, we'll show mercy all right, just like you did."

Daisy let out a sigh of relief, neither voice was that of Wilson.

Stepping back from the hole she noticed that something had been scratched into the face of a brick that was jutting out like a loose tooth. The impression was faint but clearly spelled out the words, 'A bad un'. Turning to Miss Wetherington, Daisy pointed at Big Mac and motioned for her to bring him over.

"Fetch the fat one and push him in. Let's see if Wilson's trapped down there."

"My pleasure."

The stocky teacher took a firm grip of Big Mac's jacket collar and jerked him to his feet. He made a strange guttural sound, fainted and slumped to the floor.

"Okay, let's try the other one" said Daisy, nodding at Miss Burton. But Miss Burton didn't have to oblige.

"Go through that white door" said Short Cake, cowering low in his chair and pointing a crabby finger beyond Daisy.

Daisy turned and followed the line of direction for a further twenty metres to a small white box mounted high on the wall. Beneath it, partly hidden by a ridge of gold bangles, was the right-angled, top corner of a door frame.

Daisy rushed round to the far side of the pile of bangles where a narrow strip of exposed marble floor made a pathway.

Wilson had been correct, the white box was indeed an illuminated directional sign. A sign that said: 'The Annexe'.

Daisy referred back to the two teachers.

Miss Burton nodded her approval that it was okay to proceed.

Daisy pushed open the door, stepped inside and was immediately blinded by an intense white light which forced her eyes shut. They needed a moment to acclimatise after the half shadow in the hall and to adjust to the glare and eerie spectacle of a white room filled with . . .people.

Children, men, women, the elderly, lots of the elderly, of all races and colour, were lined up in regimented row upon row, like soldiers standing on a parade ground. Except there was no ground, just whiteness — and no ceiling or roof or sky, only open space. The people were dressed in the same uniform of white polo-neck sweater, white cotton trousers and white pumps; as though an army in white had been called to attention in a featureless expanse of nothingness.

Daisy stepped up to the front line, face to face with a girl of around her own age. She passed her hand across the girl's eyes and then touched her shoulder — there was no response, no signs of life. Daisy was reminded of Sally and the words of Doctor Khan.

"Over the last few weeks, her cerebral activity has become stronger as her brain has started to repair and reorganise itself. Patients like Sally will, with time, pull through."

Then it dawned on Daisy, the role of The Annexe, the white room. The girl was in a coma, in a kind of suspended animation, along with thousands of others. She was waiting for her damaged brain to fix itself. But Daisy knew Wilson wasn't brain-damaged; he'd simply run out of charge. She did a quick calculation based on the number of rows and the people in each row, but the sum total would never be accurate, because the rows didn't seem to end. Even with the help of two hockey teachers, Daisy knew it would be hopeless, it would take forever to find Wilson - and her teachers wouldn't recognise his face anyway. They didn't know him like she did.

Wilson's face. Wilson's face! She could see Wilson's face!! Daisy half laughed in acknowledgement of her stupidity as she became aware of the obvious.

She didn't need a search party. There was no need to go looking for Wilson, because all she had to do, was bring Wilson to her. To imagine his presence. She closed her eyes and recalled all the marvellous, wonderful memories of Wilson. Thousands of images rushed to volunteer their services and Daisy slowly pored over them like the pages of a treasured scrapbook. A few minutes later, as she closed the cover and, hardly daring to look, opened her eyes – Wilson was standing there – in the white sweater and trousers she knew he'd be so embarrassed to be seen wearing. She smiled inwardly at the thought of him complaining and tears of happiness and relief ran down her cheeks.

It took the combined strength of the two teachers to carry Wilson back into the Hall of Extinguished Spirits. Daisy closed the door to The Annexe behind her.

Big Mac and Short Cake were by their desks. Short Cake was screaming insults and warning Daisy that she had no idea how much trouble she was getting into. Big Mac was chewing the nails off five fingers all at the same time, his eyes virtually popping from their sockets.

"Come on" said Daisy, "let's get out of this place."

They were just about to man-handle Wilson to the Exit to The Market Square when Daisy remembered Tom, the boy in the bed beside Wilson in the hospital.

Perhaps he's also in the White Room somewhere.

Daisy brought to mind her best recollections of his face, framed against a white pillow and ran back into The Annexe.

Three minutes later, all five of them emerged into the bright sunshine of The Market Square where a triumphant Daisy raised her arms, threw her head back and yelled at the top of her voice:

"I found him, I rescued Wilson and I don't care what you Powers That Be do about it. And don't even think about sending your monk-man to attack me again, cos I'll trap him in a cage and stick him on TV and tell everyone about your stupid gambling games!"

Miss Burton and Miss Wetherington said their goodbyes and left Daisy sitting on a bench seat by the Clock Tower with Wilson and Tom slumped either side.

Daisy knew she had done the hard part but her work was not completely over. She had pulled people into The Market Square and now she was planning to reverse the process. She wrapped her hand firmly around Wilson's and then clutched Tom's fingers.

As the effects of the knockout drops finally wore off, Daisy's presence in The Market Square dissipated like mist in the morning sun, and she didn't leave empty-handed.

When Daisy awoke, she was stretched out beside Wilson on the hospital bed and her hand was still locked on his. Still groggy from the after-effects of the sleeping pills, she propped herself up on one elbow and studied his face. There was still a trace of blue at the edge of his lips but the tinge was now barely perceptible. And his skin was losing its parchment like appearance. Daisy heard a soft bleep and was drawn to the EEG monitor above Wilson's bed. The pinhead of white light, normally flatlining across the screen, had left the trace of a spike.

She heard a bleep from a different direction and turned to see a solitary spike in the centre of Tom's screen. A moment later, Wilson's EEG bleeped again, followed quickly by Tom's. Then they both bleeped in unison for a third time and within moments all the bleeps were bleeping every bleeping second.

Wilson slowly opened his eyes. They were shining like sunbeams dancing on a rippling sea. He smiled at Daisy. Then someone tapped Daisy on the shoulder. It was Sally, the girl from the other bed.

"Your boyfriend saved my life" she said "is he a number eleven like me?"

Chapter 61

Blindsided

So that, dear reader, completes the story of Wilson Armitage. A cautionary tale in which he dies at the end. Actually, it was more a comedy of errors, because Wilson wasn't supposed to die. It was all bad timing really, what with Daisy accidentally taking the bangles from The Gateway and Wilson taking too long to break into Blamire's safe to retrieve them.

You see, we originally planned for Blamire to put the bangles in his jacket pocket, in the car park – making it easy for Wilson to then pick that pocket once he was standing outside Ward 3B. But we realised Blamire would smell a rat, as though Wilson had performed a trick and had never really given him the bangles in the first place. So we projected the traces into the future and it all looked very messy.

Vanessa is kidnapped by the thugs who bought the debt from Blamire. Wilson visits The Market Square to discover her whereabouts and the next day, confronts the thugs. The thugs give Wilson a serious beating and then the ambulance racing him to A&E, collides with a car, gravely injuring the driver. The driver is a heart surgeon racing to the airport to fly off and operate on the ruler of a politically stable republic in Africa – who as a consequence of the surgeon being injured, has a fatal coronary. So, the politically stable ruler, as a consequence of being dead, is then replaced by a politically unstable nutter, who starts a civil war – which, without major intervention on my part, looked as though it would eventually lead to Russia and America having a right old barney.

So, as I said, the prognosis for the 'bangles in the pocket scenario' didn't look good. So that's why we decided to go with the second car and make Blamire give the bangles to Dickweed, rather than put them in his pocket. And to be honest, when we ran the future projections for that scenario, they all came up trumps. No major knock-on effects.

Wilson does his stuff. Granny brings the bangles back. The Gateway are happy and call off the monk-man scaring Daisy. And Blamire gets sent down for GBH.

So my fellow Powers That Be thought the second car scenario was just the job. But yours truly didn't, I never thought it'd work. I told them Wilson's electrolyte levels were far too low to take the chance and I was right. It took Wilson far longer than anticipated to open Blamire's safe. A few seconds less spent searching would have saved him precious energy – and saved his life! Energy, eh? It's a bugger.

However, on the positive side, running with the second car scenario meant that there was an awful lot of bobs riding on Wilson. Virtually all of my colleagues thought he'd pull it off. So I'm in line for quite a windfall after backing Wilson to fall at the last fence. The good news is, the bookies have agreed to pay out early, so tonight it's my shout. We're going to have a big party here in eternity. Elvis and John Lennon have written new songs especially for the occasion. Can't wait. There's even a chance Wilson will join us, given the state the poor lad's in, weight wise. And I think that's for the best. Because, knowing Wilson, even if he's only a tad over the three ounces, he'll go straight back as a non-extinguished spirit, messing up his dad's research, mixing up the clothes in his mum's charity shop and getting up to all kinds of lovelorn nonsense with Daisy.

Let me just check the time. I've only got a few minutes and I need to prepare for the party, but before I toddle off, I thought I'd look at some of our predictive traces for the future and see what life holds in store for the rest of the cast.

Not that I can be totally certain of course. There's always the possibility of another Wilson coming along and flapping his flipping cabbage whites.

So, let's have a quick look. What's this first projection?

Oh good it's Daisy's. That's nice, really nice.

In a world without Wilson, it looks like Teaps will step in to mend her broken heart. Second best I suppose. And . . . they'll get married . . . and have a baby.

Wait a minute, the images are coming thick and fast.

Here we are. It's a baby girl.

There's the christening.

And it seems, Teaps and Daisy are going to call their daughter . . . Wilson. Oh, wouldn't you just know it.

So who's next? Kate and Megan?

Here they are, let's see.

Well, no surprises there. By the looks of it Kate and Megan are going to have a fashion label together. And very successful. World famous in fact. Designs based on Bratz dolls. Big platform boots, press studs the size of a satellite dish. It all looks good for the 'peas in a pod'.

Now here's Hoover's projection.

He goes on to uni, gets married, good job. Ditches the missing sock website. Wonder why?

Ah. They only found the one missing sock. Wilson's

411

favourite green sock I believe.

And I think I was responsible for that.

As for Wilson's mum and dad – let's have a look.

Strange, there's nothing showing on the horizon for those two. Well, actually there is, but it's fuzzy. Possibly being updated as I speak, so I can't really see what happens to them. I think someone's straddling in their neck of the woods. Blowing the smoke around. I'll come back to them in a minute.

So what about Michael? What does the future hold for him?

Blimey, he looks like a new man.

Happy, confident. Big gardening business. Doing well; will only drink wine in the future.

And finally, finally, here she is: Vanessa.The star of the show, and the cause of all the trouble.

So let. . . . me . . . see . . . what's in store for Vanessa.

Well, it doesn't look like she's going to get her memory back. Tut. And she seems to be happier living in residential care. That's a shame.

Hey, but looks like she's in a very posh nursing home, very smart, like a five-star hotel, and her son and husband go and visit her every . . . every . . .

Uh, that's odd. There's a new scenario coming along. What's this all about? That's not supposed to happen. Let's have a look.

Ah, that's better. Here's the very latest projection. Updated just a few seconds ago. In fact I was wrong. Vanessa is going to get some of her old memories back after all, and goes on to be the boss of her old firm again – but only on a part time basis, excellent news!

Wonder how she got her memory back?
Let me look at . . . Here we are.

She gets her memory back because . . . because Daisy... and . . . Wilson . . . are in The Market Square and . . . bloody hell!

"Big Mac, Short Cake! Come here! You two can't be trusted to get anything right. I thought I told you both to make sure Wilson takes the Exit to Eternity. Well, look at these projections. He didn't! Daisy has just rescued him from The Annexe and soon they'll be up to mischief again!"

The WiFi of Dreams. Book Two

Butterfly Assassins

Coming soon.

Printed in Great Britain
by Amazon